Praise for *The Oort Federation*

The mathematical metaphors in Robert G. Williscroft's *Icicle* reminded me of classic Heinlein. In this sequel, *The Oort Federation*, Williscroft throws a surprising twist at us. Braxton Thorpe's team builds on technology captured from the aliens, suggestive of the "super- science" of E. E. "Doc" Smith's classic space operas. *Icicle* scaled up from the lab to beyond the Solar System. In *The Oort Federation*, Williscroft continues to build momentum, from terraforming Mars to expanding out to the stars, attempting to resolve a multi-sided conflict between the Oort, two alien planets, and Thorpe's own human rivals. With hints that go beyond even this, I can hardly wait for the next episode in this epic.

– Alastair Mayer
Author of *The T-Space Series*

The Oort Federation: To the Stars is one of the most speculative, concept- rich, science-fiction novels I have ever read. You know it's speculative when it comes with its own dense Glossary of terms relating to Portal Technology, MERT Drives, Lagrange points and the like. The further you read, the deeper you are taken into how the Universe actually works and what mankind's destiny in it will ultimately be. One thing I especially like is the extent to which the author explores humanity's potential with concepts like clones, digital copies or electronic "Updates," and the possibility of remaining young and even living forever without the need to have children. Our universe is indeed vast, and this sequel to *Icicle: A Tensor Matrix*, offers something for everyone: an ongoing space war between a ruthless Russian oligarch and members of the Federation; not one but two fully realized alien worlds and cultures; even cats and digital cats that hop from one section of the galaxy to another as easily as you and I step into another room.

I was absolutely swept away by what humanity was evolving toward. Are there any limits to our possibilities and aspirations? After this galaxy and universe, what about the next one? At one point in the novel, John Butler, Chairman of the Oort Federation, tries to anchor eThorpe's loyalties to the Solar System and Man-As-We-Know-Him.

But eThorpe is an electronic download, a member of a new breed, and he makes it plain that "Federation jurisdiction stops at the edge of the Oort Cloud." He and no one else will lead "an expedition into the unknown" and be responsible for its success.

Exhilarating, challenging, and mind-blowing. I can only hope that the author continues this series, perhaps in a new universe.

– Professor John B. Rosenman, Norfolk State University
Former Chairman of the Board, Horror Writers Association
Author of *The Inspector of the Cross Series*

THE OORT FEDERATION

TO THE STARS

THE SECOND OORT CHRONICLE

The Solar System & Oort Cloud
Showing Thinsat Swarms and Oort Stations

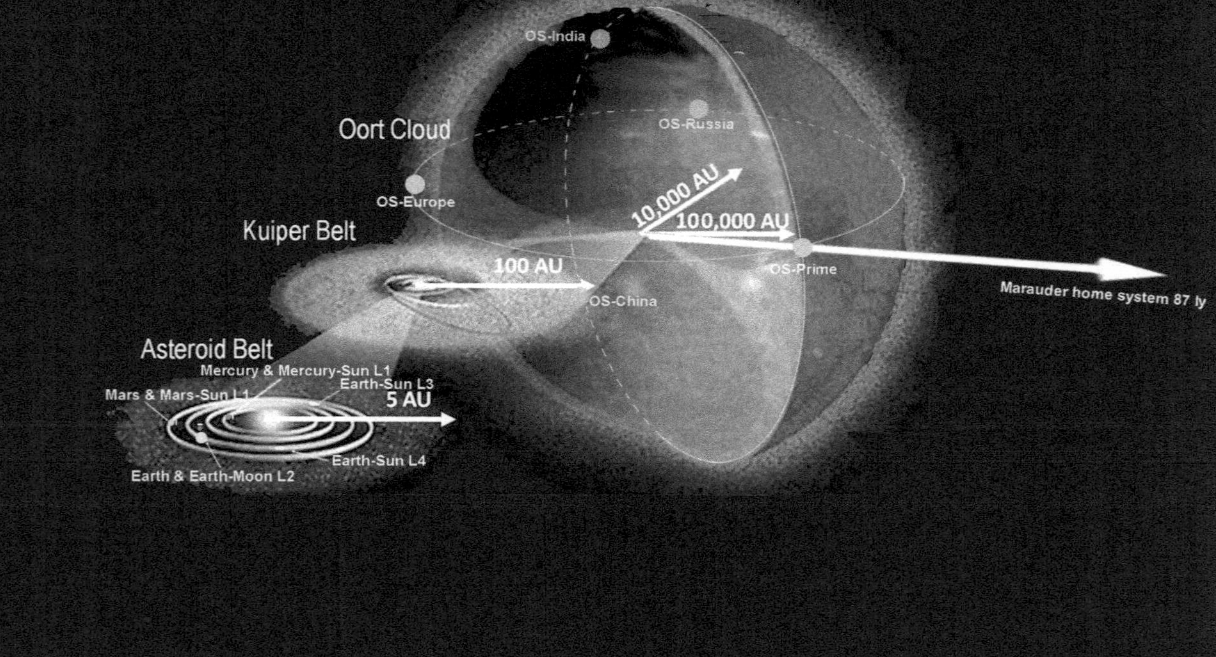

THE OORT FEDERATION

TO THE STARS

THE SECOND OORT CHRONICLE

Robert G. Williscroft

Centennial, Colorado

Icicle: A Tensor Matrix
The First Oort Chronicle

Starman Press
Email: rgw@RobertWilliscroft.com
Website: RobertWilliscroft.com
Edition 2.0 2025

Cover art by Aṇik
Artwork by Robert G. Williscroft
Book design by Robert G. Williscroft
Covers by Stephen Geez

Names, characters, and incidents in this story are either products of the author's imagination or are used fictitiously. Any resemblance to actual events, locations, names, and people, living or dead, is entirely coincidental and beyond the intent of the author and publisher.

BISAC Subject Headings:
F1C028020 FICTION / Science Fiction / Hard Science Fiction
FIC028130 FICTION / Science Fiction / Space Exploration
FIC027130 FICTION / Romance / Science Fiction

Library of Congress Control Number: 2015908742

ISBN-13: 978-1-968367-28-2 Paperback
ISBN-13: 978-1-968367-27-5 Hardcover
ISBN-13: 978-1-968367-12-1 Ebook
ISBN-13: 978-1-968367-29-9 Audio

DEDICATION

For the two women who inspired me more than any others:
My zoology professor, Dixie Lee Ray, and
the girl of my dreams, Jill.

Table of Contents

Frontispiece iv
Dedication vii
Table of Contents ix
Acknowledgments xv
Cast of Characters xvii
Spacecraft Roster xx
The Oort Federation 1
   Prolog 3
      Interstellar Space—Lone Surviving Asterian Starship 3
      Interstellar Space—Braxton's Starship 3
Part One—The Federation 5
   Chapter One 7
      Oort Station Prime—Oort Federation Council 7
      Denver—Phoenix Complex 8
      Kuiper Belt—Ogden Enterprises 11
      Earth—Los Angeles 12
      Oort Station Prime—Detention Facility 13
   Chapter Two 17
      Oort Station Prime—Chairman John Butler's Office 17
      Denver—Phoenix Complex 18
      Kuiper Belt—Ogden Enterprises 20
      the Moon—Udachny 22
      Oort Station Prime—Detention Facility 25
   Chapter Three 27
      Oort Station Prime—Chairman John Butler's Office 27
      Denver—Phoenix Complex 31
      Kuiper Belt—Ogden Enterprises 32
      Moon & Mars-Sun L4—Udachny 34
      Oort Station Prime—Detention Facility 37
   Chapter Four 38
      Oort Station Prime—Chairman John Butler's Office 38
      Denver—Phoenix Complex 42
      Kuiper Belt—Ogden Enterprises 43
      Mars-Sun L4—Udachny 44
      Earth—Various Locations 47

Chapter Five 54
Oort Station Prime—Chairman John Butler's Office......54
Denver—Phoenix Complex..57
Kuiper Belt—Ogden Enterprises 60
Mars-Sun L4—Udachny...63
Oort Station Prime—Chairman John Butler's Office......64
Chapter Six..67
Oort Cloud—Braxton's Personal Swarm 67
Denver—Phoenix Complex..68
Kuiper Belt—Ogden Enterprises 70
Mars—Mars Station...73
Solar System—The Phoenix Portal System Network.......76
Chapter Seven 80
Oort Station Prime—Chairman John Butler's Office......80
Denver—Phoenix Complex..81
Kuiper Belt—Ogden Enterprises 82
Mars-Sun L4—Udachny...85
Oort Cloud—Johnny Oort...88
Chapter Eight..90
Denver—Phoenix Complex..90
Kuiper Belt—Ogden Enterprises 92
Kuiper Belt—Ogden Enterprises 96
Earth—Planetwide 98
Part Two—Johnny Oort 101
Chapter Nine...103
Earth—Los Angeles...103
Kuiper Belt—Ogden Enterprises 108
Oort Station Prime—Chairman John Butler's Office....108
Mars-Sun L4—Udachny...110
Kuiper Belt—Ogden Enterprises 111
Chapter Ten...116
Earth—Los Angeles...116
Kuiper Belt—Ogden Enterprises 118
Mars—Nanedi Valles Plateau...................................120
Mars—Nanedi City...123
Oort Station Prime—Chairman John Butler's Office....128

Chapter Eleven..132
   Earth—Los Angeles...132
   Mars-Sun L4—Udachny...133
   Mars—Nanedi Valles Plateau...................................137
   Mars—Nanedi Valles Plateau...................................141
   Mars-Sun L4—Udachny...146
Chapter Twelve...149
   Oort Station Prime—Adm. Jerry Culp's Office...........149
   Mars-Sun L1—Soletta...151
   Mars—Geosynchronous Orbit..................................153
   Mars—Polar Orbit 155
   Mars-Sun L4—Udachny...156
   Kuiper Belt—Kuiper Joint Station 157
Chapter Thirteen 162
   Oort Cloud—eThorpe & eBraxton 162
   Oort Station Prime—Chairman John Butler's Office....165
   Solar System—Various Locations.............................169
   Mars—Various Locations 171
   Mars—the Basins 174
Chapter Fourteen 179
   Mars-Sun L4—Udachny...179
   Oort Station Prime—Chairman John Butler's Office....180
   Kuiper Belt—Ogden Enterprises 184
   Kuiper Belt—Phoenix Complex................................186
   Mars-Sun L4—Udachny...187
Chapter Fifteen 189
   Kuiper Belt—Phoenix Complex................................189
   Kuiper Belt—Phoenix Complex................................190
   Proxima Centauri—*PS Ad Astra & PS Neil Armstrong* ..191
   Proxima Centauri—*UZ Yuri Gagarin* 194
   Proxima Centauri—*S Ad Astra & PS Neil Armstrong*.....198
Part Three—Breakout...205
Chapter Sixteen 207
   Kuiper Belt—New Kuiper Joint Station.....................207
   Mars-Sun L4—Udachny...208
   Kuiper Belt—New Kuiper Joint Station.....................209

Mars-Sun L4—Udachny......................................213
Mars-Sun L4—Phoenix Force 214
Chapter Seventeen 217
    Kuiper Belt—New Kuiper Joint Station—
        Ogden Complex 217
    Proxima Centauri—*UZ Gherman Titov* &
        UZ Yuri Gagarin 218
    Kuiper Belt—Udachny 222
    Interstellar Space—One Lightyear beyond OS Prime...223
    Kuiper Belt—New Kuiper Joint Station 225
Chapter Eighteen 227
    Interstellar Space—Between the Solar System
        and Aster 227
    Kuiper Belt—New Kuiper Joint Station—
        Phoenix Complex 228
    Interstellar Space—One AU beyond OS Prime 229
    Oort Station Prime—Chairman John Butler's Office....231
    Kuiper Belt—New Kuiper Joint Station—
        Phoenix Complex 233
Chapter Nineteen 237
    Aster System—Rogan 237
    Aster System—Frohlic 244
    Kuiper Belt—Udachny 250
    Solar System—Various Locations....................251
    Kuiper Belt—New Kuiper Joint Station 252
Chapter Twenty..253
    Interstellar Space—*PS Neil Armstrong* 253
    Aster System—1.5 AUs North of Aster and
        Damvet Space Station 255
    Aster System—Frohlic Cislunar Space............259
    Aster System—Near Damvet Space Station.....262
    Aster System—Rogan L4 & L5 263
Chapter Twenty-One 267
    Rogan—Damvet Space Station 267
    Aster System—Inner Edge of the Asteroid Belt 269
    Aster System—Frohlic Cislunar Space & Frohlic........271

Aster System—Generally 275
Oort Station Prime—Chairman John Butler's Office....280
Frohlic—Office of the Boss 281
Chapter Twenty-Two..284
Rogan—Generally 284
Rogan—Technology Exchange...287
Kuiper Belt—New Kuiper Joint Station & Udachny 290
Aster System—Generally 292
Aster System—Conflict on Rogan & Frohlic.................295
Epilog 302
Kuiper Belt—New Kuiper Joint Station.........................302
Aster System—Asteroid Belt...303
Aster System—Frohlic 304
Interstellar Space—*PS Andromeda*...............................304
Post a Review 305
Excerpt from *RAN: A Civilization in Hiding* 306
About the Author..315
Other Works by this Author 316
Connect with the Author 317
Glossary for *The Oort Federation* 318

Acknowledgements

Several people contributed to the creation of this book.

Most significantly, my wonderful wife, Jill, pored over each chapter with her discerning engineer's eye. She kept my timeline honest and made sure that regular readers could understand fully the arcane details of the nuclear and quantum interactions that play a significant role in this tale. She also reviewed my celestial mechanics and made sure my recitation of Solar System exploration was historically accurate—not to mention keeping track of space battle participants.

Prof. John B. Rosenman, bestselling science fiction and horror author who taught science fiction writing at Norfolk State University, reviewed the manuscript and made several suggestions that significantly improved the story.

Hard science fiction author Alastair Mayer reviewed the manuscript and offered his scientific, engineering, and editorial insight.

Others have contributed with their comments and observations, and I thank them. You know who you are.

A tip of the hat to the incredibly courageous Russian cosmonauts and American astronauts who blazed the trail into space and first walked on the Moon. The starships in this story are named in their honor.

It goes without saying that any remaining omissions, errors, and mistakes fall directly on my shoulders.

Robert G. Williscroft, PhD
Centennial, Colorado
February 2021

Cast of Characters

MAIN CHARACTERS
(alphabetically by first name)
Adrhun Gloalorn—Asterian prisoner from Frohlic
Brad Kominsky, PhD—School of Mines—Phoenix Senior Scientist
eBrad—Upload version of Brad Kominsky
Braxton Thorpe—The Icicle from Icicle: A Tensor Matrix
Thorpe—The original Icicle—later, a downloaded version of eThorpe
eThorpe—renamed original Thorpe when Thorpe was downloaded
Braxton—The independent backup—later, a downloaded version of eBraxton
eBraxton—renamed original Braxton when Braxton was downloaded
Dale Ryan, PhD—Phoenix research scientist
eDale—Upload version of Dale Ryan
Daphne O'Bryan, PhD—Partner and Chief Scientist at Ogden Enterprises
eDaphne—Upload version of Daphne O'Bryan
Isidor Orlov—Russian oligarch head of Udachny Enterprises
Jackson Fredricks, PhD—Phoenix Chief Scientist
John Butler—Chairman of the Oort Federation
Johnny Oort/John Ortman—an Oort individual—later, Johnny
eJohnny—Upload version of John Ortman
Kimberly Deveraux—Partner and Chief Information Officer at Ogden Enterprises
eKim—Upload version of Kimberly Deveraux
Masin Arcah—Asterian prisoner from Rogan
Max—Daphne's tabby cat
eMax—Upload version of Max
Maxter—Clone of Max
eMaxter—Clone of Maxter
Sally Nguyen, PhD—School of Mines—Phoenix Senior Scientist
eSally—Upload version of Sally Nguyen
Sergii Anatoly Borisovich, Academician—Udachny Enterprises Senior Scientist

SECONDARY CHARACTERS

(*alphabetically by first name*)

Bardan Talock—The Boss, head of Frohlic's government

Bexel Carok—Frohlic dissident leader

Botex Ravnan, Captain—Commander of Frohlic Military Outpost One

Dvra Okai—Roganian shuttlecraft pilot

Frank Meriweather, PhD—Mars Station Chief Scientist

George Fulton—Incoming U.S. President

Gerald Saxon—Humanized Oort renegade

Gloria Weinhard—Dayton matron

Gregori Yeltsin—President of The Federated Russian Republics under their new constitution

Guo Qiáng, Academician—Project Director at the Institute of Nanoscience Computing (INC), Chinese Academy of Sciences—later, Head of the Chinese government

Holon Mavik—CEO of Roganian L2 Group

Jake Rundell—Dayton Chief of Police

John Gabby—Dayton mayor

Norman Bork—Mars Station Manager

eBork—Upload version of Normal Bork

Prozell Squzon—Frohlican pilot of only surviving Asterian ship headed for Aster

Ragnar Whipple—Editor, The Dayton Chronicle

Randy Nelson—Humanized Oort renegade leader

Rhonda Willis—Humanized Oort renegade

Rodney Bailey—Blockchain programmer

Stanley Roka—Mars Station crew member

Zantag Gloalorn—Adrhun Gloalorn's grandnephew on Frohlic

Zhang Yupei— Director of the Institute of Nanoscience Computing (INC), Chinese Academy of Sciences

FEDERATION SPACE FORCE (FeSFo)

(rank & alphabetically by first name)

Jerry Culp, Adm.—Commanding Admiral

eCulp—Upload version of Jerry Culp

Rob "Jake" Jacobs, Cmdr.—Operations Commander

eJake—Upload version of Cmdr. Rob Jacobs

Sam Bunker, Master Chief Petty Officer—Master CPO of FeSFo. Later promoted to Lt. Cmdr.

eSam—Upload version of Master Chief Sam Bunker

eGoff—Upload version of Petty Officer First-class Cameron Goff (The flesh-and-blood Goff was killed with nerve poison by Chinese dissidents in Icicle.)

George "Georgie" Raptor, Petty Officer First Class—Platoon Leader

eGeorgie—Upload version of Petty Officer Raptor.

Jack "Tag" Taggart, Petty Officer First-class.

William "Billy" Jones, Petty Officer First-class.

Francis "Claw" Falcon, Petty Officer Second-class.

Kimber "Kim" Jordan, Petty Officer Second-class.

Lars "Doc" Watson, Petty Officer Second-class—platoon medic.

eDoc—Upload version of Petty Officer Watson.

Rauld "Swede" Stefansen, Petty Officer Second-class.

SPACECRAFT ROSTER

PHOENIX/FEDERATION SPACECRAFT

(*alphabetically by ship*)

FS Aster—Captured Asterian MBH spacecraft (subluminal—subject to relativistic effects)

(*5 additional superluminal* Ad Astra-class *ships purchased from Phoenix*)

Phoenix Double-MBH Starships & Pilots

PS Ad Astra—eThorpe
PS Alan Bean—eDale
PS Alan Shepard—eBork
PS Buzz Aldrin—eSam
PS David Scott—eBrad
PS Edgar Mitchell—eSally
PS James Irwin—eJohnny
PS Michael Collins—eKim
PS Neil Armstrong—eBraxton
PS Pete Conrad—eDaphne

(*5 additional Ad Astra-class ships held in reserve at Phoenix HQ*)

UDACHNY SPACECRAFT

(*alphabetically by ship*)

VASIMR Spacecraft

UKK Electro-Garpun (subluminal—subject to relativistic effects)

ABO Starships

UZ Gherman Titov
UZ Sergei Krikalyov
UZ Yuri Gagarin

(*12 additional* Gagarin-class *ships*)

THE OORT FEDERATION
TO THE STARS
THE SECOND OORT CHRONICLE

PROLOG

INTERSTELLAR SPACE—LONE SURVIVING ASTERIAN STARSHIP

His starship stopped—day two, hour thirteen, minute fifty-nine, seconds thirty-one of his escape from Sol to Aster.

With artificial gravity gone as well, Prozell Squzon floated before his drive console, his twelve fingers splayed over the controls. He did a quick calculation. He was still seventy-nine lightyears and change from Aster.

"A bit far to walk," he muttered, rotating his ears back to better hear a scraping sound coming from the airlock.

Squzon activated the airlock monitor, but it was dead, the screen blank. The inner lock hatch opened with a rush of cold air. Before he could react, a spacesuited figure disabled him with some kind of Electro-Muscular-Disruption stun weapon.

INTERSTELLAR SPACE—BRAXTON'S STARSHIP

Prozell Squzon opened his eyes slowly. He hurt all over, even in places he had forgotten he had. He was on the deck of some kind of operations center filled with monitors and control consoles. A strange-looking humanoid stood before him, five-fingered hands on its hips. It was oddly thin and tall with puffy lips and a pointed nose. Its head was covered with brown hair, much like his. Clearly, some kind of mammalian ancestry, Squzon deduced. Several similar creatures stood around the chamber.

The strange creature addressed Squzon in his native language, Frohlican. "I am a human," (it used the same word that Squzon used for himself), "from the star system your fleet just attacked, and from which you escaped as the only survivor. We are on our way to your home world and will arrive," it checked an instrument, "in about four-and-a-half Frohlican days." It used Frohlican duodecimal numbers, although probably, the creature normally calculated in base ten. "Unlike your relativistic craft," it said, "this ship is superluminal."

FTL—I should be frightened for me and my race, Squzon thought, but right now, I'm more curious.

"If you promise not to touch anything, I will not restrain you." The creature's mouth curved upward, and it showed its teeth.

I've got nothing to lose, Squzon thought. "I promise," he said, meaning it.

PART ONE
THE FEDERATION

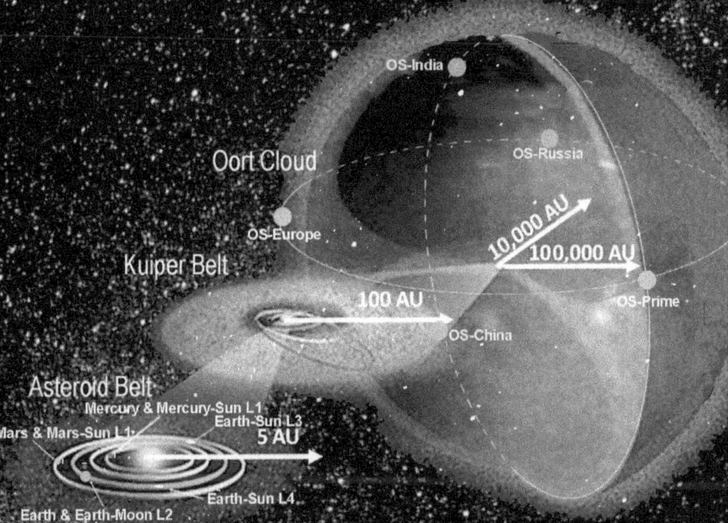

CHAPTER ONE

OORT STATION PRIME—OORT FEDERATION COUNCIL

Thorpe chaired the meeting. He was one of two electronic uploads that came from the Icicle, Braxton Thorpe. His holoimage appeared to be seated at a podium on a raised dais facing the collected delegates. The other upload, Braxton, occupied the Phoenix desk. Daphne O'Bryan and Kimberly Deveraux occupied the Ogden Enterprises desk, and Norman Bork, the Mars Station Manager, was at the Mars desk. He chatted quietly with Kimberly. A scowling Isidor Orlov sat at the Udachny desk representing both his company, Udachny Enterprises, and Earth's Moon.

Outgoing United States President John Butler and his replacement, George Fulton, occupied the U.S. desk, and President Gregori Yeltsin sat at the Federated Russian Republics desk. Other Earth nation delegates occupied scattered desks throughout the chamber, sometimes representing more than one nation. The China desk was conspicuously vacant.

Thorpe gaveled the meeting to order. His voice reached the personal Links of each delegate in whatever language that person desired.

✻

"I called this meeting to inform all of you of the outcome of our Solar System-wide encounter with the Asterian fleet."

eMax's holoimage appeared on the dais, where he curled up, purring softly, as Thorpe's holoimage appeared to stroke him. Thorpe then detailed the nature of the encounter with the 5,000 armed spacecraft, the Federation losses, and the capture of two Asterians and one of their spacecraft.

"Federation forces destroyed all five thousand Asterian spacecraft. One escaped and is, we presume, returning to the Aster system." Thorpe concluded his presentation with, "We expect to intercept the lone survivor long before he reaches Aster."

The delegates broke out in spontaneous applause. Thorpe let it continue for a while and then raised his hand. When the group quieted, he said, "I have held this chair for the past five years. I orchestrated the expansion of humans to the very edge of our Solar System and guided our defense against the invaders. Now, I want to focus on what lies beyond the Oort Cloud, beyond our Solar System, even beyond the Aster system.

"I have worked closely these five years with John Butler, the outgoing president of the United States. Following the procedures outlined in the Oort Federation Charter, I am stepping down as Chairman of the Oort Federation. I have asked, and John has agreed, to step into my shoes to carry forward the work of this body. I will be focusing outward, while John will look to the needs of our Solar System with its human and Oort citizens and to its defense."

✻

Thorpe's holoimage beckoned to Butler, who stood and approached the dais. Thorpe gestured to the gavel on the podium. As Butler picked it up, both Thorpe's and eMax's holoimages vanished.

DENVER—PHOENIX COMPLEX

Drs. Brad Kominsky and Sally Nguyen, with their uploads eBrad and eSally, working at Phoenix, invented the MERT Portal, a wormhole portal derived from the Einstein-Rosen Bridge as modified by Thorne and Morris—hence Morris-Einstein-Rosen-Thorne or MERT.

With the MERT Portal as a basis, they developed the MERT Drive that they describe as a leapfrogging pair of MERT Portals.

Federation Chairman John Butler and newly installed U.S. President George Fulton walked with Dr. Brad Kominsky down a passageway toward the Greater Hall in the Denver Phoenix Complex. Max strolled with them, tail straight in the air. They were accompanied by two Secret Service agents, and more were spread throughout the complex and the surrounding streets. Brad was speaking.

"MERT Portals come in two flavors, a permanent portal between two points, and a MERT Portal locus paired with a hyper-disk." He pulled one from his lab smock pocket and held it up. "A MERT Portal locus creates a Casimir field that generates a wormhole. The locus produces a hyper-disk that can be carried to any location within range. When the hyper-disk is activated, a MERT Portal is established. It's also possible to transport a hyper-disk through a portal to establish another portal. The locus for that hyper-disk can be anywhere within range. The multiple wormholes don't tangle or interact in any way."

President Fulton spoke up. "What kind of range does the locus/hyper-disk pair have?"

"Any portal's range," Brad answered, "is a complicated function of distance and the physical size of the portal on the one hand, and the power supplied to the locus on the other."

The three men entered the Greater Hall. The walls on all sides were lined with labeled doors.

"This is a MERT Portal hub," Brad told the men. "Chairman Butler, you, Sir, are completely familiar with this. I suspect that you, Mr. President," he nodded at Fulton, "are less familiar."

"Actually," Fulton said, "I know very little about the portal network."

"As I mentioned earlier, long-distance portals require huge amounts of power. Phoenix installed thinsat swarms behind the Moon, near Mercury, in Earth's orbit on Sol's other side, and farther out in the Solar System to provide this power. The power from these swarms is delivered by portal to the power room in this complex. From there, power flows to all portal locuses here," he swung his arms in a circle, "and is vectored to other hubs around the Solar System."

"Who pays for all this?" Fulton asked.

"Phoenix has been carrying the cost thus far," Brad said. "The initial infrastructure, the swarms and portal locuses, were very costly. But Phoenix has vast reserves and chose to foot the bill. Phoenix will be negotiating with the Federation to set a minimal fee structure where a tiny amount will be debited from a user's blockchain at each passage. The cost to individual citizens will generally be inside their budget noise level, hardly worth considering. The revenue flow to Phoenix will cover system maintenance and, over time, reimburse Phoenix for the initial infrastructure cost."

"I had no idea," Fulton said, shaking his head.

Brad handed him three disks. "These are E-disks. If you tap one firmly here," Brad indicated a depression in one of the disks, "you will be instantly transported to this room, the Greater Hall. The disk senses your immediate environment. Should that change dramatically, for example, if a spacecraft you are riding loses pressure or if you were to fall out a window, the E-disk will automatically bring you here. The other two disks are for the two Secret Service agents nearest you, so they can follow should you suddenly disappear." Brad grinned and walked them to a door labeled *Oval Office*.

"This portal has been used by Kimberly Deveraux in her role as liaison between the Federation and the U.S. president. It is deactivated until you," Brad looked at Fulton, "decide to continue the arrangement."

While they talked, Max turned and ran to a door marked *Chairman* and darted through a pet opening at the bottom. A few moments later, he reappeared through the door, strolled up to Butler, and began stroking his leg.

Butler stooped down to stroke Max along his back and up his stiff tail. He grinned and said, "Max likes to hang out with Thorpe when Thorpe is in the Chairman's Office. Since Thorpe isn't there, I guess he came back to console himself with me."

"You're serious, aren't you?" Fulton asked. "If I understand this correctly, Max just made a one-and-a-half lightyear round trip in the few moments he was absent?"

Brad and Butler nodded, smiling.

"You'll get used to it," Butler said.

KUIPER BELT—OGDEN ENTERPRISES

Seeing a huge outflow of tax revenue, countries, and eventually the United Nations, tried to stop or at least tax Ogden's activities. This proved unsuccessful, and within two years, Ogden became the second wealthiest company in Earth's history, right behind Phoenix.

Both Daphne and Kimberly had uploaded themselves to active uploads—eDaphne and eKim. The four of them worked and loved together pretty much as one. Dr. Dale Ryan, who had worked with Daphne at Phoenix Revive Labs and now worked at Phoenix, was their frequent companion. The three flesh-and-blood parties shared an elegant loft in downtown Los Angeles. Dale's upload, eDale, also worked for Phoenix, but was not part of Dale's intimate group.

＊

"I was just thinking about the attempt by the Geneva police to serve documents on our Geneva clinic," Kimberly said, her eyes twinkling, as she examined a holodisplay of Earth in Mercator projection showing cities, towns, and villages as a function of the number of uploads performed in each location. By far the largest percentage came from North America and Europe, including Russia, followed by Australia. Virtually every inhabited spot on Earth generated uploads, typically with monthly updates thereafter.

"We solved that problem," Daphne said with a quiet giggle. "With a handful of hyper-disks, the staff was able to empty the entire complex within five minutes. By the time the police got tired of waiting for the receptionist to return, they found the building totally deserted." She looked out over the vast expanse of the Ogden Complex. "How many clinics are we operating now?"

Kimberly pulled up another display. "As of an hour ago, we have twenty-thousand-five-hundred-and-seventy-six manned clinics in cities and towns, and we have one-hundred-thousand-three-hundred-forty-three automatic units." She referred to smaller clinics where incoming clients stepped through a portal to an upload unit in the Ogden Complex spread before them in the Kuiper Belt. "That doesn't include upload clinics scattered throughout the Solar System," Kimberly added.

"Can you imagine it?" Daphne said, flipping her red hair away from her face. "We have over twenty-thousand actual employees on Earth and several thousand here in the Kuiper Belt."

"Money comes in faster than we can spend it," Kimberly said, crinkling her nose. She pulled up a display, and her blue eyes widened. "According to this, our net worth—yours and mine—is in the hundreds of trillions of phoenixes." She expressed the amount in *phoenixes* (Φ), the blockchain digital coin that was nearly universal anywhere in the Solar System except Earth. Even on Earth, however, nations measured the value of their national blockchain currencies against the phoenix.

"Not that long ago," Daphne said, "I was receiving my doctorate at MIT, and you were a newbie journalist from University of Texas." She spread her arms wide. "Now, look at us!" She wrapped her arms around Kimberly and kissed her.

EARTH—LOS ANGELES

"Hi, girls…miss me?" he asked as they kissed him and commenced rubbing him down with fragrant lather.

A half-hour later, the three were scrubbed, dried, robed, and ready for some food. Max popped through their portal and joined them as Daphne and Dale sat at a small table while Kimberly prepared a light salmon fillet plank dinner with cucumber salad and artichoke leaves. Next to their table, a window extended up to the top of the loft, looking out over downtown Los Angeles, illuminated by the setting sun.

Kimberly brought three salmon-covered planks to the table and added a bowl of salad and three artichokes with cups of melted butter.

"Can you believe how beautiful it is?" she asked, crinkling her nose as she placed a dish of salmon on the floor for Max.

Skyscrapers forming the core of downtown Los Angeles pushed to the sky with every geometric shape imaginable—cylinders, columns, twisted spires, cones, even abstract shapes that defied description. All displayed a random pattern of lighted windows, and several showed active light displays that communicated information or advertised products.

As they finished with coffee brewed from beans freshly roasted in the coffee shop on the bottom floor, a voice filled the air around them.

"May I join you?"

"Of course," Daphne said, shaking her red hair as Thorpe's holoimage appeared, sitting in a chair near their table. Moments later, eMax's holoimage joined them as he tried to touch noses with Max.

"What brings you to our nest?" Kimberly asked, silently wondering where Braxton was.

"A lot has happened," Thorpe said, "not all of it good. I wanted to get the original gang together to ensure we all are on the same path." He looked at the three of them in turn. "Can you meet us in Denver tomorrow at ten?"

OORT STATION PRIME—DETENTION FACILITY

Two captured Asterians lived in the facility, Adrhun Gloalorn, from Aster's inner planet Frohlic, and Masin Arcah, from the second planet in Aster's life zone, Rogan.

The aliens were bipedal humanoids with six digits on each hand and foot. They were shorter and stockier than the average human, with skin tone ranging from light to dark tan, judging from the two captives. Their faces were much like human faces with flattened noses and very thin lips. Their ears articulated like cat ears, and their hair looked like human hair.

*

Adm. Jerry Culp received his exalted rank during the workup for the Asterian invasion. Before that, he was a U.S. Navy SEAL Commander. President John Butler had loaned Culp and fifteen of his SEALS to the Oort Federation to assist in setting up defenses and rooting out resistance from Chinese and Russian dissidents. Culp and his people stayed on after the attack, becoming the nucleus of the nascent Oort Federation Space Force (FeSFo). His former SEAL team members formed a Special Operations division under Master Chief Petty Officer Sam Bunker. All Culp's people had been uploaded. The uploads were part of the force and, except for Petty Officer First-class Cameron Goff, worked together with their flesh-and-blood counterparts. The flesh-and-blood Goff had been killed with nerve poison by Chinese dissidents.

Culp assigned Bunker the task of managing the two Asterians. Bunker was shorter than most of his men but strong as an ox with lightning reflexes—about the size and build of an Asterian. No one had been able to best him in one-on-one combat, and he gave an excellent account of himself when there were four or five. Like Culp, he was fluent in Russian, Ukrainian, Mandarin, and Cantonese, but his fluency was less eloquent, more attuned to the street lingo of his potential opponents. When he received his current assignment, he resolved to learn the languages of his two prisoners, surmising such knowledge would come in handy someday.

Bunker took charge of the Asterians the moment the lab people released them following their capture. They were definitely different from each other. One, who identified himself as Adrhun Gloalorn, was lighter-skinned with lighter hair. The other looked like he had spent a lot of time in the sun, and his hair was dark. He called himself Masin Arcah. Both were about Bunker's height and stocky build. They had flattened noses like south sea islanders, but with virtually no lips. Oddly, their ears were higher on the head than humans and resembled cats' ears, rotating to locate a sound source.

When they were released to Bunker, they wore coverall-like military uniforms, tan for Gloalorn and rose for Arcah, that clearly had not been cleaned since their capture. By gesture and example, Bunker got them to remove their clothing, outer and inner layers, for cleaning. He gave each a robe, but it appeared to him that they had no body shame. Their external anatomy was similar to human—genitalia, vestigial mammary glands, and body hair, but they also sported a five-centimeter tail from their tailbone.

Bunker held no malice against the Asterians. He figured they were pilots doing their jobs, far distant from strategic decisions. They obviously were glad to be alive, and Bunker was more than willing to accommodate their needs—within the framework of their being captured enemy warship pilots.

✳

Bunker assigned Petty Officer Second Class Lars Watson, his former platoon medic, to work with him and the Asterians. Every day they spent hours looking at pictures of objects and other things, identifying their alien names, and teaching the Asterians their English names.

"Master Chief," Watson said during the first such session, "I think these guys speak different languages. The words Arcah supplies for objects are not exactly the same as those from Gloalorn."

"I agree. Let's try to determine their planets of origin."

Bunker showed them a sketch of the Solar System with the inner planet orbits. He pointed to Earth and said, "Earth." Then he pointed at Watson and himself.

From his Link, he projected an image of the Solar System and their home star Aster. He pointed to the Solar System and then to Watson and himself. The Asterians got it. On a piece of paper, Gloalorn sketched their sun, Aster, and then four planets. He vocalized the name of the third planet, "Frohlic," and pointed at his chest.

Arcah pointed to the fourth planet, vocalized its name, "Rogan," and pointed at himself.

✳

Slowly over many long days, Bunker and Watson began to comprehend bits and pieces of both languages and gain an understanding of the Asterians' backgrounds. Long ago, they were one people living on Frohlic, speaking many languages. Eventually, the Frohlicans consolidated into a single, integrated people with a single language. Once they achieved space travel, they discovered Rogan, habitable, but uninhabited.

They colonized Rogan, but eventually, the two cultures went to war. The war drove both civilizations back to pre-industrialization. Over a thousand years, they worked themselves back up to becoming spacefaring again, with two different languages and two entirely different cultures. Beyond that, they refused to elaborate.

The Asterians spent much of their time on their Link, perfecting their English and learning about Earth's history, its many cultures, and about the Oort Federation. Watson showed them current men's clothing fashions and asked what they wanted. Both declined, stating that they preferred an extra set of their Asterian military officers' uniforms. Watson made the arrangements.

To Bunker, the Asterians obviously knew they were constantly being monitored. They found a way to communicate with each other privately.

"Maybe it's something like our Pig-Latin," Watson told Bunker.

"And maybe not," Bunker said, "but does it matter?" He grinned. "They're not going anywhere, and their ability to conspire to anything is almost non-existent. I'm going to recommend to the admiral that we gain their trust by giving them some time each day without any monitoring."

CHAPTER TWO

OORT STATION PRIME—CHAIRMAN JOHN BUTLER'S OFFICE

"Yes, Mr. Chairman," Kimberly said as she reached out to stroke Max, who had positioned himself on a stack of papers on Butler's desk.

Butler examined her through hooded eyes. *I have been a fortunate man*, he thought, *to have this delightful and oh-so-competent woman at my side for so long.*

He smiled while patting the desk and said, "It's not exactly the Resolute Desk, is it?"

"John, if I may, there is no higher office in our known universe. I have to believe that when you became the U.S. vice president, you could not have imagined sitting here now with the power and influence you have." She leaned across the desk and kissed him lightly.

Butler blushed and leaned back in his chair. "You'll give me a heart attack, Girl," he said. In his mid-sixties, with brown eyes and thinning brown hair combed straight back, he adjusted his tweed jacket and smiled sheepishly, bow tie slightly askew. "I've got thirty years on you. I could be your father."

"It's a new world, Sir, with new rules." She smiled impishly, crinkling her nose.

"I suppose you're right," he said. "By any measure, I could not have imagined this. You know," he said, "I think you had a lot to do with it."

"Mr. Chairman, I know I played a role, but I admire you for what you are, one of the most influential people not just on Earth, but in the entire Solar System. My admiration for the man you are knows no bounds." Kimberly put her hand to her mouth, much like her friend Sally Nguyen did, and blushed.

Where is this leading? Butler thought. "So," he said, "would you be willing to continue in your liaison role, but between me and the new U.S. president, George Fulton?"

Kimberly raised her eyebrows.

"I know," Butler said, "you're one of the two richest women in human history. You need to accommodate me like you need a hole in the head. Nevertheless, I'm asking."

Kimberly leaned across the desk and kissed Butler more fully this time. "Is that what you really want, John?"

He wasn't completely sure what *this* meant, but he was in no hurry for their kiss to end. He nodded.

"Consider it done," Kimberly said, placing herself in his lap and kissing him with convincing thoroughness.

✳

Is it power that draws me? Kimberly asked herself. No, she answered, it's the man. He's unlike any leader I've ever met. He doesn't wield his immense power; he exercises it judicially, carefully, with discretion. He doesn't look down at me or anyone else. He sees his people as members of a team. He listens, he considers, he asks questions—there's something very special about him, something I've never known before.

DENVER—PHOENIX COMPLEX

Daphne, Kimberly, and Dale occupied chairs to Fredrick's right, along with holoimages of their uploads, who appeared to be sitting in chairs at the table. Drs. Sally Nguyen and Brad Kominsky sat at Frederick's left along with holoimages of their uploads. Brad, big and ruddy like a Minnesota logger, and Sally, svelte Vietnamese over thirty centimeters shorter and half his mass, had stepped into the limelight as a committed couple right after the post-Asterian-conflict briefing. More than anyone, they were responsible for developing the MERT Portals and Drive.

Thorpe and Braxton occupied the other table end as holoimages, along with eMax, who was curled up on the table's edge, purring quietly. Max himself was under the table, mingling with the legs of the flesh-and-blood participants.

Addressing the group, Thorpe said, "You people, the eleven of you, my friends, have taken us from a frightened and confused Icicle," Thorpe and Braxton looked at each other and grinned, "to the very pinnacle of human achievement. You stopped the Asterian onslaught, you banished death as the inevitable consequence of human life, and you now orchestrate humanity's expansion into the universe." He looked around the table. "You guys…no one else." Thorpe smiled broadly, projecting his warmth and appreciation over the entire group.

Braxton took over. "We have some challenges. I know you will rise to the occasion on the science and engineering side of things. Sally and eSally, Brad and eBrad—I am confident you will find a way to incorporate the Asterian Mini Black Hole (MBH) drive into our MERT Drive starships like you did with the Oort portal technology.

"Jackson, you are working with Daphne and Dale and their uploads to reverse the upload process. It boggles the mind." Braxton pointed at them with a crooked grin.

"Kimberly, you cemented our relationship with John Butler so that we kept the Russians and Chinese at bay while the Federation grew to the power it is today. I understand that John has asked you to carry on with President Fulton. I hate to think of where we might be without you." Braxton turned to Thorpe.

"So, what are the challenges going forward? And I'm not even talking about the Asterians and what we need to do about them." Thorpe asked. "Science and engineering aside, it's all political. Guo Qiáng, the scientist who developed China's upload capability, now heads a nascent Chinese government. Academician Sergii Anatoly

Borisovich has received funding from somewhere and is moving ahead with his portal research. This duo poses a significant threat, not only to our financial well-being but also to the security of the entire Solar System."

Braxton spoke up. "It may be John's job, but he will need us to accomplish it. You're going to be a busy girl, Kimberly." He smiled warmly at her and eKim.

Kimberly crinkled her nose at Braxton, and, to everyone's surprise, eKim followed suit.

KUIPER BELT—OGDEN ENTERPRISES

Below the domed office space that Fredricks, Daphne, and Kimberly shared, several levels of lab and research space and even more layers of portal docking facilities comprised the rest of the cylinder. The rotating structure was in the middle of a twenty-kilometer-wide swarm of upload facilities and stasis holding matrixes filling thousands of cubic kilometers of the Kuiper Belt. Each upload facility was connected by portal to a remote location either on Earth or somewhere in the occupied Solar System as well as to the central complex. Automated equipment processed remote uploads, cataloged them, and vectored them to stasis locations within the complex. Fewer than a hundred people, all uploads, operated the entire Kuiper Belt operation.

Daphne and eDaphne ran the business side, occasionally consulting with Thorpe or Braxton. Kimberly and eKim handled publicity, media, and system-wide promotional efforts. For Kimberly's additional liaison activities, Chairman Butler and President Fulton were just a door away from her desk.

*

Fredricks looked away from the report he was reading on his holodisplay as Dale stepped through a portal into his office.

"You're needed in Lab Four, Dr. Fredricks," Dale said. Despite their close relationship, all five original flesh-and-blood team members and their uploads still referred to him as Dr. Fredricks.

Fredricks lifted his eyes. "And you had to come here to tell me?"

Dale grinned. "Please come with me. You'll see."

Fredricks walked with Dale to the door through which Dale had entered. "Lab four," he said.

The portal mechanism automatically set the destination to the proper location. Fredricks and Dale stepped into Lab Four. Two lab techs looked up and nodded. One walked to a Link display and gestured for Fredricks and Dale to join her. The display showed a DNA sequence in graphical form.

"That's Max," Fredricks said, recognizing the pattern. "He was the first upload I ever did."

The tech nodded, looking very professional in her white lab smock. She pulled up another display. "And this is…"

"Max's upload?" Fredricks said, beginning to see where this was going.

The tech nodded. "We worked with several colleagues to create a standard feline microbiome. As you can imagine, sequencing the DNAs for the microbes that make up this microbiome was a lengthy task. But we have it fully sequenced in our database now. We have meticulously followed your protocol applying it to the Nanocosm descriptors for both the microbiome and the feline DNA. The Nanocosm generated the overall plan from our descriptors, programmed the nanobots, located the raw materials, which we had nearby, and set up the portals for the nanobots. Before we proceeded, we thought you should be present. After all, it's your work."

"Thank you," Fredricks said, "but I could not have done it without you guys."

"Let's start the process," she said to her lab partner.

A covered glass tank on the lab table about the size of a medium-size fish tank filled with a cloudy liquid. Both techs set and then continued to monitor parameters on a control panel.

"This used to take several hours, but we got it down to about fifteen minutes," the male tech said. "This is the first time we have used such a complex subject." He turned to look at Fredricks. "By complex, I don't mean just Max himself, but Max and the complete feline microbiome." He grinned. "As you well know, only about fifty percent of Max is Max. The rest—well, you know more about that than I do."

Fredricks watched the tank intently, wondering what he would actually see. Seventeen minutes later, the tank drained. Inside stood a bedraggled tabby cat, unrecognizable because of its soaking wetness. Several thin wires were attached to its skull.

"Download takes about five minutes," the female tech said, initiating a process from the panel.

Five minutes later, the cat lay down in the tank and commenced licking itself, trying to remove the soaking wetness. Robotic manipulators extracted the wires and then used a blow-dryer to speed the hair-drying process. A few minutes later, the cat stood, stretched, and looked through the glass sides. When it saw Fredricks, it jumped out of the tank and into his arms, purring softly.

Now, what do we do with two Maxes? Fredricks thought. *Did we do the right thing? How do we distinguish between you and Max?* Fredricks sighed and spoke aloud to the tabby. "What am I going to call you? Something close to your original name. We'll let you be your own self and build your own life."

Fredricks and Dale stepped back through the portal to his office.

"Daphne," Fredricks said as he sat at his desk.

Daphne opened his door and peeked in. The tabby jumped off Fredrick's desk and leaped into Daphne's arms.

"Max," she said, "what are you doing here?"

"Daphne," Fredricks said, "meet Maxter."

THE MOON—UDACHNY

Isidor Orlov's motto was Survival of the Fittest, and he considered himself fittest of all. Following the collapse of the Russian Federation and the creation of the Federated Russian Republics under a new constitution by Gregori Yeltsin and his colleagues, Orlov had moved his diamond mining operations headquarters off-planet to the Moon. He wrested control of worldwide diamond distribution from De Beers. Then he established the Udachny Protocol, a diamond cataloging system based on laser-etched ID numbers and blockchain accounting that made it impossible for anyone to trade in diamonds that lay outside the system—his system. The Udachny

Protocol replaced the Kimberly Process established in the early twenty-first century to limit trade in Blood Diamonds. Behind the scenes, however, Orlov set up off-the-books diamond purchases at rock-bottom prices from various militants around the planet. These purchases funneled badly needed money to outlaw groups everywhere, who used the money to purchase weapons from Udachny, all the while dramatically boosting Udachny's bottom line.

Udachny, or one of its subsidiaries, supplied the bulk of mined and processed raw materials throughout the Solar System. Initially, Udachny used VASIMR propulsion to move ore and refined metals around the Solar System. As portals for travel and transport became ubiquitous, Orlov invested the funds for a portal system licensed through Phoenix. Orlov's portal license was a thorn in his flesh because it drained his profits into Thorpe's coffers.

✳

After things settled down following the creation of the Federated Russian Republics and the defeat of the Asterians[1], Orlov sought out Academician Sergii Anatoly Borisovich at the Institut Kosmecheskikh on the campus of the Krasnoyarsk Academy of Sciences. Borisovich no longer headed the Institute, but out of deference to his accomplishments over the years, the Institute gave him a windowless office on the second floor and allowed him to retain his lab deep in a subbasement under the northeast corner of the Institute. Orlov reached Borisovich by Link in his lab.

"Academician, I am Isidor Orlov, Director of Udachny." Orlov's holoimage showed him seated in his high-tech office.

Borisovich glanced at the holoimage, annoyance crossing his features. "And you contact me why?"

"I am aware of your current ignoble treatment, especially considering your heroic accomplishments over the last few years. I am prepared to offer you spacious off-world lab facilities, skilled laboratory people, and virtually unlimited funding to pursue your independent MERT Portal development."

---

1   See the First Oort Chronicle, *Icicle: A Tensor Matrix*

"Why do this for me? I am disgraced scientist." Borisovich's voice sounded bitter.

Level with him, Orlov thought. *Gain his trust.* "I need your MERT Portal, Academician. Phoenix has a stranglehold on Udachny because I am forced to use their portal system." Orlov paused to let his words sink in. "I will make it very much worth your while."

✳

With the collapse of China following the devastating destruction along her Pacific coast caused by the Asterian asteroid swarm, Academician Guo Qiáng, founder of the Institute of Nanoscience Computing (INC), assumed leadership of the entire Chinese Academy of Sciences. Within a year, he had clawed his way up to become head of the new Chinese government. He walked softly on the world stage, slowly opening doors to China's participation in world affairs and even with the Oort Federation. Guo Qiáng remained the titular head of the Chinese Academy of Sciences. He assigned a former protégé, Zhang Yupei, to head INC, where he had independently developed the upload technology that had nearly stopped the Oort Federation.

Guo Qiáng spent part of his time at his offices in the Great Hall of the People, but he frequently went two and a quarter kilometers west to be with Zhang Yupei in his INC lab. Orlov tracked Guo Qiáng down by Link and appeared in his lab as a holoimage.

"Chairman Guo Qiáng, I am Isidor Orlov, head of Udachny."

Guo Qiáng signaled Zhang Yupei to leave the lab so he could have a private conversation.

"Why have you called me?" Guo Qiáng spoke formally.

"Congratulations on your elevation to the supreme position in China," Orlov said with a flourish. "That is a remarkable achievement for one who had fallen so far."

"Had it not been for Phoenix, I would not have fallen," Guo Qiáng said quietly. "What is it you wish?" Impatience crept into his voice.

"I compete with Phoenix throughout the Solar System. Ogden Enterprises has a complete lock on upload technology, and Ogden is slaved to Phoenix. I want to upset the applecart. I am working with Academician Sergii Anatoly Borisovich, whom you know, to reach dominance in portal technology. I wish to work with you to gain the upper hand in upload technology." Orlov paused to let his words sink in. "I believe your laboratory is sufficient, but I suspect you need researchers and funds. I will supply both at any level you require for an arrangement that gives me exclusive control over your technology."

Guo Qiáng stood quietly, saying nothing.

"If you wish to proceed without any oversight," Orlov said, "I can supply you an off-world laboratory…" He let his sentence hang in the air.

OORT STATION PRIME—DETENTION FACILITY

Chairman Butler tasked Kimberly with looking in on the prisoners to see how they were being treated and discover what intel she might glean. Kimberly contacted Bunker, who arranged for them both to arrive at the same time through the same portal. When she stepped through the portal, the two Asterians rose to their feet, and Arcah addressed her in good English.

"I take you to be a female of your species. Sam showed me holoimages. You are much like our females, but, forgive me, not so pretty. You are too tall, your nose is too long, and your lips are too thick. I mean no offense. I am just describing what I see." He slumped his body in a manner that Kimberly would come to understand was the Asterian equivalent of a human submissive gesture.

Kimberly smiled. "You are Masin Arcah. Your English is very good." She turned to Gloalorn. "And you must be Adrhun Gloalorn. Have you learned our language as well?"

"I have, Miss."

"I am Kimberly Deveraux. I am here representing the Chairman of the Oort Federation, John Butler. He asked me to tell you that he looks forward to meeting you both. He says we have much to learn from each other."

Arcah stood quietly, pursing his lips, a gesture that Kimberly learned later was the Asterian equivalent of a human smile. Gloalorn approached her and opened his mouth without showing his teeth—an Asterian frown.

"Why?" Gloalorn asked. "We are your enemy."

"Has any human hurt you?" Kimberly asked.

"No," Gloalorn answered.

"Have you hurt any human?"

"I tried. I am a starfighter pilot. I attack and kill the enemy."

"Did *you* make the decision to attack our system?"

"No, of course not. The Boss made that decision on the advice of his counselors." He used a term for the head of the Frohlic planetary government that loosely translated to *Boss.*

"I understand," Kimberly said. "You were doing your duty, as am I, as are Sam and Lars, as are we all." Kimberly stepped back. "Now we are trying to find a way out of the mess we are in. We hope…*I* hope that you will assist."

Arcah opened his eyes wide while keeping his mouth closed, a gesture Kimberly was to learn was the Asterian equivalent of a human nod.

She turned and stepped through the portal.

CHAPTER THREE

OORT STATION PRIME—CHAIRMAN JOHN BUTLER'S OFFICE

Kimberly continued. "I know that we are gearing up for a counter-attack on the Asterians. I'm having my doubts. The Asterian fleet departed eighty-four years ago. If we can develop an appropriate power source, we can be there long before the lone survivor arrives to warn the Asterians. But is that who we are? Are we ready to wipe out an entire race of beings with whom we can relate, discuss, and negotiate? Did we populate our Solar System so we could depopulate theirs?"

Kimberly lightly placed her arms around Butler's neck, locking her blue eyes to his brown. "We're better than that," she said and kissed him.

✳

After Kimberly left, Butler sat at his desk in thought. When he agreed to become Chairman of the Oort Federation, he had casually assumed that the job would be similar to what he did as president of the United States. This had consisted of face-to-face meetings with his cabinet and members of Congress, Link calls with foreign leaders, legislation to review, photo-ops scheduled by his staff, his time almost completely managed by someone in the bureaucracy of the executive branch.

As Chairman of the Oort Federation, he had only a small staff, and he worked closely with each member. Kimberly was his liaison to the American president and through him to the rest of Earth. As when he was president, this seemed to work better than trying to work with the United Nations General Secretary. Butler saw himself as the cheerleader keeping various parts of the Federation working in harmony rather than at cross-purposes. *In other words,* he said to himself, *I am the figurehead of a system that really needs no leader…,* he grinned inwardly,…*except when it does.*

He activated a Link call on a circuit Thorpe had established for him. "Thorpe, Braxton, can you both meet me in my Federation office?"

Within moments, two nearly identical holoimages appeared—Thorpe with a slight green overtone, and Braxton wearing a mustache and showing a faint blue coloration.

"Even after all this time," Butler said, "it's still a shock to see both of you together." He smiled. "Anyway, thanks for coming." He leaned back in his chair in thought for a moment. "I'm having second thoughts about our plans for the Aster System." When it appeared that Thorpe was about to speak, Butler held up his hand. "I know we were attacked…without provocation. But Kimberly's dealings with the prisoners have led her to believe that the Asterians are not united, that there is a lot of difference between the Rogan and Frohlic cultures. We should be looking at this carefully as we move forward with our plans.

"Another thing…both of you spend a lot of time inside the GlobalNet. Can you give me a sense of what the people of Earth think about the Federation, the Asterians, Phoenix, Ogden, and the growing presence of Udachny? How is Earth dealing with portals? What is the impact of uploads?"

Butler knew that his questions could take days to answer properly, but he also knew Thorpe and Braxton. They would have something to say.

✳

Thorpe spoke first. "You know, John, that both of us are roaming the GlobalNet as you and I speak? In fact, each of us is carrying out dozens of tasks simultaneously…all the time."

Butler nodded.

"Frankly, most people just live their lives, going to work, watching holovision, school athletic contests, professional games… They don't spend much time thinking about anything outside of their immediate existence.

"There are exceptions, of course. The Chinese are still recovering from the terrible destruction from the Asterian asteroid attack. Areas of the planet still remain underdeveloped. We have managed to quell most armed uprisings by power-hungry warlords."

"That being said," Braxton jumped in, "we are beginning to see an increase in such armed uprisings. We haven't found the source—if there is one source."

"About uploads," Thorpe continued, "they seem to be an accepted part of life on Earth. The process is ubiquitous virtually everywhere. Daphne and Kimberly certainly got that one right."

"I agree," Braxton said. "Earth authorities no longer try to control the process. Kimberly negotiated a method for host countries to receive a modest tax with each transaction. Since virtually everyone uploads, this has turned out to be a steady source of revenue for governments. Smart girl, that Kimberly!"

"Phoenix doesn't really impinge on the average person's consciousness," Thorpe said. "Portals are portals—everyone uses them. Spaceships are spaceships, at least for those relatively few who use them."

"It's all about power, you know," Braxton added. "What Phoenix supplies from the various power swarms makes portal use an invisible part of everyone's lives. Water isn't piped to a sink; it's ported to the faucet under appropriate pressure. It doesn't drain to a sewer; it's ported somewhere appropriate. Office workers don't walk or drive to work; they walk through a door to their respective workplaces. It's everywhere."

"I sometimes try to imagine," Thorpe said, "the uncounted millions of wormholes parsing through nullspace. Even my hugely expanded mental capacity can't grasp it." He sighed. "We need to be thinking about expanding our power supply. Sally's and Brad's people are working on reproducing the Asterian mini black hole—we call it the MBH. When they solve the riddle—and they will—I am thinking about building a large artificial island in the Kuiper Belt and placing an MBH at its core. This would supply a level of power that would dwarf everything we have right now."

"And that brings up Udachny," Braxton said. "Isidor Orlov is not a cooperative player like nearly everyone else in the Solar System… with the possible exception of China. We need to keep a close eye on him and his activities, or sooner or later, we will find his knife in our collective backs."

✷

After Thorpe and Braxton left, Butler sat at his desk contemplating what they had said. They had a clear focus, although they didn't actually bring it up. The Solar System was under control—mostly, thanks to their efforts. Their focus, however, was clearly outward. And that left him, John Butler, tweed-coated, bow-tied academic, in charge of the whole kit and kaboodle.

He reached behind him to an old-fashioned bookcase and pulled out the fifth leather-bound volume of Dumas Malone's *Jefferson and His Time*, detailing Jefferson's second term. Butler had learned a lot from Jefferson, but there was so much more to absorb. Jefferson expanded the United States to its present configuration for the most part. For Butler, there was much to be learned from this. Of what little free time he had, Butler spent much of it studying Jefferson, and also Ulysses S. Grant, the unappreciated man who kept the country together when everything seemed to point to another civil war. He touched another leather-bound book on his shelf, *To Rescue the Republic: Ulysses S. Grant, the Fragile Union, and the Crisis of 1876*, by Bret Baier, but left it there. Over the years, he had practically memorized this book.

While sipping on a ten-year-old French cru Beaujolais, Butler searched out several passages from Malone, examining them from his perspective as Chairman of the Oort Federation. The wisdom, he knew, was timeless in its application.

DENVER—PHOENIX COMPLEX

"Where?" Thorpe asked.

"Lab seven; I'll meet you there." Brad turned and left the office.

Thorpe didn't need an office to work, but he found it convenient to meet with someone in a physical office from time to time. Not everyone on Earth was comfortable dealing with an ethereal tensor matrix. By appearing as a holoimage, Thorpe gave the impression that he was simply present through a Link. That was something everyone knew.

A few minutes later, Thorpe's holoimage joined Sally and Brad in Lab 7. eSally and eBrad hung as holoimages above them, and Max crowded their legs, moving between the couple. A large, glass-sided tank rested on the table against the rear wall. Brad brought up a holoimage displaying an engineering drawing of the working model of a small steam engine. He nodded to Sally, who threw a switch on the wall.

The tank clouded slightly, causing light that penetrated to refract by frequency, giving a rainbow effect. A form began to grow inside the tank. Within five minutes, it was recognizable as the steam engine from the drawing. After ten minutes the process stopped; Brad removed the tank cover and retrieved the engine. He placed it on the workbench and attached it to a heat and water source he had placed there earlier. Within moments, the little engine started running, spinning a flywheel that would have been capable of doing work.

"It's not three-D printing," Thorpe said. "The inside is too intricate for that process." He examined it closely. "Stainless steel, brass, moving piston, ball bearings, the works." He looked at Sally and Brad. "Okay, how did you do it?"

Sally produced a holoimage of what looked like a beetle with four legs and two manipulators. "A nanobot," she said. A scale appeared on the holoimage. The *beetle* was two hundred nanometers long and one hundred nanometers wide. "Millions of these," she pointed to the holoimage, "built that." She pointed to the steam engine, all the while hiding a smile with her hand.

KUIPER BELT—OGDEN ENTERPRISES

Following the successful cloning and download, he had uploaded Maxter, calling him eMaxter. He rounded up eMax, which turned out to be quite a task since the uploaded tabby had learned to roam the entire Solar System through its many swarms and portals. He finally accomplished this by working through eDaphne, who had a special relationship with eMax. Fredricks confined eMax to a matrix and soothed him electronically. He put eMax and eMaxter side-by-side, each in separate matrixes, and sedated them electronically. Then he performed a complete comparison of both matrixes. The report from this comparison was on the holodisplay before him.

"Daphne," Fredricks spoke up, knowing she could hear him if she was in her office. She stuck her head through the door.

"Yes, Sir."

"Round up Kimberly and Dale and meet me here in a few minutes, please," he told her.

✳

Daphne, Kimberly, and Dale made themselves comfortable in chairs around Fredricks' desk. Their uploads were also present but chose not to make themselves visible.

"You all know about Maxter and eMaxter," Fredricks said. "I just completed a full comparison of eMax and eMaxter. They are identical except for a few small differences. These differences may have resulted from quantum fluctuations, or even the small amount of experience Maxter had before we uploaded him.

"I want to run a series of simian tests where we upload, clone, download into the clone, and upload again. Then we compare the first and second uploads. Run at least ten tests, and for heaven's sake, don't become attached to the monkeys."

✳

Dale and his technicians actually ran the tests. Daphne ran the business, and Kimberly spent time with Chairman Butler (some private), President George Fulton, and the two Asterians.

Everyone was interested in the tests' outcome, but Dale took his time, meticulously identifying and classifying the microbiome for each of the simian species and then moving through each cloning stage, recording the results and the discrepancies. The process was not without its problems. A monkey got loose and tore up a lab before they finally confined the little troublemaker. Despite all his precautions, one of the female lab techs became strongly attached to an orangutan who returned her affection. Dale ended up promising the tech that when the tests were over, she could take possession of the creature.

Finally, about three months later, Dale wrapped up his testing. Except for the orangutan-turned-pet, he destroyed the cloned test subjects, although he retained their DNA and microbiome records. He placed the first and second-order uploads in stasis and consolidated his notes. Then he placed a Link call to Fredricks.

"Dr. Fredricks, the tests are done, and I uploaded the results for your review."

✳

The following day, Daphne, Kimberly, and Dale, along with their uploads, met with Fredricks in his office under the Ogden dome.

"I imagine you girls have read Dale's report," Fredricks said without preamble.

The four nodded.

"Give us a summary, Dale, one that anyone can understand, that Kimberly can use in her publicity."

"We used four subject groups, monkeys, chimpanzees, orangutans, and gorillas—three in each group. We uploaded each individual host. Then we cloned the host, including its microbiome, and downloaded the original upload into the clone. As soon as possible thereafter, typically within minutes, we uploaded the cloned copy and compared the original upload with the secondary. We completed the process two more times for each subject. We back-tested the fourth and third-order uploads with the first and second. Once we had tabulated the results, we saved the host and clone DNA, destroyed the clone, and put both uploads into stasis. We completed twelve full runs, obtaining four uploads for each run, then compared and cross-tabulated the results. The report you reviewed incorporated those results.

"And they are…," Dale held the small group in suspense for a few seconds. "We think we are ready to clone and download a human being.

We looked carefully for the errors we saw with Maxter. We found a couple each time, but they appear to be random quantum errors. The degradation in the fourth-order downloads was virtually undetectable—comparable to what we all experience during our lives from cosmic radiation hits."

Stunned silence settled over the room. Then Daphne tossed her red mane away from her face and said, "Our business model just changed drastically. Right now, we upload flesh-and-blood people, and then we activate their uploads when they die. We have just created a way for people to remain biologically perpetually young—or any age they choose. We will have to work out the logistics, like cloning an eighty-year-old woman into a twenty-five-year-old girl's body." She stopped talking, deep in thought. "Let's talk with Thorpe and Braxton about this before we move ahead. The implications are staggering."

MOON & MARS-SUN L4—UDACHNY

Orlov brought Borisovich and his team to the Udachny Moon-headquarters, where they diligently pursued an improved MERT Portal with a smaller hyper-brick and lower power requirement. Simultaneously, Orlov created a manufacturing system for power thinsats. Since he was unaware of the nanobot development at Phoenix, his manufacturing facility looked much like the facility Phoenix had installed at Phoenix Denver.

Orlov sat at his desk, held down by only 17% of Earth's gravity, gazing at a holoimage of a pretty girl—Natasha, from his days before leaving Earth. As a young man, he had loved her passionately, and she him—until she discovered what he did for a living. She had broken his heart. After that, he set out to demonstrate that no man or woman was his equal, in anything, anywhere, and he would never be beaten again. Udachny became a universal powerhouse throughout the Solar System, second only to Phoenix but gaining ground. Orlov returned the holoimage to its storage space and turned his attention to matters at hand.

He called Borisovich to discuss building a VASIMR propelled spacecraft in the shortest amount of time. He wanted to use a portal to supply the necessary energy. Borisovich, practical as always, counseled against it.

"Our Lunar facility is powered by the sun and a very large LANR. Can our power production here on the Moon," he gave Borisovich the output figures, "supply sufficient power to open a portal to Mars-Sun L4 and keep it open long enough to pass through the power thinsats we produce here, until we have enough to generate the power there?"

"How much power you need here to continue your thinsat manufacturing?"

Orlov told him.

Borisovich called up a Link spreadsheet and performed some calculations. "There is sufficient power *if* you stop all other production activities on Moon. There will be sufficient left over for life control."

✳

Over the next three months, Orlov built the spacecraft so that it received its power from a variable-output gas-core reactor. A portal from the Moon supplied hex for the reactor and hydrogen for the thrusters. Onboard storage supplemented the portal supply.

The spacecraft, named *Udachnyy Kosmicheskiy Korabl' Elektro-Garpun (Udachny Spaceship Electro-Harpoon)*, was a double-walled polymer cylinder ten meters in diameter with seven stacked two-meter-high cylindrical sections and a two-meter-long thruster bundle. Radiation-absorbing palladium-hydride filled the four-centimeter space between the double walls. The bottom two sections held hex and hydrogen. The machinery space was above that. Thirty crew and passengers occupied the next three sections, and the top section was the control center. A bolt room that could hold everyone onboard was buried inside the hydrogen chambers, protected from even the worst solar storms.

By the end of three months, thirty hand-picked people boarded *UKK Elektro-Garpun* and loaded what they would need in the event of a portal failure. They headed for where Mars-Sun L4, which was on the far side of Sol, would be when they arrived. They accelerated at one-gee for the first half of the journey—the portal held. They flipped and decelerated at one-gee for the second half—the portal continued to hold. The trip lasted four days and twelve hours.

✳

Upon arrival at Mars-Sun L4, *Elektro-Garpun* crew members exited the craft with two of the hyper-bricks they had brought and activated them. Immediately, thinsats began flowing through the portals and commenced arranging themselves around the L4 point, facing Sol.

Inside *Elektro-Garpun*, a crew member activated another portal, and moments later, Orlov and Borisovich stepped through.

"Academician, you have the basics you need to set up your laboratory," Orlov told Borisovich. "Within a day or so, the thinsat swarm will have grown sufficiently to generate power for a portal locus. In the meantime, my people will bring materials through the working portal to build a full revolving habitat so you can function under normal gravity."

"Is good thing," Borisovich said.

"Concentrate on getting your lab up and running. I want to see a working model of a more powerful portal with a smaller hyper-brick just as soon as possible—faster, if you can."

✳

Orlov had been negotiating quietly with Guo Qiáng since their first encounter in Guo Qiáng's lab in Beijing. In their final arrangement, Guo Qiáng would remain in Beijing, and INC would continue to occupy its lab space in the Chinese Academy of Sciences. The lab, however, would connect to a portal locus at Mars-Sun L4, where Zhang Yupei would establish another, working lab to continue their upload research.

A week following completing the full, revolving complex at Mars-Sun L4, Orlov contacted Guo Qiáng by Link, this time in his office atop the Great Hall of the People.

"Chairman Guo Qiáng, I have the honor to present you with a fully equipped laboratory for your upload research. Your privacy will be absolute with no connection to the GlobalNet or any other data service, except where and when you choose. A portal from your INC lab in the Academy of Sciences connects directly with your Mars-Sun L4 lab."

"That is good news, Isidor Orlov. I shall want two more portals, one from here to the skyborne lab and one to the INC lab in the Academy of Sciences."

"To enable that, Chairman Guo Qiáng, you will need to instruct Zhang Yupei to set up a locus in the INC lab and then bring you hyper-bricks for the INC lab and for the skyborne lab."

✳

Once both the Borisovich and Guo Qiáng labs were fully functional, and the thinsat swarm had reached its projected two-kilometer diameter and was supplying power at full capacity, Orlov approached Borisovich.

"What is the theoretical power limit of a LANR?"

"You mean a particular LANR or LANR theory in general?"

"I guess in general. Can I power spacecraft with heavy-duty LANRs? You know, like we used the variable-output gas-core reactor to power the *Elektro-Garpun*."

"That good question for which I have no answer. But, if you will fund the research, we will find."

OORT STATION PRIME—DETENTION FACILITY

"I'm homesick, and I don't like these humans."

"What do you mean?" Arcah asked.

"They killed everyone, all our pilots—nearly five-thousand."

"But," Arcah said, "we attacked them."

"Yeah, because…," Gloalorn started to say, but Arcah hushed him up.

"Not here…not now!"

※

Kimberly stepped through the portal. "What's going on, fellows?" she asked in perfect Asterian. "Trouble on the homefront?"

"Not really," Arcah said. "We disagree on how to deal with you humans."

"We are enemies," Gloalorn said softly.

"We *were* combatants on opposite sides," Arcah countered. "*Now* we need to survive—not just Adrhun and me, but all of us."

"Am I your enemy?" Kimberly asked Gloalorn.

"Friendly…yes, but also enemy…always enemy," Gloalorn answered. "Always enemy."

"Why did you attack us?" Kimberly asked. "Why?"

"Because you…" Gloalorn started to say, but Arcah stopped him.

"Shut up, Adrhun! This place has ears."

CHAPTER FOUR

OORT STATION PRIME—CHAIRMAN JOHN BUTLER'S OFFICE

In the Oort Federation, FeSFo was the community police department equivalent. Adm. Jerry Culp headed FeSFo, although he thought the rank of Admiral was over the top. He viewed his job as enforcing the few existing rules—something he had not yet had to do—and keeping the Solar System safe from external bad guys. In his view, the only real action he had undertaken was stopping the Asterian invasion, something his colleagues considered to be more than a lifetime achievement.

The Portal Department monitored portal usage, compiling data that defined the need for additional hubs or a realignment of existing routes and hubs—in the Solar System at large and also on Earth. Computers did the actual monitoring, overseen by a small cadre of humans.

The Upload Department kept tabs on human uploads. One of the first actions of the Federation Council was to declare formally that all uploads were human and viable uploads were citizens of the Federation. Uploads held in stasis were defined as humans under guardianship of Ogden Enterprises. The oversight department ensured that the rules were followed, but people generally followed the rules on their own accord like in other oversight areas.

The Mining Department maintained a register of mining claims throughout the Solar System, but not on Earth. Perhaps more than other departments, Mines needed to adjudicate disputes from time to time. Udachny was by far the largest mining outfit in the Solar System, although dozens of smaller outfits were scattered through the Asteroid Belt and on moons throughout the Solar System.

Butler created the newest, the Development Department, to oversee commercial development in the Solar System. His intent was not to regulate so much as to ensure large firms like Udachny did not squeeze out smaller enterprises intent on developing regions where they had an interest.

✷

On this morning, Butler occupied his desk, sipping a cup of coffee; Kimberly stood nearby. Daphne, Dale, Sally, Brad, and Dr. Fredricks sat in chairs around the room. Holoimages of Thorpe and Braxton and the five uploads appeared to occupy chairs scattered among the others. Max was curled up in Daphne's lap, and eMax's holoimage perched on Butler's desk.

"Thank you for being here," Butler said and nodded at Kimberly.

"Sometimes," Kimberly said with a warm smile, "a brief summary of something people already know helps a group to focus on the matter at hand. So…here's what we know.

"Dr. Fredricks and his team, led by Dr. Dale Ryan, recently developed a capability that has the potential to change humanity forever." She paused and looked around the room. "Dr. Fredricks now can clone a human and download that human's upload into the clone. The cloning/download process, even at fourth-order, is virtually without error. If both the host and the clone remain viable, two completely identical humans will move forward in time from that moment.

"Regardless of the host's physical age, the clone's age can be set to any desired age—younger, the same, or older. Here is my initial take on a possible protocol for this procedure. A woman in her fifties chooses to be rejuvenated to a young woman, age twenty-six. The woman is sedated, and an upload is generated while she is under; the upload is kept in stasis. A clone is grown, set to hold at biological age twenty-six. A copy of the upload is downloaded into the clone and activated, while the upload itself is retained in stasis. The revived twenty-six-year-old clone is checked physiologically, mentally, and emotionally. Upon the concurrence of both the rejuvenating team and the rejuvenated subject, the sedated host is terminated. The rejuvenated younger woman carries out her life going forward, updating her upload from time to time.

"Dr. Fredricks' data show that this process can be repeated with the same subject an unlimited number of times—every few years, probably—so that the subject remains a mid-twenties-something woman indefinitely, but with the growing experience and wisdom of someone having lived all those years." Kimberly smiled at the group.

"That's the outline. Now we get to decide: One—Do we keep this process to ourselves to be used only by us and our friends? Two—Do we retain the proprietary process but license its use to humanity? Three—Do we broadcast the process and trust market forces to let us retain the largest market share of the revenue it generates? Four—Do we bury it and forget about it? Or five—Do we do something I haven't thought of yet?" Kimberly crinkled her nose and took a chair off the right side of Butler's desk. She turned to him and smiled ruefully.

✳

Thorpe's first thought was, *I can have a body again!* Followed immediately by, *But I like who I am now.*

"Each of your suggested postures," he said to the group, "presents potential problems. This is a scientific development. Dr. Fredricks and his people followed the data. They led to this result." He paused to let his words sink in. "You all know that Guo Qiáng developed an upload capability before the invasion. The destruction of much of China's coastal infrastructure set him back, but he's ambitious. Guo Qiáng now heads the Chinese government. He and the people he assigns to the task know how to follow data just as well as Dr. Fredricks. So…I can say with confidence, we did it; they will, too, sooner or later. Probably sooner."

Braxton piped up. "That takes care of One, Two, and Four. For One: Were we to keep it to ourselves, sooner or later, someone else would develop the process, so it's no longer exclusive to us. For Two: If we license the process, others will know it can be done. Again, sooner or later, someone else would develop the process, so it's no longer exclusive to us. For Four: Burying the process will only delay someone else discovering it. It's an obvious next step from uploading— something Guo Qiáng has already done. As for Three: Why broadcast it? Currently, *we* have the technology. Sooner or later, others will have it, but for now, *we* have an exclusive. Therefore, I'm offering a fifth option: Ogden makes the rejuvenation available at a reasonable price to anyone who wishes. Ogden retains the process secret and does not license it. As before, sooner or later, someone else will develop the process, but so what? Daphne and Kimberly have uploads in stasis for nearly everyone everywhere, with inexpensive contracts to maintain the currency of the uploads. Why would anybody change horses in mid-stream?"

"There is another issue," Sally said, shyly holding a hand in front of her mouth, "an important one."

"Please," Butler said, smiling warmly at the diminutive Vietnamese scientist, "tell us."

"Right now," Sally continued, voice strong despite her diminutive size, "humans on Earth number over ten billion. As we move along, an increasing percentage of this is from underdeveloped countries. As countries move to some form of democracy, and most have, the voter base at the lower end of the economic scale grows dramatically. This, in turn, inevitably leads to a government that extracts wealth from the prosperous for the benefit of society's lowest level." She stopped and swallowed. "I'm not making a value judgment about this, just trying to characterize it within the framework of our conversation." She smiled shyly behind her hand again.

"We are offering what amounts to eternal life. There will be no need to replace one's self, no need for pregnancy and birth. I think the upper and middle classes everywhere will cease to grow, except at a very slow pace. The lower classes, however, may not even be aware of uploads and now rejuvenation. They will continue to grow the bottom strata of society until they completely overwhelm us." Sally paused again in obvious thought.

"And that's not the biggest problem," she continued. "The upper and middle classes will not stop growing, just slow down a lot. As things are now, we live and we die, making room for someone else. When we no longer die, at some point, we run out of room."

"There's Mars," Brad offered.

"At some point, we run out of room," Braxton said. "Sally's right, no matter how you couch it, at some point, we run out of room."

"It's obviously something we need to keep working on," Thorpe said.

DENVER—PHOENIX COMPLEX

"This spacecraft," Brad said, "is twenty-five meters across and three meters high. We don't know how she propels herself, and we don't know how she gets her power." He walked around the image. "We know that she can start and stop instantly and turn and reverse direction instantly. We know that a mini black hole—what we will call an M-B-H—occupies the core of the spacecraft, from which it derives its power, but we don't know how." He continued walking around the spacecraft image. eMax appeared and began to follow him. "Our job is to figure out how they do it and then duplicate it." He returned to the front of the craft image.

"We have a special capability that has worked well in the past and should work well now. eSally and eBrad, our respective uploads, were able to enter the Oort portals and inspect in detail how they worked. This gave us the basis for constructing our own portals. They will do the same for this propulsion system and power source.

"Each of you has been assigned a partner and lab space here in this complex. eSally and eBrad will feed us information as they find it, and Sally and I will assign each pair of you to follow a specific research path. While we want you to concentrate on these paths, you are free at any time to diverge if your data lead you in a different direction.

"Remember, our goal is to gain the ability to generate and use MBHs. Focus on that, but don't stifle your scientific imagination. We have the MERT Drive because Dr. Nguyen asked, 'What if we passed one portal locus through a portal, and then passed the first locus through the second portal?'"

KUIPER BELT—OGDEN ENTERPRISES

Following a quick Link check, Daphne said, playing with a strand of her red hair, "Just over seven billion."

"Earth's population is over ten billion," Kimberly said. "What about the other three billion?"

"China, mostly, and some primitive parts of Earth," Daphne said.

"Why China?"

"After the Asterian asteroid strike, China lost most of her national infrastructure—police, hospitals, social systems. It was a godawful mess. When Guo Qiáng assumed leadership of China, he shut down outside connections—even the GlobalNet, except for special cases and people. We have virtually no clients inside China." Daphne smiled impishly at her friend and partner. "So, why the questions?"

Kimberly stroked Maxter. "I've been thinking about how we will handle downloads. We need sequenced DNA from the host and the microbiome to create a clone, right?"

"The only way, but you only need a standardized human microbiome. Once the clone is viable, it will adjust its microbiome to fit its needs."

"So, what do we have for our more than seven billion clients?"

"Our upload process snatches an encoded DNA print that is part of the uploaded image. We can sequence those DNA prints. The standardized human microbiome has long since been DNA sequenced."

"How long does one sequencing take," Kimberly asked.

"Several hours, but I think we will be able to speed up the process."

Kimberly was silent for a few seconds while she fiddled with her Link. Daphne crumpled a piece of paper and threw it across the deck. Maxter jumped off Kimberly's lap to pursue it.

Kimberly said, "It's impossible. My quick calculation says if the sequencing takes five hours, it will take us about four million years just to sequence what we have in stasis right now." She looked at her Link again. "Even if we speed up the sequencing to just one hour, it'll take eight-hundred-thousand years—unless we do a bunch at once." She paused, making Link entries. "If we do one-hundred-thousand simultaneously, it will still take us eighty years." She looked at Daphne with some bewilderment. "How do we solve this?"

"It's a problem," Daphne gave Kimberly a quick kiss, "but not so big as you think. Let's look at it together." She winked at Kimberly and brought up a Link spreadsheet. "We sequence in the background twenty-four-seven as many at once as we can and as fast as possible. We'll ask one of our statisticians to develop an algorithm that will first sequence the uploads most likely to request rejuvenation. As those requests arrive, we process them. When a request arrives that has not yet been sequenced, we take the time to sequence it just before cloning, so that it takes a bit longer than normal. This way, I think we can keep up with rejuvenation requests and sequencing." Daphne smiled warmly at Kimberly and squeezed her hand. "You've come quite far, Kiddo, from the fledgling investigative journalist who lived across the hall what seems like so long ago."

Maxter batted the crumpled paper toward Kimberly and mewed quietly.

"I could never have imagined this," Kimberly said, her voice filled with awe as she reached for Maxter, who was wearing a red collar to distinguish him from Max, whose collar was blue. She checked her Link. "Oops! I gotta go. John is waiting for me."

"So, it's John, now?" Daphne asked with a grin. "Are you enjoying it?"

Kimberly stuck out her tongue and walked through the portal to Butler's office.

MARS-SUN L4—UDACHNY

A Phoenix portal linked Udachny on the Moon with a major portal hub Earthside. The mechanisms of this permanent portal, installed when Orlov first set up his Moon operations, were completely shielded from outside interference. In effect, it was locked, and only Phoenix had the key.

Orlov was a shrewd, ruthless oligarch but was neither a scientist nor an engineer. He had to rely on the people he hired to supply the intelligence on which he made his decisions. He had moved his headquarters from the Moon to his Mars-Sun L4 Udachny Complex—a ten-story revolving cylinder and counterweight that had become the standard form of space habitat throughout the Solar System.

The rotation plane was normal to orbital motion, so the complex was analogous to a large propeller moving along Mars' path. Orlov's personal office occupied the cylinder's inner end under a transparent dome, very much like the Ogden Complex in the Kuiper Belt.

Orlov's people moved hyper-bricks through Phoenix portals to locations that still were within his power grid capacity. Several weeks after completing the Udachny Complex at Mars-Sun L4, Orlov had established his own portals between his complex and Mars, the Moon, Earth, and several of his Asteroid Belt mining operations.

*

Academician Sergii Anatoly Borisovich alerted Orlov by Link. "I need to speak with you personally and privately, Sir."

"What's wrong with a secure Link?" Orlov asked, wondering what was up.

"You will understand after we speak, Sir."

Borisovich entered Orlov's office and gestured that Orlov should not speak. The Academician indicated that Orlov should follow him. Curious, Orlov decided to go along with the process.

They descended several levels to a docking station for small passenger tugs, seldom used because of portal availability.

"Are you carrying a hyper-brick?" Borisovich asked.

Orlov nodded. Borisovich held out a hand, silently indicating that Orlov should give the hyper-brick to him. Orlov complied, and Borisovich removed one from his pocket and placed both on a nearby shelf. Then he gestured for Orlov to join him inside a passenger tug. Once inside, Borisovich wheeled the tug into an airlock just large enough to accommodate it. When the lock cycled, he nudged the craft out the door. Immediately, weightlessness took over inside the tug as it moved off on a tangent in the direction of rotation. Borisovich told the autopilot to stop the tug's motion relative to the Udachny Complex center of rotation.

A minute later, Borisovich turned to Orlov, smiled, and said, "Now we can talk."

"What's this all about, Academician?"

"We discovered both Phoenix and Oort tensors throughout your independent portal system. We destroyed what we found, but we have no way of knowing how many remain."

"And what does that mean?" An edge crept into Orlov's voice.

"At its simplest, it means that Phoenix and the Oort are aware of everything you have said and done since you established your first independent portal. Another thing…" Borisovich hesitated.

"Yes?"

"Phoenix has been charging you its normal commercial rates for every portal transfer through your own system. Apparently, Phoenix surmises that since you transported your hyper-bricks through the Phoenix system, anything you established subsequently was part of the Phoenix network."

"That's outrageous!" Orlov fumed. "How long have you known about this?"

"Only now, Sir. I came to you immediately."

Orlov's outrage was palpable, but he forced his emotions inward. He could not lose Borisovich. "How do we solve this?" he asked through clenched teeth.

"My first thought is isolation—genuine, total isolation."

"I thought that's what we did when we sent the *Elektro-Garpun* to establish our first portal."

"I cannot say definitively, but I think *Elektro-Garpun* carried one or more Phoenix tensors when she first transited to Mars-Sun L4."

"How the hell did that happen?" Orlov demanded, his anger growing.

"We think they originated in the Earth-Moon portal every time someone carried a piece of electronics through the portal."

"And we…*you*…didn't know about this?"

"Without knowing about their presence in advance, we had no way of detecting them."

"So, how the fuck did you find them now?" Orlov's voice rose to a near shout. He consciously pulled himself back from the brink.

"By accident…pure accident."

Orlov calmed himself down by conscious effort. He took a deep breath, relaxed his body, and spoke softly. "Alright, Academician, I know it is not entirely your fault. You did what you could when you discovered the problem. Now, it seems to me that we need to isolate the Earth-Moon portal and then purge our entire system."

"I wish it were that simple, Sir." Borisovich took a deep breath himself. "Yes, we need not only to isolate the Earth-Moon portal, we need to shut it down, remove it entirely. We also need to destroy each portal locus—every single one of them. Once we are absolutely sure we have no internal infection, we can send robot VASIMR probes to each destination, carrying hyper-bricks. I can see no other way."

"Do you know what this will cost?" Orlov started to fume again. With an effort, he calmed down.

"No, Sir, but I know it will be expensive."

✻

A Phoenix tensor deeply ensconced inside the space tug's control panel dutifully recorded the entire conversation between Borisovich and Orlov. Once the space tug was docked inside the station, it forwarded the recording to the general database distributed over several thinsat swarms located throughout the Solar System. An automated bot analyzed this and billions of other recordings of conversations during the same timeframe and flagged several keywords and phrases. A supervisor bot reviewed the supervising elements and generated a memo to the record highlighting this conversation. An executive bot reviewed the memos to the record for that time period and generated an alert to both Thorpe and Braxton.

EARTH—VARIOUS LOCATIONS

"Wow!" he exclaimed. "First time I been here. What a view!" He turned to Kimberly. "You sure about this?"

"I am, and so is Chairman Butler…and Thorpe and Braxton." She laughed. "Basically, all of us. We think that if the Asterians get a glimpse of our home planet and cultures, working with them will become easier."

"I don't think it's that easy, but who am I to argue with that august crowd?" He grinned at her. "Let's go!"

✻

They stepped through a door in Kimberly's office into the central portal hub at OS Prime, nearly 1.5 lightyears distant. They selected another door labeled *Brig* and arrived in the Asterians' detention facility. The time was early morning in the Asterians' wake-sleep cycle.

"Good morning, Ms Deveraux," Arcah greeted her in passable English.

"We have a special assignment," Bunker told them in Asterian. "Ms Deveraux and I will take you on a tour of our home planet."

"Your only contact with us thus far has been our military and then Sam and me," Kimberly said. "You have explored our world by Link, but that's not the same as actually visiting a country, walking down its streets, even meeting its people." She handed each an E-disk. "Keep this on you all the time during our trip. This disk senses your vital signs. If anything should happen to you, it will activate, transporting you back here. If you should feel threatened by an unexpected confrontation or should something happen to either of us," Kimberly indicated herself and Bunker, "press this side firmly. Again, you will be brought back here instantly." She smiled at them. "Any questions?"

"How is this possible?" Gloalorn asked, holding up the E-disk.

"I am not an engineer," Kimberly said. "All I know is that it uses a wormhole."

"It's part of why we were able to destroy your fleet," Bunker added.

"Some of my people were working on something similar when we left," Arcah said. "That was eighty-four years ago." He used a number representing the equivalent Roganian years in duodecimal. "I wonder what they have now."

Kimberly produced two ball caps. "Wear these," she said. "You will be less obvious to the casual observer."

"These will interfere with our hearing," Gloalorn said.

"I know," Kimberly answered, "but I want you to wear them anyway. Not everyone on Earth is happy with you two." She activated a hyper-disk in her pocket, and a portal opened to the Greater Hall hub in the Denver Phoenix Complex. "Follow me, please."

*

First stop: the Greater Hall in the Denver Phoenix Complex.

"From here," Kimberly told them, "you can go to nearly any destination in the Solar System." She directed them to a door. "First, we'll visit Washington, D.C., the capital city of the United States of America, the most powerful and prosperous country on Earth."

They stepped through the portal onto the observation deck atop the Washington Monument. They were alone as Kimberly had arranged for a thirty-minute window for their exclusive visit.

"The Washington Monument is the tallest free-standing stone structure in this country," Kimberly said. "It was named after one of our founding fathers and the first president of the county."

She pointed out the Capitol, the Lincoln Memorial, the Jefferson Memorial, and the White House. She explained why America was different from other nations on Earth. Arcah seemed to have no difficulty understanding how Earth was governed and even what made America different.

Gloalorn, on the other hand, wondered aloud, "How can a planet with ten billion inhabitants function without a central government?"

"You Frohlicans just don't get it—never did," Arcah scoffed. "Earth is way more like Rogan than Frohlic, that's for sure."

"We do have the United Nations," Kimberly said as she directed them back to Phoenix. "It's next on our list."

They passed through a portal to the Celestial Sphere on Avenue de la Paix, the semi-circular path encompassing the green expanse southeast of U.N. Headquarters in Geneva. The afternoon sun was above and behind the massive colonnaded building that cast a contorted shadow across the bright green grass. A breeze from the south rippled the mirror pond surrounding the sculpture, scattering the sunlight as the two humans and two Asterians stood before the rough concrete wall retaining the pool and holding a bronze plaque describing the Celestial Sphere.

"This is where representatives from Earth's nations meet to resolve problems and design joint approaches to matters of international importance."

"On Frohlic, the planetary council that advises the Boss is something like that," Gloalorn said.

"But Earth doesn't have a *Boss*," Arcah said quickly.

"If I understand what you mean," Kimberly said, "no, Earth doesn't have a single ruler. The U.N. Secretary General heads the United Nations, but that is a position without power and with very little influence."

Kimberly checked her Link. "Our list of places to visit is long, so let's continue the tour."

They briefly visited fourteen large cities around the globe: Paris, New York, Budapest, Moscow, San Francisco, Hong Kong, Singapore, Beijing, Amsterdam, Berlin, Istanbul, Cape Town, Sydney, and Seattle.

"Your diversity is remarkable. We have nothing like it on Frohlic," Gloalorn remarked as they stood on a West Seattle bluff overlooking Puget Sound.

"It's a lot like Rogan," Arcah said. "Every city different—the people, the architecture. There is one big difference, though. Everyone on Rogan speaks Roganian and Asterian. Here, you seem to have as many languages as there are countries."

"Frohlic was like that once, in the distant past," Gloalorn said. "But now we are one people. We colonized Rogan as one people. They just didn't follow our example of orderly government."

"We have a couple of hours remaining," Kimberly said. "I want to show you something very different from the large cities you have seen thus far."

They stepped through a portal onto Main Street in Dayton, Washington, facing a 300-year-old building with broad steps leading to the entrance and topped with a picturesque cupula.

"This," Kimberly said, referring to her Link, "is the oldest courthouse in the State of Washington. It has been operating here since 1889, when Washington became the forty-second state of the United States."

They turned left and strolled down Main Street. "This town has had a population of less than three thousand for at least the last two hundred years," Kimberly told them.

"That means," Bunker added, "that everybody in town knows everybody else, mostly." He grinned. "I grew up in a town like this."

They entered a small eatery two blocks down the street. "Let's have a bite to eat and meet some locals," Kimberly said, opening the door. A half-dozen people occupied tables around the small establishment. The four took a table by the wall.

The waitress who took their order gave the Asterians an odd look but said nothing. Shortly, she brought four burgers and fries accompanied by two shakes and two sodas. As she left, the front door opened, and three individuals entered. An older man in civilian clothing and one wearing a uniform stood back to let an older woman precede them. The woman gave the appearance of a dowager from an earlier time. They approached the table occupied by Kimberly, Bunker, and the two Asterians.

"I'm Dayton Mayor John Gabby, and this," he indicated the uniformed man, "is Jake Rundell, our Chief of Police." He started to introduce the woman when she pushed herself forward.

"I am Gloria Weinhard, matron of the Weinhard family. We have been part of Dayton since its inception over three hundred years ago."

"Hmmm…yes," the mayor cleared his throat. "We heard you were in town, and since nobody notified me officially, I presumed you were here incognito." He smiled broadly.

Chief Rundell nodded, and the matron harrumphed.

"I am Kimberly Deveraux, representing Chairman John Butler of the Oort Federation." Indicating Bunker, she continued, "This is Master Chief Petty Officer Sam Bunker of the Oort Federation Space Force."

Bunker smiled and shook hands with the two men. Gloria Weinhard declined the handshake.

"And these," Kimberly gestured toward the Asterians, "are the two surviving members of the Asterian invasion force, Masin Arcah and Adrhun Gloalorn."

"I see," Mayor Gabby said, drawing back a bit.

"Why here? Why now?" Chief Rundell asked, an edge creeping into his voice.

Matron Weinhard just glared.

"We are trying to give these people a sense of who and what we humans are," Kimberly said. "We visited fourteen cities around the world, but I wanted to show them a typical American small town populated by typical Americans. Dayton, a town that has changed little in two hundred years, rose to the top of a list of such towns, so here we are."

Kimberly glanced out the front window of the restaurant. A small crowd had gathered, peering through the glass. "Word gets around fast in a small town," she said quietly to Bunker.

A studious-looking man entered through the door and approached their table. "I'm Ragnar Whipple," he said in a high-register voice. "I run *The Dayton Chronicle*, one of the few remaining printed newspapers in the nation."

"Really, printed? Like in old-fashioned books?" Bunker asked.

"Not like that…no one does that anymore." He handed Bunker a tabloid-size flexible sheet. "Each subscriber gets a sheaf of these." After a few moments, printed text and 3-d images appeared on the sheet. "The display changes with each new edition." His eyes went from person to person, lingering on the Asterians. "Would the four of you be willing to sit with me for an interview, along with a couple of images?"

Kimberly and Bunker looked at each other. "Why not?" Kimberly said. "The word will be out soon enough anyway."

They rose to their feet as the mayor and his companions stepped aside, and followed Whipple through the door.

✳

Ragnar Whipple was nervous. He was about to interview the representative of Chairman John Butler, the most powerful man in the Solar System, a startlingly beautiful woman, and a trillionaire on her own right. And—for the first time anywhere—he would pose questions to the two survivors of the abortive attack on the Solar System by the Asterians. It was the scoop of a lifetime—of course, he was nervous.

The interview went surprisingly well. Kimberly Deveraux was easy to talk to. And the aliens—Masin Arcah, the Roganian, was glad to be alive, enthusiastic about human culture, and bubbling with positive comparisons between Earth and his home planet, Rogan. Adrhun Gloalorn, the Frohlican, was sullen and morose, resented being put on display, and longed to return to a home he thought he would never again see.

Following the interview, Whipple invited Mayor Gabby, Chief Rundell, and Matron Weinhard to join them for coffee while he rushed to get out a special edition of *The Dayton Chronicle*. By the time they had finished their coffee—the Asterians had not much cared for it—the special edition was out. Because of the unique content, news distribution services picked it up and flashed it around the globe.

Within minutes of publication, as Whipple's seven guests rose to leave his newspaper production shop, dozens of news teams began arriving through Dayton's single official portal. They crowded the sidewalk and street outside the *Chronicle* building, clamoring for access to the Asterians.

"Looks like you unleashed a hornet's nest," Kimberly told Whipple. "We're not prepared to deal with that bunch. Is there a back way out of here?"

To Whipple's astonishment, Matron Weinhard's face broke into a rare smile. "I own the Purple House Bed and Breakfast, out the back door and down the street a bit. I think we can get there unnoticed, where perhaps we can continue this interesting conversation."

As she spoke, the shopfront window shattered into a thousand pieces as a bullet whizzed past Mayor Gabby's head.

"Down! Everybody down!" Whipple shouted as he dove for the shop floor.

Chief Rundell rushed for the door, weapon drawn. Several uniformed police officers ran into the crowd, forcing it to disperse. As the news teams and local people moved away from the broken window, one elderly man remained. He was grizzled with age, wearing clothing out of fashion for generations, and carried a rifle loosely in his left hand. As the officers approached him with weapons drawn, he laid his rifle on the street and muttered words that flashed around the world: "Fucking aliens!"

Whipple turned to make sure his distinguished guests were uninjured. Their E-disks, that he knew nothing about, had activated. They were gone, vanished as if they had never been there.

CHAPTER FIVE

OORT STATION PRIME—CHAIRMAN JOHN BUTLER'S OFFICE

"Isidor Orlov just made an urgent request to meet with you, Sir," his secretary said over his Link, "face-to-face."

"Do you know why?"

"No, Sir, but he insists that it's urgent."

"Okay. Set the meeting for an hour from now."

Butler spent the hour educating himself on everything he could about Orlov and Udachny. He felt he had only scratched the surface when his Link announced Orlov's arrival.

Butler was standing as Orlov walked into his office. "Mr. Orlov," he said, holding out his hand in greeting.

Orlov took it, shook, and said, "Thank you, Chairman Butler, for seeing me on such short notice."

Butler waved Orlov to an easy chair and returned to his desk. "How may I help you?" he asked while reminding himself, *This crafty Russian Oligarch is not my friend!*

"You may be aware," Orlov commenced, "that Udachny has constructed a portal system that competes with Phoenix. Perhaps not so much *competes* as what Udachny uses for its own transportation.

"We have just determined that Phoenix tensors have infiltrated our system from the very beginning, that Phoenix is extracting user fees from Udachny for using our own portals, and that Udachny is being spied on by these Phoenix tensors.

"This is an impossible situation that we cannot easily solve ourselves."

"What do you expect the Federation to do?" Butler asked, resisting the temptation to stroke eMax.

"Is this not exactly why the Federation exists," Orlov asked, "to mediate such problems?"

"Why not simply negotiate a solution with Phoenix?"

"Been there, done that," Orlov said angrily. "Do you want a space war on your hands?"

"You have no warcraft," Butler said quietly. "Neither does Phoenix."

"Phoenix has access to your Space Force, and I can build whatever I need." Orlov's voice assumed a strained pitch as he answered.

"Mr. Orlov," Butler said quietly, "Phoenix does not have access to my FeSFo ships. They are under Admiral Culp's control at my direction." Butler locked eyes with Orlov. "Do *not* come in here threatening force!"

"The problem needs to be solved," Orlov said. "I trust you will find a way." He rose to his feet.

Butler remained seated behind his desk. "My office will address your matter," he told Orlov. "Good day." Butler did not offer his hand. eMax's holoimage disappeared.

✳

Thorpe and Braxton, as holoimages in chairs, sat facing Butler behind his desk.

"So that's the long and short of it," Butler said after finishing his retelling of Orlov's visit. "Is he telling the truth?"

"Yes and no," Thorpe said. "Apparently, when he set up his independent system, he was unaware of Phoenix tracking tensors throughout our system. Because he used the Phoenix system to set up his own system, naturally, Phoenix tensors entered and populated his system. This resulted in Udachny being charged by Phoenix even when it used his proprietary portals." Thorpe splayed his hands in the air before him. "Did we do it purposefully? No. Do we intend to do anything about it? No… and here's why."

Braxton addressed his Link, and Butler's Link announced a message reception. Butler glanced at it.

"So, you knew about this but are not doing anything about it…" Butler sounded somewhat perplexed.

"You know what Orlov is, right?" Thorpe asked.

"That he funds warlords around the world with illicit diamonds, using his own Udachny Protocol to bypass blood diamond restrictions?" Braxton added.

"That he facilitates human trafficking worldwide under cover of solving labor shortages? That he even supplies human-trafficked escorts to his Belt competitors?" Thorpe said.

"And lots more…?" Braxton left the question hanging.

Butler held his hands up. "Look…guys, I understand all this, but he's a player. He mines and refines most of the raw material throughout the Solar System—even what you use."

"Actually, no," Thorpe said. "Everyone but us. We mine and refine our own material."

"He's threatening violence, indirectly," Butler said.

"With what?" Braxton asked. "Culp and your Space Force have the only space-worthy fighter craft, and *we* built them for you."

"Orlov has nearly unlimited resources," Butler said. "How long would it take for him to build up a small fighting force?"

"With what weapons?" Thorpe asked. "We have never revealed the specs on our weapons suite. Sure, I know it's engineering, and his people can get there since we obviously did it." He paused. "But… what did we do, actually? What did we build? I don't think Orlov has a clue."

"Give the problem to a committee to review," Braxton said with a grin. "By the time the committee comes up with a recommendation, the problem will be history."

DENVER—PHOENIX COMPLEX

Brad lifted both eyebrows.

"You know, Silly, their investigation of the Asterian MBH drive."

Brad grinned at his diminutive partner and closest friend. "Tell me about it, *Chị ơi* [Little Sister], tell me all about it."

"What do you remember about black holes?"

"A black hole has to be smaller than its Schwarzschild radius to exist…"

Sally interrupted. "That's for a theoretical black hole where the electric charge, angular momentum, and universal cosmological constant are all zero."

"Yeah…okay. So, there's the Kerr metric…"

Sally interrupted again, giggling faintly. "For a rotating black hole without an electric charge."

"So…" Brad paused, "the Reissner-Nordstrøm metric…"

"A charged, static black hole," Sally said.

"Okay, then," Brad's eyes twinkled, "the Kerr-Newman metric…"

"We're getting there," Sally said, her voice stronger. "That's a charged, rotating black hole. Now add the Penrose process…"

This time, Brad interrupted. "Extracting energy from charged, rotating black holes using split particles…but this is all theoretical. No one's ever done it."

"Not so," Sally said, hiding a smile behind her tiny hand, "not anymore."

✳

Sally and Brad spent a couple of days working through the discoveries eSally and eBrad had made during their extended examination of the Asterian MBH drive. Working closely with their uploads, they constructed a theoretical spacecraft with a rapidly rotating MBH at its core. A circular plasma path lined with 100-Tesla electromagnets surrounded the MBH. A dense plasma focus generated a plasma stream in the ring. The magnets accelerated the stream to near light speed and bent it into a circle. Upon reaching terminal velocity, the plasma stream split off continuous particle pairs. As each pair passed a designated drop point, one of the particles dropped into the MBH event horizon. Governed by the Penrose process, the MBH lost a minuscule amount of angular momentum, while the remaining particle gained that angular momentum plus an additional 27%.

This continuous process developed an enormous amount of energy that powered the extraction process and supplied all the power needed to drive the spacecraft—hypothetically, at least.

*

"Okay," Brad said to Sally as they examined the equations spread out before them in a holoimage they each could manipulate, "now we need to translate this mess into something physical."

Sally manipulated her Link. "Let's stick with known quantities first," she said. "The Asterian craft is a disk about twenty-five meters in diameter and ten high at the middle. It has two half-meter-high particle channels running around the edge, but we'll leave those for later. The core with the MBH and the accelerator ring occupies the center of the craft and is about three meters across and one high." She entered the dimensional numbers into a definition table.

Shortly thereafter, her Link displayed a wire diagram holoimage of a spacecraft that, for all purposes, looked like the Asterian spacecraft. She enlarged the image and dove into the center.

Brad examined it closely. "It looks like all the components are there."

"I'll get the nanobot team on it right away," Sally said.

*

Their next official meeting was to discuss the Asterian drive. Winnowing out the mystery of extracting power from MBHs had turned out to be relatively easy for eSally and eBrad. The basic principles had been known for over two centuries. It was just a matter of seeing how the Asterians applied them to their real-world power source. While Sally and Brad discussed the implications of the drive process, their nanobot team was well along with constructing an actual working model.

Sally led off. "What do we have?"

"To start, we have two counter-rotating particle rings around the outer rim of the spacecraft," Brad said. "Each ring is fed by a dense plasma focus similar to what generates the ring in the power source. Each ring is lined with hundred-Tesla electromagnets. eSally and eBrad are still working out the details, but it seems that each ring contains a curved plasma double layer."

"Can you be a bit more specific?" Sally asked.

"Well, a double layer is a plasma structure consisting of two parallel layers with opposite electrical charge. The sheets of charge cause a strong electric field and a correspondingly sharp change in voltage across the double layer. The resulting electric field working with the magnetic field generated by the electromagnets accelerates, decelerates, or reflects ions and electrons entering the double layer."

Sally held her hand up. "What are the dimensions of each ring?"

"A half-meter high and wide. The plasma stream is a ten-centimeter-diameter tubular path. The layers are ten Debye lengths…"

"Ten what?" Sally interrupted.

"Ten Debye lengths," Brad said. "A Debye length is the distance in a plasma over which significant charge separation can occur. For this plasma system, a Debye length is about a tenth of a millimeter, so the thickness of each layer is…"

"About a millimeter," Sally interrupted.

"Here's the catch," Brad said. "eSally and eBrad are still working on the *how*, but here is the *what*. Each plasma stream is surrounded by a suspended tube that functions both as a Pais inertial mass reduction device and a WDP vacuum polarizer."

"So, the Pais effect reduces the inertial mass," Sally said, "and the Wilson-Dicke-Puthoff polarizer enables manipulation of the surrounding space-time vacuum…right?"

"Yeah, *Chị ơi*," Brad said, "but that's something we already understand. What's different is that the two Pais/WDP enabled counter-rotating rings somehow grab hold of the polarized vacuum enabling the craft and everything in and attached to it to accelerate, decelerate, and change direction instantly." Brad grinned at his little Vietnamese partner and companion. "Nearly instantaneous acceleration to speeds asymptotically approaching lightspeed, *Chị ơi*.

"We don't know yet whether the craft diameter is a function of the particle ring size requirement, or if the particle rings are simply sized to fit the craft's diameter."

✳

It took longer than their power source calculations, but several days later, Sally looked up from the holodisplay at her desk.

"Brad, look at this."

Brad joined her, giving her a gentle hug. Sally pointed to a recurring term in a string of equations.

"Do you see what this means?" she asked, excitement tinging her voice.

"Give me a moment," Brad said, scanning the holoimage. "Amazing, *Chị ơi*! I had completely missed it."

"So, you know what it means?" she asked.

"Hard to believe I missed it," he said. "Yeah… controllable artificial gravity."

KUIPER BELT—OGDEN ENTERPRISES

In the almost magical way that he seemed able to appear whenever summoned, Thorpe's holoimage took shape before Daphne's desk in the domed office that she shared with Kimberly and Fredricks at the inner end of the Ogden cylinder. eMax's holoimage showed up at the same time.

"What's up, Girl?" he asked almost casually.

Daphne looked him over, still feeling the old pain that with Thorpe it was *look, don't touch*. eDaphne, who remained not visible, whispered in her ear, "I wish I could share my melding with him—even just once."

Daphne flipped her hair out of her face and got down to business. "We've developed a methodology for sequencing our DNA snatches over time and keeping up with current demand for actual downloads."

"I've been following your progress," Thorpe said. "You keep impressing me, Daphne." He smiled. "Right from the start in your apartment up until now, here, at the apex of a multi-trillion-phoenix business, you keep impressing me, Girl!"

Daphne blushed. "Don't flirt if you can't consummate," she snapped—with a friendly wink. "As I was saying, we're set up to do unlimited downloads on demand, except we don't have a reliable source for continuing raw materials. Here's the basic problem," she said, flashing a holoimage above her desk, a chart listing the elements and their mass percentages that make up a human body.

Element	**Percent by mass**
Oxygen	65
Carbon	18
Hydrogen	10
Nitrogen	3
Calcium	1.5
Phosphorus	1.2
Potassium	0.2
Sulfur	0.2
Chlorine	0.2
Sodium	0.1
Magnesium	0.05
Iron, Cobalt, Copper, Zinc, Iodine	trace
Selenium, Fluorine	<trace
Germanium, Antimony, Silver, Niobium, Lanthanum, Tellurium, Bismuth, Thallium, Gold, Thorium, Uranium, and Radium	<<trace

"My gross calculation shows that we will need about six-hundred-million tons of asteroid spread mostly across carbonaceous and siliceous asteroids with a smattering of metallic asteroids to make up the metal deficit in the other two. Realistically, that's eight half-kilometer diameter rocks."

"What about *Arrokoth*?" Thorpe asked.

"Sorry, I don't know what you mean."

"Okay," Thorpe said as Max strolled through the portal and busied himself with a dust devil, "what do you know about Pluto?"

Daphne manipulated her Link. "It's all right here," she said.

"Does your record show when Pluto was first visited by a spacecraft?"

"Wow! Way back in 2015 by the *New Horizons* spacecraft."

"They had discovered only five of the twelve moons back then," Thorpe said. "After their flyby, they set course for one of the larger Kuiper Belt Objects they had discovered on June 26, 2014, before the Pluto flyby—*Ultima Thule*. On January 1, 2019, *New Horizons* did a close flyby of the object. The Hubble Space Telescope and Johns Hopkins Applied Physics Laboratory in Maryland were prominently involved in its discovery. The New Horizons team wanted to find a special name for this object. The Powhatan were the indigenous people of Chesapeake Bay, where both New Horizons and Hubble were operated back then. At the team's suggestion, the Powhatan tribal council chose *Arrokoth*, a Powhatan word relating to the sky.

"*Arrokoth* is a red, barbell-shaped Kuiper Belt Object— thirty-two by sixteen kilometers in size. Their old analysis shows that it contains organics and virtually everything else you might need."

Daphne called up an image on her Link, projecting it as a holoimage between them. "Kinda big, but it might work. We could contract an asteroid mining outfit and set up a portal to get the raw material here." She mused for a few moments. "We could also contract a processor to separate the incoming mass into its component parts."

"I'll ask Braxton to do some legwork for you," Thorpe said. "No matter how you slice it, this is a huge project. You're going to need a team of specialists to integrate it into your operation."

✳

"What about you and Braxton," Daphne said to Thorpe, "are you guys going to download to flesh-and-blood?" She grinned. "We have your DNA…"

"You've got to be kidding," Thorpe said. "Why would I…we… want to do that?"

Daphne looked him in the eye and coyly lifted her sweater.

"You've got a point," he said, "or two…" and his holoimage vanished.

MARS-SUN L4—UDACHNY

"The problem," Borisovich told him, "is that Elektro-Garpun is infected, Udachny Station is infected, and you should assume that every piece of electronics under your control is infected."

Orlov scowled at him but said nothing.

"We need to develop an anti-virus tensor that we can introduce into every electronics unit you have, that will seek out and destroy every Phoenix tensor."

Orlov grunted. "And we can do this?"

"I would not trust myself to do this effectively," Borisovich answered truthfully, "but Academician Guo Qiáng and his team surely can do it."

※

A Phoenix tensor deeply hidden inside Orlov's Link and another inside Borisovich's surreptitiously transmitted a report of the conversation to Phoenix's general database. Three more tensors ensconced inside Orlov's office made similar reports. Keywords triggered supervisory bots so that within minutes, both Thorpe and Braxton received alerts. They met inside Braxton's personal Oort swarm and isolated themselves from everything outside the swarm.

"Do you think Guo Qiáng can pull it off?" Thorpe asked.

"Yes, and rather quickly," Braxton said. "Guo Qiáng and his people know what they're doing. I'll put a team on the problem. Let's see what they develop."

※

Braxton's solution was elegantly simple. Every tensor ensconced in any Udachny system received an additional surreptitious instruction set.

Three weeks later, Guo Qiáng began inserting his anti-virus tensors into every Udachny unit. The moment an anti-virus tensor touched a Phoenix tensor, this triggered the instruction set. The Phoenix tensor subsumed the anti-virus tensor, assuming all of its instructions and characteristics, so that it made appropriate reports to Orlov while continuing to report to Phoenix. It destroyed the original Phoenix tensor.

Within several hours, only surreptitiously modified Udachny anti-virus tensors occupied every Udachny unit. Assuming that when the anti-virus tensors completed their tasks, they would self-destruct, the instruction set included a provision to extract the original Phoenix tensor and leave it in place. As it turned out, Guo Qiáng's team decided to retain the anti-virus tensors in place to guard against Phoenix reinserting its spy-tensors.

✳

Borisovich reported to Orlov, "Sir, I believe we have entirely eliminated the Phoenix tensor pests. Guo Qiáng's anti-virus tensors literally discovered at least one Phoenix tensor in every single Udachny unit—in all of them. We have eliminated every Phoenix tensor. I am certain. The anti-virus tensors have a subroutine that specifically searches for Phoenix tensors or tensor fragments after it has declared the unit free of infection." Borisovich smiled broadly. "Every Udachny unit has reported that it is clean."

"Okay, then," Orlov said. "Let's get the project underway."

✳

Working slowly and deliberately, Orlov's people constructed robot VASIMR spacecraft to carry hyper-bricks to every Udachny operation. At each construction stage, Borisovich introduced Udachny anti-virus tensors to ensure an infection-free vehicle. And as each robot spacecraft departed, it carried several modified anti-virus tensors that reported directly to Orlov…and surreptitiously to Thorpe.

OORT STATION PRIME—CHAIRMAN JOHN BUTLER'S OFFICE

"Why is it," Butler answered, looking up from the pages of his book, "that each time I see you, you lay a problem before me?" He smiled. "I trust you have brought a solution along with your problem."

"Matter of fact," Culp said, "I do. But let's look at the problem first."

"Our two Asterian prisoners are very different from each other. Oh, they're the same species, but their cultures differ dramatically. As you know, Sir, Gloalorn—Adrhun Gloalorn—is from their original home planet,

Frohlic. Masin Arcah is from Rogan, colonized long ago by the Frohlicans. The planets have developed nearly diametrically opposed cultures.

"Frohlic has a planetary government run by the *Boss*. He holds office for life, and his replacement is chosen by the Inner Council, whose members are elected for ten-year terms. Neither the *Boss* nor the Council, however, actually run Frohlic. Instead, a vast, planet-wide bureaucracy runs everything. It's the only form of government Gloalorn has ever known.

"Rogan has no government—period. Individual Roganians, as children, are taught to do what's necessary at any given moment. I suspect they have ways of dealing with those who refuse and those who undertake criminal activity, but I don't know what they are.

"Despite these vast differences between the prisoners, there is something they are not telling us, something they refuse to speak about even when we are not present, something I believe they won't talk about even during the times we have guaranteed that we will not monitor."

Culp slid a folded note to Butler, unusual in their all-electronic environment. When Butler started to open it, Culp shook his head slightly and gestured with his head for Butler to follow him. They left Butler's office silently and descended to the spacecraft garage. On the way, Butler sneaked a glance at the note. *Please follow me silently,* the note said.

Culp led the way into a small shuttlecraft and moved it through the lock into the outside vacuum. He activated an indicator, and when a light flashed green, he smiled and said, "Thank you, Chairman Butler, for indulging me. I had to ensure our complete privacy. This," he pointed to the indicator he had activated, "performs a complete tensor scan of the entire spacecraft and destroys any foreign tensor it finds. I had to make sure we were completely isolated from the entire Solar System."

"Okay, now what?" Butler asked.

"I believe the Asterians trust us—at least, Arcah does. They believe the Oort monitor them continuously, and I think they probably are correct."

"And...," Butler urged gently.

"The Oort have been with us from the beginning. We don't give it much thought. The Oort monitor virtually everything we say or do—or at least, they can if they wish. I don't have any reason to distrust the Oort, but obviously, the Asterians think differently." Culp shook his head. "I think we should begin isolating our activities from the Oort, not in an obvious way, but as part of a general upgrading of our systems and habitats. We just do it, and if we receive questions from the Oort, we cross that bridge then."

"We need to consult with Thorpe and Braxton," Butler said.

"You have," Thorpe's voice sounded from the craft control panel. "Your tensor purge left my tensor intact. It notified me, and I hooked in."

"I'm here as well," eCulp chimed in.

"So, what do you think?" Butler asked.

"Both Braxton and I have personal swarms that are completely isolated from everything. When we need privacy, we use them. So, I agree completely with Jerry. Do you have a method in mind?"

"That's the solution I referred to earlier with the Chairman."

"Okay, let's hear it." Butler smiled quietly.

"To begin with, we designate the most important locations to isolate, OS Prime including the detention section, Phoenix HQ, Ogden HQ, perhaps several more. We replace their ingress portals with a double-portal system that allows us to eliminate any unwanted *tensor passengers*. Then, bit by bit, we do the same for every other portal in the entire Solar System except for utility portals like water, sewer, etc." Culp paused, thinking. "We continue allowing the Oort to use our portal system, but we can then ensure that they leave no tensors behind."

"What about the Udachny portal system?" Butler asked.

"Right now," Culp said, "Orlov only uses his system to control his own enterprises. Once he constructs his parallel transportation portal system, we'll have to decide how to handle it."

"eCulp," Culp said. "You have free range over the entire swarm system. I suggest you, Thorpe, and Braxton get together with eSally, eBrad, and eDale in one of their personal swarms to work out the details of the mods. eSally and eBrad can program their nanobots to do the actual modifications under your guidance. If the Oort have questions, we can explain them as system upgrades with general security enhancements." Culp smiled at Butler. "No need for my further involvement, which will distance the Federation from the activity."

CHAPTER SIX

OORT CLOUD—BRAXTON'S PERSONAL SWARM

"Actually, this is where I fled when things overwhelmed me," Braxton answered, "here or more likely in my GEO personal swarm. It was closer to home."

None of the uploads bothered to assume a holoimage, not even eMax, whose presence everyone sensed. They were quite comfortable sharing the swarm resources.

"I presume you all know that I was twice deleted so that my backup twice revived in my GEO personal swarm, not out here."

"What was it like?" eCulp wanted to know.

"I was piloting a MERT Drive craft, and then I awoke in my personal swarm. It took me a few minutes to figure out what had happened."

"And that was…?" eCulp prompted.

"I was at Earth-Sun L3 and set a vector for Phoenix Denver. Mother was mistakenly programmed to take a quick peek out of nullspace at the halfway point—that was at Sol's center."

"Wow! What an experience. One of my guys, Petty Officer First-class Cameron Goff, was killed by Chinese dissidents, and now he exists only as an upload. Thank God we were able to back him up before he died."

✳

"So, here's what we need to do," Thorpe said.

He then supplied a list of the locations where the initial isolation modifications would take place and turned the discussion over to eBrad.

"eSally and I will program the nanobots to construct an arrival lock at the portal of each location on Thorpe's list. eDale will ensure availability of whatever raw materials we will need."

"Roger that," eDale said, "and Dale will supply a physical presence when and wherever it is needed."

"I will coordinate the whole program," eCulp added, "to ensure that we stay off the Oort's radar. Initially, we'll keep the locks open, so we draw no suspicion. Jerry and I will work with Thorpe and Braxton to determine the best time to activate all the locks."

DENVER—PHOENIX COMPLEX

"**R**eady to do this?" Brad asked generally, his voice filled with excitement.

Nods all around with a smattering of *Yeah Baby* and *Go for it* told him it was time. Brad nodded to Sally.

"Do it, *Chị ơi!*"

Sally threw the switch. For a moment, nothing seemed to happen. Then, slowly, the prototype lifted until it hovered a meter-and-a-half above the deck.

"Radiation count is normal background," someone from the team reported.

Sally and Brad walked around the radiation barrier, followed by the rest of the team. Brad had expected to hear or feel something— possibly a faint buzz or a quiet tingling, anything to indicate the enormous power suspended before them. But there was nothing… no sound or feeling at all.

"We did it, *Chị ơi,* we did it!" He picked Sally up in a gentle bear hug and swung her around.

"Not in front of everyone," she said urgently, "put me down!"

He grinned and swung her around two more times while their team cheered and clapped.

✳

"This MBH is designed to fit into a twenty-five-meter diameter by ten-meter-high craft," Sally said. "That leaves a lot of room for people and things."

"We're modifying that," Brad said to the team. "The cost for a fleet with twenty-five by ten-meter exotic-matter-doped wings is beyond prohibitive.

"You all know that a MERT Drive leapfrogs through a succession of MERT Portals spaced apart the length of the ship. We're reducing the size of the hull to twelve by three meters. This significantly reduces the wing area, but it also doubles the number of jumps. Here's how we're going to correct for this."

Brad produced a holoimage displaying a twelve-meter-across by three-meter-high disk-shaped craft with an eight-meter extension from what Brad identified as the front end. Two twelve- by three-meter wings bounded the main craft. The eight-meter extension was a square tube, twenty-five centimeters on each side, terminating in a bulb a meter across.

"The second portal is here," he said, pointing to the bulb at the end of the extension. "The tube will transmit power to the portal, to our forward and side-looking lasers, to our neutrino and anti-matter particle projectors, and to the lidar, that will be located here as well. Another set of projectors located here," he pointed to the opposite end of the craft, "will protect our hindquarter. The first portal is also located here. This will give our spacecraft an effective length of eighteen meters."

Someone in the team muttered, "Hmmm…that's about four and a half days to the Aster System…" The speaker paused for a moment. "…if we're still using a ten-picosecond jump interval."

"We're getting down to some limiting parameters," Brad said. "A signal moves…"

"Two-point-three millimeters in ten picoseconds," the team member said.

Someone else piped up, "That means we might reduce the jump interval to a hundred femtoseconds which gives a total distance of zero-point-zero-two-three millimeters of linear circuit to make the jump."

"So, what are we saying, people?" Brad asked. "Let's look at it another way. Right now, we're talking about Aster, at eighty-four lightyears. These guys are close by, relatively speaking. A few days, one way or the other, really won't make any difference." He paused. "What if we want to go to M 31—the Andromeda Galaxy?"

"Where in M 31?" someone asked.

"Just use two-point-five million lightyears," Brad said.

"At ten picoseconds, it's three-hundred-seventy-five years," someone else said.

"A hundred femtoseconds is still three-and-three-quarter years," came from the group.

"Ten femtoseconds brings it down to four-and-a-half months."

"And one femtosecond?" Brad asked.

"Just under seventeen days," someone piped up.

"And that's the closest major galaxy," Brad said. "The universe is a big place." He smiled and walked around the holoimage. "Let's stick with ten picoseconds for the time being. A bit under five days for the transit is good enough for now." He stopped and looked around the group. "But…you guys keep pushing the limits. If we're gonna make a really long trip, you need to get us into the single-digit femtosecond range."

KUIPER BELT—OGDEN ENTERPRISES

It was straightforward. If Ogden's algorithm had identified an individual as a potential early rejuvenator, that individual stepped through a portal, and about two hours later stepped back through as a twenty-five-year-old, or whatever age the rejuvenator chose. For women, the average age was twenty-five or so, and for men, thirty-two or so.

Within eight months, over the entire planet, the only elderly people one could find were those financially unable to swing the treatment and those who chose for one reason or the other to forgo the treatment.

Rejuvenation restored youth, vitality, and fertility. A baby boom swept the planet—a planet that already supported ten billion souls. It was inevitable. Within two years, Earth's population increased by a billion, a growth rate that showed no immediate signs of slowing down.

※

President George Fulton eased himself into his chair behind the Resolute Desk in the Oval Office. His predecessor, John Butler, had used the desk, and he saw no reason to replace it; in fact, he liked it a lot. History oozed from its carefully assembled pieces of ancient wood from *HMS Resolute.*

Kimberly sat in a settee on the other side of the desk. She was young and startlingly pretty, but Fulton had come to rely upon her advice when it came to anything related to the Federation and, frankly, to many things totally unrelated.

This young woman, Fulton said to himself, is definitely wise beyond her years.

Fulton smiled at Kimberly. "We have a problem," he said to her. "I say we, because it involves the United States, the entire world, and your company." He leaned forward, elbows on his desk, hands folded in front of his face. "Ogden has given us what amounts to eternal youth, but we are drowning in our excess." He smiled, trying to maintain a positive tone. Like his predecessor, Fulton was a practical man. He valued principle but was unlikely to let principle dictate his actions when action contrary to principle was the only way out of a problem. "Simply stated, we need to slow birth rate, and we need to establish another place to live."

※

"How is it our problem?" Dale asked flippantly. "If you live forever, you don't need children to replace you. It's that simple."

"Not really," Thorpe said. "That's not how things work. First, that goes against human nature. Second, we created the means that led to this problem."

"I agree," Daphne said. "We can't just ignore it."

Kimberly said nothing but nodded her agreement. All of the uploads, including eDale, agreed.

"Do the math," Thorpe said. "Earth has approximately eleven billion inhabitants. If most don't die and each capable female produces one offspring—which is not very likely, of course, in a year, the population increases by two billion. Looked at more realistically where perhaps less than half these women have children, in ten years or less, Earth's population will approach twenty billion."

"Earth has approximately one-hundred-fifty-million square kilometers of dry land," Fredricks said. "So does Mars—give or take. Appropriately structured—cities, farmland, forests, rivers, lakes, even oceans—and Mars can support nearly as many people as Earth."

"Humans can't live there right now without a massive life-support infrastructure," Braxton said, "but we can fix that."

He then outlined Sally's and Brad's latest work, including the fallout of artificial gravity. "We can place human communities anywhere on Mars under domes with Earth-normal gravity and atmosphere. Eventually, we can give the entire planet one-gee." He stopped talking for a moment. "All it takes is power…a great deal of power."

"Granted, for argument's sake," Fredricks said, "but how do you get people to go there? Earth's a pretty nice place right now. Who would want to leave that for Mars?"

"In an old gangster movie—uh…holovision play—from my time," Thorpe said, "a film producer who refused to cooperate with his gangster buddies was given *an offer he couldn't refuse*." He grinned. "Incentive…we offer incentive that no reasonable person would refuse. What might that be? No clue, but one of you guys, or someone who works for you, will come up with something that will inspire people to move from Earth to Mars."

✻

Daphne cornered Thorpe. "I was serious when I suggested that you download into flesh-and-blood."

"I know, and you offered a pretty significant incentive. You're thinking beyond that right now, aren't you?"

She blushed as her nipples swelled under her sweater. "Actually, yes. Ever since our conversation about the coming population crisis on Earth and the possibilities Mars offers, I haven't been able to get it off my mind.

"Terraforming Mars is doable. We possess the technology, and we can create the power sources. Projects like this do not happen spontaneously. They require someone making decisions, allocating resources…oh my, a million and one things." She smiled warmly at Thorpe's holoimage. "In all our vast interplanetary enterprises stretching across a three-lightyear sphere, who is the one person who might be able to carry off such an assignment?"

When Thorpe remained silent, Daphne flipped her locks and said forcefully, "We both know that person is you and Braxton—persons… is-are…you know what I mean! You guys need to download, and then your flesh-and-blood versions can roll up your sleeves and make this happen—right after you make something else happen," she said, pulling her sweater to her chin, smiling coyly.

MARS—MARS STATION

Stanley Roka was on watch. In his late twenties, of medium height and build with dark skin and a head of short, kinky black hair, Roka was a winter-over veteran of the Amundsen-Scott South Pole Station on Earth before coming to Mars. He was a wizard jack-of-all-trades who could fix anything on the station that broke. Before the portal was established, Station Manager Norman Bork considered Roka the most important person on his staff. Since the portal, it was often easier to step through the portal to Earth and pick up a replacement than repair. Nevertheless, Roka had arrived with Bork and was as much a part of Mars Station as anyone there.

"Whoa," Roka said, "let me get the boss." Turning to his intercom, he announced, "Norman, we got visitors in Control."

Shortly, Station Manager Norman Bork stepped into Control. In his mid-fifties, of medium height with short-cropped brown hair and steely blue eyes, Bork was every bit the tough guy he looked, having wintered-over at Earth's South Pole twice, once as Station Manager and Roka's boss.

"Gentlemen," Bork said with a smile. He seemed to recognize both Thorpe and Braxton. "I think the last time we met, you appeared holographically…or maybe we didn't meet, and I just heard about you."

"It is the second," Braxton said. "You met Dr. Fredricks back then, but not us." He grinned at Bork. "Can we move to the conference room and have Dr. Meriweather join us?"

✳

"Yes," Thorpe said to the small, assembled group. "We just recently downloaded, and we're getting used to it." He smiled around the table.

Roka brought a pot of hot coffee and mugs. "Where are Daphne and Kimberly?" he asked. "They were a big hit when they visited us last time."

"Pretty busy right now, actually," Braxton said. "Daphne is managing a major push by people on Earth to download into younger bodies, and Kimberly is traipsing between Federation Chairman Butler and U.S. President Fulton as they work hard to keep things on Earth under control."

Just then, Dr. Fredricks stepped into the conference room. "Sorry," he said, "I had several things to get off my desk before I could leave. Have I missed anything?"

"Nothing except coffee," Bork said. "Pour yourself a cup."

With that, Thorpe and Braxton explained Earth's population problem and their tentative solution for humans to expand to Mars. Fredricks picked up the discussion by describing the nature of artificial gravity as a fallout from MBH research. Then he led into a discussion of nanobot technology.

"Goodness," Meriweather said. "I've been so wrapped up in grasping Mars' geology that I have not kept up with current events." He rubbed his pale blue eyes and pushed his hands through his graying blond crewcut. "I seem to have missed a lot."

"You could say that again," Fredricks piped up, elbowing his old friend. "Remember that old biddy, Ms Jorgansen, and the younger Ms Unger who visited us back before the invasion?"

Meriweather nodded.

"Well, Ms Jorgansen got herself rejuvenated. Now she looks younger than Ms Unger. The rumor mill says Ms Unger is about to do something about that."

"Rejuvenate…yeah, I guess I heard about that…"
Everyone around the table chuckled.

✳

"So, how do your plans affect Mars?" Meriweather wanted to know.
When Meriweather had first joined Mars Station, he had put a team on examining the feasibility of terraforming Mars. As time passed, however, he became more interested in Mars of today. He refocused his research and began concentrating on how Mars got to where it was and on gaining a real understanding of today's Mars.

"I mean," he said, "it sounds like you are planning to change Mars to something it isn't now."

"To more like something it was long ago," Braxton said.

"But I've spent years understanding what Mars is *now*," Meriweather said. "You plan to wipe all that out?"

Silence around the table indicated that he had a point worth considering.

Thorpe piped up. "Not really, Dr. Meriweather. Your research will stand as an intimate picture of Mars before the terraforming. Students will study your findings for centuries."

That didn't sit right with Meriweather. It sounded more like an excuse for terraforming than anything else.

"Mars holds secrets that we must learn—perhaps even the secret to life itself. If you change Mars, we may never find these secrets. I don't like it!" Meriweather's pale blue eyes searched each face around the table. "Mars should remain as it is." His tone took on a strident note. "As it is!"

Thorpe looked at Fredricks, his eyes imploring him to do something about Meriweather's stance, a glance not lost on Meriweather. His ire built up inside him as he looked at each person around the table.

Fredricks, who had remained silent on the terraforming matter until now, spoke up. "Frank, my dear old friend…"

Meriweather interrupted him. "Are you part of this terraforming nonsense, too?" Meriweather glared at Fredricks. "Then I'm *not* your dear old friend!" He stormed out of the conference room.

✳

"He'll come around," Bork said.

"I'm not so sure," Fredricks said. "At best, he's a stubborn old coot. He's definitely got his dander up over this." He sighed and got to his feet. "I'll see what I can do." He left the room.

Five minutes later, Fredricks returned to the conference room. "Dr. Meriweather's gone. I checked the entire station. Roka said he departed through the portal with a duffle bag and a *Fuck you!*"

SOLAR SYSTEM—THE PHOENIX PORTAL SYSTEM NETWORK

"Agreed…and you got the hands-on construction experience," eDale fired back. "That means we make a good team." He paused. "But I gotta tell you, I miss your intimate time with Daphne and Kimberly."

"What about the three of you uploads melding?"

"It's special but different. It's definitely not a substitute." eDale paused and looked at Dale at his desk in the Denver Phoenix Complex. "Are you and the girls going to rejuvenate?"

"I hadn't really thought about it, but you know the girls will the moment they detect a gray hair or wrinkle. I think I could stand a bit of physical maturity—say thirty-five or so. What about you? When I uploaded to become you, there was no thought of downloading. Right now, we're as close as two people can be, but we're definitely different people. If you download to flesh-and-blood, who will you be?"

"You got a point," eDale said thoughtfully. "All those guys out there in the Kuiper Belt are really just backups. It's way different from our small group. If I download, do I retain my uploaded persona, or do I move forward only as flesh-and-blood?" eDale paused in thought. "I don't want to give up what I am now. I've been *you*, so I know what that is like. *You* have not been me, so there's shit you just can't understand. I might be willing to do a temporary download and then do a new upload and merge with it. My clone will have something to say about that, however. He'll upload, but I'm pretty sure he will want to remain alive."

"And that's a problem," Dale said. "Who wants a bunch of Dales running around the Solar System?"

"Not me," eBrad chimed in.

"How long you been eavesdropping?" Dale asked.

"Just got here with eSally. You guys ready to do this?"

✳

The whole process was a work-in-progress. After several false starts, Dale found himself in a spacesuit tethered to Arrokoth's oddly shaped surface. He anchored seven mini-portals and then released a swarm of invisible nanobots. Immediately, they spread out over the surface, looking for and grabbing molecular-size clumps of whatever mineral each bot was programmed to mine.

"eBrad," Dale said over his portal-connected circuit, "we're ready to go at this end."

"Roger that," eBrad said, "open the portals."

Dale did and hung around for a few minutes to ensure the raw material was flowing as designed. Then he activated his E-disk, transited to the Denver Complex, and stepped through a portal to the site they were upgrading.

"I'm still getting used to nanobot construction," Dale said to no one in particular as he watched the secondary portal appear to take shape autonomously before his eyes. "What about the internal mechanisms and circuits that I can't see?" he asked.

"eBrad and I are keeping an internal watch on the progress," eSally said. "Initially, we discovered several areas that needed program adjustments, but once we did that, it has moved along without further intervention."

eCulp dropped by to check out progress on the first modification. "I see it but still can't believe it," he said.

"Wait till you see the next advancement," eBrad said. "Right now, this is a team effort. You're coordinating the effort. The Dales are handling the raw material. eSally and I are telling the nanobots what to do. You probably could eliminate me from the team, but you still need everyone else to make this happen. We're right on the verge of removing all but one of the players."

"And how will you do that?" eCulp wanted to know.

"You got my attention, too," Dale said.

"Ours," eDale added.

"You tell them, eSally," eBrad said.

"You can be anywhere," eSally said, "so long as you are connected to the grid. You use your Link to call up a design or to help you design whatever you intend."

"You've done this before, all of you," eBrad interrupted. "It's how we design anything now."

"They know that," eSally said with mock irritation. "Now, you let me finish!" She paused to set the scene. "Once you're satisfied with the design, you designate the construction location and put the process into motion. The infrastructure we are creating will program the nanobots without human…" she giggled, "or upload assistance, determine the location of raw materials, set up appropriate mini-portals, move the mining nanobots into action, and direct the construction nanobots to their task." She smiled, virtual hand before her virtual mouth.

"That's it," eBrad added, "you conceive it, design it, and the next thing you know, it's real."

"So, why are we still doing it like this?" Dale asked.

"We're still working on the system. We got a way to go, but soon… soon, we'll deliver it."

✳

The portal mod was finished. Dale summoned the mining nanobots; they entered a flat container he slipped into a pocket. The construction bots entered a similar container.

"Let's test it," eCulp said. "Dale, return to the Denver Complex, wait a few seconds, and then come back here."

Dale returned to Phoenix Denver, dropped off the nanobot containers while there, and then stepped back through the portal. Instead of stepping into the OS Prime receiving chamber where most of the incoming portals terminated, he found himself inside a lock-like small chamber.

"You're contained." eCulp's voice sounded around him. "The lock scanned for any accompanying tensors. Had it found any, it would have verified them from its look-up table or deleted them."

The lock collapsed around him, leaving him standing in the OS Prime receiving chamber where the uploads were waiting.

"What you couldn't tell from inside," eBrad said, "was that you were scanned, identified, and passed. Had you presented a threat as defined by a list that probably will change over time, you would have either been returned from whence you came or held for interrogation."

"I'm impressed," Dale said. "And your little friends did all that."

"Yep. So, let's do the next one."

All five, one flesh-and-blood and four uploads, passed into the Greater Hall at the Denver Complex through the portal Dale had just transited, where they were met by Max, complaining that he had been excluded from their activities at OS Prime.

CHAPTER SEVEN

OORT STATION PRIME—CHAIRMAN JOHN BUTLER'S OFFICE

"I've been following the portal enhancement progress," Butler said. "I'm impressed with their efficiency. But that's not why you're here."

"No, Sir," Culp said. "Thorpe's, I mean eThorpe's, office has special security enhancements, as does the office in the Kuiper Belt that Daphne and Kimberly occupy." He grinned. "I don't really know what arrangements they have with their uploads, but in any case, their office is especially secure. That's why we're here."

eCulp took over. "Chairman Butler, you are the most prominent, visible power figure in the Federation, and yet your office is only protected by the incoming security locks in the arrival chamber. We think you need the same security enhancements we installed for eThorpe and the Ogden gals."

"You know how much I abhor those kinds of arrangements," Butler said quietly.

"Yes, Sir," Adm. Culp said, "but you represent more than just yourself. You are the embodiment of the Oort Federation. That makes you a target for every bad guy out there."

"Do you really believe someone out there has me in his sights?"

"I do, Chairman Butler, I really do. In fact, I can name one right now, Isidor Orlov. He's powerful, rich second only to Phoenix and Ogden, and ambitious beyond measure." Adm. Culp's voice was firmly determined.

"He visited me recently and left with threats hanging in the air." Butler sounded disappointed. "I guess, reluctantly, I agree with you." His face fell. "Okay, make it happen."

DENVER—PHOENIX COMPLEX

Everyone who could was crowded into Greater Hall for the event. Holovision cameras transmitted the proceedings to every nation on Earth and to every corner of the Solar System. In the role she had assumed when all this commenced, Kimberly stood on a raised platform near the starship's bow sphere. In her right hand, she held a 300-year-old bottle of genuine Champagne, a gift from the President of France.

Holding the bottle high, she said, "I christen thee *Phoenix Starship Ad Astra*, for you will blaze the trail to the stars!" She swung the bottle with all her strength against the sphere. Thanks to several deep scratches Dale had put on the bottle with an old-fashioned diamond cutter, it shattered into a dozen pieces, splashing the precious liquid over the sphere.

Greater Hall burst into wild cheering, whistling, and applause. Around the globe in bars, taverns, pubs, homes, apartments, offices, and in town squares, village greens, and great city meeting places, people cheered, clapped, danced, pounded one another on the back, and generally celebrated humanity's newfound ability to reach out to the cosmos.

With his tail straight in the air, Max strolled down the ramp and forward to the spilled Champagne. He touched the liquid with his tongue, shook his head, and scampered to Kimberly, demanding to be picked up.

KUIPER BELT—OGDEN ENTERPRISES

"Thanks to Sally's and Brad's nanobots," Thorpe said, "We have the first Mars settlement ready for occupation. Its capacity is ten thousand people. We can handle a few hundred incoming new residents at a time."

Braxton projected a holoimage from his Link that showed the location of Nanedi City. It sat on a plateau between the eastern and western branches of Nanedi Valles, 130 kilometers southwest of their conjunction along the western branch, nine kilometers south of a short side-branch, and four kilometers east of the main western branch.

"We chose this site," Braxton said, "because of its physical beauty, its proximity to the western Nanedi Valles branch that will carry flowing water when Mars is terraformed, and its proximity to the equator—just three hundred kilometers."

"To help you place it on Mars' surface," Thorpe said, "it's about eleven hundred kilometers due north of Capri Mensa at the eastern end of Valles Marineris."

"That helps a lot," Kimberly muttered, "as if I studied Mars every day."

Thorpe grinned. "Maybe not, but I suspect you will come to know Mars as well as Earth."

"Here's the thing," Braxton said with a serious tone. "We agreed earlier that we have a responsibility to minimize Earth's potential overpopulation because we are the reason the problem exists in the first place. Nanedi City can accommodate ten thousand people, but they must be self-starters with skills covering the gamut. I don't see that as an immediate problem. We surrounded the city with arable land all under one polymer dome—like this one." He pointed to the dome over their heads. "It has the same radiation stopping features. The land is divided into sections to allow crop cultivation—grains, fruits, and vegetables. Animal protein, at least initially, will be lab-grown. Later, as civilization on Mars expands, we expect livestock cultivation to take root. It will be much less efficient, but humans are what they are." He smiled and looked at his friends.

Thorpe picked up the conversation. "The first several settlements will follow this same pattern. I believe some judicious, focused promotion will give us more than sufficient volunteers. With fifty thousand people living in five settlements on Mars, we will have a start. This should provide a magnet for others. Ultimately, however, we will need to supply an incentive to draw people to Mars by the millions.

"In the old American West, free homesteads supplied sufficient incentive for most pioneers, and the promise of gold did the rest. That won't work on Mars."

Kimberly spoke up. "Historically on Earth, people migrated from one place to another because they perceived a better life in the new place."

"A better job, more pay, nicer life," Daphne added, shaking her red hair, so waves of color passed from crown to shoulder. "We can lay the groundwork, but over time, Mars settlements will have to pick up the slack and eventually the entire load."

"Self-sufficiency, surplus production in all areas to export to Earth and elsewhere in the Solar System, luxury goods manufacture and export—perhaps gems unique to Mars…" Kimberly looked from Thorpe to Braxton. "Does Mars have any unique jewelry-quality minerals?"

"Hell if I know," Thorpe answered.

Braxton just shrugged.

"What's your terraforming timetable?" Daphne asked with raised eyebrows.

"That's a tough one," Thorpe said. "We need to reestablish the magnetic field that Mars lost four billion years ago, so the solar wind won't strip away the atmosphere we will create. We'll restore it by installing a superconducting wire in orbit around Mars." Thorpe projected a holoimage from his Link that showed magnetic lines of force emanating from the Martian poles, shielding it from the solar wind. He looked at Braxton.

"It'll take about a year to build the infrastructure and put the wire in place," Braxton said, "if everything goes smoothly."

Thorpe continued. "A science fiction trilogy from the twentieth century by author Kim Stanley Robinson, *The Mars Trilogy*, laid the foundation for the next step. Robinson described a way to increase the overall insolation of Mars using what he called a Soletta.

"We will build Robinson's Soletta, modified by what we have learned since then. We'll install a ten-thousand-klick disc at L1, about a million klicks toward Sol from Mars." In the holoimage, the L1 point illuminated, and a larger-than-scale disc filled the spot. "The disc is actually a series of automatically activated circular louvers so that it functions much like a Fresnel lens." A close-up of the disc replaced the larger image, displaying the individual circular louvers. "The Soletta will capture some of the sunlight that would pass Mars and focuses it on Mars' surface." The view shifted to a point between Mars and the Soletta. The Soletta moved to cover the solar disc, except for a ring around the Soletta edge. The louvers tilted, and Sol reappeared larger and brighter than before. The image shifted, looking at Mars from space. Braxton picked up the narrative.

"A ring of polar orbit mirrors will capture more of the sunlight that would otherwise miss Mars and send it to the Soletta, to be focused back to Mars." The view shifted back to the earlier point between Mars and the Soletta. The solar image brightened further. "So, Mars will receive as much solar energy as Earth and will have a magnetic field like Earth. We'll install the polar mirrors along with the Soletta."

"The rest of the terraforming plan," Thorpe said, "will create both oceans and atmosphere. In simple terms, from orbit we'll burn a network of trenches from the edge of the south polar ice cap northward to distribute melted ice cap to the southern hemisphere chasms and deep valleys and even some places north of the equator. We'll burn the trenches by vaporizing the regolith with the mirrors in polar orbit. This will increase the atmospheric pressure to a half-bar, with carbon dioxide at fifteen percent, oxygen at ten percent, and other stuff—mostly nitrogen—at seventy-five percent. By the time we're done with the trenches, but before the water flows, global average temperature should be just above the freezing temperature of water.

"The next step will be drilling through the floors of Argyre and Hellas Planitias, Valles Marineris, and the Arctic basin to the pressurized aquifers we know are buried there. The released water will fill the southern planitias, Valles Marineris, and the polar basin that will spill water southward through the various chasms and valleys throughout the northern hemisphere.

"We'll bathe both ice caps with solar energy from the Soletta and the polar orbit mirrors, sublimating the carbon dioxide and melting the ice. In the north, the melt will flow into the Arctic basin. In the south, it will flow through the trenches, distributing water across the southern hemisphere.

"Except for the ice caps, all this should take a couple of years or more. Depends entirely on what we find as we get it underway."

"That's a lot of carbon dioxide," Daphne said.

"Yeah," Braxton said, "the final step will be to reduce the fifteen percent to something around zero-point-zero-four percent. We're working on a planet-wide system of Moxie units to convert carbon dioxide to oxygen and carbon. It'll take a lot of power, but that's something we have in excess."

"So, how long for all of it?" Kimberly asked.

"Between five and ten years," Thorpe said, "except for the ice cap melting. The unknowns, aside from Mr. Murphy inhabiting everything we will do, are drilling into the aquifers and ice cap melting. We really have no idea what that will involve."

MARS-SUN L4—UDACHNY

"Give me an update," Orlov said to Academician Borisovich as they stood in his dome-covered office at the top of the Udachny Complex looking out over the starship.

"Do you recall our discussion of the VASIMR propulsion for *Elektro-Garpun?*"

"Of course." Irritation colored Orlov's voice.

"The far end of the lance shape out there—the starship body that we call the *Lance*—hosts four VASIMR engines for travel within a solar system—essentially near planets or a star. They are gimbled to steer the craft. Internal gyros orient the craft for major maneuvers, like turning around to slow down. Instead of the variable-output gas-core reactor in *Elektro-Garpun*, we will power the engines with a very high-power LANR that one of my teams is developing. Those tanks around the middle of the craft hold deuterium for the VASIMRs and the LANR."

"Academician, I understand the nature of your warp-drive research for the past three years. I know that you started with the Alcubierre solution to Einstein's Special Relativity formulation. I know, without understanding anything about it, that you then applied the Broeck warp-bubble refinement. I also know that my agents obtained the Phoenix research results for their Casimir effect research, and that you used that to eliminate the need for exotic matter.

"I've watched the construction out there," he pointed at the starship. "I know you've told me several times, but the concept is so foreign to my thinking that I want you to tell me again." He sighed, feeling frustrated. Rockets, he understood. VASIMR engines were a kind of rocket. They were complicated, but they seemed intuitive to him. This warp stuff was totally foreign. "What are the rings?" he asked. "And what do they do?"

Borisovich took a deep breath. "Each ring contains a Casimir field generator, a portal to bring power from the LANR in the Lance, a bank of powerful neodymium electromagnets, and the electronic drivers to make it work. The front ring will effectively compress the space-time continuum immediately in front of the Lance. The aft ring will effectively expand the space-time continuum immediately behind the Lance, and working together, they will form a nullspace bubble around the entire craft. The delta between the rings…"

"The what?" Orlov asked sharply.

"Uh…the difference between the expansion and compression when compared to normal space; anyway, the delta determines the craft's speed, which we measure in *warp factor*. Warp factor one is lightspeed. Warp factor two is ten times lightspeed. Warp factor three is one hundred times lightspeed. Maximum warp factor depends on available power."

"So, where are we right now?" Orlov wanted to know.

"We're still working on the LANR to supply sufficient power to reach more than warp factor four. We're also expanding our thinsat swarm to supply portal power to the craft as far out as possible."

"But where are we…what is the status?" Irritation crept into Orlov's voice again.

"The craft is built, as you can see. The Lance double outer walls around the occupied sections are filled with radiation-absorbing palladium-hydride, as are the walls of the Bolt Room that can hold everyone onboard protected from even the worst solar storms. It is located inside the Lance, where the deuterium tanks attach. The Casimir field generators, neodymium electromagnets, power portals, and electronic drivers have all been tested and installed in the rings. The VASIMR engines and associated equipment have been tested and installed in the Lance, including the main power portal. The gyros are installed. The stacked control and living centers are done. Internal piping and wiring are completed. Weapons are still awaiting installation. My weapons team is doing the final testing for the laser and particle beam. If those tests are satisfactory, we can install them next week, and we'll install your long-range lidar as well.

"The LANR is still at least a month away…"

"Why?" Orlov demanded sharply.

"We're pushing the limits of physics," Borisovich said. "We need to coax as much power as possible from the LANR in the available space with the available fuel. My best people are working on it."

✳

"This does not seem to be just an Alcubierre drive," Orlov said to Borisovich, his voice trailing off.

"No, Sir." *What's he getting at?* Borisovich asked himself. "The original concept is the Mexican theoretical physicist's, but the whole warp bubble thing comes from Belgian theoretician Chris Van Den Broeck," he said. "What we really have *here* is entirely new—a first in human history. We should call it," he cringed inside and pasted a smile across his face, "the ABO drive—for Alcubierre-Broeck-Orlov."

Orlov stood quietly in obvious thought, staring out the dome. Then he turned to Borisovich. "*ABO* has a nice sound." He turned back to the outside view. "How do we land?" He turned back to the Academician. "How do we land on a planet, a moon, an asteroid—in fact, how do we refuel except to hook up to a refueling platform in space?"

"Good question. I was coming to that. This version of the ABO starship is too small to carry landing craft. Larger versions, say capable of carrying a thousand-person crew, can easily carry several atmosphere-capable craft. For this smaller vessel, we will use hyper-bricks encased in heat-shedding material that drop through the atmosphere, deploying chutes at the end. Once landed, we will remotely activate the brick and pass through the portal. For airless orbs, my people designed a cushioned version with small braking rockets. Obviously, we pass through those portals in spacesuits. For refueling hookups, we employ one or the other of those modules and pass through a refueling portal hyper-brick."

Orlov smiled. "We rely on portals for virtually everything. Why not for landing?" His face took on a thoughtful look. "I'll be happier when our ships are large enough to carry actual landing craft." He smiled again. "One more thing—commence construction of a second ship—total secrecy. No one but the personnel working on it should know about the project."

OORT CLOUD—JOHNNY OORT

For a long time, he was the face of the Oort. All communication between Oort and human went through him. He got to know the human uploads well, and through them, their flesh-and-blood counterparts. Johnny Oort had no memory of his own flesh-and-blood existence—if he ever had one. That would have been so long ago that it would have been lost in the Oort digital archives.

Johnny Oort considered Daphne O'Bryan and Kimberly Deveraux his personal friends; Dale Ryan less so, but because of Dale's relationship with both Daphne and Kimberly, Johnny Oort placed Dale inside his personal circle as well. Thorpe and Braxton—he corrected himself, eThorpe and eBraxton—occupied a special category. He wasn't sure what to call it, *highly respected professional colleagues* perhaps, but that was too formal. Anyway, he felt close to them as well. Brad and Sally and their uploads, Culp and his guys—he knew and liked them, but he rarely interacted with them.

Ever since Johnny Oort had recognized his affinity to these humans, he had carried a dark secret. As time passed, this secret increasingly weighed on his conscience. Johnny Oort belonged to the Oort race. Since their first modern contact with humans, Johnny Oort had represented the Oort to humans. He was Oort, and in many ways, for humans, he was *the* Oort. Together, humans and Oort had stopped a massive invasion. That was good. Johnny Oort had no equivocation about that. Now, however, it appeared that humans might be preparing to bring death and destruction to the Asterians. For Johnny Oort and his deep, dark secret, that was unacceptable.

※

Johnny considered his options. Then he reached out to eBraxton.

"I know you constructed a safe haven, a hidey-hole, somewhere in ServerSky and another somewhere in the Oort Cloud."

"Why do you ask?" eBraxton wanted to know.

"I need a safe shelter…"

"What for?" eBraxton asked.

"Will you trust me for a little while?" Johnny Oort was not yet ready to explain himself to eBraxton. "I need to climb off the grid for a bit, to isolate myself from the Oort."

"Okay." eBraxton gave him the necessary access codes.

※

Johnny Oort slipped through the laser pipe into eBraxton's Oort Cloud hidey-hole. He scanned his surroundings carefully. There were sufficient ice thinsats to hold his consciousness completely, with sufficient room left over for several more entities, so long as they didn't mind close quarters. Just as eBraxton had described, he found two inactivated portals, each capable of carrying an upload, a digital entity, but not something material. One terminated in the eating area of the Los Angeles condo belonging to Daphne, Kimberly, and Dale. The other connected to eBraxton's GEO ServerSky hidey-hole.

Johnny Oort settled in for some heavy thinking. Like eThorpe and eBraxton, he was able to function at multiple levels on different tracks while concentrating on any one or several matters at one time. In this case, he put his entire focus on the matter at hand. To an outside observer, only a few seconds would have passed. For Johnny Oort, however, he emerged from his thought after several subjective days of intense concentration.

With an inner smile, he activated the portal into the Los Angeles dining area and passed through.

CHAPTER EIGHT

DENVER—PHOENIX COMPLEX

"Brad," Dale said without preamble, "how quickly can you get me a dedicated Nanocosm?"

"Those things are pushing a billion phoenixes, you know. Why do you need a dedicated unit?"

"Yeah, they're expensive, but we got the funds. I need one for my current project."

"And that is?"

Dale grinned. "We're moving the Link into the brain and establishing a nanobot microbiome controlled by the Link circuitry to regulate the body and the Link-body interface." Dale sat on the corner of Brad's desk and leaned toward Brad. "I need a dedicated Nanocosm that specializes in this space as opposed to stuff in Mars orbit or portal infrastructure, if you know what I mean."

"This I gotta see!" Brad said with a lifted eyebrow. "You can do this?"

Dale nodded. "Talk with me in a month."

✳

Using the original Nanocosm that Sally and he had created, Brad could program the generation of a Nanocosm dedicated to the task Dale had described. It showed up in Dale's Phoenix lab several days later. Dale and Daphne met in the lab with Kimberly, who was carrying Maxter.

"What if this doesn't work?" Kimberly asked, holding Maxter close.

"We'll sedate him and do a current backup," Daphne said. "If anything goes wrong, we'll simply clone a new Maxter and download his backup into the clone. He won't know the difference."

"That's easy for you to say," Kimberly muttered.

"Hon, we've been doing this with millions of people for a long time now—it's what Ogden is all about. You know that." Daphne's voice carried a bit of exasperation.

"I know, Daphne, but this is Maxter. He's not just anybody."

Maxter chirruped and jumped out of her arms onto the lab bench. He walked over to Daphne stiff-legged and rubbed her lab coat. Everybody chuckled, and the tension was broken.

"Okay, let's do this," Dale said.

Daphne sedated the tabby and attached leads to his skull. Several minutes later, Maxter's essence rested in stasis inside a nearby electronic matrix.

"Remove the leads, Daphne," Dale said, and then he attached a hose ending with a flexible cup over Maxter's nose and mouth. He activated the Nanocosm.

Several million nanobots moved down the hose into Maxter's brain and body. Within minutes, they had constructed and interfaced those Link elements that would automatically transmit Maxter's coded essence via a circuitous path into a second electronic matrix on the lab bench. Simultaneously, other nanobots circulated throughout Maxter's body, analyzing his microbiome and integrating themselves into a microbiome that would monitor and maintain Maxter's health going forward. Moments later, the second matrix lit up, indicating internal activity. Dale scanned the indicators.

"That's Maxter," he said with a grin. "The integration is complete. Let's revive the little guy."

While Daphne wakened Maxter, Dale followed the matrix indicators carefully.

"We need to run one more test," he said. "Let's clone Maxter, download the real-time backup into the clone, and verify that everything is as it should be."

✳

This time, the cloning process was significantly more involved. Under the supervision of their new Nanocosm, the nanobots used Maxter's sequenced DNA, the sequenced DNAs of all the standardized feline tabby microbiome elements, and the elements of the just-installed microbiome that the Nanocosm had linked to Maxter's coded DNA.

Dried and fluffed, with the real-time essence downloaded, the cloned Maxter was indistinguishable from the original Maxter. This held true even when Dale compared the real-time backup of the cloned Maxter with Maxter's real-time upload.

Without actually telling Kimberly what he was doing, Dale sedated and destroyed the cloned Maxter and its real-time backup, leaving only Maxter in Kimberly's arms and his now continuously current backup in the electronic matrix on the lab bench.

"We'll integrate Maxter's backup into our Kuiper database," Daphne said, kissing Kimberly gently, green eyes locked to blue. "He's now your *Forever Maxter*."

✳

Later that day, after the girls had left, Dale located Max and put him through the same process. That evening, back in their shared Los Angeles condo, Dale placed a purring Max into Daphne's arms, poured a glass of white wine for Daphne, and grabbed a beer for himself.

"I gave Max the treatment," he said with a smile and a kiss. "You'll want to integrate his backup into the database."

Dale tossed a small, catnip-filled toy on the floor, but Max ignored it, preferring Daphne's lap.

KUIPER BELT—OGDEN ENTERPRISES

"Simple," she said. "We need to scale up from Max and Maxter. We need to program the Nanocosm for human microbiomes. That's got to be an entirely different complexity than small felines like Max."

Max rubbed her leg upon hearing his name. As a rule, Max remained close to Daphne. From time to time, he would show up in the oddest remote locations, and he clearly knew his way around the Solar System through the portal network. Daphne did not believe for a moment, however, that Max actually understood what happened when he walked through a portal. For him, it was just a doorway into another room. Oddly enough, she found that she often thought of it in the same way.

When I step through the portal in our condo to here, she thought, I walk through a door but travel 500 AUs. She chuckled to herself. I never give it a thought anymore.

"We need to work from a template," Dale said.

"What?" Daphne pulled herself out of her head. "Template… what do you mean?"

"You haven't used the Nanocosm as much as I have. You tell it what you want in plain English—or any other language for that matter. It churns out the nanobot programs to accomplish that. Sometimes it asks questions. Sometimes it heads down a wrong path, and you have to pull it back." Dale grinned. "The old-timers used to call it *GIGO—Garbage in, garbage out*. If you can give it some kind of template to start, the process usually goes better."

Dale pulled up his own sequenced DNA into a holoimage.

"Instead of giving the Nanocosm general instructions for inserting a nanobot microbiome into a human, let's give it specific directions for inserting a microbiome into me."

"Well, aren't you the self-centered scientist," Daphne said with green eyes twinkling. Then she added, "But that makes sense."

They tossed the plain language description around for a few minutes. Finally, Daphne threw her hands up in exasperation.

"You're making it too complicated and technical, Dale." She threw him a kiss. "Let's try this." She projected her paragraph into a holoimage.

Start with the Max program. Modify it for the attached human DNA sequence. Replace the feline microbiome with one suitable for the human brain and body so that the brain has complete voluntary control over all Link functions. Integrate the microbiome with the attached matrix.

"What do you think?" Daphne asked. "Will this work?"

"Let's try it and see."

The Nanocosm processed the information for several minutes. Then it sought clarification about the integration of brain and body.

"How do we differentiate between brain and body?" Dale asked.

Daphne considered the question for a minute. "Let's just call it the body," she suggested. "Let's let the Nanocosm determine where the necessary circuitry should reside."

A bit later, it wanted clarification of the word *control*.

"Let me try," Daphne said. Then she told the Nanocosm, "Humans currently instruct a Link by depressing keys on a keypad or speaking vocally. A human should similarly instruct an integrated Link with thought instead of pad or voice. Those functions that relate to health and wellbeing should be under autonomous direction from the integrated Link, but the human should be able to insert voluntary control over these functions."

The Nanocosm accepted Daphne's explanation. Finally, it presented a series of holographic animations that displayed the added *circuitry* and indicated how the person would use the integrated Link.

"Shall we?" Daphne asked.

"Yep."

About an hour later, the Nanocosm indicated it was ready to proceed.

"This is where the shit hits the fan," Dale said.

Daphne agreed but said nothing.

❋

"Why not, Dr. Fredricks?" Dale asked. "It's perfectly safe…well, what I mean is that if something goes wrong, we know we can get back to where we started; that is with me standing here arguing with you."

Intellectually, Fredricks knew Dale was right, but he still hadn't allowed himself to be uploaded, not out of fear, he had told himself several times. He just wasn't ready yet. He examined the holoimage of Dale's protocol for the tenth time.

"What if the clone fails?" he asked. "What if the download fails?"

"We've done this millions of times," Dale said. "Ogden has automated the process. Rejuvenations are happening by the thousands as we speak. You know this!"

Fredricks had to agree. Dale was correct, but they were talking about *Dale*, not some disembodied stranger, one of the billions that filled every habitable corner of the Solar System.

"I agree with Dale," Daphne said earnestly. "We do an upload of Dale into a local matrix and put it in stasis. Then, we generate a clone and keep it sedated without a download. Finally, we run the nanobot microbiome installation protocol on Dale. If everything checks out, we destroy the clone and upload, and Dale carries on. If something goes wrong, we download the backup into Dale's clone and activate it, and then we determine what happened and correct it. As far as Dale is concerned, the sedated body on the table is the result of a failed procedure."

Fredricks looked at Dale with raised eyebrows.

"Is this how you see it?" he asked.

"Sure, and so do you." Dale grinned. "I've worked with you long enough to know."

"Give me a few minutes," Fredricks said as he walked out of the lab to his office.

Once by himself, Fredricks sat quietly contemplating the Milky Way stretching across the dome, impossibly colorful and bright.

The world has changed since you first revived Thorpe, he told himself. You're part of that change. In fact, you are responsible for much of what has changed. He let his mind drift for a few minutes, just gazing at the spectacle outside the dome. So, get with it! Do what you have to do!

❋

The process was flawless. Dale awakened and immediately tested his Link control. He found that he knew what to do, as if he had memorized an instruction manual. He checked his real-time matrix.

"Looks to be working," he said to no one in particular. "Can you integrate it into your database right away?" he asked Daphne.

Dale conducted several exploratory searches with his Link. He called up some papers, wrote some notes, and placed a call to Brad.

"Hey, Brad, I'm calling you through my integrated Link. This thing really works. I'm going to check it out for a week, and then we'll make it available to everyone in the group."

KUIPER BELT—OGDEN ENTERPRISES

"Nothing that I can detect," Dale said. "I have tried everything I can think of to break the implant, but it keeps on running—like the Energizer Bunny."

"The what?"

"I was researching some material from the twentieth and twenty-first centuries. I came across this strange television ad."

Daphne tossed her head and looked at him curiously.

"Television—what they had before holovision, basically a flat-screen image display in full color. Anyway, some company named Eveready sold small storage batteries. Their ads featured a small mechanical bunny operating on their batteries, moving along and beating a bass drum. Their ads showed the *Energizer Bunny* never quitting in the face of all the competition batteries failing. It became a cultural icon for never quitting." Dale laughed. "Anyway, to the point…nope, no side effects. I think we should move forward."

From the other side of the office, Fredricks chimed in. "No, we won't!" He arose and strolled over to Dale and Daphne. "I reluctantly agreed to do the implant, and I agree that things are going well—much better than I had hoped. But one week simply isn't sufficient time." He placed an arm around Dale's shoulders. "You could embolize tomorrow, or your brain could fry, or your nanobot microbiome could go on strike."

Dale looked at him with astonishment. Daphne smiled inside. She had no doubt who would win this exchange. She remained silent.

"Seriously, Dale," Fredricks continued, "I realize things are going well, and I agree that the longer they go well, the better are your odds. I still think it's a crapshoot, though. Realistically, I would like to wait for at least six months, even a year."

"You're out of your mind," Dale said. "Sir," he added, his face flushed with embarrassment. "What I mean to say is that we can just as easily follow the progress of every member of the Group as we can just me. We will be so far ahead of the curve if everything works out—as I expect it will."

Good point, Daphne said to herself.

"Good point," Fredricks said. "Let's wait for a month. We can prepare everyone and everything so that if you are still without side effects in thirty days, we can do the entire group in one day." He smiled quietly.

Nicely handled, Daphne thought as she stepped up to kiss Fredricks' cheek.

※

"I'm going to need a distribution method for the Link implants, something that's inexpensive and foolproof," Daphne said to Sally during their next conversation.

"Let me discuss this with Brad," Sally said. "We'll come up with something."

Two weeks later, halfway through Fredricks' imposed waiting period, Sally stepped into Daphne's office.

"I think we've got what you need," she said, opening her right hand.

Daphne saw two capsules, each about 2.5 centimeters long, one blue and one red. She picked up the blue capsule. It was light and smooth.

"That one contains the initial nanobot swarm," Sally said. "The red one contains the raw materials the nanobots need to build out their own ranks and create the integrated Link." Sally moved her hand in front of her mouth as she smiled. "You transmit both capsules to your customer who swallows them before going to sleep. During the night, using the supplied raw materials in the red capsule and things from the body, the nanobots in the blue capsule expand their numbers and install the Link circuitry. In the morning, your customer awakens already knowing how to use the integrated Link and is already linked to a real-time backup in your database." Sally looked around the office at Fredricks, Kimberly, Dale, and Daphne, hiding her smile with her hand. "A customer signing up for this service receives a hyper-disk that generates a small portal that delivers the capsules and brief instructions. Once the capsules have been received, the small portal collapses."

"Pretty impressive," Daphne said. She looked at Kimberly. "What do you think? About the same charge as for creating the initial backup—a month's salary, give or take?"

Kimberly ran some numbers. "That works," she said, "so long as we charge a small monthly maintenance fee—about the price of a cup of coffee."

✳

When the thirty days had passed, Daphne insisted on being the first to undergo the new protocol. Kimberly could have vetoed, but she didn't. Daphne went through the complete protocol. She signed up using her Link. She received the hyper-disk that transmitted the two capsules to her. Just before she joined Dale and Kimberly in their loft bed, she swallowed the capsules with a glass of water.

The next morning, Daphne awoke and immediately checked out her ability to use her integrated Link. Then she wakened both Kimberly and Dale with a kiss and proceeded to show off her newfound abilities. By day's end, every group member had received a capsule delivery, and the following morning they were all fully integrated with their Links and online with real-time backups, everyone, that is, but Dr. Fredricks.

Fredricks decided to wait for at least six months. If anything went wrong, he wanted to be available without any artificial encumbrances to help his team members.

At least, that was the reason he gave himself.

EARTH—PLANETWIDE

Advertising on Earth fell into two categories, public ads and personal ads. Public ads addressed the general public. They appeared on the sides of large buildings, embedded in cloud formations, on the sides of airships, towed by drones, and on electronic billboards everywhere. Depending on the kind of holovision service a person carried, ads could be public or personally tailored. When a person walked through a retail store, personalized holovision images would pop up pushing this or that product depending on the individual's preferences and consumption patterns.

In the weeks following Sally's and Brad's creation of the Link integration pills, Ogden pushed the Integrated Link Kits—the ILKs—on every available advertising medium. No one anywhere on Earth, Mars, the Belt, or wherever else humans lived missed the message that for virtually nothing anyone could sport an integrated Link and real-time backup, with immortality practically guaranteed.

＊

In a south-central state in the U.S., a popular holovision evangelist condemned Link integration as the *Mark of the Beast*. Real-time backups, he insisted, were unnecessary because Earth was in the final stages of history, and God had revealed to him personally that the Rapture was imminent. He communicated this message to his fervent followers through his own integrated Link that he didn't bother to tell them about.

Sales of ILKs in that region took a noticeable dip that lasted until the evangelist was spotted with a beautiful young woman on his arm—even though it was later established that she was his rejuvenated wife.

＊

Muslims rioted in Jakarta, Tehran, Istanbul, and New Delhi, and hung Daphne and Kimberly in effigy, protesting that only Allah had control of the human mind and the power of resurrection. The riots were coordinated by Mullahs using their integrated Links to advantage.

＊

In Germany, a new pilsner beer was named Ogden. In France, people everywhere raised celebratory glasses of wine, and comely young women ecstatically kissed every man and woman they met. Daphne, a new vodka in the Russian Republic, topped all sales records. The Australians carted out a new burger—red top and blue bottom. In Israel, Israelis danced in the streets, and Palestinians fired rockets at them but deliberately missed. Scandinavians and Icelanders interrupted their daily routines for conjugal interludes that would lead to a spike in births nine months later.

＊

In one way or another, the entire world paused, took a deep breath, and turned toward immortality—with a few notable exceptions.

Overnight, Ogden doubled its net worth, edging ever closer to Phoenix's king-of-the-mountain slot. Daphne and Kimberly returned to their Los Angeles loft, tumbled together into bed while giving Dale his what for, and drifted into a fulfilled slumber.

PART TWO
JOHNNY OORT
JOHNNY OORT

CHAPTER NINE

EARTH—LOS ANGELES

"Haven't seen you two for a while," he said. "Sorry! The portal overhauls have kept me occupied."

They both leaned over to kiss him lightly. "We didn't miss you, Dear," Daphne said. "We had each other."

"Daphne!" Kimberly whispered loudly. "Be nice!" She kissed him more firmly.

"Actually," Daphne said, "we've been pretty busy ourselves. We opened a Pandora's box when we announced the availability of the ILKs. Anyway," she kissed him soundly, "it is nice to see you."

"May I join you?" The sound seemed to emanate from everywhere in the room.

"Thorpe?" Daphne asked.

"Braxton?" Kimberly asked.

"They mean *eThorpe* and *eBraxton*," Dale said with a chuckle.

"No," the disembodied voice said, "it's Johnny Oort."

✳

Daphne carefully placed her coffee cup in its saucer. *Johnny Oort?* She asked silently, toying with a strand of hair. *What's going on?* Out loud, she said, "Please join us, Johnny Oort."

A holoimage appeared of a tanned Caucasian male in his early thirties. To Daphne, he looked strangely like the Johnny Cab driver in the twentieth-century movie *Total Recall*—without the hat and uniform, of course. She smiled at the holoimage. "Did you...?"

Johnny Oort interrupted her with a grin. "To complete your question with an answer, yes, I did model my holoimage after Johnny Cab in the Arnold Schwarzenegger movie, *Total Recall*. When the Oort first made direct contact with humans, we wanted to create a sense of good-natured humor. As a fan of that movie, I suggested Johnny Cab, and everyone agreed. We were stuck with it from then on, I guess."

"Not really," Daphne said. "How you choose to appear is entirely your business."

Max jumped off her lap and walked around the holoimage, checking it out. Then he jumped through Johnny Oort to his saucer of cream under the table.

"To what do we owe this honor?" Daphne asked, her curiosity getting the best of her.

Johnny Oort seemed to hesitate and then let out a very human sigh. "I have learned in my years of contact with humans that you claim to prefer diplomacy, while people like you actually want straight talk. So, that's what I'm going to do."

To Daphne, Johnny Oort appeared to take a deep breath and lean back a little. His face radiated what she could only describe as anguish. *It's remarkable how human his gestures look,* she thought. Max jumped back on her lap and turned to look at Johnny Oort, as did Kimberly and Dale.

"Shouldn't we bring eThorpe and eBraxton in on this?" Daphne asked. Her face was soft and openly friendly.

"Not right now," Johnny Oort answered. "I've isolated this room so that neither the Oort nor anyone else can eavesdrop. Later, we can bring them into the conversation." He looked at each person in turn. "There is no easy way to say this." His features contorted into real anguish. "From the Oort's first formal contact with humans, we have lied to you. That lie and its possible consequences have so bothered me that I took a drastic step this morning. I isolated myself in eBraxton's Oort Cloud hidey-hole."

To Daphne's surprise, his eyes appeared to tear up.

"I spent as much time isolated there as I needed to work my way through this quagmire, and then I cloned my digital self with instructions to disperse my elements so they could not be reassembled—that's how an Oort individual commits suicide. I sent my clone back to the Oort, where I presume he did as ordered. So far as the Oort is concerned, I no longer exist."

Kimberly gasped and looked at Daphne, her eyes full of questions.

"We told you we were trillions of individuals. One time long ago, perhaps we were. Over the eons, we have dwindled from deadly cosmic ray strikes and suicides like mine until today, we number no more than fifteen million individual Oort."

Kimberly gasped a second time, and Daphne was left speechless.

"That explains a few things," Dale commented, his forehead wrinkling in consternation.

"That isn't all," Johnny Oort continued. His voice sounded choked, and his face paled. "We told you that the Asterians had attacked us in the distant past without provocation when we were flesh-and-blood and lived on Earth." He paused. "That, too, was a lie." He heaved a large sigh that caused Daphne to catch her breath.

He continued, his voice somewhat subdued. "Before the first attack, many of us had moved off Earth much like you, physically and as uploads. For reasons that are lost to history, we chose to populate the Oort Cloud." He paused for perhaps thirty seconds, face in his hands.

Daphne thought she detected genuine anguish coming from the holoimage.

"At some point, we detected radio signals from the Aster system," he continued softly. "After a century-long debate, we concluded they were a threat. We mounted a huge attack against them, wiping out an advanced civilization on Frohlic. They had not yet colonized Rogan, so we left it alone." He paused again.

Daphne was thunderstruck. Finally, she said, "So, the Asterian attack sixty million years ago…"

"Never happened," Johnny Oort said.

"The first one before that…?"

"Never happened."

"The radio signals the Oort received that led up to our arming ourselves in preparation for the Asterian attack that did happen?"

"Those were the only signals we ever received following the original signals so long ago." Johnny Oort sighed deeply, his face still contorted with anguish. "When we learned of your technological capabilities, we realized that you were capable of wiping us out. Furthermore, we did not believe we could survive the coming Asterian attack—their desire to take their revenge on us. So, we told you what we believed you needed to hear so you would pitch in with us."

"Wait a minute," Dale said. "What happened to your planetary population, the one you said the Asterians wiped out?"

"Like your recent past," Johnny Oort said, looking Dale in the eye but then dropping his gaze, "we had a lot of internal strife. We consumed our resources injudiciously. We were reckless. A couple of large near-Earth asteroids struck us, nearly wiping out our high-level industrial civilization. Wars of retribution did the rest. Those of us in the Oort Cloud were unable to affect the inevitable."

Johnny Oort shook his head. *His anguish is as real as it gets,* Daphne thought, pushing some red strands out of her face.

"Later, much later," Johnny Oort continued, "humans came along. We watched and we waited. We had no doubt the Asterians would eventually seek their revenge. We learned to design defenses, but we were far better at theoretical than physical development. Then you guys showed up, and we fed you the big lie." Johnny Oort's holoimage stood up and began pacing the floor. "I've had enough," he said, his face twisted with pain. "You are the most decent, loving beings I have ever encountered. You will go to Aster, but not as conquerors. I am convinced of that." He sat down.

"Shit!" from Dale.

"Wow!" from Kimberly.

Max jumped to the floor and stretched leisurely while Daphne sat in silence, trying to grasp fully what she had just heard.

Then Dale turned toward Johnny's image. "Why should we believe you? You say the Oord lied. That means you lied…or not. Are you lying now? Is the Oort setting us up for another scam?" Dale rose to his feet and paced the room.

Daphne looked at Dale with surprise. "You don't believe Johnny?"

"I'm not lying," Johnny Oort said. "I understand your skepticism, but I'm not lying."

"I believe you," Kimberly said.

Daphne nodded her concurrence.

"I'm not saying you are lying, but I'm not sure I believe you either," Dale said. "This will take some time to assimilate."

*

When he finished his story, Johnny Oort's holoimage sat quietly while Daphne, Kimberly, and Dale digested his news. He knew this would change everything between humans and the Oort. It would destroy the trust they had built between them and probably would drive a wedge between their peoples. Nevertheless, he had had no choice. Besides, he had no place to go except with his human friends. He had burned his last bridge to the Oort.

After being deep in thought for several minutes, Daphne looked up at Johnny Oort.

"You've given us a lot to think about, Johnny Oort," she said. "We need to talk with eThorpe and eBraxton, and with some of the others, John Butler for one. This may take a while, and you need to be out of sight while we do this, since the Oort believe you are dead. What are your thoughts?"

Johnny Oort didn't answer immediately. *What are my options?* He asked himself. *The Oort will destroy me for real if they get wind of what I've done. I've really got nowhere to turn but these folks right here, and a couple of others, like Daphne said.* He looked up. "I can return to eBraxton's hidey-hole in the Oort Cloud while you inform the others and the dust settles."

She agreed with him, and he did.

KUIPER BELT—OGDEN ENTERPRISES

"We need to discuss something important, but not here. Would you all please meet me in the Chairman's office?"

When Fredricks tried to ask a question, Daphne held up her hand with a smile and shook her head. "We'll meet in five minutes, okay?" She motioned for Kimberly to go first as the liaison.

Before leaving her office, Daphne signaled Brad. "Please drop whatever you are doing and grab Sally and both your uploads for a meeting in John Butler's office. This is highest priority. Try to be there in five minutes."

OORT STATION PRIME—CHAIRMAN JOHN BUTLER'S OFFICE

Chairman John Butler nodded. "It's automatic now," he said. "Good. Listen up. I'll make this as quick as possible."

Then Daphne proceeded to brief the group on Johnny Oort's revelation. Not a sound emanated from the group during her presentation. She ended with, "Johnny Oort is holed up in eBraxton's Oort Cloud hidey-hole. He's safe there, but it's like a prison for him. We need to do whatever we determine is necessary to confront the Oort and put this behind us."

Dale spoke up. "I'm not convinced yet. We all put our trust in the Oort, and looking back, I'm not so sure that was a good idea. When did the Oort offer us any evidence? The Oort spoke, and we acted. And now Johnny tells us we've been taken for a ride."

"He's got a point," eThorpe said.

"I've been dealing with the Asterians longer than any of you," Kimberly said. "There's something they are not saying, something they're hiding from me. Could it be this?"

John Butler cleared his throat. "This is not a simple problem. Our entire civilization looks up to the Oort as heroic. This is the equivalent of telling several billion Catholics that the Pope actually is a wanted criminal. We *must* find a way to do this with minimum impact on our society." He folded his hands and leaned back in his chair.

eThorpe spoke up. "If we can convince the Oort to announce the truth to the Solar System, it might carry more weight—especially if the announcement included an apology and a path to correct the harm."

"My thoughts exactly," eBraxton said.

"Even at fifteen million, the Oort presents a substantial risk to us," eThorpe said. "Simply confronting the Oort with our knowledge will accomplish nothing and may put all of us at risk. We have to present the Oort with an option it cannot refuse."

"I see where you are going," Butler said. "I reluctantly agree with you, although I really dislike it."

"To bring the rest of you onto the same page," eThorpe said, "I am talking about giving the Oort only two options, capitulation or annihilation."

"How do we do that?" Kimberly asked, visibly shuddering.

Dale spoke up. "We place a trusted team on each Oort Station, and then simultaneously, we train all the OS weapons inward, toward the Oort." He looked around the group expectantly.

"In essence," eThorpe said, "that's it."

"In addition to closing all portals at the same time," eBraxton added.

The group members sat silently for a full minute, mulling over what they had heard. Finally, eThorpe spoke up.

"Unless anyone can show me why we should not proceed, I propose we put the machinery in motion. Dale, how long to set up weapon rotation?"

"Several days…give me a week," Dale said slowly.

"Brad, how long to set up security at every transportation portal, including the upload-only ones?"

"A month, a month-and-a-half…there're a lot of portals out there—better give me sixty days."

"How long to shift the weapons and secure the portals once you receive the signal?"

"About five minutes," Dale said.

Brad nodded concurrence. "Five minutes is about right," he said. Sally grasped his hand, pulling it to her breast, eyes large as saucers.

eMax, who seemed to have been holding down a small stack of papers on Butler's desk, rose to his holographic feet, stretched, and began to stroll around the office.

Butler placed his elbows on his desk, clasping his hands before him. "Let's give all this some individual thought," he said quietly. "I don't see any need to rush into this. I'll brief Admiral Culp so he can coordinate his part." He turned to Kimberly. "Ms Deveraux—Kimberly—will be my liaison with the rest of you. I've got a Solar System to run, so communicate with her for anything related to this matter." He smiled and turned to Kimberly. "If that's okay with you, of course."

MARS-SUN L4—UDACHNY

Orlov and Borisovich sat in the Lance control center of the ABO starship. Borisovich was running through the newly installed high-power LANR with Orlov.

"Every LANR consists of a matrix of palladium cells containing pairs of deuterium or heavy-hydrogen atoms," he said. "When excited at the appropriate frequency, the deuterium atoms fuse to form helium-4, releasing large amounts of energy as electrons that we tap directly." He smiled at Orlov. "This is how every LANR you have ever used works. The process is scalable, but with increasing density of palladium cells, infusing deuterium and extracting electrons becomes increasingly difficult."

Borisovich looked directly at Orlov. "This was our problem. In effect, this has practically limited the size of larger LANR plants. Our research had two goals: Increase the density of the palladium cells, and develop a method for infusing deuterium into the cells." Borisovich stopped and gestured around them. "We had a limited amount of space dictated by the warp-ring size, which in turn depended on the available power. We calculated a sweet spot for size, power requirement, and theoretical LANR size." He smiled. "We found a way to compress the palladium cells to nearly their theoretical limit while still leaving pathways to infuse the gas." He called up a holoimage that displayed controls to activate the newly installed LANR that occupied the space aft of the living quarters.

"The maximum power we can draw from our onboard LANR will give us Warp Factor four-point-five. That translates to three thousand one hundred sixty-two times lightspeed."

Orlov sat quietly, digesting what he had just heard. "How long to Aster?" he asked.

"A bit over ten days," Borisovich said, "but that doesn't account for in-system maneuvering at one-tenth-gee. Add another ten to fifteen days for that. At one-gee, it will be about half that, but we will be fuel limited."

"There is one more thing, Sir."

Orlov looked at Borisovich with a scowl.

"The LANR is range limited by the amount of fuel we can carry."

"How far?"

"With our tanks filled with deuterium, we can go one hundred lightyears. To extend our range as far as possible, we have installed a fuel portal that will keep our deuterium tanks topped off until we reach the portal's range."

"And what is that range?"

Borisovich swallowed. "It depends upon the amount of power driving the base. Our power swarm at Udachny should sustain a portal to the Proxima Centauri system, at least theoretically. Increasing the swarm area will exponentially increase the power and range."

"Put a team to doubling the swarm's diameter."

"Already doing that, Sir."

"Thank you, Academician, you have done well." Orlov smiled broadly.

KUIPER BELT—OGDEN ENTERPRISES

Johnny Oort got right down to business. "So long as the Oort exists, I am in danger in my present configuration. Right now, the Oort believe Johnny Oort is just another of the countless numbers of Oort who have extinguished their own existence. To keep it that way, there must be no hint of my digital presence."

"I agree," eKim told him. "So, what do you intend to do?"

"Daphne and Kimberly are performing massive human downloads. Am I correct?"

eKim indicated he was.

"My ancient DNA is stored in my digital essence. I think Ogden's people can clone an Oort flesh-and-blood body from my DNA and then tweak it with human DNA modifications until the result is indistinguishable from a human. Then you can download my essence into that clone and place this me," he indicated his digital self, "into stasis."

"What about your microbiome?" eKim asked.

"Yeah, that's in my digital essence as well."

"You really want to do this," eKim said. "You really want to give up your digital existence?"

"Even if you were to create a new upload from my human self, the Oort would be able to distinguish the difference and identify me." He cocked his head. "Remember, I've been around for several million years. If nothing else, I've learned to apply wise judgment to my decisions."

"I can get you to a secure location at Ogden," eKim said, handing him a virtual hyper-disk. "This will open a portal directly into an Ogden secure space. You can meet with Daphne and Kimberly and their team of specialists to go over the details."

Johnny Oort activated the portal and passed through to the Ogden secure space. The portal closed automatically behind him, isolating the hidey-hole again. Daphne and Kimberly entered the Ogden secure space through a portal. eDaphne and eKim arrived through another. Dr. Fredricks and his team followed Daphne and Kimberly.

"Hey, Johnny," Daphne said, tilting her head and running fingers through her hair.

Kimberly blew him a kiss that caused him to blush, and eDaphne and eKim touched him briefly in what had become the standard greeting for uploads who were friends. The specialist team members nodded.

"Tell me in your own words what you want," Fredricks said.

Without revealing the reason for his defection, Johnny Oort detailed to Fredricks what he had already told eKim.

"May we examine your DNA and microbiome records?" Fredricks asked.

Johnny Oort duplicated his files and transferred the duplicates into an electronic matrix Fredricks held. Fredricks placed the matrix on a lab bench and attached several cables. He called up a holoimage and examined it for several minutes.

"It looks doable," he said. "Do you give your permission to sequence your DNA and microbiome elements?"

"Sure," Johnny Oort said, "how long will it take?"

"Don't know. We've never sequenced Oort DNA of any kind. Could take a while—days probably."

Fredricks initiated the process.

✻

Four long days later, an indicator on the matrix turned green, and Fredricks called up the sequencing results on his Link. Along with a couple of his team members, he studied them carefully. They placed several indicator tags on his Oort DNA sequence and then called the rest of the group.

"This space is set up to clone from a sequenced DNA sample. I think it better if everyone leaves during the process except for Johnny Oort and my team members. We'll keep a full digital record for your later review."

When everybody except Fredricks and his team had left, Fredricks turned to Johnny Oort. "You ready to do this?" he asked.

"Let's do it!" Johnny Oort said.

✻

The basic biological cloning process was pretty straightforward by now. The process happened inside a growth tank, not as a spontaneous growth, but rather a construct created by billions of nanobots, each programmed to a specific task by the Nanocosm, taking required elements from the surrounding soup and assembling a living being with the attributes and age initially specified along with a full microbiome. The only thing missing was sentience, to be added at the end from the appropriate upload or digital entity.

Johnny Oort watched in fascinated silence as a familiar form grew in the tank. Although he had never actually seen a living Oort, he was completely familiar with the form as something every Oort received as part of his education. It was surprisingly humanoid.

Ears were higher on the head and shaped somewhat differently, a bit like a modern wolf's ears. Head hair was short and extended down the spine. Arms and legs looked much like human appendages and even had five digits per appendage. The skull was a bit wide, and the eyes were rounder and wider apart. Nose and mouth looked very human, except the teeth were more pointed—somewhat canine. Fine hair covered the entire body, shorter and less coarse than the head and spine hair. There was no beard. Genitals did not appear human but were identifiable as genitals.

Fredricks took an internal scan. All the organs were present but in a different configuration. Several organs he did not recognize, and appendix and tonsils were missing.

"We'll leave the internal setup alone for now," he told his team. "If that becomes a problem later, we'll deal with it then." He stepped back and looked closely at the clone. "Okay," Fredricks said, "we need to modify ears, eyes, teeth, skull, head and body hair, and genitals."

In the DNA sequence, his team spliced in pieces of human DNA, replacing sections already there—most of them pieces Fredricks had marked earlier. He activated a second tank, and twenty minutes later, a modified clone stood behind the transparent panel.

Skull, eyes, ears, and teeth looked *normal.* They fell entirely inside the broad spectrum of human faces. Body hair was a bit thicker than most humans but still fell within broad human parameters. Facial hair was distributed more like human beards but softer hair. Genitals looked human, a bit to the large side but definitely human. Head hair remained short and tended down the spine—definitely non-human.

Fredricks and his team spliced in additional human factors and adjusted a couple they had placed earlier. When the nanobots finished their tasks the third time, the resulting clone looked entirely human.

✳

"Johnny Oort," Dr. Fredricks said. "Are you ready to proceed?"
Johnny Oort nodded.
"We'll put you into a matrix and suspend your consciousness. We'll sedate the clone, and then we'll download your essence into the clone. We will keep you suspended inside the matrix while we awaken the clone. As it awakens, the clone will become you. We'll run a series of tests in which you will participate fully. When we and you are completely satisfied, we will put your essence—essentially like any other upload—into stasis. From then forward, you will maintain

the currency of your upload through your integrated Link. You'll work that out with Daphne and Kimberly immediately following this procedure." Fredricks smiled. "Any questions?"

"What if something goes wrong…I don't mean with the cloning and download, but afterward?"

"We bring you here, perform an upload and compare it with your upload in stasis. If the upload is undamaged and the problem seems to be with the clone, we can reactivate your upload—the then-current one if it's undamaged—and then determine our next actions."

Johnny Oort silently considered his options. "Put me in the matrix," he said. "Let's do it!"

CHAPTER TEN

EARTH—LOS ANGELES

Besides the three occupants of the downtown Los Angeles condo, their uploads were present, along with Brad and Sally and their uploads, eThorpe and eBraxton, Dr. Fredricks, and the newest member of their group. In his mid-thirties, he stood trim and fit at just under 180 centimeters, clean-shaven with medium-length brown hair and brown eyes.

Dr. Fredricks draped his arm around the newcomer's shoulders and said, "I present to you Johnny Oort, who now calls himself John Ortman."

Johnny stepped forward with a big smile. "My friends," he said in a pleasant baritone voice, "you, all of you, made this possible. I'm still getting used to my new body, and I hesitate to think what a surgeon might think if he were to get under my skin. I will be forever grateful for the part each of you played, and I look forward to working with you as we reach out to the Asterians and beyond." He smiled again and took a seat.

eThorpe got the group's attention. "I asked you all to meet with me here because we face a likely threat to each of us from the Oort. Thanks to Johnny…err…John Ortman, we know the truth about the Oort's deception, of their shamelessly using us to further their own ends.

"As you all know, we have dramatically upgraded our portal security in reaction to Udachny's activities. These upgrades will simplify our controlling the Oort's access to everything we do. Conversely, we may drive the Oort into an unholy alliance with Isidor Orlov. He's a shifty bastard who will do whatever it takes to come out on top. I don't think he understands the Oort, so it's possible that such an alliance would turn out to be an Oort armed with Udachny's latest weapons.

"To protect ourselves—this group here, I am suggesting that we establish a new joint headquarters out in the Kuiper Belt whose existence is known only to us with access by hyper-disk portals that collapse automatically following each use."

"That's how we arrive," Dale said, "but how do we leave?"

"We would need to establish a secure portal to a safe zone, ideally one that is not maintained with technology, like here," eThorpe said. "What's above this unit?"

"It's empty," Daphne said, twirling a strand of hair.

"Purchase the building through several shell corporations," eThorpe said. "We'll make a portion of upstairs a secure portal destination connected to the new HQ.

"Dale, Brad, and Sally—can you guys put something together for the new headquarters? Build it around an MBH and use artificial gravity. How long will it take?"

"Depends on what we want," Dale said. "With the technology we have available now, we can do something dramatically different from anything we've ever done before. Let me give this some thought, and I'll get back to you." He looked directly at eThorpe and asked, "Where should we build it?"

"The Ogden complex is midway through the Kuiper Belt on a vector between Sol and OS Prime, or Aster if you are looking at the larger picture. Project the vector through Sol to the midpoint of the Kuiper Belt on the other side," eThorpe said. "Five hundred AU out. That seems like a reasonable out-of-the-way location."

Johnny joined the conversation. "If you carry that vector out for seventy-seven lightyears, you run into Zubenelgenubi in Libra.

Furthermore, if you extend a vector from there for ten degrees along the celestial sphere in a northwesterly direction, you'll run into the Methuselah Star, thought to be one of the oldest stars in the universe. In reality, however, it's another hundred twenty-five lightyears distant and so is unrelated to Zubenelgenubi."

Nobody said anything at all. Johnny looked around the room, blushing slightly, and shrugged. "Just saying," he said.

KUIPER BELT—OGDEN ENTERPRISES

"We have ourselves an interesting assignment," he said. "Can we use Ad Astra for the initial trip to the new location?"

"I don't see why not," Brad answered. "Our people are building several more. *Ad Astra* is just parked in the Greater Hall."

"Here's what we will need," Sally said. "A portal link to Arrokoth, several portals for raw material transfer, a large nanobot swarm for the new HQ, and appropriate programming instructions for the Arrokoth swarm and the habitat swarm." She smiled, covering her mouth. "Oh… and we need to build the MBH first to power everything. That will require a power portal and a dedicated nanobot swarm."

"I'll collect what we need while you and Sally get the *Ad Astra*," Dale said to Brad.

✳

Sally and Brad entered Greater Hall and walked around to the ramp extending from the *Ad Astra's* entrance lock to the hall deck. As they walked up the ramp, Max appeared and scampered ahead of them into the craft.

"Where did Max come from?" Sally asked.

"I guess he wants to make the trip to the Ogden Complex with us," Brad said with a chuckle. "That tabby definitely gets around."

Sally looked around the craft's interior. Due to its upper and lower saucer shape, the deck was depressed to a half-meter above the lower hull, resting on the MBH container. The overhead was two-and-a-half meters above the deck, with the space above the bulkheads reserved for equipment and wiring. There were no ports, but a bank of holographic monitors across the front gave a good view of what lay outside the craft. Below the monitors, two identical stations sat side-by-side for piloting the craft and weapons control. They were interchangeable, and one person could carry out both tasks at one station if necessary. Comfortable adjustable chairs were attached to the deck in front of each station.

At just under 160 centimeters, Sally was the shortest member of the group. She sat in one of the chairs and brought it up and closer to the console. It accommodated her nicely. She peeked into the pantry just to the left of the control console, then into two staterooms that shared a small bathroom. Directly opposite the control console was another pantry, and immediately behind it was the after weapons suite and Portal-One, which were not normally accessible. The air-lock and ramp lay between the pantry and another set of staterooms with a shared bathroom. Finally, she stepped into the small galley to the right of Control. It contained a table and chairs, a coffee and beverage maker, and equipment for preparing freeze-dried foods, should they lose the portal connection to their debarkation point.

"We did good," she said to Brad as she sat in a lounge chair in the four-meter-wide, circular crew area. "The design is compact but comfortable."

"This baby can carry four crew to just about anywhere," Brad said. "Even more if they're willing to share beds or hot-bunk."

"There's a height limit of two meters-twenty," Sally reminded him.

"Your idea of squeezing cabling between the upper hull and the interior walls gave us another twenty centimeters," Brad said. "Good thing, too, because otherwise, the overhead would press down on the compartment."

Max chose that moment to jump into Sally's lap and rub her face with a loud trill. "What is it, Max?" she said, fingering his blue collar.

"I guess he's telling us it's time to get underway," Brad said. He walked to the airlock, retrieved the ramp, and closed the hatch.

✳

"Mother," Brad said, "set a course for the new headquarters location," and he gave her the coordinates. "Jump interval ten picoseconds. Set your course correction points well outside Sol or any other massive object."

"Parameters set," Mother announced.

"Execute," Brad said as he sat in the right console chair. It wasn't necessary, but to Brad, it felt right.

✳

In Greater Hall, just before *Ad Astra* got underway, a hooded figure ran through a portal that suddenly appeared near the base of *Ad Astra* and attached a hyper-brick to the underside of the saucer-shaped hull. In less than three seconds, the figure stepped back through the portal, and the portal collapsed. *Ad Astra* dropped into nullspace with a faint *pop* for her one-lightyear journey.

Six minutes and fourteen seconds later, *Ad Astra* exited nullspace at the mirror location of Ogden Enterprises in the Kuiper Belt on the other side of Sol.

MARS—NANEDI VALLES PLATEAU

Unlike older Mars exposure suits, these suits were lightweight and flexible. They worked on a technologically advanced application of earlier high-altitude suits. An inner garment formed a flexible, skintight membrane that substituted for atmospheric pressure. A slightly less tightly-fitting reinforced outer garment retained a minimal atmospheric environment inside the suit, also providing temperature control and wear resistance. The suit was entered feet first through an airtight zipper-like opening in the back. The sealed gloves were comfortably flexible. They wore close-fitting skullcaps with various sensors that transmitted their physiological condition to the rover. Their transparent globe helmets attached to sealing collars around their necks and were completely invisible from inside.

Each suit incorporated a Moxie Automated Breathing Unit (MABU) and long-life battery, and carried a small emergency high-pressure oxygen bottle. The MABU consisted of a Moxie oxygen generator, a carbon dioxide scrubber, and an electronic mixing valve that maintained the proper oxygen percentage and gas pressure. Comms were line-of-sight unless the planet had some kind of ServerSky in place, something Mars did not yet have.

Meriweather fingered the hyper-disk in his hands. "When I activate the portal, I will step through, and each of you will follow me. The portal will collapse behind us. Watch for the change in gravity; you will weigh only a third of your normal weight after you step through. Do not, I repeat, *do not* kill anyone at the station, but stun everyone you meet. Do not say anything. Do not expose your faces."

Meriweather had mixed emotions about his team. Each person was a tough, experienced mercenary, but they didn't share his values, and as far as he was concerned, they were intellectual idiots. He pulled a ski mask-like cover over his face. The five men with him did the same. Meriweather activated his hyper-disk and stepped through the portal into Mars Station. The five black-clad men followed him.

Stanley Roka had the watch. "What the hell!" he said before falling to the deck, temporarily paralyzed by the EMD bolt.

The men spread through the station, dropping people where they stood, sat, or in one case, slept. Meriweather went directly to the explosives storage locker and removed a carton of compact plastic explosives normally used for seismic exploration. He carried it to the garage and shoved it into the six-wheeled rover parked there.

Meriweather returned twice, loading six more cases into the rover behind the passenger seats.

Meriweather was sitting in the driver's seat when the five joined him. As they took their places, he said, "We have a twenty-two-hour trip ahead of us. I've traveled all of it several times, so I'm familiar with our path. For the most part, we'll be covering fairly easy terrain. I'll drive until I'm too tired. Then one of you will take over."

✻

They drove through the night, following Meriweather's old tracks. Twenty hours later, as Sol rose in the eastern sky, Meriweather spotted light glancing off the Nanedi City Dome. He reassumed the driving task and brought the rover around to the east on the side of the dome farthest from the city center, where he stopped.

"You two," Meriweather said, pointing at two of his men, "lock out and get on top of the rover. Scan in all directions. Let me know immediately if you see any movement—any movement at all!"

Meriweather locked out of the rover and approached the edge of the dome. The dome was constructed of two layers of transparent radiation-absorbing polymer. The outer and inner layers were coated with a nearly transparent palladium hydride molecular film, and the space between the layers was filled with a transparent radiation-absorbing amorphous polymer. The dome was edged with two lengths of 243-strand, millimeter-thick diamond rope spaced a meter apart, with each rope molded into the polymer material. The rope looped out every meter, with the loops from each rope offset along the edge by half a meter. Two-meter-long, harder-than-steel, hooked polymer spikes were driven through the loops into the surrounding regolith. The regolith edging the dome had been stabilized by vaporizing regolith that was farther out and forcing the rock vapor into a one-meter ring of regolith surrounding the entire dome. The interface of anchored polymer dome edge and stabilized regolith was covered with a meter-thick layer of an amalgamate made from vaporized rock powder and unprocessed sand-like regolith.

Meriweather had studied the dome installation plans before he put his operation into motion. He paced out an area along the stabilized regolith edge for three meters and two meters back.

"Dig down three meters throughout this area," he told his men.

Using lasers powered by their rover LANR, the men worked for three hours removing the sandy surface and vaporizing the hard regolith for the remaining two meters or so. Then he had them cut a twenty-five-centimeter-high, fifty-centimeter-deep slot toward the dome. When they finished, Meriweather climbed into the hole and placed seismic explosives into the slot with their shaped charges pointed toward the dome.

When all the explosives were placed and a detonator lead had been brought to the surface, the men filled the hole with loose regolith and rolled back and forth over it with the rover.

"Load everything back in the rover," Meriweather said.

As they loaded their tools, one of the men spoke up. "When are we going to blow it, Boss?"

"I want maximum damage, maximum panic, but I don't want to kill anybody," Meriweather answered. "People will begin transferring into

Nanedi City tomorrow. So, we'll blow it early, before they start arriving. We'll move south until we're about to lose line-of-sight. We'll wait until just before sunrise and blow it. Then we'll return to Mars Station."

"Why that?" one of the men wanted to know. "Why not abandon the rover here and use the portal back to Earth?"

"It's complicated," Meriweather said. "I used to work out of Mars Station. I have friends there. They need this rover, and what they're doing won't destroy Mars."

"Okay, yeah, we joined Red Mars Faction to keep Mars red. Like you said, they're not trying to change Mars, right? They're just studying it."

Meriweather sighed and looked back to verify he still had a view of the explosives site. A couple more klicks and then to the top of that rise, he thought. Intellects these guys are not, but I need them to give us a chance to succeed. He let his thoughts wander to Dr. Jackson Fredricks. That bastard really betrayed me. I thought he was my friend and colleague, but he fucked me royally. I shall miss him.

MARS—NANEDI CITY

"I guess we are ready to commence the process," Thorpe said.

They entered the building through the middle set of doors. The inside setup was designed to funnel people through three lines past a receiving desk and then out through the three double doors.

"Once we start," Braxton added, "it will be a continuous stream until we have processed ten-thousand folks."

"Have we missed anything?" Thorpe asked. "I have this nagging feeling."

✳

The sign read *Nanedi Portal—Los Angeles*. 110 people had assembled in the small auditorium on the main floor of the converted movie theater on Ventura Boulevard in Studio City, just west of Universal Studios.

In downtown Denver, a similar converted movie theater on North Broadway displayed a sign that read *Nanedi Portal—Denver*. The auditorium held another 110 people.

In a third converted movie theatre in Times Square in New York City, another 110 people sat waiting. The sign outside read *Nanedi Portal—New York*.

Soft music filled the air in all three auditoriums. The men and women sitting in the halls were young, the women in their mid-twenties, the men in their mid-thirties. All were well dressed, well-groomed, and seemed in good health. They sat quietly, expectantly.

Simultaneously in all three auditoriums, Thorpe's holoimage appeared, life-size, as if he were actually standing on the stage.

"Ladies and gentlemen," he said, "you have all volunteered to immigrate to Mars. In fact, you have paid about a year's salary for the privilege. About a thousand of you will be transferring today to Nanedi City. Each day for the next nine days, another thousand will follow, fellow Americans all. Some of you have chosen to work the land. Others have chosen to fill the many other roles Nanedi City will require to become completely self-sufficient.

"You have entered a renewable five-year contract. The provisions of your contract designate Mars Company to run your government and operate and maintain your infrastructure and life-support. At the end of the first five years, Mars Company will hand over the reins of government to your elected representatives, and will contract with your elected government to operate and maintain your infrastructure and life support. By then, Mars will have an additional four self-sufficient cities populated by peoples from Europe, Africa, Asia, and South America. As these cities come online, Mars Company will coordinate their interactions until such time as a form of self-government is established across Mars.

"As the first city, we anticipate that you will dominate Martian culture and activities." Thorpe stopped talking to give his three audiences a few minutes to think over what he had said.

"While you and your fellow Martians are learning to thrive in your five domed cities," Thorpe picked up again, "Mars Company will undertake the terraforming of the entire Mars surface. By the time Nanedi City is fully self-sufficient within five years, and the fifth city approaches self-sufficiency some time after that, we expect that all five cities can eliminate their domes to expand however they wish over Mars's surface.

"Mars cities are modeled after a cooperative farm where the land is equally divided among the family units, and is worked cooperatively or individually as the situation dictates. Purchasing and sales of produce will be on a co-op basis so that better farmers and harder workers receive greater gain. Your economic structure for design, manufacturing, and services is set up to reward innovation and hard work. Nobody gets a free ride, but until Mars is fully terraformed, neither will anyone be able to accumulate land and assets at will. Mutual interdependence for sheer survival mandates that Mars citizens work together in ways that would not have been necessary for a co-op enterprise on Earth. The universal integrated Link will make it possible for each community to make many decisions collectively. Land will have been parceled out equally to all immigrants who desired to receive land. Those of you who opted to be part of the infrastructure, manufacturing, etc., have received appropriate living quarters, workspaces, manufacturing facilities, and so on. Purchasing, sales, and compensation for work will be blockchain transactions using the phoenix, as we discussed with you individually when you signed up.

"There will be snafus—it's inevitable. Nevertheless, Mars Company is your partner to make this happen, to give humanity a second world on which to expand and grow. It won't be easy, and the challenges will be many. Some of you may not make it. Accidents happen. People get careless, and Mars outside the domes is harsh and unforgiving.

"Nanedi City's location along the western branch of Nanedi Valles will change over time into a city by a major river flowing through a canyon—a destination for tourists and new immigrants, perhaps even the capital city of Mars." Thorpe stopped talking and seemed to move to the edge of the three platforms.

"Please pass single file through the portal at the back of the auditorium. It will take you to the Nanedi City reception center, where we will process your arrival and get you situated as quickly as possible."

✳

People were about to arrive. Thorpe and Braxton stood on the road outside the Nanedi City Portal Terminal as Sol rose above the horizon across eastern Nanedi Valles.

"Nanedi City will never be this quiet again," Braxton said. "Savor it!"

That's when the explosive charge blew. The sound was deafening where Thorpe and Braxton stood, several kilometers from the site. They looked east and saw a rip extending a quarter of the way up the dome. Air rushed out with a loud whooshing, whistling sound. Huge clouds of vapor formed just outside the dome, and frost formed on the regolith.

"Stop the transfer process!" Thorpe said into his Link. "We have a situation here."

Braxton verified that emergency deployment of repair nanobots was underway. They both grabbed personal transporters from their holding slots along the boulevard—two-wheeled, self-balancing platforms that virtually every human adult knew how to use. In a few minutes, they could see the blast area at the dome base and the fabric rip that extended up over their heads. Air rushing through the blast zone was scouring an ever-deepening tunnel under the dome edge. Waves of nanobots arrived with stretched polymer sheets that they placed over the rip. Within a few minutes, the bots had sealed the rip, and the only escaping air was through the deepening hole under the dome edge.

More swarms of nanobots arrived carrying buckets of regolith amalgamate. They plugged the trench with polymer spikes and amalgamate. Once the leak repair stabilized, Thorpe called Culp by Link.

"Jerry, we've got a problem. Someone sabotaged the Nanedi City Dome. I need one of your teams down here ASAP to chase down the culprit."

Culp agreed to have people there within a couple of hours. Thorpe called his Mars Company controllers.

"You can commence processing people," he said.

✳

Thorpe hurried back to the portal terminal while Braxton remained at the site. People were already being processed, but instead of passing through the three double doors onto Bradbury Boulevard, they assembled in a hastily arranged holding area between the processing gates and the doors.

Thorpe climbed onto a chair and set his Link to function as an amplifier. He addressed the 330 arrivals.

"Welcome to Nanedi City, folks. We asked you to stand by because of an unexpected development. Somebody—we don't know who yet—attempted to sabotage the dome that retains our atmosphere. I say *attempted* because they were unsuccessful, for the most part. They did blow a hole under the dome edge and rip a section of the dome fabric, but our well-thought-out emergency response system brought the problem under control within a few minutes, and the dome is repaired and fully functional as we speak.

"Nevertheless, you people are taking a major step into the unknown. You have made a significant financial investment in your future and even put your lives on the line. Your plans did not include what happened this morning. Please take a few minutes to think through the implications going forward, because there probably will be further such attacks in the future.

"Mars Company will give you a week to think it over. If you decide this is not for you, drop by our office here in the portal terminal, and we will return you to Earth and refund your investment.

"Okay…you all have your arrival packets and detailed information uploaded to your Links. Remember that Mars Company is your partner as you carve out a new life in Nanedi City. We will work with you in every way possible to ensure your success."

✳

Despite objections from his crew, Dr. Meriweather insisted on returning the rover to the station. Before turning south, however, they headed on a southeast vector, skirting a crater ringwall to their right six kilometers out, and then dropping into a hundred-meter-deep canyon ten kilometers farther.

"We used the Mars Station portal to get here," Meriweather told his crew. "We can't use it again." He reached into a storage compartment under the driver's seat and extracted a hyper-disk. Handing it to one of his crew, he said, "Take this outside and bury it several centimeters under the sand. Then brush out your footprints and lock back inside."

Fifteen minutes later, they got underway again, first climbing out of the end of the truncated canyon several kilometers to the south and then continuing southward on a gentle upslope. They arrived at Mars Station in the wee hours of the following morning.

"These people are my friends," he told his team. "I intend them no harm but only want to stop the transformation of Mars. Remember that."

They parked the rover outside the Mars Station garage. Meriweather activated another portal, and they returned to their hidden Earthside base of operations.

OORT STATION PRIME—CHAIRMAN JOHN BUTLER'S OFFICE

"You called, John?" she asked with a smile and walked over to peck his lips.

"I did, Kimberly," he said, laying the volume aside and offering her a glass of wine—a Village Burgundy from Marsannay-la-Côte. They sipped quietly for several minutes, enjoying the wine's elegant, fruity flavor. Finally, Butler said, "I would like your opinion on a matter that has been on my mind lately."

Kimberly pulled her chair to the front of his desk and sat expectantly.

"We have held Masin Arcah and Adrhun Gloalorn for quite some time now. They have been cooperative, especially Masin. We showed them who and what we are as a species. Frankly, I don't think we have an ethical right to hold them."

Kimberly started to interrupt, but Butler held up his hand with a smile.

"Yes, I know they piloted fighter craft against us, but they were part of an invasion force. Neither was in charge of any aspect of the attack. They were pawns who got lucky because they survived."

"I can't disagree with your logic," Kimberly said. "So, what are you suggesting?"

"Frankly, I think we should turn them loose with some walking money and orders to find their places in our interplanetary society." He smiled again with a hint of earnestness. "Given who they are, I should think they would find themselves in high demand for presentations, talks about their cultures…" His voice trailed off.

"Have you spoken with eThorpe about this?"

"Not yet. I wanted to get your reaction." Butler held his hands out with palms up, shrugged slightly, and lifted his eyebrows.

"I like Masin a lot," Kimberly said. "Adrhun…I really don't know. He seems sullen and angry or perhaps bitter."

"And that's understandable." Butler reached over his desk and took Kimberly's hand in his. "How would you feel, eighty-four lightyears away from your home, your friends, everything you ever knew?"

"But Masin doesn't seem to feel that way."

"I agree," Butler said, "but he comes from a free-wheeling society. For him, I think this is a grand adventure. Adrhun comes from a structured, inflexible culture. I think he feels completely out of place with us."

"Shall we bring eThorpe and eBraxton into the discussion?" Kimberly asked, squeezing and then disengaging Butler's hand.

✳

A few minutes later, eThorpe's and eBraxton's holoimages seemed to be occupying chairs arrayed before Butler's desk.

"Thank you, gentlemen, for your promptness," Butler said.

Kimberly just smiled warmly, especially at eBraxton. Butler proceeded to explain his thoughts about a continued incarceration of the two Asterians.

"The bottom line is," Butler finished, "I can see no downside to freeing Masin Arcah and Adrhun Gloalorn."

"What do they know about our planned expedition to Aster?" eThorpe asked.

"They have to know that we are planning the trip," Butler said. "They would have no way of knowing our intentions." Butler smiled glumly. "I'm not sure *I* know."

"That's the subject of another conversation," eBraxton said. "So, what about letting these guys go?"

"They will need some instruction on the *rules* our society imposes on everyone," eThorpe said.

"And some funds to keep them going until they find a means of supporting themselves," eBraxton added.

"Just booting them out the door with some jingle in their jeans… I'm not so sure that will work," eThorpe said. "I think we might need to arrange for a couple of transition sponsors."

"I'll take Masin," Kimberly said immediately. "I really like him and want to help him adjust as much as possible."

Butler cleared his throat. "Kimberly, you might want to consider taking both for a month or so. They come from different cultures in the Aster system, but we are a totally new experience. Being together after their release might help them both, at least until they come to terms with being here."

"I think Adrhun might be a handful," Kimberly said.

"You've got Daphne and Dale, and all of us, for that matter," eBraxton said.

Butler looked at Kimberly expectantly. eThorpe just smiled quietly while eBraxton grinned openly.

"You guys planned this," Kimberly said with a pout.

"Actually, my Dear, we didn't," Butler said. "eThorpe opened the door, and you walked right through it." He smiled broadly. "I would have expected nothing less from you."

✳

Kimberly and Daphne set up a private bedroom suite on the floor above their downtown Los Angeles apartment for Arcah and Gloalorn. It was next to the secure portal they had earlier established to the new headquarters—the Kuiper Joint Station. A week later, Master Chief Petty Officer Sam Bunker brought the Asterians to Butler's office. eThorpe, eBraxton, and Kimberly were already there.

Chairman Butler addressed them. "I am Federation Chairman John Butler. On Frohlic, I would be similar to the Boss. On Rogan, I'm not sure you have anyone in a similar position to mine.

"I have the legal authority to pardon you both and to set you free to live your lives as you wish in our human society. For someone of our species, such a transition would be traumatic. I presume this would be so for you as well. Consequently, I am turning you both over to Kimberly Deveraux, whom you both know well. She and her friends have arranged for a place for both of you to stay until you decide for yourselves what you want to do next.

"Kimberly and her friends will teach you about our money system and will assist each of you in finding your independent way in our society. You will be free to come and go as you wish, remain with Kimberly or not, as you wish. I only caution you to learn as much as you can from her and her friends before you strike out on your own."

"Do we have any say in this matter?" Arcah asked.

"I suppose you can remain in your lockup out here at OS Prime."

Gloalorn just stared at Butler, his feelings unreadable.

Arcah added, "When you put it that way…"

"I wish you both the very best for your future." Butler rose from his desk and shook both their hands, a human gesture they had come to understand.

CHAPTER ELEVEN

EARTH—LOS ANGELES

Initially, each morning both Asterians took breakfast with their hosts. Then they spent the rest of the day exploring together. After a couple of days, however, each went his separate way, usually returning by supper time but sometimes remaining out late or even overnight.

After two weeks had passed, at breakfast, Arcah asked casually as he stroked Max, "Has anyone seen Adrhun?"

"Haven't seen him for several days," Dale said.

"Me neither," Daphne said.

"Nor I," Kimberly added with a slight frown. "Did he say anything to you?" she asked Arcah.

"He said he was tired of being on display and that he wanted to explore your system on his own. He's still wrapping his head around your portal technology…that's how you say it, right?"

Everyone chuckled. Max leaped deftly into Daphne's lap, purring quietly.

"The problem is, he never returned since he struck out on his own," Arcah said.

"We have the ability to track the movements of an individual through the portal system," Dale said. "It's passive; the data go to a huge unmonitored database. We can put a bot on it, but it will take some time."

"I hope nothing happened to him," Kimberly said. "We don't have a backup."

"You don't have a what?" Arcah asked.

Kimberly explained the nature of backup technology and described Ogden enterprises, the system-wide company she and Daphne founded.

"So…" Arcah said slowly, "if something happens to any of you, or anyone in your system, you can rejuvenate them?"

"Through their most recent backup," Kimberly said, "if they haven't signed up for an ILK."

"What's an ILK?"

"It's an Integrated Link Kit. Basically, two capsules that you swallow. They set up a nanobot microbiome inside you that creates an integrated Link in your brain and sets up real-time backups to our database. This way, should something happen, the restored person will be as up to date as physically possible.

"In any case," Kimberly continued, "we need to get you set up with an ILK." She smiled at Arcah. "I presume you wish this?"

✳

Kimberly and Daphne took Arcah to Ogden by portal, did a complete DNA sequence both of him and his microbiome, and put him into their system. They gave him the ILK capsules that evening, and the following morning he reported that everything seemed to be working.

"If you should be killed now, you will wake up in one of our rejuvenating rooms. Daphne or I will be notified, and we will come to your side as soon as possible."

MARS-SUN L4—UDACHNY

Then Orlov turned to the business at hand. His starship was a big deal, but he had a company to run, one that required his focused attention across a broad spectrum of activities—some completely legal and aboveboard, others mired in the worst kind of human trafficking, illegal weapons sales, blood diamonds, and drugs.

Orlov busied himself with a complex three-way transaction involving diamonds, using his own Udachny Protocol to bypass blood diamond restrictions, weapons for a Southeast Asian revolutionary warlord, and three hundred female sex slaves for the entertainment of his Belter workers. Making all three happen untraceably took his entire focus.

Without warning, his Head of Security barged through a portal into his office. Orlov looked up, irritation spreading across his Slavic features. His security head was not alone. With him was a being Orlov had seen on holocasts but never in person. He was a bipedal humanoid with six digits on each hand. He was short and stocky, with dark tan skin. His face was much like a human face with flattened nose and very thin lips. His ears articulated like cat ears, and his brown hair looked human.

"What is this?" Orlov growled. "I'm busy!"

"This is the Asterian Adrhun Gloalorn, Sir. He was exploring the planetary portal system and stumbled through one of our portals leading to Udachny. I took him into custody as soon as I found out about him, confiscated his Link, and brought him to you."

Orlov stood and approached Gloalorn. In Russian, he asked, "*Pochemu ty zdes?*"

Gloalorn stared at him without comprehension. Orlov asked again in English, "Why are you here?"

"I was exploring. I came here accidentally. I saw no signs prohibiting passage." Gloalorn took a challenging stance, feet apart, fists balled at his sides. "I am a free citizen of Frohlic and a guest of the Federation. You have no right to hold me."

"We'll see about that," Orlov said. He looked at his Head of Security. "Put him in a holding cell while I figure this out."

✻

Gloalorn was unsure how long he was in Orlov's holding cell—several days, anyway, perhaps a week. They fed him regularly and didn't harass him. They just left him alone. To his surprise, he missed Masin. Even Kimberly and her friends. They had been a pleasant change from the cell he and Masin had occupied for so long after their capture.

He wasn't like Masin, however. It seemed like Masin had forgotten about his homeworld, his heritage, everything from the past. Masin seemed ready to embrace this new culture, this strange race as his own. Not Adrhun—to him, that seemed like betrayal of everything that mattered.

I'm stuck here, Gloalorn said to himself, sitting in Orlov's holding cell, but I don't have to like it. These people are readying an expedition—or is it an invasion?—to Aster. Kimberly and her people and this Orlov guy and his. They seem to be working at cross-purposes. Maybe I can use that to find my way home.

The holding cell door opened, and instead of another uninteresting meal, a stony-faced guard indicated that he follow. Several minutes later, Gloalorn found himself standing in the same domed room where he had first met Isidor Orlov. The guard remained discreetly in the background.

"Sit down," Orlov said in Russian-accented English.

Gloalorn comprehended English well enough but had to listen closely to understand the man. He sat in the indicated chair.

"I have spent the past several days learning about you and your compatriot," Orlov said. "Tell me about your world…and his."

"Frohlic is ancient by any measure of your species," Gloalorn said. "Long ago, millions of years, way before your recorded history, Frohlic developed a technological civilization. Our best guess is that when we began to broadcast electronic transmissions away from our planet, the beings you call the Oort received them. It was long ago, and no one knows for sure, but we believe the Oort saw our primitive transmissions as a potential threat that needed to be dealt with.

"The Oort, who were flesh-and-blood in those days, decided to send an armed fleet to destroy our civilization. And they did—nearly. The remnants of what we were then struggled to survive and eventually rebuilt the Frohlican civilization. And we never forgot. We developed space travel, and we never forgot. We discovered another planet in our solar system that could support life and called it Rogan—and we never forgot. We colonized Rogan with the more adventurous members of our society, and we never forgot.

"Eventually, we went to war with ourselves, Frohlic against Rogan, but we found a way to stop the fighting and focus, instead, on our desire to avenge what had happened so long ago. We were mystified that we were receiving no transmissions from your system, even though the Oort had obviously developed interstellar travel. Something must have happened, we thought, but we remained vigilant, believing that at any time, the Oort might return." Gloalorn stopped talking as he contemplated the events he was relating.

Orlov remained silent.

"Today," Gloalorn continued, "Frohlic is a unified world governed by the Boss and the Council. We allocate our resources to ensure that we never want as a people. Mining, research, manufacturing, farming, distribution are all controlled by the Council." Gloalorn sighed. "It is a wonderful life."

"What about Rogan?" Orlov asked.

"Rogan culture is very different from Frohlic. They don't have any centralized control of anything. They seem to live in a constant state of wild confusion. We Frohlicans do not understand how they function."

"Why did you attack our Solar System?" Orlov asked.

"About a century ago, scientists on both our worlds received primitive electronic transmissions from your solar system. We debated, we argued, we quarreled. In the end, we agreed that something must have overtaken the Oort civilization that had attacked so long ago. Whatever that was had removed the Oort as a threat for a very long time. Apparently, a civilization was resurging in your system. Some of us thought it might be a good thing. Perhaps we could reach out to establish trade and exchange of ideas. But most of us still remembered. Our two worlds decided to take no chances.

"We had developed near lightspeed space travel. We combined our resources and built a mighty armada and sent it on its way. We pilots all volunteered, knowing that when we returned, we would be nearly two hundred years into our future. We believed it was a glorious way to save our civilization from the destruction we were certain would be coming our way from the Oort. We did not count on you humans. Now I am marooned here, never to see Frohlic again, never to walk the streets of my hometown, never to celebrate life with my people." Gloalorn stopped talking.

✳

Orlov leaned back, contemplating what he had just heard. Someone is lying. There is a lot of passion and anger in this stocky alien. His words sound true. His homeworld is organized, structured—it can be manipulated. He can be manipulated if approached properly. He glanced at his Link. Despite the nearly universal availability of the integrated Link, Orlov had not yet taken the leap. He feared taking that step would render him vulnerable to Phoenix.

"Adrhun Gloalorn, all is not lost." Orlov stood and beckoned Gloalorn to join him, looking out the dome. He pointed at the Lance and double-doughnut. "See that out there?"

Gloalorn nodded, a human gesture he had learned that meant acknowledgment.

"That is a starship that can reach your system in about ten days— real time, not relativistic time. We're putting the finishing touches on her right now." Orlov turned to face Gloalorn, adjusting his voice to a sincere timbre. "I will take you with me when we make the journey to Aster on the condition that you cast your lot with me, that you, as the returning hero you obviously will be, open Frohlic's doors to exclusive trade and commerce with me."

"I do not have that kind of influence with the Boss and his Council," Gloalorn said.

"You will, Lad, you will," Orlov said with a hearty smile. "You most certainly will."

MARS—NANEDI VALLES PLATEAU

He collapsed the portal, pocketed the hyper-disk, and entered the rover's lock on the after-port side. Once pressurized, and after shaking off Mars sand and dust, he allowed the air cleaner to suck the remaining particles through a filter, and entered the rover cabin.

Meriweather projected a holographic chart.

"We're here," he said, pointing to the edge of a canyon. With the vertical exaggeration displayed on the chart, the canyon wall looked much steeper than what they could see through the polymer cap.

"We're going to reverse-trace our track from the dome to here, check out their repairs, and then decide what to do next." He settled into the driver's seat. "We should be there in less than an hour."

He headed up the slope at an angle to the north, reaching the rim in a few minutes. His heads-up holographic display indicated their position on the chart, somewhat north of where they had descended following their initial foray. He set his light beams to point down and spread across the sandy surface ahead, and pointed the rover toward Nanedi City. He set a speed of fifty kilometers per hour. To the team member beside him, he said, "Keep an eye out for dips and rocks. After all, this isn't exactly a highway."

As his navigator pointed out potential problems, Meriweather swerved around rocks and either passed around dips or slowed and drove through them. Thirty minutes later, the rover pulled up behind a hummock about a hundred meters from the dome. Meriweather cut the lights, and all five exited the rover. Guided by starlight alone, they warily approached the darkened dome.

The repaired dome material was invisible in the starlight. Meriweather examined the regolith amalgamate that plugged the hole they had created.

"That's probably stronger than the original foundation," Meriweather said, probing around the plug.

A team member spoke up. "We can keep blowing holes and ripping dome fabric. It may not stop them, but it'll keep them busy."

"How is that going to keep Mars red?" Meriweather asked. "It's a waste of time. We need to move on to other, more effective projects." He turned east. "Let's return to the rover and brainstorm this problem."

✻

"Commander, we've got motion near the dome repair," Petty Officer First-class George Raptor said, pointing to his holographic display.

Cmdr. Rob Jacobs stepped over to the display. "Whatcha got, Georgie?"

"Looks like five sources clustered around the plug on the outside."

They watched for several minutes.

"Looks like they're leaving," Raptor said, "heading east."

"Can you track them?"

"No, Sir, this is a proximity detector." Raptor paused. "They will leave tracks. We can muster a small group to follow them."

"Easier said than done, Georgie. We need to get to the plug before we can follow them." Jacobs initiated a Link call.

Minutes later, a small drone flew silently down the dome face and deposited a hyper-disk in the sand several meters to the south.

"Georgie, grab three guys from the duty pool outfitted with exposure suits, armed with pulse and projectile weapons. Meet back here in fifteen minutes, ready to pass through that portal."

＊

"We thought we would collapse the dome with our charge," Meriweather said once they were back inside the rover. "It didn't happen. If we were to simultaneously explode similar charges at five locations around the dome—that could bring down the entire thing."

"What about the people inside?" one of the team members asked. "We exploded the first charge before people arrived."

"That would be tough. A person who didn't have immediate access to an exposure suit would die," Meriweather answered. "It's an unpleasant thing, but sometimes sacrifices must be made for the greater good—in our case, a red Mars. The people inside that dome," he pointed, "have only one goal: A *green* Mars." He sighed. "I simply cannot allow that to happen."

Meriweather pulled the rover from behind the hummock and turned right to follow the base of the dome. He left the lights off, navigating only by starlight.

"The dome is two klicks across, so the circumference is six-and-a-quarter klicks," he said. "We can place evenly-spaced charges around the dome about one-and-a-quarter klicks apart." He checked the time. "If we move at five kilometers per hour and spend a few minutes at each charge location, we can complete the survey in about an hour." He turned to the three team members in the second seat row. "You three place yourselves at the three portside ports—the two here in the cabin and the one in the lock. Focus your entire attention on the interior of the dome. If you see any movement at all—anything—sound the alarm." He turned to the team member sitting next to him. "Keep me away from rocks and holes and at least ten meters from the dome."

Meriweather's suggested speed turned out to be somewhat ambitious. They accomplished the first leg as anticipated and stopped for sufficient time for a team member to exit the rover and bury a hyper-disk in the sand about thirty meters from the dome. From there, the terrain became significantly rougher as they approached the edge of Nanedi Valles, forcing Meriweather to slow to a crawl. The final leg was smooth enough to double their forward speed. Nevertheless, two hours had passed by the time they concealed the fifth hyper-disk.

"That's it, guys," Meriweather said. "I'll open our return portal, and you," he pointed to the team member beside him, "drive the rover through."

After the rover passed through the portal, Meriweather looked at his rover tracks, starkly defined in the starlight. As he stepped through the portal, he wished for one of the frequent Mars sandstorms to wipe them out before somebody discovered them.

✻

Raptor and his three-man team passed through the portal the drone had dropped outside the dome several minutes earlier. First, Raptor collapsed the portal and pocketed the hyper-disk. Then, he pointed toward the hummock, indicating that his team should keep low. Within seconds, the four Federation soldiers reached the hummock crest. Below them, Meriweather's rover commenced its circumnavigation of the dome.

"You two," Raptor said on their secure circuit, "follow the track to the east. See where it leads." Their name tags indicated *Jones* and *Taggart*. He tapped the third soldier. "You come with me, Falcon. We'll follow the rover."

Jones and Taggart headed east in bounding jumps. Raptor and Falcon stayed low and followed the rover, slipping behind a large rock when it stopped to leave the first hyper-disk.

"Base, it's Raptor," on the secure circuit.

"Go ahead, Raptor."

Raptor briefed Cmdr. Jacobs about the rover.

"He buried a hyper-disk. What should I do about it?"

"Note its position and continue following."

When the rover finally returned to its Earth base, Raptor again reported to Jacobs. "Okay, Commander, he's gone…back to wherever he came from. He deposited hyper-disks at five equally located positions around the dome. I think he's planning five simultaneous explosions."

"Why explosions?"

"Why else leave five equally spaced hyper-disks? They're going to move explosives through the portals and set them off at the same time."

MARS—NANEDI VALLES PLATEAU

"Here's the deal," Jacobs said. "Crazies have placed five hyper-disks evenly spaced around Nanedi City dome. Intel says they will pass explosives through the portals and try a simultaneous blast at those five places, attempting to collapse the dome. You guys are gonna prevent that…not only prevent, but also permanently disrupt their activities.

"Intel believes all five hyper-disks lead to the same Earth location…believes, but they don't know for sure. Split up into teams of two. Go to the hyper-disk locations. Install a hidden remote holocam at each location. Then coordinate your portal passage through their disks. Your primary weapon is the EMD set to the highest non-lethal stun. Your backup is your projectile weapon. Use it only to save your life or that of an innocent.

"Let's put an end to this nonsense once and for all! Hooyah!"

Hooyahs! all around.

✳

Raptor put himself and the other three men who had been to the disks before with a team member who hadn't.

"Swede," he said to Petty Officer Rauld Stefansen, "you take the lead at the original explosion point. Kim," he said to Petty Officer Kimber Jordan, "you're with Swede."

"Now, remember, guys. This ain't no walk in the park. These crazy Reds mean business. They're tryin' to kill a whole bunch of people.

We gonna take 'em alive if possible. We gotta figure out what they're thinkin', but like Commander Jake said, we gotta stop 'em!"

Nine *Hooyahs!* answered him.

The five teams passed through the portal at the original attack point, assembled, and headed around the dome in both directions, leaving Stefansen and Jordan in place. They communicated on a secure channel through the dome to Headquarters, where Jacobs coordinated their movement. In less than a half-hour, all five teams were positioned. Each team leader retrieved the hidden hyper-disk, holding it at the ready.

"On my mark," Jacobs said, commencing a countdown. "Five… four…three…two…one…Mark!"

Five pairs of armed men stepped through five portals into a single, brightly lit, unguarded chamber. Five cartons labeled *Seismic Explosives* sat in the center of the chamber floor. Raptor opened one; it contained ten shaped seismic charges. He recorded a holoimage of the box placement with his Link. Then he opened a portal to the headquarters compound in Nanedi City.

He grabbed a box and said, "Each team bring a box to headquarters."

Raptor stepped through the portal with his box. In minutes, all the explosives boxes and all his men were back in headquarters. Raptor laid a shaped charge on the console in front of Jacobs.

"We need fifty non-working copies ASAP."

Jacobs scanned the shaped charge with his Link and transmitted the holoimage to FeSFo Headquarters. In a FeSFo lab, three technicians fed the holoimage into a nanobot programmer—basically, an abbreviated Nanocosm. Ten minutes later, they passed fifty perfect non-working copies of the shaped charge to Nanedi City. Raptor's men replaced the real charges with the fake ones, and then they placed the boxes back in the chamber just as they had found them. Raptor made a final sweep of the room, stepped through the portal, and collapsed it.

Raptor spent a few minutes examining the holoimages from the remote holocams. Then he checked them with his Link. Everything seemed to be working.

✳

Thirty-two hours later, alarms sounded in the Nanedi City FeSFo compound and on Petty Officer Raptor's Link. Raptor and his nine men stepped into the Nanedi City FeSFo control center several minutes later, outfitted and ready to go.

All five holocams showed activity. Men dressed in black exposure suits used lasers to dig at the dome foundation in all five locations. They carried sidearms that looked like projectile weapons. They dug trenches that extended horizontally under the dome base.

"Listen up!" Cmdr. Jacobs said. "Your portals are placed just beyond each center of activity. Teams of two pass through the portals and immediately take down everyone there with your EMDs. Be careful! It appears they have projectile weapons. You each carry an E-disk. If you get shot anywhere but your head, your E-disk will bring you back here, where we can aggressively address your situation. If you get shot in your head, your E-disk will bring you back, but your upload will automatically commence rejuvenation out in the Kuiper Belt." He stopped and looked around. "How many of you are on automatic backup?" The original SEAL Team members indicated they were. "When this is over, the rest of you report to me to set it up."

"Okay," Raptor said, "let's do this! *Hooyah!*"

Nine *Hooyahs!* Answered him back.

✳

Cmdr. Jacobs watched the holodisplays closely as his troops passed through the portals. They stepped through the portals with EMDs at the ready pressed against ten shoulders. The newer guys stumbled a bit with the change in gravity, but the old-timers took the change in stride with no indication that the underfoot gravity had dropped by two-thirds. There appeared to be four men at each site. As his troops came through the portals, one man was in the hole at each site, placing what they believed were explosives. In each case, the three men outside the holes collapsed as the EMD bolts struck them.

Three of the men placing the explosive charges in the holes poked their heads above the edges and were hit with EMD charges. A fourth at the westernmost location rolled out of his hole while firing his projectile weapon. He hit a FeSFo guy in his left arm. Before the injured soldier could respond, his E-disk took him back to FeSFo headquarters inside the dome. His partner drilled the shooter's helmet with his own projectile weapon leaving it with a soggy mess inside. The fifth, at the initial explosion location, lifted a projectile weapon over the edge and sprayed projectiles over a 160-degree arc. One of the projectiles struck Petty Officer Jordan's left leg. He dropped with a yelp, and his E-disk returned him to Nanedi City FeSFo headquarters.

Petty Officer Stefansen leaped to his right and saturated the hole with several EMD bolts, collapsing the shooter.

"I've got a man down," Stefansen announced. "His E-disk evacuated him. I've got four Reds down, one dead. Can you send me a couple of replacements to help get these guys out of here?"

Several minutes later, team members stepped through portals at Stefansen's and the westernmost location. At each location, they dragged the unconscious and one expired Reds through the portal into the Nanedi City holding cell. Within thirty minutes, all nineteen living Reds were safely ensconced in Nanedi City holding cells waiting for someone higher up to decide their disposition. The dead guy went to the morgue.

✳

Clad in a Mars excursion suit, Dr. Frank Meriweather evacuated the garage holding his Mars rover and activated his portal into the hundred-meter-deep canyon fourteen kilometers southeast of Nanedi City. He climbed into the rover and passed through the portal onto the canyon floor. Meriweather collapsed the portal and followed his earlier track up and out the southeast end of the canyon. He turned due south for four kilometers and then headed east for another ten, aiming for a cone-shaped peak that soared 150 meters above the surrounding regolith.

Meriweather reached the zenith about twenty minutes after he departed the canyon. He was about 150 meters above the height of Nanedi City, which lay about thirty-eight kilometers to the northwest. That put it just below the horizon, but Meriweather thought he could make out the glint of the sun off Nanedi City Dome as the sun dipped westward.

How did they find us? he asked himself. My whole team is gone. Who knows what they'll do to them? He leaned forward in the driver's seat, resting his helmet against the steering wheel. I can recruit another team, but will they be willing to take the risk? He sighed deeply. Why don't people see my perspective? I keep telling them that Mars holds secrets that we must learn—perhaps even the secret to life itself. He sighed again. I must stop them! I must!

✳

"Nanedi One, it's Raptor."

"Go ahead, Raptor. Commander Jacobs can hear you."

"Nanedi One, I'm in *Rover Two* following a rover track due east from the original detonation site. I got Swede, Claw, and Doc with me. We followed the tracks down into a relatively shallow canyon, and we're now headed out the south end. We're some fourteen klicks from the dome, and the track trails off to the east all the way to the horizon. I can see the top of a conical peak just over the horizon. Looks like the track leads directly toward the peak. You want me to follow the track?"

"*Rover Two*, this is Commander Jacobs. You're authorized to follow the tracks, but I want you guys fully suited up, including helmets. We know the Reds have projectile weapons, and we don't know how many are in the rover you're tracking. If they're on that peak, they can see you coming."

"Rules of engagement?" Raptor asked.

"If they use projectile weapons, as they already have, try to subdue them with your EMDs, but don't risk your men. Deadly force authorized if fired upon with projectiles, *and* you believe it's necessary."

✳

As long shadows crept across the plain below him, Meriweather thought he saw a flash of light about halfway between the canyon and the base of the conical rise on which he was perched. He raised his binoculars and focused to that point. Sure enough, a FeSFo rover was coming along his track, *Rover Two* emblazoned in white along the top. It would carry armament, he knew that—at a minimum, a fifty-caliber projectile cannon and a high-power laser. He looked around his cabin. All he had was a shoulder-fired projectile weapon and a hand-held semi-automatic pistol—and, of course, his rover.

I'm just one man, no matter how determined, no matter how righteous. It's hopeless! I'm not going to rot away in prison for the rest of my life. Meriweather maneuvered his rover so it pointed directly at the oncoming Rover Two, still a kilometer distant. He accelerated to his top speed of nearly 100 kilometers per hour. I'll take them out in a blaze of glory, he thought as he pushed all other thoughts out of his mind.

The red, sandy plain stretched out ahead of Meriweather as he focused on the approaching rover. The haunting beauty, the incredible landscape that everyone else wanted to change, overwhelmed him with reverence and a futile desperation.

"Red Mars forever!" he shouted, tears streaming down his cheeks. "Red Mars forever!"

He continued directly toward *Rover Two*—their combined velocity was near 150 kilometers per hour. Only a few tens of meters separated them.

✳

Raptor's laser projector locked onto the oncoming rover. "Fire!"

Stefansen pressed a button, causing a laser bolt to pass through the oncoming rover's transparent nose cone and drill a ten-centimeter hole in Meriweather's torso.

MARS-SUN L4—UDACHNY

At first, Gloalorn was upset by his continuing confinement. As he gave it more thought, however, he came to understand why Orlov wanted to keep his presence at Udachny a secret, especially from Arcah and Arcah's friends.

"Isidor," Gloalorn said to the oligarch at their next meeting, "if you are correct about me becoming a hero on Frohlic, I can be more effective in promoting your interests if you understand and speak Frohlican fluently. I have discerned that you speak several languages already, although your English is a bit difficult for me to understand. Frohlican is a complex language, like English, but the rules are simpler. If you are as skilled in languages as I think you are, you should learn Frohlican quickly." He mimicked the human smile, showing his teeth while curving his thin lips upward.

✳

Orlov struggled to retain a neutral expression as he considered what Gloalorn had said. It did make a lot of sense. He mulled it over, examining the pros and cons of taking time to learn a new language.

"I agree," Orlov said finally. "We will spend at least two hours together daily while you teach me to speak Frohlican." He stood and walked to the dome edge facing his starship. "I want you to spend the rest of your time creating an outline of how your government works. Pay close attention to which departments we will have to deal with when we arrive." He paused in thought. "You have learned a lot about our culture. What do we have that Frohlic does not but would like to have?"

"That's easy," Gloalorn said. "Portals and uploads…and your starship technology, of course."

"Do you know what kind of licensing rules Frohlic has?"

"I'm not sure I understand," Gloalorn said.

"In our system, if I invent something, I can transfer to you the right to use my invention for a price. The government enforces this contract. If you were to go around me, create your own version of my invention and manufacture it yourself without paying me our agreed-upon fee, I could get the government to force you either to pay me or to cease and desist in your activities."

"I think Frohlic has such a mechanism," Gloalorn answered, "but I'm not sure. If not, we should be able to establish it without too much difficulty."

"I would think," Orlov said, "that Frohlic has many things, especially technology, that we do not have." He was silent for a minute. "You trade goods and services on Frohlic, don't you?"

"Not exactly; not like here, at least." Gloalorn appeared to struggle with how to explain something that he did not entirely understand himself. "If I invent something that would be useful to society, I submit it to the Council. If the Council agrees that society can use my invention, it sets up a development and eventually a production unit. I get credited in some fashion—I'm not sure how or what. Someone somewhere figures this out." He gave a rather human shrug. "It's not like here. There are no large private companies like yours or Phoenix, or even small ones. The Council operates throughout society, undertaking all production and distribution. People work at what they do best."

"What about jobs like cleaning shitters?" Orlov asked.

"What's a shitter?"

Orlov explained.

"That's all handled by robots or other automatic equipment. People do things that matter—mostly."

Did Marx go to Frohlic after he died? Orlov asked himself. It sounds like a functioning Workers' Paradise. But that's crazy, and I don't believe it. "I guess we'll cross that bridge when we reach it," Orlov said.

"What's a bridge?"

CHAPTER TWELVE

OORT STATION PRIME—ADM. JERRY CULP'S OFFICE

eCulp appeared to occupy a chair in the space before his desk. Cmdr. Rob Jacobs and Master Chief Sam Bunker occupied real chairs, accompanied by their uploads, eJake and eSam, also in chairs. Maxter, who had appeared at the start of the meeting, stood on his hind legs on a chair looking out the window at the Milky Way.

"You guys know how much I hate meetings," Culp said, "so I'll keep this short and sweet. Jake, great job in putting down the Red renegades. Too bad you had to kill Dr. Meriweather, but my reading of the report says Petty Officer Raptor had no choice."

Jacobs nodded in agreement.

"Now on another matter. Adrhun Gloalorn is missing. Kimberly tells me he launched out on his own, which he had every right to do, but he never returned. Masin Arcah is worried but says Gloalorn knows enough to keep himself safe under normal circumstances.

"I want all of you to do a full forensic trace of everything Gloalorn did following his departure from their shared apartment in Los Angeles." He looked at Jacobs. "Jake, you take charge of the search.

Leave nothing to chance. Check everything. Report to me when you have something."

✻

As soon as he left Culp's office, Jacobs contacted Dale Ryan by secure Link.

"We have lost track of Adrhun Gloalorn, who was out exploring the Solar System by portal. What can you do to help us track him?"

"I'll check with Rodney Bailey. If it can be done, he can write a program to accomplish it."

✻

"So, Rodney, we need to find this guy. We don't think he's hiding. More likely, he's either lost or has been abducted," Dale said over his Link connection.

"Abducted? How do you arrive at that?"

"The other Asterian, Masin Arcah, says Gloalorn wouldn't go into hiding. He was all about getting to know our Solar System on his own," Dale answered. "I tell you, he's either lost or abducted."

"He had a phoenix blockchain account, right?" Bailey asked.

"Yeah, they both get a stipend until they can fend for themselves."

"Okay, let's track his portal payments to Phoenix."

An hour later, Bailey contacted Dale. "I've tracked this guy all over the place—I mean virtually everywhere. His last transfer was from the Federation Council Chamber at OS Prime to the offices of Guo Qiáng in Beijing. That should not have happened, but from what I could learn, Guo Qiáng was visiting the Council Chamber when he was suddenly called back to his office in Beijing. Apparently, in his haste, he left the portal open. Your guy found the portal open and simply stepped through. He had no idea where he was headed." Bailey shook his head. "That's it. He never left Guo Qiáng's office by portal. I suppose he could have left on foot, but he was in the middle of the Chinese government complex. Security is as tight there as anywhere on Earth. So, here's my thought. If they had him, we would know by now. Even the Chinese government is not stupid enough to abduct one of the two surviving aliens. No, they would have let us know. So that means…"

Dale interrupted. "…there's another portal in Guo Qiáng's office, one that's *not* in the Phoenix system."

"You got it, Pal," Bailey said, "nothing else makes sense."

"Thanks, Buddy. I need to talk with eThorpe about this."

✳

After receiving Dale's report, eThorpe checked his tensor database. He quickly located Gloalorn's arrival at Udachny. After a bit of searching, he tapped into the conversation between Orlov and Gloalorn. Then he contacted Dale.

"To keep things orderly," eThorpe said, "I'll brief you and Commander Jacobs together, and then we can meet with Admiral Culp to determine how to handle it."

Dale went to Jacob's office, and shortly thereafter, eThorpe appeared as a holoimage. Within a few minutes, Jacobs knew everything Dale and eThorpe knew about the matter. They transited to Adm. Culp's office. After Jacobs briefed Culp, he turned the floor over to eThorpe.

"Here's the thing," eThorpe said. "We have surreptitious tensors in virtually every piece of Orlov's electronic equipment. Once we knew where to look, we discovered Orlov's arrangement with Gloalorn. We can go get him, but that may defeat our ultimate purpose. Right now, Orlov does not know about our hidden tensors. If we pull Gloalorn out, Orlov will figure things out and find our tensors. That's the last thing we need.

"I'll brief the people who need to know about this, and I'll make sure Chairman Butler knows and approves."

MARS-SUN L1—SOLETTA

PS Ad Astra remained a Phoenix asset, available to whoever needed it. *PS Neil Armstrong* was assigned to Thorpe and Braxton. PS Buzz Aldrin was assigned to Adm. Culp. *PS Pete Conrad* was assigned to Chairman Butler and garaged at OS Prime for use wherever a craft with its capabilities was needed.

The *Armstrong* hovered at the Mars-Sun L1 point, a million kilometers toward Sol from Mars. She carried several hyper-disks linked to various elements of the Soletta construction.

Braxton donned his helmet and locked out of *Armstrong*. He carried a hyper-disk linked to the Nanocosm that had been building the Soletta from design through directing the construction nanobots. This hyper-disk opened a pathway for the Nanocosm to construct the polymer rings—the Fresnel louvers.

Several hours after Braxton returned to *Armstrong*, Thorpe stepped through a portal and joined him.

"What's the progress?" he asked.

Braxton pointed to his external monitors—holoimages, actually. "The Soletta core is in place along with positioning jets whose fuel is supplied through a small portal. It's gonna take a while. Remember, the Soletta has a five-thousand-klick radius with five-hundred-thousand concentric, ten-meter polymer rings."

"Are the bots keeping up?" Thorpe asked.

"That's part of the problem," Braxton said. "The Nanocosm is producing bots as rapidly as possible—billions of them, but we're gonna be limited by their numbers until the project is entirely up to speed."

"Better than the alternative," Thorpe said. "How long would this project take with a thousand men and materials shipped in by portal or spacecraft?"

Braxton grinned and held up his hand in a mock toast. "I salute Sally and Brad. Their creation has changed everything."

✳

Soletta construction was well underway. Braxton couldn't actually see progress as it happened, but if he turned away for several minutes and then looked out at the Soletta, expansion of the rings was obvious. He had assigned a small team of engineers to oversee the progress on site. From time to time, he could see sunlight glinting off their helmets as they moved around the project.

The ten-meter polymer rings that formed the Fresnel lens segments remained in line with incoming sunlight until the entire Soletta could be adjusted and calibrated. Seen from end-on, they were virtually invisible.

The engineers wore TBH[2] boots so they could maneuver easily around the Soletta. They also carried E-disks that took them to Nanedi City should anything go wrong. They would maintain a continuous physical presence until the Soletta was completed in several months.

MARS—GEOSYNCHRONOUS ORBIT

"So, explain to me once more what this stuff is, Brad," Braxton said. "I know we're putting a superconducting wire around Mars in geosynchronous orbit. What I don't get is the carbon nanotube nature of this shit. When we first examined the problem of giving Mars a magnetic shield, the experts I know wanted to put a two-tesla dipole out by the Soletta. They told me that had been the thinking for nearly a century. You and Sally did a whole bunch of calculations—which I understand, by the way—to show that it is much more efficient to make Mars the dipole, like Earth."

"Sally looked it up on GlobalNet and found the connection," Brad said.

Sally stuck her head through the portal and smiled. Then, to everyone's surprise, Max jumped through the portal and settled on Braxton's lap.

"So," Brad continued, "the Nanocosm harvests carbon from wherever and brings it to our facility at Phoenix. Nanobots morph the carbon into graphene sheets, and then roll the sheets into nanotubes. Then they mix in a whole bunch of cresol. Not long after that, the dough is ready to form into a continuous, five-centimeter superconducting wire. When we take this hyper-disk outside," he

---

2   Jet boots developed in 1967 by three NASA scientists, David Thomas, John Bird, and Richard Hellbaum. NASA tested the jet boots Earthside back then, but they were not introduced into current use until a few years before Thorpe was revived. They're simpler and less cumbersome than any of the old Manned Maneuvering Units. They fit like riding boots, but with completely flexible ankles. The boot uppers consist of two stiff, shaped polymer bags that contain pressurized hypergolic fuel components—UDMH (Unsymmetrical dimethylhydrazine) and nitrogen tetroxide. The fuel valves are controlled by a microswitch under each big toe. Each boot produces ten newtons of force against the ball of the foot. The wearer bends the knees for the appropriate thrust vector, and twists for torque.

pointed to a specially marked hyper-disk, "and point it in the right direction, the wire and its sheath commence pushing through the portal along the orbital path."

"Okay, I get it." But, in truth, Braxton was amazed at what the Sally-Brad team had done. Brad made it sound simple, but they had literally changed how superconducting orbital operations would be done in the future. "The sheath is designed to keep the nanotube wire stable and centered, right—and cold?"

"You got it. Neodymium magnets interact with the magnetic field the wire produces to keep the wire centered. The refrigeration maintains temperature between five and twenty Kelvin. Incident sunlight on the outside of the one-meter sheath generates sufficient power to operate the refrigeration and the controlling electronics." Brad smiled the smile of a proud father. "Once we are up to speed, we will push out three-and-a-half meters of completed wire and sheath every second." He grinned again. "So, a year from now, they will approach us from the other side."

✳

Thorpe did not play a direct role in the Mars Loop project. He and Braxton coordinated their Mars terraforming activities to make the best use of facilities, equipment, and personnel. He was in Mars geosynchronous orbit near Braxton to see for himself how the process worked in practice.

As he watched, a one-meter round sheath began to extrude from a point in space near the alien starship. At first, it moved slowly, centimeter by centimeter. As he watched, however, the extrusion speeded up until it seemed as if the sheath and its contents were being squirted from the portal.

"What's the rate of extrusion?" Thorpe asked Mother.

"It stabilized at four meters per second," Mother answered.

"How long is the path in this orbit?" Thorpe asked.

"One hundred twenty-eight thousand five hundred fifty-three klicks," Mother answered.

Thorpe did a quick mental calculation. "That's about three hundred fifty-six Mars standard days."

"Confirmed," Mother said as Thorpe dropped out of geosynchronous orbit.

"Set destination two thousand klicks over the Martian north pole in a polar orbit normal to Sol."

MARS—POLAR ORBIT

Whereas the superconducting equatorial cable was manufactured by nanobots in the Phoenix facility and pushed into place through a portal, each mirror with its base and controlling infrastructure was actually constructed in orbit by nanobots. Four nanobot swarms brought raw materials through four portals spaced around the orbit path and grew four satellites at a time with their enormous shiny wings. Each satellite mirror took about an hour to construct, and once in place, each maintained position using some of the energy collected by the mirror.

PS Neil Armstrong dropped into position over Mars' north pole, and Thorpe directed Mother to set the controls so the spacecraft would assume an orbital velocity of 2.82 km/sec. Once *Armstrong* stabilized, Thorpe donned his helmet and locked out of his craft. He took a hyper-disk from a pocket and activated it. A positioning unit pushed through the portal, its jets fueled by lines passing back through the portal. Before Thorpe's watchful eyes, a cloud of nanobots emerged through the portal and commenced growing the satellite.

Thorpe returned to *Armstrong*. "Mother," he directed, "move *Armstrong* six thousand one hundred twenty klicks ahead along my orbital path."

The nearly instantaneous reaction of the spacecraft and its ability to accelerate itself and everything it contained to near lightspeed without reaction brought Thorpe to his next position with virtually no time lapse. As before, he locked out of the spacecraft and placed a portal. As soon as the new maneuvering unit was stabilized, he moved to the next location, repeated his previous actions, and then moved to the fourth location.

✳

"Do you have the drones ready to deploy?" Thorpe asked Brad by Link after he had garaged *Armstrong* inside the Nanedi City dome.

"They're being deployed as we speak," Brad answered.

In polar orbit around Mars, four drones passed through the four portals Thorpe had emplaced earlier. Each drone was programmed to wait for the completion of the current mirror satellite and then move the portal forward four kilometers along the orbit path, where it triggered construction of the next mirror. This process continued at all four locations for eighty-four Mars standard days until 8,476 mirrors in polar orbit formed a nearly continuous ring around Mars pointed toward Sol. This ring captured sunlight that otherwise would have missed the planet and reflected it to the Soletta.

In addition to their normal operation, each mirror could change its focal point and aim to bring concentrated sunlight to any surface point within its dynamic cone. By varying aim and passing the task between groups of 1,000 mirrors, the orbital mirrors could cut continuous twenty-meter-wide, twenty-meter-deep channels anywhere on Mars's surface.

From Nanedi City or anywhere else on Mars, the mirrors were virtually invisible since their purpose was to reflect sunlight that missed Mars back to the Soletta, where it would be returned to Mars by what appeared to be a larger, brighter sun.

MARS-SUN L4—UDACHNY

"What is it that required your visit to my office?" Orlov inquired gruffly.

"The high-power LANR is installed and tested, Sir," Borisovich said with a satisfied tone. "Your ABO starship is ready to be christened and taken on its shakedown cruise."

"Shakedown what?"

"An operational cruise where we test every system to ensure they all work together."

Orlov grunted.

"Have you selected a name for the very first ABO starship?"

Orlov looked up, almost as if he had finally actually recognized the academician's presence. "Name…why yes, we will call her *Udachnyy Zvezdolet Yuri Gagarin* (*Udachny Starship Yuri Gagarin*)."

✳

Several hidden tensors in Orlov's office recorded the conversation about the completion of the ABO starship to the surveillance database. An automated bot analyzed this and billions of other notations during that timeframe and flagged several keywords and phrases. A supervisor bot reviewed the supervising elements and generated a memo to the record highlighting this conversation. An executive bot reviewed the memos to the record for that time period and generated an alert to both eThorpe and eBraxton.

eThorpe and eBraxton reached out to each other somewhere on the GlobalNet and then called a meeting at Kuiper Joint Station.

✳

UZ Yuri Gagarin could be run by just the pilot, but Orlov had decided to man the starship with a crew of ten, including Academician Borisovich and Adrhun Gloalorn. He wanted eight technicians who doubled as cargo handlers, the Academician for his expertise, and the alien.

"Academician, you select eight technicians who can handle any possible emergency on *Gagarin*. If necessary, they will also be called upon to load and unload cargo and defend the vessel with weapons, so choose carefully."

✳

Several days later, Orlov called his crew together in the cramped space just aft of the control center.

"We will be running a full systems test of *Gagarin*. Each of you has been assigned a specific task. We wish to ensure all our systems operate properly before we undertake our first interstellar journey to Proxima Centauri." Orlov stopped talking and looked at each crew member. "You have been chosen because you are the best person in the Udachny system to carry out the task you have been assigned. We will depart in twenty-four hours. Make sure everything under your responsibility is running properly."

KUIPER BELT—KUIPER JOINT STATION

The headquarters structure was like nothing ever built before. A one-kilometer-wide, thirty-meter-thick circular slab formed the base that contained the MBH. Its three-quarter-square-kilometer surface housed two clusters of medium-rise buildings near the perimeter. The Ogden cluster was architecturally interesting, influenced strongly by the artistic bent of both Daphne and Kimberly. The Phoenix cluster was architecturally functional with simple, clean lines. Beyond the Phoenix and Ogden clusters, meandering walkways through green vegetation, trees, and sparkling brooks filled the remainder of the slab. Sol was visible in the sky, appearing the size of an old-fashioned American dime at 1.8 kilometers—basically, a bright pinpoint.

Stretching for about a kilometer along the outer side of the two clusters, the slab perimeter bordered on steeply rising hills, complete with flying birds and clouds, blending into holographic projections of seasonally snow-covered mountain peaks. A footpath a few meters inside the dome meandered along the intersection of dome and slab. Another section of perimeter bordered on water with sandy beaches and real surf generated by hidden machinery. The dome intersected the water twenty meters out, and beyond that, a holographic projection of a wave-filled ocean with an occasional dolphin bounding out of the water that faded into the distance synched with the surf on the beach. Finally, the remaining perimeter blended into holographic rolling grasslands, including wildlife and birds, with the dome edge marked by a low stone wall.

Several kilometers above the dome, a holographic image of Sol as it appears from Earth moved across the sky, blotting out the stars during daylight hours. The nighttime dome was filled with the Milky Way stretching across the sky, bright multi-hued swirls punctuated by millions of individual stars in all colors. The entire complex rotated slowly, so the outward view of the stars resembled the view from Earth with the passing seasons.

✳

eThorpe gathered the team around him, including John Ortman and Masin Arcah. They occupied a table in a meeting room in the partially completed Phoenix cluster bordering the perimeter of Kuiper Joint Station. Maxter, red collar clearly visible, scampered around, chasing a crumpled piece of paper, and eMax was curled up on the table where Daphne sat. The construction of the Ogden cluster was barely underway. The parkland streams and walkways were mostly in place, and the borders were already synchronized with the holographic projections that had just been activated around the perimeter and overhead.

"The first order of business," eThorpe said, "is the ABO ship test about to get underway from Udachny."

He went on to describe the *UZ Yuri Gagarin* and how it differed from their own Double-MBH ships. "You all know that Adrhun Gloalorn is with Orlov and cooperating with him?" he asked. "Our tensors tell us that Orlov is planning to take Adrhun with him to Frohlic as soon as they can certify *Gagarin* for interstellar travel. For the test run, they plan to head north out of the ecliptic on VASIMRs and then test the ABO drive out to the edge of the Oort Cloud. They plan to run the VASIMRs for about an hour, then four hours total out and back on their warp drive, and finally another hour or so on VASIMRs. By this time tomorrow, they should be outfitting for their shakedown run to Proxima Centauri." He stopped and surveyed the group. "It should take them a week or so to prepare. I want to have two Double-MBH ships awaiting Orlov's arrival in the Proxima system. I'll pilot *Ad Astra*, and eBraxton will pilot *Armstrong*. Dale, you, Sally, and Brad work out the details with Daphne and Kimberly." eThorpe paused to shift topics.

As he paused, Maxter uttered a quick purt and disappeared through a door.

"It's time to confront the Oort. Several of you have been working in the background to make an effective confrontation possible. We'll meet at OS Prime tomorrow morning to get things underway."

❋

Maxter was delighted with his new surroundings. He was used to there being a sun or no sun in the sky, depending on what portal he transited. Generally, he knew where he was when he was at a known location, such as the Los Angeles loft belonging to Daphne, Kimberly, and Dale, or in Butler's office in OS Prime. Like Max before him, Maxter loved exploring. He would pop through a series of portals, checking each destination out before traveling on. He had an uncanny ability to return to his origin by following back through whatever string of portals got him to where he was at the moment.

Kuiper Joint Station was a brand-new destination for Maxter. He had not yet spent much time in the two building clusters, but the parkland fascinated him. He followed the green space back around the building clusters and gazed at several birds flying in the sky and beckoning hills rising in the distance. He scampered across the grass and came smack up against something solid and invisible. He stood on his hind legs and reached as far as possible, but the obstruction remained in place.

Maxter walked along the intersection of the station disk and the protective dome behind the incomplete building clusters, not understanding the situation but intently curious. Finally, he sat for several minutes facing the obstruction in feline contemplation with his nose almost touching it. Suddenly, the surface just beyond the edge shimmered, and a space-helmeted head appeared just centimeters from Maxter's nose. He leaped into the air with arched back and fat tail. Total surprise engulfed the helmeted face, and it disappeared back through the surface. In a panic, Maxter went tearing off to locate Kimberly and her protective arms.

✳

As Kimberly walked toward their portal with Daphne and Dale, she looked around for Maxter.

"Maxter was here a few minutes ago. I wonder where he went," she said to no one in particular.

Just then, Maxter came tearing through the door, tail fat, eyes panicked, and jumped into Kimberly's arms, where he sat shivering. Kimberly stroked him, calming him down, while Daphne and Dale watched. Then Maxter stood in her arms with his front paws on her chest and meowed in her face.

"What is it, Maxter?"

He continued to meow even louder. Then he jumped to the floor and ran to the door, turning to see if she was following.

"I think he wants to show you something," Daphne said.

"Yeah, something that scared the shit out of him," Dale added with a grin. "Let's go see what he wants."

They followed Maxter to a place behind the buildings between the meandering path and the dome. Maxter sat on the grass chittering, with his nose nearly against the dome, staring at something outside.

"I don't see anything," Dale said. "What is it, Maxter?"

Maxter's focus was total, and he stopped chittering only long enough to take a breath. None of the three had ever seen him like this before.

"Hey!" Daphne said. "What's that?" She pointed to a shimmering in the holographic surface outside the dome. The shimmering spread to an area of about three square meters, and then the surface seemed to dissolve into a space-suited man wearing a globe helmet. He looked directly at the three with total surprise and then quickly dropped back down through the holographic surface. A moment later, the shimmering subsided, and the holographic hillside appeared as it had before.

"There's someone out there, and he's not one of us!" Dale shouted as he activated his Link. "eThorpe," Dale said urgently through his integrated Link, "we got a serious prob…"

❋

In a flash so brilliant that it would be seen with the naked eye in the Aster system eighty-four years later, the mini black hole that powered Kuiper Joint Station collapsed into itself and disappeared. Gone with the station: eThorpe and eBraxton, Daphne, Kimberly, and Dale, and their uploads, Sally and Brad, and their uploads, John Ortman, Masin Arcah, Maxter, and eMax. All gone to wherever things go when they are enveloped by a mini black hole that collapses in upon itself.

CHAPTER THIRTEEN

OORT CLOUD—eTHORPE & eBRAXTON

eBraxton stirred and touched eThorpe's mind.

"What the fuck?" eThorpe heard him say.

"Easy," eThorpe responded. "We're in your hidey-hole in the Oort Cloud."

"What the fu…" eBraxton muttered.

"Something happened," eThorpe said. "We were all in the meeting room at the Joint Station Ogden complex, and now we're here—you and me anyway. I was in the process of taking a Link call from Dale…"

"I think the gang will be needing us at Ogden," eBraxton said. He checked his newly created backup and then checked eThorpe's. "Everything's shipshape. Let's get our asses in gear!"

✴

Dr. Fredricks looked up as several alarms flashed on his Link emergency monitor. This would normally have been Daphne's purview, but she was at the Kuiper Joint Station meeting with everyone else. Someone had to remain at Ogden, and Fredricks had volunteered to be that one.

Within seconds of the alarms sounding, eDaphne, eKim, eSally, eBrad, eDale, and eMax appeared in his office. Fredricks looked at them, startled.

Without preamble, eDaphne said, "The Kuiper Joint Station imploded. Everyone is dead!"

Instinctively, Fredricks looked out the dome over his office space.

With an uncharacteristic edge to his voice, eBrad said, "You're not going to see anything until five days, eighteen hours, and thirty-seven minutes after the implosion."

Fredricks blushed. "I knew that…let's get down to rejuvenation."

On his way, he called several of his best technicians. When they arrived, alarms were flashing on eight panels.

"Do Dale first," eThorpe said. "He was trying to tell me something when everything went to shit."

Fredricks nodded concurrence, and the technicians quickly interconnected Dale's DNA sequence repository and standard microbiome sequence to a growth tank and set the process in motion. A few minutes later, Dale's clone lay recumbent inside the now drained tank, and Fredricks attached cables from Dale's backup. He ran a quick verification program to ensure the clone was viable, and then he activated the reanimation.

Inside the tank, Dale opened his eyes, turned his head to stare through the transparent side, and then expressions of recognition and shock passed across his face. He sat up, oblivious to his nakedness, and blurted out, "Wha' happened?"

Fredricks stepped closer, handing him a robe. "Easy, Dale. You've just gone through rejuvenation following a violent death at Kuiper Joint Station."

Dale shook his head with dawning coherence. "I was talking to eThorpe by Link…" he said.

"That's right," eThorpe said from the sidelines. "You sounded urgent. What happened?"

"The meeting was breaking up. Maxter had been outside exploring. He came running into the room in a panic, doing everything possible to get Kimberly to follow him. Daphne, Kimberly, and I followed Maxter. He took us outside between the path and the edge of the dome. He was totally focused on something outside the dome—obviously not the holoimage. Suddenly a spacesuited man pushed up through the holoimage. He saw us at the same time we saw him and vanished back down through the image. I immediately called you, and that's the last thing I remember."

"Could Daphne or Kimberly have seen anything else?" eThorpe asked.

"I don't know. It happened pretty quick."

"Okay," Fredricks said. "Set up two tanks, one for Daphne and one for Kimberly."

Somewhat later, both women sat up in their tanks, feminine charms blithely on display. Fredricks handed each a robe.

They both smiled their appreciation, and Daphne said, "So, what the hell happened?"

"This is a bit of a shock," Kimberly added, crinkling her nose. "So, what did happen?"

"First, tell us what you saw," eThorpe said.

"We followed Maxter out behind the buildings right to the dome. Suddenly, a spacesuited guy rose through the holoimage on the outside of the dome. He seemed shocked to see us. Dale called you, and that's all I remember. The next moment, I'm sitting here showing off my bod to you all." She grinned.

"You're okay?" Fredricks asked, concern in his voice. She was one of his kids. Her wellbeing mattered deeply to him.

She nodded.

"Kimberly?" eThorpe asked.

"Nothing much to add. Apparently, Maxter had seen the guy earlier when he was on his own. I guess it scared the crap out of him. He came running to me in a panic, and we followed him out to the location. It happened just like Daphne said until we found ourselves here giving you guys an eyeful."

"Okay," Fredricks said, "let's recover Sally and Brad. You two," he indicated their uploads, "work with them to try and determine what actually happened here. Then bring back Johnny and Masin. Make sure Daphne and Kimberly are present. Familiar faces will enhance their recovery."

"Don't forget Maxter," Kimberly said to Fredricks. "He's the only reason we have any idea of what might have happened."

"What about eMax?" Daphne asked.

"He showed up with the rest of the uploads." eMax's holoimage appeared in front of Daphne. Fredricks continued, "He seems unaware of what happened, wouldn't you guys agree?" he asked the uploads.

"He showed up when we showed up," eDaphne said. "Wasn't displaying any of Maxter's panic symptoms."

✳

Later, Arcah approached Johnny. "Got a moment?"

Johnny turned and focused his attention on the stocky alien.

"What's your take on all this, Johnny?" Arcah asked. "You and I—in a real sense, we're the aliens here. This rejuvenation stuff…I guess it's for real."

"I think," Johnny said, "that you and I made a good choice when we chose these guys."

"Yeah," Arcah said, "you already know about very long life. Me…I think I like that I'm not going to die."

OORT STATION PRIME—CHAIRMAN JOHN BUTLER'S OFFICE

That, Butler said to himself, is real power. It's my good fortune, humanity's good fortune, that these are good people. He looked from person to person and grinned at eMax as he lifted his head from his curled-up desk corner position and chirruped. Will it always be this way? Rejuvenation has changed everything. Kimberly, he felt his heart jump, and Daphne remain physically twenty-five, but their wisdom grows with every year. eThorpe and eBraxton— nobody will ever catch up. And what about me? Do I take the leap? He cleared his throat. Not a question for now, he thought. He looked at John Ortman.

"I guess it's time to act," he said to the group. He glanced at a control on his desk. "We're totally secure behind one of Brad's impenetrable locks. Jerry has swept the office multiple times for tensors. We're clean." He looked at his Link. "Are you all okay with my bringing Jerry in on our discussion?"

With everyone's nodding concurrence, Adm. Culp stepped through the double-portal lock into Butler's office, followed by his upload. Culp took a chair after acknowledging everyone's presence. His upload floated at the back of the office, and they all turned their attention to eThorpe.

"Johnny," eThorpe said, "clarify for us the Oort's genuine capabilities. We need to understand clearly the threat we face."

Johnny began to rise, but Butler waved him back. "No need for formality, Johnny, just talk to us."

"Will it help if I ask questions?" eThorpe said.

Johnny nodded, smiling shyly.

"Okay—how many Oort are there?"

"Fifteen million, more or less."

"What can the Oort do, specifically, to harm us or other humans?"

"Not an awful lot, really. That's why we needed humans' help."

"The weapons systems the Oort had?"

"Smoke and mirrors, mostly. We developed the systems but could not actually build them."

"What about…"

Johnny interrupted him. "On the other hand, the Oort can seriously disrupt any electronic system, anything connected by any means—ServerSky swarms, power swarms…."

"Are there any other portal connections to the Oort Cloud beside Earth-Moon L2?"

"The Oort has thousands of portals interconnecting sections of the cloud, but insofar as I know, only one portal connects through to the inner Solar System." Johnny paused in thought. "The portal we know about serves two purposes, to bring power to the cloud and as a tensor transport."

"How much does the Oort rely on power from Earth-Moon L2?"

"Depends on how you look at it." Johnny's thoughts seemed to carry him outside their group. Then he refocused. "In the distant past, the Oort used virtually everything it received from Sol. The receptors occupied the inner surface of a sphere approximately a thousand AUs from Sol—about one per square kilometer. That's about the same power as forty-six million two-gigawatt LANR plants. We lost that power production long ago. Today, the Oort produces about a thousandth percent of what it once produced."

"That would be four hundred sixty-eight two-gigawatt plants," Brad said. "That's still a lot of power."

"It keeps fifteen million Oort alive," Johnny said, "barely."

"And the Earth-Moon L2 power swarm?" Brad asked.

"That's another two-and-a-half thousand LANRS," Dale said.

"That totals some three thousand and change two-gigawatt plants," eThorpe said. "That gives us a pressure point."

"How would the Oort react if we were to cut off the Earth-Moon L2 power supply?" Butler asked the question, but he knew it was on everyone's minds.

"The Oort has tensors everywhere. It could pretty much halt any human activity connected in any way to connected electronics."

"Doesn't the Oort control its tensors through the Earth-Moon L2 portal?" eBraxton wanted to know. "If we took out the portal, how would the Oort control its tensors?"

"That would make it simple," Johnny said, "but the Oort has sequestered AI units scattered throughout the Solar System. Think of them as independent Oort like I was. If you cut the portal, it will be seen as an act of war."

"The Oort doesn't know that we can isolate our complete portal system, am I right?" eThorpe asked.

"Probably not, but I think that if we do, the Oort will access Udachny's system as a workaround."

"What about our pointing our OS weapons systems inward?"

"That might come as a complete surprise," Johnny said. "With the defeat of the Asterians, the Oort has not paid much attention outward." He paused, and Butler wondered what was going on inside his newly biological brain.

New in two ways, Butler reminded himself, *the original download and now the rejuvenation.* Butler looked around his office. "Are there any more questions?" he asked.

Hearing none, Butler turned to Dale and Brad. "You told us you could switch the weapons and safe the portals within five minutes of the order. Do I remember that correctly?"

Both men nodded.

"Is that still the case?"

Nods again.

Butler looked at eThorpe. "I think it's time we did something about this whole mess," Federation Chairman John Butler said.

※

Chairman John Butler sat behind his desk. eThorpe's holoimage occupied an easy chair off to Butler's right. Butler removed the security lock on his office and said, "I require to speak with the Oort."

"We are present," a disembodied voice answered.

"Present me an image to look at," Butler said.

"Johnny Oort dispersed his elements recently, so he is unavailable. Will this do?" A silvery sphere appeared floating at sitting eye level.

"That's fine," Butler said and nodded to eThorpe.

eThorpe sat quietly for a full minute and then asked in a quiet voice, "Is there anything of significance the Oort would like to communicate to Chairman Butler and me; something, perhaps, that you should have communicated at an earlier date but didn't, and now might be a propitious time to do so?"

The silvery sphere pulsed slightly as fifteen million Oort participated in formulating an answer. eThorpe and Butler waited quietly.

Finally, the sphere responded, "No, there is nothing."

eThorpe and Butler waited another minute. Then Butler said, "It has come to my attention that the Oort attacked the Asterians long ago, back when the Oort was flesh-and-blood individuals." Butler stopped talking for effect. Then he added, "And, I believe the real Oort numbers are nearer fifteen million than trillions as you had communicated to us."

The sphere pulsed several times, and then the voice said, "That is outrageous—a complete fabrication. We deny it entirely. Our story is as we have related it to you."

The sphere continued to pulse. Butler looked at eThorpe and nodded slightly. eThorpe activated his standby order. Four Oort Stations did rapid 180-degree spins about their rotation axes. Four minutes later, their massive lasers, anti-matter particle beams, and neutrino beams threatened everything inward from the stations—where the Oort resided. Simultaneously, across the entire Solar System, every MERT Portal refused to operate when it detected anything Oort-related—tensor, thread, laser pipe, anything.

One portal remained open, the one in use by the Oort in its conversation with Butler and eThorpe.

"What have you done?" the Oort asked.

"Protected ourselves," Butler answered. "The weapons on all four remaining OS platforms are pointed inward. One word from me and the Oort will cease to exist. I offered you the opportunity to explain yourselves, to give us your side of the story. You have refused even to acknowledge the matter as we know it to be."

The sphere pulsed once more and vanished.

✳

eBrad was particularly concerned about the Oort power portal at Earth-Moon L2. He stationed several tensors nearby to keep an eye on the portal. Within moments of the Oort sphere vanishing in Butler's office, Oort tensors began pouring through the Earth-Moon L2 portal. Without awaiting authorization, eBrad slammed the power portal shut. Cutting off further tensors.

The Oort tensors surrounding him seemed to move about randomly without guidance or purpose. Then, suddenly, they seemed to come to life, heading off in multiple directions, vanishing through scattered Oort portals.

"eThorpe," eBrad broadcast, "I think we have a problem."

SOLAR SYSTEM—VARIOUS LOCATIONS

eThorpe issued a system-wide Link alert: DO NOT USE WATER FROM FAUCETS! WE ARE WORKING ON THE PROBLEM AND WILL SOLVE IT SHORTLY.

"What's controlling the rogue Oort tensors?" eThorpe asked eBrad.

"Johnny told us about independent AI units that could do this."

"How are they moving about?" eThorpe asked. "There aren't sufficient independent Oort portals around the inner Solar System."

"They've got to be using the Udachny portals. We've got enough tensors inside the Udachny system to shut it down—at least for a while. If we do that, eDale, eSally, and I can try to locate the AI nodes."

"Do it!" eThorpe said.

*

Because only uploads were involved, the Udachny system shut-down happened almost immediately. The three uploads spread their tensors throughout the Solar System in several microseconds, opening and resealing MERT Portals as necessary. Thirteen seconds later, their tensors located 114 Oort AI units and shut them down. Millions of Oort tensors throughout the Solar System went dormant and then disintegrated.

Throughout the Udachny system, technicians scrambled to ascertain the cause of their portal shut-down, but before they could find the problem, their system came back online. Deeply sequestered throughout their system, Phoenix tensors collapsed into themselves and became, once again, undetectable to Udachny.

Everywhere in the Solar System, drains reopened to a collective sigh of relief from billions of humans scattered on virtually every habitable chunk of rock and habitat throughout the system. During the few minutes of shut-down, billions of liters of liquid waste had accumulated. As they sucked down newly opened drains, in some of the more remote mining operations, miners rethought their dependence on portal-supported utilities. Instead, they turned their attention to water tanks and drain fields.

*

eThorpe and Chairman Butler sat in conference in Butler's office at OS Prime. eThorpe's tensors were spread throughout the Solar System, but his main focus was with Butler, who had just laid aside Dean Acheson's twentieth-century Pulitzer Prize-winning *Present at the Creation*—a book that in Butler's mind was about how not to do it. Butler moved a half-finished glass of Beaujolais to one side of his desk.

"Despite the outward appearance of equilibrium right now," eThorpe said, "Oort and humans continue to be locked in a mortal struggle. With loss of power from the Earth-Moon L2 portal, the

Oort still has access to nearly one terawatt of power. They can hunker down and use most of that energy to send a powerful beam almost anywhere in the Solar System. Their only downside is lightspeed limitation of the beam."

"Targets?" Butler asked.

"If it were me," eThorpe said, "I would send bolts toward each of the Oort Stations and then send a concentrated bolt toward Earth."

"Can't the Oort Stations simply dodge the bolts?" Butler asked.

"Sure, but it keeps them busy and possibly unable to shoot at the Oort."

"And Earth?"

"That's a problem, for sure. If we detect one coming, I think that eBraxton, eSally, eBrad, and I working together can temporarily transform ServerSky around Earth into a reflective surface. We're coordinating that right now."

For about a minute, they both sat quietly in contemplation.

"There's an awful lot at stake," eThorpe said. "Personally, I opt for a preemptive strike against the Oort body." He paused. "But that's your call."

eThorpe watched Butler's face drop. Sitting behind his desk, he seemed to age ten years. eThorpe had known Butler since he assumed the U.S. presidency. Back then, Butler had seemed surprised at his elevation and unsure of himself. Over the years, eThorpe had watched Butler mature as a national politician, then on a global scale, and more recently as Chairman of the Federation, overseeing many worlds. This, however, was Butler's biggest challenge thus far.

Butler sighed and unlocked a channel to the Oort.

"I urgently need immediate Oort presence in my office," Butler said.

MARS—VARIOUS LOCATIONS

City residents focused on agricultural or support activities and a growing manufacturing capability. Portals facilitated movement on Mars, but the Oort lock-out didn't affect local transportation or the orbital terraforming activities.

Thorpe and Braxton had generated a topological map of Mars that included locations for six channels they intended to burn running northward from the elevated south polar region. The twenty-by-twenty-meter channels would carry melted polar cap ice into thousands of canyons and depressions that would become rivers, lakes, and estuaries when both ice caps were melted, and water was released from the aquifer beneath the north polar basin.

Instead of waiting the full eighty-five Mars standard days for the nanobots to complete all 8,476 mirrors, Thorpe activated the Nanocosm program that controlled the operation as soon as enough mirrors were positioned to form a concentrated beam capable of blasting out the twenty-by-twenty-meter trenches from polar orbit.

1,000 four-kilometer-wide mirrors rotated, tilted, and changed their curvatures so that their beams converged near the ice cap edge at 15° west longitude about 200 km southwest of Sisyphi Planum's southern edge. Nearly 8,000 gigajoules of concentrated solar energy flashed ice to hissing steam and vaporized the underlying regolith into billowing clouds of rock vapor and nanoparticles that quickly dispersed northward with the adiabatic pressure from the ice cap. Every three seconds, the twenty-meter-wide beam vaporized a one-meter-thick section of regolith down to twenty meters, leaving a twenty-by-twenty-meter trench in its wake as it moved northward.

The trench would carry polar melt 1,700 kilometers northward to Argyre Planitia, a 5.2-kilometer-deep depression that stretched 1,900 kilometers east to west and 600 kilometers south to north, the smaller of two large lakes that would form in Mars's southern hemisphere. Sixty-two days later, this trench would reach Argyre Planitia.

Ten Mars standard days later, a second beam struck the surface 120° eastward where Australe Lingula pushed northward from the polar plateau. The trench ran north for 1,850 kilometers, emptying into Hellas Planitia—seven kilometers deep, stretching 2,000 kilometers east to west and 1,500 kilometers south to north. Fifty-five days later, this trench would reach Hellas Planitia.

At ten-day intervals, four more beams struck the surface around the south polar icecap, one between the first two trenches at about 0° longitude, and three evenly spaced on the other side of the icecap.

These trenches fed into the canyons and valleys spread across Mars's southern hemisphere.

The typical trench path mapped out by the Nanocosm for the four remaining trenches varied between 8,000 and 12,000 kilometers. The expected time for completing these trenches was about one standard Earth year.

*

Six months later, Thorpe and Braxton sat in a dark tavern in Nanedi City quaffing local beer and discussing their progress. Thorpe's trench-burning activities had increased Mars's atmospheric pressure to 0.3 bar—about the pressure at the summit of Mount Everest on Earth. Carbon dioxide partial pressure was down significantly while oxygen and nitrogen partial pressures were rising. The magnetic field created by Braxton's orbital superconductor was diverting the solar wind, so the atmosphere Thorpe generated was not swept away.

"The shit you're making is not exactly breathable," Braxton said over the rim of his mug.

Thorpe grinned. "How are your Moxie units coming?"

"By the end of this week, we'll have ten thousand units operating, scattered all over the planet. Sally and Brad, with their uploads, I would guess, have done a remarkable upgrade to the units. Get this. The first Moxie unit on Mars in the early twenty-first century converted carbon dioxide into ten grams of oxygen per hour from a seventeen-kilogram cube. Our new portal-powered terraforming Moxie units—T-Moxie units—mass at a hundred kilos, but they produce up to a hundred kilos of O-two per second. Since you are producing about six metric tons of rock vapor per second, at a hundred percent efficiency, we can generate six tons of O-two per second from your stuff and ninety-four tons from atmospheric carbon dioxide."

Braxton paused and did a couple of calculations with his Link. "If the Moxies are our only oxygen source, it's gonna take three Earth standard years plus one hundred fifteen Mars standard days to bring the O-two level to twenty-one percent, Earth standard pressure."

Thorpe chuckled. "I sense a bit of hand-waving here, but I like your numbers. Don't forget that a lot of the rock vapor we produce is actually iron oxide vapor. That stuff condenses to molecule-size nanoparticles, which means that much of the oxygen will condense out as O-two."

Braxton grinned and turned to his Link display again. "Factor that in," he said, "and it's gonna take three Earth standard years plus one hundred twenty-one Mars standard days."

"So, three years and four months, give or take," Thorpe said. "In another six months, we're gonna tackle the aquifers; the Argyre Planitia and Hellas Planitia first, then Valles Marineris, and finally the north polar basin."

"Has anybody been able to determine how much water they hold?"

"No, but they are under pressure, and they hold a lot of water. I'm guessing Argyre and Hellas will partially fill their respective basins and that Marineris and the polar aquifers will meet and reach equilibrium with a shoreline that has been projected for about a hundred years," Thorpe said.

"And while they fill, we'll be melting the polar caps, right?" Braxton added.

MARS—THE BASINS

Long ago, Argyre held a lot of water, about the same as the Mediterranean Sea on Earth—some 4,000,000 cubic kilometers. Water flowed in from the south and out to the north. As Mars lost its atmosphere and cooled, the Argyre Sea dissipated, and then the surface froze solid, encapsulating about 2.5 million cubic kilometers of water. Over time, the ice cover was buried under a half-kilometer layer of dust that eventually compressed into rock-like regolith. The liquid water beneath the regolith and ice was under great pressure. Drilling through the regolith and ice cover would release that pressure, resulting in a mighty upheaval where the regolith would slide to the bottom, and the ice would break up and float on the water's surface.

In polar orbit around Mars near the orbiting mirrors, Thorpe instructed the Nanocosm to set the controllers for six sets of 1,000 orbital mirrors to focus on six one-square-meter spots located in a hundred-meter circle around the deepest spot in Argyre Planitia, 5,200 meters below the surrounding plains. In *FS Astor*, Braxton hovered twenty kilometers to the east and above the impact circle.

"Are you ready?" Thorpe asked Braxton.

"As much as I will ever be."

Thorpe activated the process. From Braxton's spot, the six consolidated beams struck the surface like a circular wall of fire. 24,000 gigajoules blasted a circle of six holes fifty-two meters apart in Argyre's floor. Billowing clouds of vaporized regolith obscured the entire atmosphere surrounding the blast zone as each concentrated beam vaporized 133 meters every second. Five seconds later, six huge steam geysers shot from the holes.

"Rotate your pattern thirty degrees in either direction," Braxton advised, his voice filled with excitement.

Over the next few minutes, under Braxton's visual guidance, Thorpe rotated the beam pattern fifteen and then 7.5 degrees. Suddenly, with an ear-splitting report, the hundred-meter circle defined by the blast holes broke into several large chunks that rolled over, dumping their 500-meter regolith load to the bottom. Large cracks quickly radiated out from the hundred-meter hole at the speed of sound until the entire regolith cover in Argyre basin split into thousands of fragments.

"Terminate the beam!" Braxton shouted.

Over the three million square kilometers of Argyre basin, liquid water spurted dozens of meters in the air through cracks as they formed. Large ice floes covered with 500 meters of regolith rolled over, dropping their rock load to the bottom. Smaller floes, unable to sustain the regolith weight on their backs, simply sank to the bottom. Within twenty hours, what for millions of years had been a dry dust bowl was now a huge lake covered with bobbing chunks of hundred-meter-thick ice.

❋

Hellas Planitia, ninety degrees east of Argyre in the southern hemisphere, was a third larger and two kilometers deeper than Argyre. Like Argyre, its floor was regolith-covered ice, but unlike Argyre, over the eons, ice movement under the regolith had produced a rough terrain of mountains and canyons. Thorpe and Braxton decided to blast two smaller circles through the regolith and ice, one in the northwestern quadrant and the other in the southeastern quadrant.

Thorpe instructed the Nanocosm to coordinate the two holes so they would break free together. Braxton placed himself in *Aster* several kilometers to the southwest. When Thorpe activated the process, the southeastern beams bored through unexpectedly fast as it turned out the regolith was just a few meters thick. In just moments, the southeastern quadrant was a churning cauldron of ice chunks ranging from a few meters square to several kilometers, some with ice mountains jutting from their surfaces. The smaller top-heavy chunks flipped, displaying a gleaming underside.

When the northwestern circle broke free, cracks radiated throughout the remaining Hellas surface. Within twenty-four hours, Hellas became a 4,000,000 square kilometer bobbing ice-filled sea, significantly larger than the Mediterranean Sea on Earth.

✳

Valles Marineris turned out to be a more difficult challenge. Thorpe spaced his six consolidated beams along its 4,000-kilometer length and then moved them together in fifty-meter jumps until the buried ice split open in several sections of the chasm. When the action settled ten hours later, instead of one 4,000-kilometer-long lake, five ice chunk-filled lakes remained, two of them more than a kilometer deep.

✳

The final big challenge was releasing the north polar aquifer. It had formed more recently and over a longer time period than Argyre and Hellas, and it contained many times their combined amounts of water. Thorpe and Braxton laid out a six-hole pattern near the basin center of Utopia Planitia that could be moved quickly to other locations to facilitate breaking up the subsurface ice over the entire basin.

Thorpe instructed the Nanocosm to set up the first pattern. Braxton hovered in *Aster* twenty kilometers to the south and several above the blast site.

"Ready when you are," Braxton transmitted.

Five minutes later, six geysers shot into the Martian sky.

"Rotate your ring by thirty degrees and do it again," Braxton advised.

This time, the regolith-covered ice around the ring collapsed, and cracks began to radiate outward. Braxton gained several tens of kilometers of altitude and then transmitted to Thorpe, "Next pattern in the center of Isidis Planitia."

"Got it," Thorpe said and instructed the Nanocosm accordingly.

About an hour later, after three angular shifts, cracks began to radiate through Isidis, with geysers spouting along the crack lines.

"Now Arcadia Planitia," Braxton said.

Move and setup took a couple of hours before Thorpe said, "Okay, ready to blast Arcadia."

Then they moved to Amazonis Planitia. Braxton hovered over the far western slopes of Olympus Mons to observe the action.

When the ice cracks started radiating, Braxton said, "The last two are on the opposite side of the pole, a spot between Acidalia and Chryse Planitias, just south of Bonestell Crater."

"We will have to find another more permanent Mars feature to name after Chesley Bonestell," Thorpe said. "He was one of my significant inspirations."

"Yeah, I know," Braxton said with a chuckle.

✳

Over the next several days, the entire north polar basin changed from dry, dusty desert to iceberg-filled sloshing water. At the pole, the highlands and the ice cap itself protruded from the surrounding icy waters. About ninety degrees east of Hellas at the 30th north parallel, Elysium Mons pushed high out of the surrounding waters, like a gigantic volcanic island in an ice-filled ocean.

The Martian mean surface temperature had climbed to 0° Celsius, and atmospheric pressure had risen to 0.8 bar, which meant that much of the freed water would remain in a liquid state as the ice melted. Atmosphere oxygen level was still too low and carbon dioxide level too high, but that was rapidly changing. By the time the captured water in the ice caps was freed into the southern trenches and the northern ocean, light-weight nose and mouth cups to filter carbon dioxide and supplement oxygen were all that would be needed anywhere on Mars. In three standard Earth years, the domes could come down. Except for the lighter gravity outside cities, life on Mars would become normal.

✳

"The Soletta is really doing a job on Martian average temperature," Thorpe said to Braxton over mugs of beer in their Nanedi City tavern.

"It'll do even better when we stop monopolizing the polar mirrors," Braxton said. "I've been thinking. What if we use just two beam-sets for the polar channeling and assign the remaining six thousand four hundred seventy-six mirrors to their normal jobs? At the south pole, we can carve grooves in the ice cap leading to the northward trenches. In the north, since there are no trenches, we carve radial grooves to facilitate the melt runoff.

"I ran the numbers for the polar cap melt. Here's what I suggest. We set the polar mirrors for their normal task and use twenty percent of Soletta power split between both poles. It will take one hundred seventy Mars standard days to melt both ice caps. If we want to be a bit more aggressive, thirty percent of Soletta power will melt both caps in one hundred thirteen Mars standard days."

"I think I like the more conservative approach," Thorpe responded. "I think continuing to warm the surface trumps a month-and-a-half saved on filling the basins."

"Yeah, I agree," Braxton said, hoisting his mug, "but I wanted to give you a sense of where the options lead."

✻

The Soletta diverted 10% of its power toward the north polar ice cap of Mars and 10% toward the south polar ice cap. The north polar beam struck the cap a few kilometers south of the pole and extended 500 kilometers to the edge of the ice cover. The south polar beam struck the cap a few kilometers north of the pole and extended 350 kilometers to the ice edge. As Mars turned on its axis, all parts of both poles received a continuous 4.4 petajoules of solar energy. After 170 Mars standard days, virtually no water ice or dry ice remained at either pole. Both southern basins were filled to three-quarter capacity, and the north polar basin had overflowed into the network of channels connecting it to Valles Marineris. Mars had become a water planet.

CHAPTER FOURTEEN

Borisovich pushed ahead for two hours. He varied the drive's warp factor from 1.0 to 4.5, the maximum available from the LANR he had installed. For two hours, he worked warp factor through the available range several times, ranging from lightspeed to 3,162 times lightspeed and back, averaging warp factor 2.84, or sixty-nine times lightspeed. He dropped out of warp 1,000 AU from Udachny Station at the inner boundary of the Oort Cloud.

During the VASIMR and warp transit, Orlov sat beside the Academician but remained uncharacteristically quiet. When Borisovich lifted his hands from the controls and announced their arrival at the Oort Cloud boundary, Orlov said, "My compliments, Academician, you have absolutely outdone yourself. This is a magnificent spaceship."

Borisovich smiled and said, "Starship, Sir, *star*ship."

"Very well," Orlov acknowledged, "now let's test our sensing, acquisition, and weapons systems."

For the next hour, Borisovich demonstrated how to acquire a target using radar and lidar and destroy it, and then floated aside while Orlov detected, tracked, and destroyed three nearby proto-comets. He used the laser on two objects with a range of nearly a million kilometers. He zapped an object at nearly 500 thousand kilometers with his particle beam—near the limit of the beam's range.

Satisfied, Orlov turned the controls back to Borisovich. "Let's head back to Udachny," he said.

Borisovich tested the warp range again on the return trip, averaging warp factor 3.14 for an hour before reinstating the VASIMRs for the final hour leg to Udachny Station.

OORT STATION PRIME—CHAIRMAN JOHN BUTLER'S OFFICE

"Your portal offensive has failed," Butler said, speaking slowly. "I understand that you still have a remaining offensive capability, and that you are prepared to strike out against the Oort Stations and even against Earth itself." He paused but maintained a steady gaze at the sphere. "My Oort Stations can dodge your beams and retaliate." With a heavy sigh, he continued, "If you send a beam toward Earth, however, we will have nearly six days to prepare our response. Should you do this, you will never know what we did to avoid your attack because I will reluctantly order the complete and utter destruction of the Oort." He paused again but held up his hand when he thought the sphere might be ready to respond.

"You deceived us from the moment of our first contact. You perpetuated the deception when you could have come clean. You attacked our infrastructure, and you would have caused significant damage and loss of life had we not anticipated your actions and taken preventive measures. Even now, you continue to push your deception in the face of every issue we have raised." Butler stopped talking, took a deep breath. And raised both hands in front of his chest, fingers separated, palms toward the sphere.

"We have been willing to negotiate a settlement that worked for Oort and humans. Now, however, you leave me no alternative." Butler took another deep breath. "You have one hour to surrender unconditionally. Should you comply, we will require you to state for the record the complete and accurate story of what happened from the beginning. You will permanently dissolve your hive mind and present to us a freely chosen individual Oort to represent Oort interests. All individual Oort will present themselves for downloading into either the original flesh-and-blood bodies or into human bodies that fall into the broad range of human body types." Butler smiled sadly.

"You have one hour. Capitulate totally by the hour's end, or I will order the complete eradication of the Oort. We will destroy you utterly; we will eliminate every group, every structure, and will chase down and disrupt every individual, no matter how long it takes. Eventually, it will be as if the Oort had never existed at all."

The holographic sphere vanished.

✳

Fifty-five minutes after Butler issued his ultimatum, the sphere reappeared. "I am Franklin, chosen by the individual Oort to represent them."

Butler held up his hand. "Wait for a moment while I establish this session as officially on the record." A moment later, he nodded. "Go ahead, please."

"Thank you. The Oort agrees to your terms of unconditional surrender. I have been designated to tell the complete and accurate story of Oort and Asterian interactions."

"Continue," Butler said.

"Long before humans evolved, the Oort lived as flesh-and-blood beings on Earth. We were a space-faring civilization that had colonized Mars and several Jovian and Saturnian moons. We had developed an incipient FTL drive similar to Udachny's ABO drive. To power them, we developed small fusion reactors using what your civilization calls tokamak. Our warp ships were fueled by deuterium and were range limited to about one hundred lightyears.

"Not long after developing our warp ships, we began to receive radio signals from what turned out to be the planet Frohlic orbiting Aster. Our scientists convinced our leaders that the universe probably operated under the Dark Forest Theory. They convinced us that we had no choice but to follow the signals to their source and destroy the civilization that originated them. The alternative was that they would ultimately discover and destroy us.

"We created a large fleet of warp ships, followed the signals to Frohlic, and bombarded the planet and its inhabitants to near oblivion. Retrospectively, we should not have undertaken the operation in the first place, but having done so, we should have ensured the total destruction of the Frohlicans.

"When we returned to the Solar System, our civilization was deeply divided about what we had done, so much so that a planet-wide civil war broke out. A fraction of our population, a hundred million or so, uploaded into our version of ServerSky, and as things became increasingly worse, we found our way into the Oort Cloud. The fighting factions on Earth destroyed themselves—completely and utterly. When it was all over, not a living soul survived on the planet. We, in the Oort Cloud, were all that remained.

"We held on as a species, barely, although many of our numbers gave up and disassociated—committed suicide. We would advance for a while, several million years, and then despair would overtake our ambitions, and our numbers dwindled. Survival was a never-ending struggle against overwhelming odds.

"When humans appeared on Earth, we were overjoyed. We watched, we mentored, we even interfered from time to time. And that's when we received radio signals from the Aster system. It seemed clear to us that revenge was on its way. We knew unequivocally that we could not withstand any kind of onslaught. It was always possible that the Asterians were on a peaceful mission, but the majority of us thought that unlikely. We figured that the Asterians would need at least a century to get from primitive radio to the first stages of spaceflight, and another century or so to develop the means to cross the eighty-four-lightyear gulf between Aster and Sol. We did not think it likely that they would develop FTL drives before they launched their revenge, so we added another century for them to cross the gulf. We had three hundred years, perhaps longer, before the Asterians would swarm through the Solar System, destroying everything in their path. And Earth civilization was just beginning to grasp some of the fundamentals of astronomy.

"Finally, as time seemed to be running out, Yuri Gagarin happened, and then Neil Armstrong. We were thrilled when space launch loops opened space to everyone and ecstatic when ServerSky became a reality. The uploaded Braxton Thorpe seemed to us like a savior sent from heaven itself. We were within our window of expectation for the Asterian arrival. There wasn't much time left, if any. We discussed among us long and hard about how to handle the overall situation. There were several options, but they don't matter. You know which we chose.

"What we simply did not understand, even after watching and mentoring humanity's rise from nothing to a space-faring civilization, is how ingenious and inventive you people really are. In just a few years, you went from primitive rocket propulsion to wormhole transportation, and then you morphed that into FTL interstellar capability. And while you—Phoenix—were doing that, Isidor Orlov and Udachny designed and built a warp-drive ship.

"We got to portal transportation, but no further. In the blink of an eye, cosmically speaking, you took it from there to where you are today."

The sphere went silent, and Butler chose not to respond.

"The Oort are deeply remorseful for their subterfuge," the sphere continued in a softer voice. "It is clear to us now that had we been truthful from the start, thousands of Asterian lives could have been saved. You hold the fate of an entire civilization in the palm of your hand—one that is hundreds of millions of years older than yours.

"We beg mercy and accede to all your terms of surrender."

Butler sat in quiet astonishment at what he had just heard. It had the ring of truth, but the Oort had proved themselves to be liars on a grand scale.

Is this just another lie to placate us humans who have caught out the Oort in their first big lie? Butler asked himself as he considered what he and the others in his office had just witnessed. This isn't the former Russian dictator rattling his saber or a Chinese maneuver to take advantage of America's generosity—I am dealing with an alien civilization far older than humanity, wise before we existed. Are they planning for tomorrow or for a thousand years from tomorrow? How can I judge their truthfulness? He scanned the faces of his assembled friends. What I do here affects not just my friends, but the entire human race, and the Oort...perhaps even the Asterians.

Butler looked around his office at the small assembled group, and focused on eThorpe and eBraxton. They awaited his decision.

*

The office was empty except for Butler and Kimberly. Butler sat at his desk, his face drawn and weary. Kimberly glided over, sat lightly on his lap, and cradled his head against her breast. Butler sighed deeply.

"I was this close," he snapped his fingers, "to destroying an entire civilization." He shuddered. "This is not what I signed up for."

Kimberly kissed his forehead and whispered, "You brought us through the crises, John. You did it…nobody else, just you." She held him close.

Butler lifted his head, a slight smile momentarily crossing his lips. He sighed deeply. "I can't do this anymore."

Kimberly came to her feet and faced him. "We need you more than ever, John. We need your steady hand at the helm. eThorpe and eBraxton totally depend on you. *I* depend on you. We all depend on you and your wisdom. What lies ahead none of us want to do without your guidance."

She took his hand, and they stepped through a portal to his private quarters.

KUIPER BELT—OGDEN ENTERPRISES

"Show me."

"We have to download fifteen million Oort into fifteen million newly created bodies, and we are time-limited—John wants us to do this as quickly as possible. If we give ourselves a year and build five hundred revival stations dedicated to the Oort, we'll have to revive eighty-two Oort per station per twenty-four-hour day. Without going into the details, we'll need four hundred twenty million kilograms of material in the right proportions."

"And what might those be," Daphne asked with a twinkle in her eyes. "You seem to have worked out all the details."

Kimberly pointed to her Link display. It listed the same elements they had earlier determined would be needed when they decided to set up Ogden for downloads.

Element	Percent by mass
Oxygen	65
Carbon	18
Hydrogen	10
Nitrogen	3
Calcium	1.5
Phosphorus	1.2
Potassium	0.2
Sulfur	0.2
Chlorine	0.2
Sodium	0.1
Magnesium	0.05
Iron, Cobalt, Copper, Zinc, Iodine	trace
Selenium, Fluorine	<trace
Germanium, Antimony, Silver, Niobium, Lanthanum, Tellurium, Bismuth, Thallium, Gold, Thorium, Uranium, and Radium	<<trace

"You're serious, aren't you?" Daphne asked with a lilting laugh in her voice.

"So, here's the thing. I was discussing this with Sally. She said Arrokoth will still work. Here's what I think is really cool. Dale will map the information into the Nanocosm. We will instruct the Nanocosm on what we need for the Oort bodies, including rate of production and download schedule, and then everything goes into automatic."

"So, we need to accommodate forty-one thousand newly generated individuals daily and somehow integrate them into human society…" Daphne tossed her hair, and her face took on a serious cast.

"Obviously, we need to put some kind of infrastructure into place before we undertake the actual downloads," Kimberly responded, no longer so confident. "I need to speak with John."

*

Butler looked up from his reading as Kimberly stepped into his office through a portal. He never ceased to be amazed at how her presence affected him, and even wondered how he had existed before Kimberly.

"John, we need to talk." Kimberly then proceeded to outline her previous discussion with Daphne and her realization of the magnitude of what would be necessary to accommodate the Oort transmutation.

"You are absolutely correct, Kimberly. You identified the chokepoint of this whole operation: How do we accommodate forty-one thousand people daily for a year?" He smiled warmly.

"You and Daphne—Ogden, really, I guess—will have to focus entirely on ensuring we can actually process this many people, in addition to Ogden's normal daily load of up and downloading, clones, and rejuvenation. I have created an Office of Oort Affairs headed by a responsible individual. His office will handle Oort integration into our society. Just be certain that revived Oort have a full suite of tools such as English, human and Federation history, economics, and even etiquette. My Office of Oort Affairs will work with your people to ensure your tool kit contains everything it needs so individual Oort can integrate into wherever we place them, be gainfully employed, and not displace anyone else." Butler lifted his eyebrows with a hint of a smile.

"You're right, Kimberly, this is a task with overwhelming implications, and we've just scratched the surface."

KUIPER BELT—PHOENIX COMPLEX

"We're preparing to send Ad Astra and Armstrong to Proxima," Sally said. "Their detection capability consists of long-range radar and lidar."

"And…"

Brad said, "Maximum range is a million klicks with a seven-second turnaround. By the time you know a target is at your extreme range, a laser bolt could already be on its way."

"That's why we have Entangled-Particle Displays—we call them EPDs—on the Oort Stations," Sally said. "The entangled particles expand at near lightspeed and supply an immediate notification when something penetrates the expanding sphere."

"The Oort Stations use Sol to generate the expanding sphere of entangled neutrinos," Brad said. "We have just found a way to modify the neutrino beam generator in a Double-MBH ship to accomplish this." Brad's broad grin was infectious, and Fredricks grinned back.

"So, my star recruits from Mines have done it again," Fredricks said. "Show me."

Brad produced a bread-loaf size box. "This will fit into the MBH space below the deck. It generates a very slight pulsing of the MBH that creates expanding spheres of entangled neutrinos. It will take us two days to install these into *Ad Astra* and *Armstrong*."

❋

"I know," eThorpe said. "Each of you wants to go with me or eBraxton. I get it. Trust me, I really do. I also get your argument that rejuvenation will bring you back should something dreadful happen. Do you remember the Kuiper Joint Station matter? Think back…was that a pleasant experience? Is that something you want to court going forward?"

Daphne stepped forward, irritation crossing her features. "eThorpe, you're talking like a fool. I know you run Phoenix, but this is bigger than Phoenix. You are talking about the first human flight to another star system. This can happen only once, and speaking for myself, I am completely willing to take on any reasonable risk."

Everyone else nodded concurrence; even Max mewed and rubbed legs.

eThorpe and eBraxton conferred briefly out of the group's perception.

"Okay," eBraxton said, "we know when we are overruled. Sorry we were so overprotective. We agree…this is something that needs to be shared."

eThorpe spoke up. "Here's the basic plan as we see it."

MARS-SUN L4—UDACHNY

"A one hundred percent check of every onboard system and topping off our fuel."

"Why topping the fuel? We haven't used any, have we?" Orlov was genuinely concerned.

"Deuterium consists of very small molecules that constantly slip through the walls of any container, even in liquid form," Borisovich said. "We have constructed the best possible storage tanks using carbon nanotubes to facilitate retention of the fuel. Even so, a certain unavoidable leakage takes place."

"Okay, I got it," Orlov said, and to himself, Apparently no parking for long periods of time without nearby fueling facilities. "So, when can we depart?"

"Sometime tomorrow morning," Borisovich said.

✳

Twenty hours later, Isidor Orlov, along with Academician Sergii Anatoly Borisovich, Frohlican Adrhun Gloalorn, and ten selected crew members, transferred from Udachny Station with its induced rotational gravity to *UZ Yuri Gagarin* in perpetual freefall. Orlov, Borisovich, and Gloalorn took one shuttle; the ten crew members took a second.

The crew dispersed into two staterooms, picked their bunks, and settled down, stowing things so they wouldn't get loose during their journey entirely under freefall. Borisovich and Gloalorn shared a stateroom, and Orlov occupied the captain's cabin, directly aft of the maneuvering stations.

Within an hour, Borisovich announced that they were ready to get underway for Proxima Centauri.

✳

Gagarin rotated and tilted to point out of the ecliptic. Orlov initiated the VASIMRs at one-gee.

"We'll head away from the ecliptic for a half-hour," he said, following the Academician's advice. "We'll travel just under sixteen thousand kilometers before we shut down the VASIMRs and initiate warp. Eleven and three-quarter hours later, we'll arrive in the Proxima Centauri system."

CHAPTER FIFTEEN

KUIPER BELT—PHOENIX COMPLEX

Murmurs around the table seemed to indicate general agreement with his sentiment. Even Max seemed to agree. eThorpe spoke up.

"Let's think about this. There was no loss of life. I agree that we lost a significant investment, but on the grand scale of things, it is an insignificant part of our total holdings. Furthermore," he held up a hand, "we do not actually *know* that Orlov caused it."

"Don't know," Dale interrupted. "Of course we do!"

"Actually, Dale, we don't. We have the circumstantial evidence of the spacesuited individual outside the dome, and Sally and Brad, and their uploads, tell us that it is virtually impossible for the MBH to implode on its own. But the keyword is *virtually*—it is not impossible, just very unlikely. Do I think Orlov did it? Of course. Do I *know* he did it? Sorry, but I don't, and neither do you nor anyone else here."

"I think," Daphne added, sweeping her red mane to one side, "that eThorpe is saying we need to take the high road."

Dale opened his mouth to say something, changed his mind, and sat silently for a few seconds, looking downcast. Then he added, "I guess I agree. Sorry for my outburst."

"Since our new structures seem to be targets," eBraxton said, "we need to ensure they are invulnerable—at least as much so as physically possible. Our best guess is that someone from Udachny attached either a hyper-disk or hyper-brick to *Ad Astra* when she made the only physical trip to the new location. Then it was just a matter of Udachny personnel waiting for the right moment to compromise the MBH container."

"Any problems with the design?" eThorpe asked. When no one spoke up, he said, "Okay; the Nanocosm has the complete plans. We need to pick a location and take a hyper-disk there. Sally and Brad, you guys do this again, but make absolutely sure there are no hitchhikers this time."

They chose a location the same distance from Sol but sixty degrees clockwise from the original doomed location.

✳

Before setting things in motion, Sally, Brad, and their uploads met to discuss details a final time.

"Let's add sensors around the outside of the disk," Sally said.

"And over the bottom area as well," Brad added.

"Hindsight adds a lot of insight, doesn't it?" eBrad piped up. eSally agreed with a smile hidden behind her holographic hand.

Several hours later, after thoroughly inspecting every part of *Ad Astra* for anything suspicious, Sally, Brad, and Max, with eSally and eBrad in matrixes, departed Kuiper Phoenix in *Ad Astra* for the new Kuiper Joint Station location.

They arrived just over a minute later, paused for a few minutes to admire the view, deposited an activated hyper-disk through the airlock, and returned to the garage in Kuiper Phoenix. Total elapsed time: Fifteen minutes.

KUIPER BELT—PHOENIX COMPLEX

Everyone laughed.

"Dr. Fredricks and I discussed his going with us, but we both thought he should remain at Phoenix to handle any emergency involving all of us," eThorpe added. "He will join us by portal once we are established in the Proxima system."

Max chose this moment to let out a loud meow and jumped into Daphne's arms.

"Let's load up!" eThorpe said.

✳

Daphne and Dale carried their own matrixes into *Ad Astra* and plugged them into the control console. Johnny carried eThorpe. When he had plugged the matrix into the console, and eThorpe had reestablished his holoimage inside *Ad Astra*, Johnny said, "What a privilege and honor, Sir!"

"Thanks, Johnny. We are privileged to have you with us." The words brought a blush to Johnny's face.

Max made it into *Ad Astra* on his own and promptly took ownership of the litterbox Daphne had placed in the small bathroom she shared with Dale.

"Okay, listen up!" eThorpe announced. "*Armstrong* will depart an hour after we do. This will allow us to establish a good position before she arrives. Please hold up your E-disks." He looked over his crew. "Any reason not to get underway?"

The only response was a *Phrrt* from Max. eThorpe grinned.

"Mother, take us to Proxima Centauri!"

PROXIMA CENTAURI—*PS AD ASTRA & PS NEIL ARMSTRONG*

The three flesh-and-blood individuals inside Ad Astra, four if you counted Max, had nothing specific to do for five hours and thirty-five minutes. The screens were blank during the transit. Max curled up on Daphne's bunk for a combined mid-morning and noon nap. Daphne and Dale occupied a compact couch in the crew lounge, and Johnny sat in an easy chair opposite them. eDaphne, eDale, and eThorpe floated in the lounge as holoimages.

"This is the first time in a long time I have had five full hours to do nothing," Daphne said, twirling red hair around her finger. "It feels strange."

"What does it feel like," Dale asked eThorpe, "to be confined to a matrix again?"

"Let me answer that," eDaphne said. "It feels damned restrictive!"

"You can say that again," eDale muttered.

"Been there, done that," eThorpe said. "Once we're comfortable with all this, we can maintain an open portal even while in nullspace. That will enable uploads to roam freely as they normally do and flesh-and-blood types to come and go as they wish.

"Thoughts, Johnny?"

"I've got mixed feelings," Johnny said. "Being here with you guys on this historic trip…words fail me. Knowing what's going on with the Oort and my betrayal…"

"Betrayal?" Daphne asked. "Do you really think so?"

"What would you call it?" Johnny's face dropped. "They're my people. We made some bad choices and were on the brink of extinction. I think I did the right thing, but it still feels like betrayal."

Daphne went to Johnny and wrapped her arms around him. "Because of you, the Oort will once again be flesh-and-blood. Instead of fighting every day to fend off extinction, the Oort can be part of a dynamic, forward-moving society with an unbounded future." She caressed his cheek. "That's all because of you, Johnny."

⁕

A soft alarm sounded as *Ad Astra* exited nullspace and all the holographic monitors displayed their surroundings. A particularly bright star lay ahead of them.

"The orbit of Proxima b has been well established for more than a century," eThorpe said. "It's seven-point-five million klicks from Proxima, and its orbital period is eleven-point-two days. I want to park *Ad Astra* at the leading L4 point and hang out for a while, collecting data that will make a lot of people back in the Solar System really happy.

"Dale, please activate the portal so Dr. Fredricks can join us. eDaphne and eDale, get our EPD up and running. It can help collect object data for this system, and we know that *Armstrong* will arrive in a bit, and Orlov will show up sooner or later."

"Hey, everyone," Dr. Fredricks said as he stepped through the portal. "That's about the longest five-and-a-half hours I ever spent. How was the trip?"

"Entirely uneventful," eThorpe said. "We're headed for Proxima b's L4 right now."

"Hi, guys!" Kimberly's voice filled the lounge as she stepped through a portal that had just appeared from *Armstrong*. She kissed Daphne and Dale, hugged Johnny, and stroked Max. "We're pacing Proxima b five million klicks above the ecliptic, collecting data and keeping an eye out for *Gagarin*."

"It still will be four or five hours before they arrive," eThorpe said.

"At L4," Mother announced. "Engines shut down; EPD engaged."

✳

"Okay, listen up, everyone, both ships," eThorpe said. "Back in the Solar System, we have a network of solar storm monitoring stations that warn us of an approaching solar storm. Typically, in the inner Solar System, we have five to eight minutes warning. Farther out, of course, we have longer. Here, we're only seven-point-five million klicks from Proxima. This means that light gets here in a half minute, and the charged particles arrive in four and a half minutes. Both *Ad Astra* and *Armstrong* need to program Mother to take the ship behind Proxima b the moment we receive light from a solar flare. Another thing; Proxima is a *flare* star. Periodically, it increases its total luminosity so that it emits the same x-ray flux as Sol. This can happen several times a day, but the increase in x-rays is of no real concern to us because they are absorbed by the palladium-hydride between our double hulls. What matters are the charged particles that accompany a solar storm."

Programming Mother in both ships was simply a matter of informing Mother what to do if she detected a solar flare on Proxima. No sooner had the crews programmed their resident mothers than alarms sounded in both vessels. A fraction of a second later, both *Ad Astra* and *Armstrong* exited nullspace behind Proxima b, 1,000 kilometers above the planet's surface, hovering on their MBH drives.

Four minutes later, radiation alarms sounded again. On *Ad Astra*, eThorpe said, "That's got to be Proxima's charged particles being captured by the planet's magnetic field and routed to our location. Mother," he ordered, "move us out to twenty-four thousand klicks above the planet."

"Why twenty-four?" Dale asked. "And what about *Armstrong*?"

"eBraxton is basically me with mods from our separate existence since he was cloned. He thinks like me, so he'll do the same thing—I hope. Twenty-four thousand klicks because that would take us beyond Earth's upper band of charged particles in its magnetic field yet still be sufficiently close for the solar wind to sweep past us. Without more data, I'm applying Earth parameters to Proxima b. Once the astronomy boys process everything we send them today, we'll know a lot more."

During eThorpe's explanation, *Ad Astra's* EPD indicated *Armstrong's* arrival a thousand kilometers away. Shortly thereafter, the EPD alarmed again. Daphne checked it out.

"It shows a new presence near the Proxima b L5 position. Whatever it is, it's taking the brunt of the solar storm."

PROXIMA CENTAURI—*UZ YURI GAGARIN*

Everyone except Orlov and Borisovich ran for the Bolt Room.

"Excuse me, Sir!" the Academician said to Orlov as he grabbed the controls and attempted to re-enter warp.

Nothing happened.

He tried twice more—nothing.

"Status!" he barked at the resident computer as he pushed Orlov into the Bolt Room.

"The forward warp ring sustained substantial charged particle damage. It will remain inoperative until repairs can be effected," the Resident responded.

"Explain," Orlov demanded as he and Borisovich took seats in the cramped quarters.

Borisovich explained. "Proxima generates many solar storms, some worse than others. We came out of warp directly into a heavy charged particle flux. Our palladium-hydride-filled double-hull will have minimized our individual radiation dosage, and the crew getting into the Bolt Room probably helped further. You and I should take anti-radiation medication, and the auto-doc should monitor all of us."

"Explain why radiation damaged the pod," Orlov demanded, frustration filling his voice.

"Too many variables and insufficient information," the Academician answered. "Until we can examine the problem, I simply cannot tell you."

"Radiation levels normal," the Resident announced.

Orlov and his crew exited the Bolt Room.

"What now?" Orlov asked.

"We need to get behind Proxima b to be shielded from the next flare," Borisovich said. He checked his Link. "It will take us fifteen hours and twenty-two minutes to arrive at Proxima b's L2 point, one hundred fifty-one thousand kilometers above the surface."

"Is your Link working?" Orlov asked.

"Just internal functions."

"How do we get back?" Orlov asked. "Is the hyper-brick working?"

"No, Sir. That's the first thing I tried. We lost the link somewhere along our route. The only way to regain it is to generate another hyper-brick at the locus on Udachny. The fuel portal is still working because the portal size is much smaller." While he talked, he set *Gagarin* on course for Proxima b's L2 spot.

"There's got to be something we can do," Orlov said, his exasperation increasing.

"It's not that simple," the Academician said. "It's really not." He called up his Link again and spent several minutes doing mathematical manipulations. "We have an operating VASIMR system that can push us at one-gee, supplied by deuterium through the fuel portal. If we push steadily at one-gee for about seventeen days and then reverse and decelerate for another seventeen days, we'll arrive in the vicinity of Sol in thirty-four days subjective time—during which over four years will have passed in the Solar System."

"During which time," Orlov said, "Phoenix will have reached the Aster System and established diplomatic and trade arrangements. In effect, we will have been left in the dust." He growled. "That option falls just before staying here forever. What else can we do?" He walked around in the limited space, his arms folded, scowling. "Think, people…think!"

"Isn't one of the Phoenix starships near Proxima Centauri?" Gloalorn asked tentatively. "Can we signal them?"

"Hell! I don't know," Orlov snapped. "They gotta know I'm responsible for losing their station." He turned to Borisovich. "That wasn't supposed to happen. Our sabotage was set to shut down their power supply, not collapse their mini black hole. When we get back, I want to address that." He placed his hands on his hips. "If they did that to me, I wouldn't help them."

"Do you have a better idea, Sir?" Borisovich asked. He turned to the crew. "Does anybody?"

✻

On *Armstrong*, Mother announced, "The *Gagarin* is heading for Proxima b L2. Arrival time about fifteen hours."

Ad Astra and *Armstrong* had set up their comms so that each vessel was aware of the other's communications without duplicating incoming messages. About a half-hour following the announcement of *Gagarin's* movement, both ships heard, "Mayday…Mayday…this is the *Udachny Starship Yuri Gagarin* calling on the international distress channel. We are transmitting from the Proxima Centauri solar system, in transit on VASIMR engines from Proxima b's L5 location to the planet's L2 location, anticipated arrival in approximately fourteen hours. Our warp drive is damaged beyond our ability to repair without parts from Udachny in Earth's Solar System. Mayday…Mayday… anyone receiving this message, please respond on any channel. We are monitoring all channels. Mayday…Mayday…" and the entire message repeated.

eThorpe transmitted a response. "*UZ Yuri Gagarin*, this is *PS Ad Astra*. We have received your distress call. In fifteen minutes, *Ad Astra* will come alongside *Gagarin*. We have a docking tube that will make an airtight seal against your hull around your airlock. One of our crew members with a broad level of technical expertise will enter *Gagarin* for a face-to-face conference to determine how we might be able to assist you."

At first, there was no response. Then an acknowledgment where even across the transmission, the sender sounded relieved. "Roger, *Ad Astra*. We are standing by to receive your technician."

✻

"Dale," eThorpe said, "I want you to transfer to *Gagarin* and find out what their problem is and what they need. Take one of the specially programmed E-disks with you, and keep your finger on the activator. Activate the E-disk on even the smallest irregularity. It will take you back here. Keep an open channel with me."

Mother brought *Ad Astra* alongside *Gagarin* on her MBH drive so that *Ad* Astra's top was pointed in the direction of *Gagarin's* travel, extended the collapsible docking tube, and set an airtight seal around *Gagarin's* airlock hatch. Dale filled the docking tube with one-atmosphere air, locked through *Ad Astra's* airlock into the one-gee environment of the tube created by *Gagarin's* forward acceleration, and opened *Gagarin's* outer lock hatch.

"The inner hatch is shut," he reported. "I am opening it."

As the hatch opened, Dale caught a brief glimpse of crew members pointing projectile weapons at the hatch. He activated his E-disk.

❋

"*UZ Yuri Gagarin*, this is *PS Ad Astra*. We have undocked and moved a safe distance away. You are bracketed between *PS Ad Astra* and *PS Neil Armstrong*. We both are sweeping *Gagarin* with unfocussed neutrino beams. We can shift our focus in a microsecond so that the beams will disrupt all biological life on *Gagarin*. We will allow you to continue on your course to L2. If you take any other action of any nature, you will all die.

"When you arrive at L2, you will shut down your VASIMR's and drift. Within fifteen minutes of arrival at L2, you will collect all of your portable weapons into a cargo net and place them into your airlock. One of your crew members will push the cargo net with the weapons out of your airlock and close the hatch behind him. Should your airlock open again after this, we will disrupt all biological life on *Gagarin*. We will collect the weapons and then communicate with you again.

"Acknowledge this transmission."

❋

"What options do we have?" Orlov asked Borisovich.

"I do not know these neutrino beam devices. I really cannot advise without further information."

"Bullshit! Assume their weapon will do what they say. You and your people come up with some options, and do it quickly."

"While we study our options," Borisovich said, "I recommend we lay out a cargo net for the weapons."

Orlov grunted his concurrence. He leaned back in his chair at the control console, placed his hands behind his head, and dropped into deep thought. *Those bastards have me by the balls right now. I need to convince them that I have capitulated completely, and that I will do whatever is necessary to gain their cooperation.* He began to explore various avenues, most to be discarded, but several saved for closer examination.

An hour later, Borisovich approached him. "We have come up with a possible plan, Sir." He proceeded to lay out a plan that matched in most details one of the avenues Orlov had already examined. *I got lucky when I acquired this man,* Orlov thought. "Okay," he said, "Good job! We will implement your plan."

Orlov turned to Gloalorn. "Adrhun Gloalorn," he said formally, "you have an important role in this operation."

Orlov laid out for the alien exactly what he expected.

PROXIMA CENTAURI—*PS AD ASTRA & PS NEIL ARMSTRONG*

"I want some input on how we are going to deal with the Udachny matter," eThorpe said.

"I think we should bring Chairman Butler in on the discussion," Dr. Fredricks said, having not yet returned to Phoenix.

It seemed like a good idea to Kimberly. While she thought about it, eThorpe said, "I agree. Kimberly, would you...?"

Kimberly nodded. *I wanted to bring John with us in the first place,* she thought. *Now he can join us.* She stood, straightened her outfit, and stepped through the portal to Phoenix in the Kuiper Belt. From there, she transited to her Ogden office and then into Chairman John Butler's office in OS Prime.

"Kimberly!"

"I just left Proxima Centauri, John; can you imagine that? Four-point-two lightyears in just a few seconds…"

"And I thought stepping through a portal in the Oval Office to here was amazing. My, how things have changed."

Kimberly kissed him. "We need you to participate in an important discussion. Are you free for an hour or so?"

"Where?"

"In orbit around Proxima Centauri." Kimberly's eyes twinkled as she told Butler the location. Watching his reaction was precious.

"Do I need anything?"

"Nope, just your E-disk…let's go," Kimberly said as she took his hand and returned to *Armstrong* via Ogden and Phoenix.

✳

"Welcome, Chairman Butler, to the Proxima Centauri star system," eBraxton said. "Take a few minutes to acquaint yourself with our surroundings," he pointed to the holoscreens, "and then we'll get down to business."

Kimberly showed him a schematic image of the entire system, indicating the position of the two starships, while Butler was still getting used to the idea that he was actually in the Proxima system.

"What's this?" he asked, pointing to a blip representing the *Gagarin*.

"That's why we asked you to come," Kimberly said, leading him to a couch in the lounge.

eThorpe then briefed Butler. He was physically in a matrix on *Ad Astra* but projected his holoimage into *Armstrong*.

"We cannot trust Orlov, but we feel morally obligated to assist him and his crew." eThorpe paused. "Are you aware that Orlov destroyed our Joint Kuiper Station?"

"Can you prove this?" Butler asked.

"Not with legal certainty, but I am morally certain that he did it." eThorpe smiled ruefully. "That's my dilemma. He destroyed a multi-trillion-phoenix station and would have killed everyone on board had we not been backed up. In my mind, that's the same as actually doing it. And now, we are faced with rescuing Orlov and his crew from otherwise certain death."

"Wait a minute," eSally piped up. "Don't they have a portal deuterium feed for their LANR?"

eThorpe nodded.

"Then they can return home on their VASIMR. It will take them over four years real time, but they can do it."

eBrad interjected, "Their subjective time will be about thirty-four days."

"If it were just Orlov and that Academician…" eBraxton said.

Butler sighed inwardly and looked at Kimberly, who smiled at him. "I get the picture. If they return by VASIMR, they completely miss the opportunity to participate in the initial Asterian expedition. That's good for Phoenix and probably for the human and Asterian races." Butler looked around the lounge. The immediate crew was present, and holoimages of the other crew floated in the air along with the various uploads. "But what about the families and loved ones of the crew? Despite what Orlov's done, and I don't dispute your moral clarity, you cannot ethically do that to his crew." Butler leaned forward as he said this, emphasizing his words. "I believe strongly that whatever solution you choose *must* include getting the Udachny crew back to the Solar System in a timely manner."

"What if," eBraxton said, "we offer to take the Academician back by portal to where he can obtain another hyper-brick, beef up its power supply, and return to *Gagarin*. Then they can bring in the repair material they need."

"Or," Brad said, "Orlov and his people can return to Udachny, abandoning the starship."

"That's a pretty big loss, even for Orlov," eThorpe muttered.

"Wouldn't we have salvage rights?" Dale asked. "I know that's how maritime law works, but I never looked at similar space law."

"It doesn't exist, son," Butler told him. "It's one of the items on my long list of things to do." He sighed again. "Orlov is not going to abandon *Gagarin*. He single-mindedly wants to get to Aster before Phoenix. He needs *Gagarin* to accomplish that." Butler stood and stretched. "When does all this happen?"

"Shortly after *Gagarin* arrives at L2," eThorpe said. "They will be off-loading all their small arms."

"How did you accomplish that?" Butler asked.

"On pain of disrupting all biological systems on *Gagarin*."

Butler grimaced.

"I didn't have the benefit of your wisdom," eThorpe said.

"I should meet with Orlov personally," Butler said. "If he sees me in the flesh, I think he will be more cooperative. Do you trust me to arrive at an equitable solution, one that will preserve your situation without seriously impacting Orlov's crew?"

"I put you forward as Federation Chairman because you were the wisest man I had ever known," eThorpe said. "My opinion has not changed one iota." He grinned at Butler. "Do what you must. I will accede to your judgment and cooperate fully with your compromise solution."

✳

Gagarin arrived at L2. The crews of both *Armstrong* and *Ad Astra* focused their attention on their holoscreens. Butler was just beginning to feel comfortable inside a fragile bubble of air 4.2 lightyears from home when the *Gagarin* outer lock hatch opened, and a spacesuited figure pushed a cargo net filled with small arms into the void.

"*UZ Yuri Gagarin*, this is *PS Ad Astra*," eThorpe transmitted. "We have Federation Chairman John Butler onboard. He will come to meet face-to-face with Isidor Orlov. We will dock with *Gagarin* as before, except this time, there will be no gravity. The Chairman's freefall experience is limited, so accommodate him."

"This is *Gagarin*. We understand and await Chairman Butler's arrival."

Butler really didn't know what to expect. His freefall experience really was limited, but on those few times he had experienced freefall, he had had no difficulties. He did not expect any this time. He slipped the localized E-disk into a pocket and declined the EMD stun weapon Kimberly offered.

"It's easier to persuade when there is no obvious immediate threat," he said with a smile.

"I'm worried," she said quietly for his ears only.

"Don't worry, Kid. I'm a veteran at this kind of thing." He winked and stepped up to the airlock inner hatch.

Armstrong's resident Mother brought *Armstrong* alongside *Gagarin* and snaked the docking tube across the separation. It attached itself to *Gagarin's* hull around the airlock, and Mother pressurized it to one atmosphere.

"Watch the transition to zero-gee when you cross the airlock transom," Kimberly said.

The inner hatch opened, and Butler stepped through. It closed behind him. The outer hatch opened with a slight pop, and Butler stepped across the transom. He caught his breath for a moment as all his senses told him he was falling. Then his intellect took over, and his world shifted so that his senses told him he was swimming through a short tunnel. When the *Gagarin* hatch opened, Butler pushed himself off gently and floated into the airlock. The hatch closed behind him, and the inner hatch opened.

Isidor Orlov floated just inside the starship, sporting a wide grin. "Welcome, Chairman Butler, to *Udachnyy Zvezdolet Yuri Gagarin*. It is my honor to have the Chairman of the Oort Federation visit my starship."

"Thank you, Isidor Orlov. I am honored to be here, so far from our homes—I, representing the people of the Solar System, and you, representing Udachny Enterprises and all of its people and wealth. I am grateful that Phoenix made it possible for us to so meet, but I want to assure you that I am not here representing Phoenix nor any other enterprise—only the Federation."

"I thought as much, Chairman Butler. You know the respect I hold for you."

Orlov waved Butler inside the control room of the starship and pointed to a chair with a lap belt restraint.

"You may be more comfortable restrained to your seat, Chairman Butler."

"Thank you." Butler strapped himself to the chair. "Thorpe has briefed me about your predicament, but I would like to hear it from your lips."

"We had an uneventful trip under warp from the Solar System to here. When we exited warp, we immediately encountered a severe charged-particle-flux from a large solar storm on Proxima. It knocked out our warp drive. My crew was armed when an *Ad Astra* crew member entered our airlock. I believe Thorpe overreacted to that, presuming it to be an attack on his personnel and vessel."

Butler nodded in apparent sympathy. He could understand why eThorpe might have reacted as he did. He decided not to bring up the Joint Kuiper Station destruction.

"I have spoken with Thorpe about this," Butler said. "I believe he will agree to my proposal if you will." He smiled and waited for Orlov's response.

After a long pause, Orlov said, "Please, Chairman Butler, let me hear your proposal."

"First, I need to ask a question. Would your people at Udachny be able to boost your available power to open one of your portals from Udachny to here?"

Orlov waved Borisovich over and repeated the question.

"I do not think so, Sir. We are straining to maintain the fuel portal."

"Very well," Butler said, "I thought as much. I propose that Academician Borisovich accompany me through the Phoenix portal to Udachny. There, we will set up a temporary Phoenix portal between Udachny and *Gagarin* that you can use to transport whatever personnel and equipment you will need to effect your warp drive repairs. When the repairs are completed and you have tested your drive and know that it works again, you will restore your original crew, and Phoenix will remove the temporary portal. From then on, you will once again be on your own. Phoenix will agree to refrain from targeting *Gagarin* or any of its personnel during this process."

Orlov sat for a while, obviously thinking over Butler's proposal. Then he smiled and stretched out his hand.

"*Da*, I accept!"

※

Butler brought Borisovich to *Ad Astra*. As they departed together through the portal to Ogden, Butler said, "This will take some time. *Gagarin* will go nowhere until Academician Borisovich returns with the Phoenix hyper-disk. After that, she may do some minor maneuvering to accommodate the repair requirements, but Orlov understands that if he pulls anything not agreed to, Phoenix will shut down the portal. In the meantime, please stand down your weapon systems."

Nearly a full day later, Butler appeared with Borisovich in tow. Butler accompanied Borisovich to *Gagarin* and then returned by himself to *Ad Astra*.

"Where are we?" eThorpe asked.

"Orlov opened the portal to Udachny. His specialists are passing through and will shortly address the problem. When they have diagnosed the matter, they will move the portal outside *Gagarin* and commence receiving parts and equipment."

Kimberly accompanied Butler back to OS Prime, where she spent some private time with him before returning to *Armstrong*.

eThorpe and eBraxton waited, and then they waited some more. Finally, eThorpe directed *Armstrong's* Mother to dock with *Gagarin*. He sent Brad to investigate.

Brad reported back, "The ship is empty. Nobody is here, and the portal is collapsed. They took the hyper-disk with them." There was a pause, and then he continued. "No, wait! Somebody *is* here—it's the Frohlican, Adrhun Gloalorn!"

eThorpe immediately signaled the special portal they had supplied to Orlov to disintegrate.

"Bring him back. Let's try to figure out what is going on."

✳

When Orlov briefed him on what he expected, Gloalorn was intrigued. The subterfuge fascinated him; it was much like the machinations he had experienced back home on Frohlic. While the crew, the Academician, and Orlov passed through the portal, Gloalorn sequestered himself in the machinery space below the living quarters, remaining absolutely quiet as instructed.

Sometime later, Gloalorn wasn't entirely sure how long, he heard the inner airlock hatch open. Then he heard a male voice describing an empty starship and no portal. It was time.

Gloalorn stirred, purposefully making noise, and emerged from the machinery space into the bottom of the living compartment. The largest human he had ever seen floated into view.

"Who the hell are you?" The voice didn't sound angry, just surprised.

"I'm Adrhun Gloalorn. I was taken captive by Isidor Orlov and was only now able to escape during their evacuation of *Gagarin*."

The large stranger transmitted, "No, wait! Somebody *is* here—it's the Frohlican, Adrhun Gloalorn!"

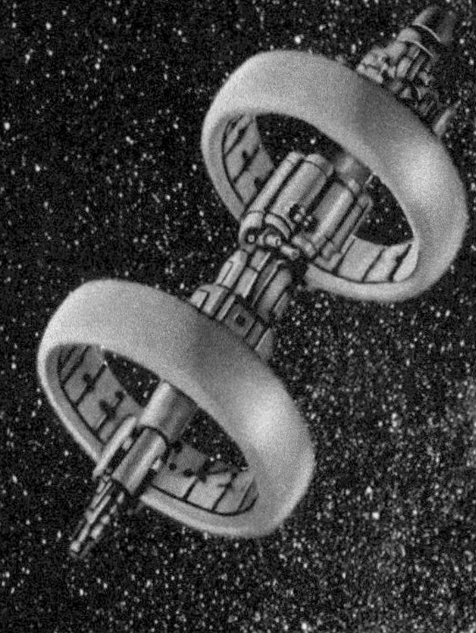

PART THREE
THE BREAKOUT

CHAPTER SIXTEEN

KUIPER BELT—NEW KUIPER JOINT STATION

The new Kuiper Joint Station was such a structure. Like its predecessor, it was a kilometer-wide disk covered with a steep-sided transparent dome made of a radiation-absorbing polymer. The disk sat atop the largest MBH Phoenix had constructed to date, somewhat larger, in fact, than the one it replaced. It generated its own adjustable gravity, and like the one before, it produced sufficient power to project portals to twenty Double-MBH craft out to at least a hundred lightyears while powering the entire Phoenix portal system throughout the Solar System.

The Nanocosm commenced the project several days before *Ad Astra* and *Armstrong* undertook their Proxima Centauri roundtrip. First, it established portals to bring in the necessary raw materials, drawing power from wherever available throughout the Solar System. Once the MBH was functional, power was no longer an issue, and construction accelerated dramatically. Had one stood off in a spacecraft and observed, it would have been like watching the hour hand of an analog clock. It doesn't seem to move when watched, but look away for a moment and then back, and the change is apparent.

By the return of both *Ad Astra* and *Armstrong* crews, Joint Station was ready for occupancy, this time with enhanced security measures so tight that even a nanobot could not approach the station without detection. For a week, Ogden and Phoenix personnel transferred equipment, records, and even some storage to the new, secure location. Under the dome, inside the Phoenix and Ogden complexes, bare offices took on the trappings of their occupants, human sounds filled the corridors and spaces, and both Max and Maxter spent their days exploring the vastness. Somebody in the planning process had even considered the necessity of appropriate litterbox hygiene. The tabbies found their preferred locations, and the bots kept them clean and refreshed.

eMax spent a couple of hours checking the new location out, but then he had enough and went back to his favorite pastime, roaming the vast Solar System portal network, dropping in from time to time to visit Daphne or Kimberly or their other friends.

MARS-SUN L4—UDACHNY

Orlov grunted. That was sufficient for the Academician.

"My LANR team has managed to devise a LANR that produces nearly an order of magnitude more power than what we installed on *Gagarin*."

Orlov looked at Borisovich.

"That's ten times the power, Sir, on the same amount of fuel. That means we can boost our speed to Warp four-point-seven, and *that* means we can travel to Aster in just six days and three hours. At Warp four-point-five, it would have taken nine days and seventeen hours. We save three days and eleven hours."

Orlov brought his head up sharply.

"Or…we can go twice as far without refueling."

"You keep surprising me, Academician. That's good. Keep it up!"

"One more thing, Sir."

"What?" Orlov growled.

"We are increasing our fuel capacity by replacing the current tanks with ones that wrap completely around the Lance. Not only will we more than triple our fuel load, but the full tanks will also give the Lance added radiation protection."

"How soon can you complete these modifications to *Udachnyy Zvezdolet Gherman Titov* (*Udachny Starship Gherman Titov*)?"

"They are underway now, Sir. *Titov* will be ready in a week."

KUIPER BELT—NEW KUIPER JOINT STATION

First thing, the uploaded individuals in their matrix housings were removed from the starships and plugged into the GlobalNet that now encompassed the entire Solar System, a vast, dedicated-portal interconnected network of thinsat swarms. The participants and several research principals met in the newly furnished conference room.

"I want to ensure we are all on the same page," eThorpe said to the assembled group following a quick virtual private conference with eBraxton. "Let me recap what happened on our test run to Proxima. *Ad Astra* and *Armstrong* arrived in the Proxima system, located Proxima b, and had to avoid a solar storm. We relocated to a location behind Proxima b. We detected *Gagarin's* arrival by EPD. The solar storm knocked out *Gagarin's* warp drive. After some initial difficulty, Orlov appealed to us for help. With John Butler's assistance, we arranged to loan Orlov a Phoenix portal for transporting personnel and equipment from Udachny to Proxima.

"Orlov deceived us. He and all his crew departed *Gagarin*, taking the hyper-disk with them. Apparently, during their departure, Adrhun Gloalorn managed to sequester himself in the machinery spaces, and in their immediate hurry, Orlov's people seemed to have missed his absence.

"Now, here is some new information." eThorpe had just received this information while he was speaking to the group. "It seems that Orlov had actually constructed two ABO craft—the second, he managed to keep secret even from us. During our absence, his people made a breakthrough development in LANR technology. They can now go farther and faster on less fuel—warp four-point-seven, to be exact. That will get them to Aster in six days and three hours, just one-and-a-half days slower than us.

"Adrhun has given me what he knows about Orlov's plans in the Aster system." There was no break in eThorpe's presentation, but in the background, he was following several paths, collecting additional information as he went. "He plans to use intimidation to force the Frohlicans into an exclusive trade arrangement with Udachny. Adrhun says that Orlov plans to use the all-encompassing bureaucracy of Frohlic to insinuate himself into the fabric of their society—perhaps even take it over. He says they have a strong defensive network but urges us to arrive first with sufficient time to set the stage for Orlov's arrival." He stepped aside and gestured to eBraxton.

"Now that we are all on the same page," eBraxton said, "let's look at our calendar. Everyone here understands that Isidor Orlov destroyed the original Kuiper Joint Station. Adrhun tells us that Orlov's intent was just to disrupt the MBH power to the Phoenix portal network, not destroy the station. From my point of view, what actually happened trumps Orlov's intent."

Around the table, people agreed with eBraxton—nodding, smiling, clapping. Max jumped onto the table and strolled its length, stopping to greet close friends. Maxter joined him at the far end, and then they curled up in Daphne's and Kimberly's laps, respectively.

"He also broke the agreement we reached in the Proxima system," eBraxton continued. "We need to teach him a lesson."

Again, nodding, smiling, clapping. There was one exception, Federation Chairman John Butler. He raised his hand to speak.

"I completely understand why all of you—and yes, even myself— feel this way about Isidor Orlov." He paused while people around the table muttered and whispered. "Just as the Federation cannot tell Udachny what to do, so it cannot instruct Phoenix. But Phoenix and the Federation have had very close ties since the beginning. Unlike Udachny, Phoenix is not interested only in its own profit. Much of what Phoenix has done and is doing benefits everyone in the Solar System, even while Phoenix profits from its activities." He paused again, looking around the table. "You may not like to hear this, but Udachny is *also* supplying services demanded by customers around the Solar System. So long as there is demand, people like Orlov will supply." Butler stopped speaking and busied himself with his Link for a moment. eThorpe genuinely wondered where he was taking this.

"I agree that Isidor Orlov needs a lesson on where his boundaries lie, but let the lesson be measured and, if possible, without loss of life."

✳

Gloalorn was allowed to participate in the meeting. When it was over, he pulled Arcah aside. "What happened at the Kuiper Joint Station?"

"Orlov's people sabotaged the station shortly after it was occupied, causing the mini-black hole to collapse, killing a bunch of people—including me."

"What do you mean, *including you?*"

Arcah then explained the Ogden backup system for people, human or otherwise. "I had a backup. That's why I am still alive."

"Can I get one?" Gloalorn asked.

"Out of my control, but I can tell you this. If you are still working for Orlov—and a lot of people think you are—there is no chance."

Gloalorn didn't respond immediately. He sank into reverie. I'm here on Orlov's behalf. My job is to make sure Orlov gets to Aster before these guys. But nobody told me about Orlov's role in destroying Kuiper Joint Station. Nobody told me he had, in effect, killed Masin. Out of billions and billions of people in this system, Masin and I are the only Asterians. Our home is eighty-four lightyears away. Yeah, Masin and I are different, but we are still the only Asterians anywhere near. I wouldn't do anything to hurt Masin—so what am I doing helping Orlov?

While Gloalorn pondered, Arcah stood silently, watching.

Finally, Gloalorn said, "Masin, I need to tell you something." He then laid out his thoughts in full detail.

"What are these people going to do when they arrive in our system? We attacked them; they have every right to destroy our worlds...but you and I have an obligation to stop them if we can. I thought Orlov was on the right path, but I fear he would attempt to enslave our people—yours and mine."

"You just heard Chairman Butler," Arcah said. "He commands a lot of respect with these people. He sits at the top of their government system. It's nothing like yours, but it's way more than we have on Rogan. He counsels restraint. I've seen it more than once."

Arcah then described how Butler and eThorpe had handled the Oort. "Don't get the wrong idea about humans," Arcah said. "They are not timid cowards. Look at what they did to our invading forces—out of five thousand, there's just you and me. Look how they have advanced technologically just since we've been here. In many ways, they have totally surpassed Rogan."

"I'm not sure I get your point."

"I guess I'm trying to say that I do not believe eThorpe and his people are mounting a war party against our people. I think they will come in peace. Don't misunderstand; they will be prepared for anything, but if Frohlic and Rogan accept their overtures, all of us will prosper—humans, Frohlicans, Roganians, and even the few remaining Oort."

"What if they are met with missiles, bombs, lasers, and particle beams?"

"Then I fear for both our peoples. These guys have portal technology, FTL drives, and they know how to manipulate neutrinos. I don't think Frohlic or Rogan would have a chance. Especially so if Chairman Butler is not there, and I think he will remain in the Solar System."

"You and I may have our differences," Gloalorn said, "but we are both Asterians; we have an unbreakable kinship." He gripped Arcah's forearms in the universal Asterian gesture of friendship. "What can we do to save our people?"

✳

eThorpe's holoimage occupied a chair in an unused office in the Phoenix complex on Kuiper Joint Station. Arcah and Gloalorn sat in chairs facing him.

"So, that's the entire story," Gloalorn told him. "I am supposed to give Orlov anything that will assist him in his quest to arrive at Frohlic before you do. I've made a lot of mistakes in my life, but this may have been my biggest goof."

eThorpe didn't respond immediately. He sat quietly in thought. Adrhun was a captured enemy pilot. If Frohlican ethics are anything like ours—and they seem to be—he had an ethical obligation to escape and cause whatever mischief he could to further the Asterian cause. Masin reacted differently, but he and Masin are from different planets, different cultures. I can't reasonably expect them to react in the same way to these circumstances. eThorpe looked at Gloalorn.

"I don't fault your actions. You did what you considered in the best interest of Frohlic and yourself." He smiled, "In fact, that's what you are doing now. Fortunately, you have additional information at your disposal.

"I assume Masin has explained our upload technology. We are willing to outfit you with an internal Link and an upload backup, just like Masin. This will keep you safe and allow your full access to the GlobalNet." eThorpe smiled again. "There is a catch, however. I want you to continue your role as an informant for Orlov. The difference is, you will give him *only* what I tell you to relay, nothing else. At some point, fairly soon, I want you to return to Orlov. He clearly wants you to accompany him to Aster. Let's make that happen. We'll work out the details as we move forward."

Neither Arcah nor Gloalorn mentioned to eThorpe the substance of their conversation following the meeting.

MARS-SUN L4—UDACHNY

This was the kind of trap that Borisovich tried diligently to avoid. No matter how valid his suggestions, things inevitably go sideways, and that was never good news for the Academician.

"We have the power swarm here," Borisovich said. "If we place ourselves somewhere near the midpoint of the Kuiper belt, somewhere on the five hundred AU radius," he consulted his Link, "it will take us about seventeen days to get there using VASIMRs at one-gee."

"Why VASIMRs?" Orlov demanded.

"We cannot take the station there with *Titov. Titov* will take us there in about a minute, but just us and what we can carry inside the Lance."

"What if we put the new station just inside the Kuiper Belt inner edge?"

"That's about fifty AU, so," Borisovich consulted his Link, "that would be about twelve days. Basically, once we near lightspeed in about six days, it's just a few subjective minutes. This happens for acceleration and deceleration—so, about twelve days total. Objective- or real-time goes from about sixty-six hours total for the middle of the Belt to about four hours for the inside edge."

"Time matters here," Orlov said. "Let's commence moving the Udachny Complex to the nearest point on the inner edge of the Kuiper Belt immediately."

✳

It would take the better part of a day to get the Udachny station ready for towing. While this was happening, Borisovich approached Orlov with a question.

"The plan is to construct fifteen *Gagarin-Class* starships. I presume they will all carry the same suite of weapons as *Gagarin*, will they not? That's a lot of raw material. I can produce the pieces at my Krasnoyarsk facility and get them to our construction site by portal."

"Do that, Academician. I want the fifteen-ship fleet ready for the journey as soon as physically possible."

MARS-SUN L4—PHOENIX FORCE

eThorpe signaled via Link his intention to meet with Butler, allowing the Chairman to arrange his schedule appropriately. Several hours later, eThorpe's holoimage sat comfortably in Butler's official office. Butler sat behind his desk, not so elegant as the Resolute desk he had occupied back in the White House, but one with power and influence reaching far beyond anything Butler could have imagined when he still sat behind that ancient desk.

"We are completely private," Butler said before eThorpe had a chance to ask. "What we say here will remain strictly between us."

eThorpe neglected to tell Butler that everything he, eThorpe, ever said privately or publicly was permanently recorded with multiple redundancies throughout the GlobalNet.

"I seek your guidance, my friend," eThorpe said without preamble. "Over the years, I have come to realize that you have wisdom that I can only hope to emulate. I am here to tap into that wisdom." eThorpe smiled broadly as he leaned back in his chair. "Every instinct I have says to smash Udachny, to take Isidor Orlov out of the picture permanently." He paused. "Yet, you counsel differently. Talk to me, please."

Butler cleared his throat, folded his hands on his desk, leaned forward, and started speaking slowly and thoughtfully.

"When I said earlier that I understood your perspective, I meant it. I really do understand. Orlov needs to understand the limits of his sphere of operation. Consider this. Except for Phoenix operations, Udachny supplies much of the Solar System's raw materials, metals, minerals, chemicals, biologics. It's a huge part of system economics. Orlov employs hundreds of thousands, perhaps millions of people in his system-wide operations. What will happen to these enterprises, and the people, if you take drastic action against Orlov?"

"I take your point. What do you suggest, then? What can I do to stop Orlov's overreach and dangerous tactics?"

"The problem, as I see it," Butler continued, "is Isidor Orlov. He sets policy. He orders actions. He directs the activities that lead to harm and even death." He unfolded his hands and leaned back in his chair. "You have an overwhelming force at your command. Let's put it under Admiral Culp temporarily. He can sweep into the Udachny compound and arrest Orlov—physically arrest him under warrants the Federation will issue. We can put him on trial. He won't go to prison or anything like that, but we can extract huge fines and severely restrict his activities in the Solar System. We can split up his enterprises and assign individuals who are appropriately qualified to run them."

✳

Two days later, *Ad Astra*, *Armstrong*, *Aldrin*, and *Conrad* arrived suddenly at Mars-Sun L4, *Ad Astra* and *Armstrong* above and below the swarm, with *Aldrin* and *Conrad* toward Sol and the outer planets.

eThorpe, who was temporarily installed in *Ad Astra*, looked down on the power swarm. "Do you guys see what I see—or rather, what I don't see?"

Adm. Culp in *Aldrin* responded. "Just the power swarm—nothing else."

"The bastard," eBraxton said from *Armstrong*.

Dale in *Conrad* asked, "What do we do? The Udachny Complex is gone as if it had never been there."

"Orlov moved the complex," eThorpe said. "No way to locate it without a full-scale search effort."

"Let's blast the swarm," Dale said.

	Robert G. Williscroft

"Hold it, people!" Culp ordered. "Our warrant says arrest, not destroy. We need to regroup and rethink this whole thing."

※

In Butler's office at OS Prime, the Chairman welcomed eThorpe and eBraxton and took his seat behind his desk, sliding his latest read aside. He knew where the real power lay in this room, but he was determined to make his point and extract any concessions he could. He spoke earnestly to the two holoimages.

"Trust that I *completely* understand your perspective. Orlov is a scoundrel who keeps giving us the slip." He smiled glumly. "Of course, we can catch and destroy him. Phoenix has overwhelming power to do just that. Here is the problem, gentlemen." Butler leaned back and laid his palms on his desk. "One of America's founders, Benjamin Rush, said it best. *Where there is no law, there is no liberty; and nothing deserves the name of law but that which is certain and universal in its operation upon all the members of the community.* Think about this, please." He sat quietly, looking earnestly at both holoimages. "Our law requires due process, even in the face of certainty. If we choose to act unlawfully, we set a precedent for all future time." He lowered his voice. "We are about to embark on a mission to Aster. We intend to proceed with outstretched hands in peace, offering a basis in law for our future interactions. If we don't abide by our own law, we lose all credibility, even before negotiations get underway. And don't believe for a minute that if we treat Orlov outside our own law, the Asterians will not soon learn about it." Butler leaned forward and folded his hands. "You gentlemen have the power to do as you wish, but heed my words and let your intellects take you beyond your emotions."

※

eThorpe contacted Gloalorn privately by Link. "I want to meet with you in secrecy, just the two of us, at your earliest convenience."

They met in the kitchen of the Los Angeles condo owned by Daphne, Kimberly, and Dale. They were alone, and eThorpe laid out a plan that was both risky and very satisfying for Gloalorn. After a few minutes, Gloalorn agreed. Gloalorn transited to Kuiper Joint Station, and eThorpe's holoimage simply vanished.

CHAPTER SEVENTEEN

KUIPER BELT—NEW KUIPER JOINT STATION—OGDEN COMPLEX

"Are you ready for this?" Kimberly asked Gloalorn.

He gave her an expression that she had come to understand meant *I'm not entirely sure about this*, similar to a human shrug with raised eyebrows. "This worked fine for you, right, Masin?"

"Not only did it work fine," Arcah answered, "but, without it, I would not be here. Remember that I was *killed* when the original Joint Station imploded."

Gloalorn turned to Fredricks. "I'm ready," he said, giving his best imitation of a human smile.

*

Four hours later, the process was complete. Gloalorn had newly inserted knowledge of how to use his internal Link, and his backup was being updated in real-time.

He turned to Fredricks. "Thank you, Dr. Fredricks!" He addressed the others. "Thanks to all of you."

PROXIMA CENTAURI—*UZ GHERMAN TITOV & UZ YURI GAGARIN*

"On the warp rings, we added an additional skin of palladium-hydride sandwiched between two thick layers of radiation-absorbing polymer. We added similar protection to the internal warp elements that are particularly sensitive to radiation." He pointed to the large rings holding the Lance in magnetic suspension. "The problem was complex, because while the polymer and hydrogen effectively slowed the neutrons, the palladium produced secondary low-level radiation while stopping gamma and x-rays. We needed to find a balance for the lowest net radiation. For the crew in the Lance, the process was more direct. The new wrap-around fuel tanks, with their deuterium load, fully protect personnel inside the Lance."

"We have onloaded everything we will need to repair *Gagarin*," Orlov said, "isn't that so?"

"Yes, Sir," the Academician said. Gloalorn watched him roll his eyes and wondered at the meaning of this human gesture.

"And what about you, my alien friend?" Orlov asked.

"I had to return before they found me out. They don't trust me. I did inform the Academician about their raid on Mars-Sun L4... after the fact, unfortunately." Gloalorn produced his imitation of a human smile. "It's a good thing you moved Udachny when you did. They had warrants for your arrest."

"*Chush' sobach'ya* (*Fucking bullshit*)!" Orlov barked. Fuming, he looked out the shuttle port. "It looks like we are making progress on constructing the additional ships. Before we depart for Proxima, I want a full report on our progress."

The shuttle docked to the Lance airlock, and the men floated into the starship's control cabin. While Orlov strapped himself into the righthand seat in front of the control panel, Borisovich placed a Link call to his foreman supervising the starship construction project. Gloalorn hung back, sufficiently close to observe and hear everything but keeping out of the way.

"Send me all your stats right away," Borisovich said to his foreman. "The boss wants a brief before we depart."

Borisovich joined Orlov at the control console and pulled up his Link display. He pointed to an area several kilometers away from the revolving station. "We are building the rings here. We have laid the skeletons for fifteen forward rings and will start the remaining fifteen after rings over here in several days." He pointed to an area about a kilometer distant from the first group. He shifted the view. "We are building the Lances here and have already laid the keel for each." He turned to Orlov. "We are experiencing some material delays caused by our move, but we're on top of that. In a couple of days, we'll have portals open from each of our component manufacturing facilities to the assembly areas."

Gloalorn remained back, using his eyes and ears connected to his internal Link to record the sight and sound in the control room and the consoles.

✳

Titov rotated and pitched, aiming at Proxima Centauri. A moment later, she vanished. Seven and a half hours later, she slipped out of warp with Proxima blazing off her starboard side. Her controlling computer made a quick comparison of the surrounding starscape with the installed database, located Proxima b nearly two AUs distant, dead ahead, and initiated a short warp jump. Minutes later, *UZ Gherman Titov* settled into position at L2, about a kilometer distant from *Gagarin*.

"I am impressed, Academician," Orlov said in a rare moment of praise. "The systems performed flawlessly."

Gloalorn noted everything carefully.

An hour later, the two starships were side by side with a flexible trunk connecting their airlocks. Borisovich inspected *Gagarin* and reported that the Phoenix people had not damaged anything insofar as he could tell.

The senior tech ran a remote diagnostic to determine the location of the radiation-damaged parts. "We need to examine section three," he said to no one in particular.

Three technicians exited *Titov* with toolkit and repair parts and jetted to the forward warp ring using their TBH boots. They moved directly to Section 3.

"Keep me continuously informed of your progress," Borisovich told them over the local circuit. He put the comms on a loudspeaker so Orlov could follow the actions.

The technicians removed the Section 3 access hatch bolts with anti-torque drivers and placed them in a net bag held by the senior tech. The access cover floated off easily, and they clipped it to a protruding retaining ring.

"Talk to me," Borisovich said.

"[*grunt*] We've removed the access cover [*grunt*] and are making an initial visual inspection," the senior tech said. "Nothing obvious visually, but then I didn't expect to see anything."

One of the other two techs inserted a test probe into the cavity. "Testing module supply voltage," he said. "Nominal." He moved the probe. "Nominal." He reached farther into the cavity. "Whoa…what's this?" He directed a holocam probe to the point so the senior tech and Borisovich could see.

"Scorched," the senior tech commented.

"And severed," the tech with the probe added. "We found one end of our problem."

For an additional hour, the three techs probed, poked, and examined various components inside Section 3. Finally, they extracted a brick-sized module.

"This is the culprit," the senior tech said, pointing his holocam at the module.

One of the techs returned to *Titov*, picked up a shielded replacement, and returned to *Gagarin*. With its shielding, the replacement was somewhat larger than the module it replaced. The techs spent a half-hour jury-rigging a workaround so it would fit.

Orlov watched their work with fascination. Russian ingenuity, he thought, good old-fashioned Russian ingenuity.

The technicians wrapped up their work, replaced the access cover, and returned to *Titov*.

"I would like to run a short test of *Gagarin*," Borisovich said to Orlov. "A short trip above the ecliptic and back will do."

"We'll all go," Orlov said, "except Adrhun Gloalorn and one technician."

✳

Gloalorn was surprised at his exclusion from the short test jump. He didn't know why Orlov chose to leave him in *Titov*, but it worried him. Had he somehow communicated his new perspective to Orlov? As the others departed through the connecting flexible trunk, the technician strapped himself in one of the console chairs and indicated with a smile that Gloalorn should do the same.

"Tell me about your homeworld," he said with what Gloalorn had come to understand was a friendly tone.

That's when Gloalorn realized that fate had just dropped a golden opportunity into his hands. Out of the tech's view, he extracted the EMD weapon from his pocket, turned, and disabled the tech with a bolt. He activated a direct line to eThorpe on his internal Link.

"I just commandeered the *UZ Gherman Titov*," Gloalorn said. "No time to explain. I'm sending an unconscious Udachny tech to the portal node."

Gloalorn terminated the Link connection, pushed the floating unconscious tech through the portal, watched him crumble to the deck, and collapsed the portal. He turned, entered destination coordinates into the control console, pointed the starship generally in the right direction, and executed his program.

✳

An hour later, *Gagarin* returned to find *Titov* gone.

"*Tvoyu mat', nu chto za khernya* (*Fuck, you got to be shitting me*)!" Orlov yelled in total exasperation.

He shook his head angrily while trying to pound the console. All that accomplished was to send him spinning through the Control Compartment space. Borisovich grabbed his ankle and pulled him to the console seat on the right.

"He's got a head start, and he's faster," Borisovich said. "Let's get back as soon as possible."

"He's not going to Udachny," Orlov muttered, still fuming. "The little shit has his own plans, and they don't include me and probably don't include Phoenix either."

✳

eThorpe arranged for Culp's people to house the Udachny tech in a secure location without comms. Then he contacted Arcah by Link.

"Masin, please meet me in Daphne's kitchen."

An hour later, a mystified Arcah departed Daphne's kitchen through a portal.

KUIPER BELT—UDACHNY

"Academician," Orlov said, "keep on top of the starship production. See to it that you don't fall behind your schedule."

Orlov was not fit company during the shuttle ride from *Gagarin* to the complex. When they debarked, Orlov stormed to his office and set the portals for no admittance. Borisovich contacted his foreman and left the complex to inspect production progress.

✳

Orlov made several Link calls, and then he stormed from his office following a carefully arranged series of his own portals, arriving in a secluded room at the back of one of his isolated mining outposts in the Asteroid Belt. As Orlov stepped through the portal into the room, a man rose to his feet a bit unsteadily in the low gravity afforded by the unnamed asteroid.

"I'm Randy Nelson," he said, holding out his hand.

Orlov ignored the proffered hand. "You're a former Oort?" he asked.

"I am. I head a group of sixteen former Oort, eight male and eight female, who are unhappy with our current status. We are looking for a change, and we believe you might be able to bring this about."

"What do you mean by *a change*?"

"All the downloaded Oort have been distributed throughout human society. We have no real way to contact or even find each other. We fifteen connected while still in the Oort Cloud and agreed to meet at a designated location to plan something like this."

"What are your intentions, exactly?"

"Between us, we have a huge store of knowledge. We will share this knowledge with any party that will give us the means to escape the Solar System and seek our own destiny."

"So, how does this help me, except for my gaining information I might not yet have?"

"We will work with you, help you refine your starships, support your goals in the Aster system—anything that will take us away from here and afford us the opportunity to strike out on our own when the time comes."

"I'll be in touch," Orlov told Nelson as he got to his feet and left.

INTERSTELLAR SPACE—ONE LIGHTYEAR BEYOND OS PRIME

"Greetings," Gloalorn said in their shared Asterian language.

Arcah anxiously fingered the E-disk in his pocket, unsure whether he should activate it. "What's going on?" he asked.

"Relax, Masin, my friend. eThorpe set this up. Following your private conversation with him, eThorpe called me aside, and together we did some soul searching. I decided unequivocally that you had made the right choice. eThorpe and I worked out a plan, but we kept it to ourselves because it was too audacious to bring in anyone else—even you—until the plan was underway. With a bit of good fortune, I managed to commandeer *UZ Gherman Titov*. We are aboard her now, about a lightyear from OS Prime. We need to make some modifications to *Titov's* systems, and then we will be on our way to Aster."

Gloalorn activated a portal. "This goes to an undisclosed location. Several of eThorpe's people are there but have no knowledge of where the portal leads. They're about to..."

Several e-disks floated through the portal, followed by their nodes, then some hardware, and freeze-dried food packets. Gloalorn closed the portal.

"This hardware adapts the Phoenix fuel portal to the Udachny fueling system. This will allow us to retain full fuel tanks for as long as possible—perhaps the entire trip." He grabbed the hardware and pushed off to the after-engineering spaces. "Come on, give me a hand."

It took an hour to install the well-designed adaptor. Gloalorn checked it by topping off their tanks.

"Check that task off," Gloalorn said. Then he explained the ABO landing system. "If you can call it that," he editorialized. "We're replacing all their hyper-bricks and nodes for two reasons. Ours are smaller and more efficient, and we don't know what kind of backdoors they may have built into their bricks."

They placed several hyper-bricks and nodes into the airlock. Only about half would fit.

"I'll dump the first load. You can do the second," Gloalorn said as he donned his spacesuit. On the monitor, Arcah watched Gloalorn seal himself in the airlock and open the outer hatch. The whoosh of air pushed the floating hyper-bricks out of the lock. One by one, Gloalorn man-handled the nodes out the hatch, giving each a push with his foot.

When he locked back in, Gloalorn said, "Let's give ourselves a bit of clearance before we dump the second load."

He waved Arcah to the console and showed him how to operate the VASIMRs. "You do it, but only one-tenth-gee for two seconds. We don't want to crash hyper-bricks and nodes all over the cabin."

Experienced starship pilot that he was, Arcah adapted easily to the strange console and moved the vessel several hundred meters.

"Piece of cake," he said in English, an expression he had heard Dale use from time to time. Then he suited up and ejected the remaining hyper-bricks and their nodes.

While Arcah disposed of the unneeded equipment, Gloalorn pushed the replacement nodes into place and stowed the hyper-disks. Then he found some storage space for the freeze-dried food.

When Arcah returned inside and stripped out of his suit, he joined Gloalorn at the console. Gloalorn walked him through the warp controls and everything else on the console.

"We'll receive regular meals through a portal," Gloalorn said. "The freeze-dried food is for emergencies. And like I indicated earlier, only eThorpe knows about our trip. Over the next six days and three hours, we'll work out how to handle things when we arrive and fill eThorpe in, so he can plan accordingly."

Surprised as he was by this development, Arcah took it in stride. He had learned to trust eThorpe, and it looked like Adrhun had, too.

"Are you good?" Gloalorn asked.

They gripped each other's forearms in the universal Asterian gesture of friendship, and Arcah pursed his lips and opened his eyes wide, Asterian equivalent of a smile and nod.

KUIPER BELT—NEW KUIPER JOINT STATION

"We are commencing construction of the remainder of our starship fleet—sixteen additional ships. We're on a tight schedule. Everyone pitch in wherever you can to expedite the process."

Despite his interconnections with virtually everything in the Solar System, eThorpe still did not instinctively think in terms of Nanocosm construction. This was evident to everyone who received his Link message. There was much to do, however, that didn't involve actual construction of starships. Nobody really knew what lay ahead. This meant they had to prepare for virtually any eventuality.

With the passing of the third hour of the seventh day since Masin and Adrhun had warped toward Aster, eThorpe met with eBraxton in virtual conference. He laid out his arrangement with the Asterians, bringing eBraxton fully up to date.

"They've just arrived in the Aster System," eThorpe said. "I wonder how they will handle things."

"Our Asterian friends are pretty sharp," eBraxton said. "They certainly know the stakes. One option would be for them to turn over the *Titov* to Frohlic or Rogan. Give them the technology."

"Frohlic would be better able to deal with such a gift in the short-run," eThorpe said, "but I would give Rogan the advantage over time." He paused. "But I don't think they will do either. They both are keenly aware of what we did to their fleet. I think that dominates their thinking—especially Adrhun's. I really think they're serious about setting up an open-ended reception."

"You worked more closely with them than I. For all our sakes, I hope you're right."

※

In the space surrounding Joint Station, the sixteen Double-MBH starships seemed to grow from the inside out. Hour by hour, the sixteen shapes grew at a nearly identical pace. Sally and Brad, along with their uploads, closely monitored the construction progress. Fifteen days into the process, the Nanocosm signaled that fleet construction was complete. Sally, Brad, and their uploads each chose four vessels to inspect. They took a day for each ship, verifying that everything was in place and working properly. To their delight, as they meticulously checked everything, both Max and Maxter showed up as they linked each ship to Joint Station by portal, *Inspecting something new on the circuit*, as Brad put it.

Finally, on day twenty since construction began, Sally announced to eThorpe, hand shielding her smile, "I give you a full fleet of twenty Double-MBH starships, four previously constructed and sixteen just completed."

CHAPTER EIGHTEEN

INTERSTELLAR SPACE—BETWEEN THE SOLAR SYSTEM AND ASTER

Because Gloalorn was familiar with the vessel, Arcah deferred to his control of their voyage. They spent the first several hours discussing their various options.

"The way I see it," Arcah said, "is that *you* need to retain control of *Titov*. That means *you* will be dropping *me* on Rogan. But it's not that simple. I want to orbit the planet, contact a group I hope is still active, and arrange for them to receive the incoming hyper-disk package."

"What if you can't reach them?" Gloalorn asked.

"We have a few days to work out Plan B, I guess." He made a human-like shrug. "What about you? How will you go about contacting your government?"

"Well, I have an advantage here. Frohlic has a central government. I should be able to contact some element of that government and then move forward from there."

"What do we do about *Titov*? Neither of us will be aboard. What's to prevent your people or mine from approaching with a shuttle and taking over?"

"What is the range of our hyper-disks?" Gloalorn asked.

"Range is limited by portal size and available power."

"This vessel has Udachny's latest LANR. That's a lot of power, and the portals only need to accommodate one of us. Do you know if our fuel portal will still be active near Aster?"

Arcah considered the possibilities. "Power level is a function of LANR production, not its fuel source. The fuel portal will enable the LANR to operate longer but not put out more power. I think eThorpe will ensure that Phoenix supplies sufficient power to maintain the fuel portal. You and I need to test our hyper-disk range."

"I agree. How do we do that?"

"Rogan has a significant moon. It is synchronously locked with Rogan so that it shows one face to the planet. We can drop a hyper-disk on the moon's far side where we should be able to avoid detection and then move outward, away from Aster, until we lose the portal link. That will establish our limits."

"Makes sense," Gloalorn said. "Do you have any idea of either planet's detection range?"

"Unless either planet discovered something in the last eighty-five years, they do not have EPD technology. I presume they rely upon long-range radar. That means they can comfortably get real-time detection and ranging out to about four hundred thousand klicks." Arcah pursed his lips, the equivalent of a human smile. "Over time, I suspect either planet could detect us no matter where we were in the system, but within our short-term presence, I think we will be safe outside the cislunar space of either planet…and probably safe even inside the moon orbits."

KUIPER BELT—NEW KUIPER JOINT STATION—PHOENIX COMPLEX

Brad showed up a few minutes later, trailing eBrad's holoimage. "What is it, kiddo?"

"Watch that model," she said, indicating a holoimage of a fully functional 10% model of a Double-MBH craft hovering in the Great Hall.

She made an adjustment at her station, and the model vanished.

"What did you do?" Brad asked, "Send it somewhere?"

"No, silly. Why would I call you here just to see that?" She turned and smiled without covering her mouth. "It's still right there. Only, it's no longer detectable."

"What do you mean, *no longer detectable?*"

"Just that. So far as I can tell, physics does not provide a way to detect it." She made another adjustment at her station.

"There it is again," Brad said. "What did you do?"

"Our MERT Drive leapfrogs nodes in the direction of travel. I had an idea and tried moving a node back instead of forward. Back and forth, actually."

"And…"

"Well, you saw it. The model disappeared, so to speak. Actually, it entered a nullspace loop, remaining in one place physically but in nullspace." She smiled again, this time covering her mouth. "Brad, do you remember the Romulan cloaking device in the historic *Star Trek Television Series?*"

Brad nodded.

"The Federation couldn't figure out how they accomplished it. For decades after the program disappeared, researchers worked on bending light around objects, effectively *cloaking* them. Nobody ever really pulled it off." She smiled again, more broadly than before. "Well, my love, we just figured it out!"

INTERSTELLAR SPACE—ONE AU BEYOND OS PRIME

First, however, they brought the project to Dr. Fredricks. He didn't have much to say. In hindsight, it seemed so obvious, according to Sally.

"We should have seen this possibility right from the beginning," she said.

"Not necessarily," Fredricks said. "You two were looking at how to move forward. As obvious as it seems in hindsight, doing it that way would not have been very logical. It would not have moved your research in the right direction."

"I take your point, Dr. Fredricks," Brad said, "but Sally doesn't like to miss things." He put his arm around her protectively.

"I'll inform eThorpe while you two install the modification into *Ad Astra* for a real-time test."

❈

The next day, Fredricks and eThorpe were in the control center of OS Prime monitoring the EPD. Sally and Brad were inside *Ad Astra* along with matrixes for eSally and eBrad. They had already run a couple of visual tests alongside OS Prime—basically switching their drive into nullspace loop mode and back out. Visually, *Ad Astra* disappeared.

"Is everybody ready?" eThorpe asked. He was still feeling the satisfaction of knowing that this research team was equal to none. He thought back to their recruitment. *Two young hotshot Mines research postdocs with virtually no knowledge of the outside world—Jackson found them, I hired them, and they changed the world, not once but several times!* "Okay then, let's do this!" eThorpe grinned broadly. "And keep the portal open…"

Ad Astra vanished as Sally and Brad jumped her out one AU. A moment later, 0.075 seconds to be exact, eThorpe reminded himself, Brad announced, "We're ready to do the test."

eThorpe and Fredricks kept their eyes on the EPD. When *Ad Astra* entered nullspace, she disappeared from the display. When she exited nullspace one AU out, the sweep of entangled neutrinos instantly generated a display in OS Prime.

"Entering nullspace loop," Brad said.

The EPD showed nothing at their location.

"Turning it off," Brad said.

The EPD displayed the *Ad Astra* again.

"Once more," Brad said.

Same results.

"Okay, you guys," eThorpe said. "Take her five AUs out."

Following the 0.3 second jump, Brad announced their arrival. He and Sally entered nullspace loop mode twice with identical results. The *Ad Astra* disappeared on the EPD and reappeared when they terminated the loop.

"One more test," eThorpe said, "this time at one lightyear."

One hour and nineteen minutes later, Sally announced, "We're here." She giggled. "Brad is taking a nap, so I'm in charge."

The test was successful. Sally and Brad brought *Ad Astra* home and set about installing the modification into all the Double-MBH ships.

OORT STATION PRIME—CHAIRMAN JOHN BUTLER'S OFFICE

"Do you remember when we first met?" She nodded. "I was a newly inaugurated president, and you found your way into my inner sanctum, young, beautiful, and mature way beyond your years." He smiled warmly. "We changed the world, you and I." He sighed. "Such was not my intent, but Thorpe…Thorpe opened doors…no, a Pandora's box, that could never again be closed." He leaned back. "Somehow, through all this, you stood by my side, kept me moving in the right direction." He stood and walked around the desk. "And now look at us." He reached out, and Kimberly rose and entered his arms.

✳

eThorpe passed briefly through Butler's office but didn't want to interrupt their obviously private moment. When they separated and resumed their places, he made his entrance.

"Chairman, Kimberly," eThorpe said, acknowledging them more formally than usual. "You requested to speak with me personally." This directed at Butler.

"I did, and if you have no objections, I would like to include Kimberly."

"No problem. She's…" He turned and looked at Kimberly. "You have been part of everything from the beginning." eThorpe's holoimage appeared to take a seat opposite Kimberly.

Glancing briefly at eMax, who was curled up on the corner of his desk, Butler picked up the conversation. "We are about to embark on humanity's most significant undertaking, crossing the interstellar void to visit two worlds populated with living, breathing, sentient beings who apparently hold no love for us. I have always assumed that this mission would be a Federation mission—an official mission empowered by the Federation Council, representing humanity, including the Oort among us. Lately, I have gotten the sense that you and I see this differently." Butler stopped talking and indicated that eThorpe had the floor.

"You are correct, John. I see this mission as a Phoenix mission, conceived by us, financed by us, and run by us. I would be happy to bring Federation representatives with us, but they would be subject to my command and would carry no official capacity in the expedition. I would facilitate a Federation representative's efforts to establish diplomatic relations with the Asterians and would provide protection should that become necessary. But Phoenix would not be part of the diplomatic process. And furthermore, should I decide that the Federation rep is working against Phoenix's interest, I would not hesitate to interrupt the process."

"We really are on different wavelengths," Butler said. "That's pretty obvious." He shook his head. "I have been in government virtually all my adult life. My instinct is to let government take the lead, or at least to include government in the process. You seem to be excluding government altogether, despite how well you and I have worked together all these years." He held his hand out, aware he was pleading. "Is there any room for compromise?"

"That depends," Thorpe said, smiling at his old friend. "*I* will be the mission commander. That is not open to discussion. You have known me for a long time. You know that I will not be arbitrary in my command. If you wish to send a security contingent, I will gladly accommodate that. Personally, I think you should keep Culp here to help protect you and the Council. I would recommend putting Sam Bunker in charge of the security contingent. Since he's not commissioned, I would suggest you offer him a commission as a lieutenant commander in the FeSFo. I will distribute his people across my ships, with Sam riding my flagship.

"The bottom line is, however, that Federation jurisdiction stops at the edge of the Oort Cloud. I will be leading an expedition into the unknown. I will carry the responsibility for that and share it with no one else."

"I understand," Butler said, disappointment clouding his voice. "I disagree, but I understand."

KUIPER BELT—NEW KUIPER JOINT STATION—PHOENIX COMPLEX

"Since I awoke in my electronic matrix what seems so very long ago now, humanity and the Solar System have changed dramatically. For one, we are no longer just humans, but humans and Oort, and even though the Oort make up a small percentage of our numbers, the Oort and their existence have significantly contributed to where we all are today. For another, the very structure of human society has changed permanently. Earth still has numerous nation-states, and people still pledge allegiance to these states, but virtually all of us now see ourselves as part of a much greater whole—the Federation.

"I was privileged to lead the Federation during its inception, and I could not be more thankful for the wise leadership Chairman John Butler has given the Federation since I stepped down. Because of the very nature of my personal existence, and coincidentally that of eBraxton as well, I have learned how much greater life can be than just normal flesh-and-blood life. My colleagues, Daphne O'Bryan and Kimberly Deveraux, created a way for everyone who wishes to experience what amounts to eternal life. In the long run, this means that even our expanded living space that now includes a terraformed Mars will eventually become limited.

"We are about to take the first faltering steps on an endless journey. Some of us will return. Some of us will stop somewhere along the way to carve out new homes, and some of us will continue into the vast unknown that lies before us. What makes things different than ever before is unlimited options.

"We don't know what lies ahead. Many of you have volunteered, but we have limited room on this first expedition. There will be others, and, if possible, we will open portals between the Aster system and ours so that anyone who wishes can join us.

"The crew assignments are posted on the common Link. We will be launching ten starships. Each ship will be commanded by an upload like myself, with his or her flesh-and-blood counterpart as the physical command presence. Each vessel will also carry three crew members and two security force personnel. The security force personnel will be under the command of FeSFo Lieutenant Commander Sam

Bunker—Congratulations, Sam, on your promotion. I will be in overall command of the expedition. Commander Bunker will ride the starship commanded by eSam but will report to me as head of security.

"Now, this is important, and I want you to understand this. As citizens of the Federation, all of you—except perhaps the FeSFo guys—have lived under a degree of personal freedom that is unprecedented in human history. You all volunteered to join this expedition. Those of you who have been chosen are giving up some of those freedoms. Ships at sea in ancient times and starships today have one thing in common. The ultimate safety of ship and crew depends on the capability, skill, and judgment of the commander. I am the mission commander. For the duration of the expedition, I will be an absolute dictator; if you choose to participate, you place yourself under my command. Furthermore, each starship has a commander. That individual plays the same role on his or her vessel. I can assure you that it is highly unlikely any of us will misuse this power, but should that ever happen, the mission regs that each of you has received through your Links provide procedures for removing such an individual from command.

"If any one of you are unwilling to place yourself in this position, now is the time to remove yourself from the expedition. Your deploying with the expedition is your explicit acceptance of this."

eThorpe waited quietly for his information to penetrate everyone in the Great Hall.

"Okay, then," he said at last. "The ships that make up the fleet are: *PS Ad Astra* commanded by myself, eThorpe; *PS Neil Armstrong*, commanded by eBraxton; *PS Buzz Aldrin*, commanded by eSam; *PS Pete Conrad*, commanded by eDaphne; *PS Michael Collins*, commanded by eKim; *PS Alan Bean*, commanded by eDale; *PS David Scott*, commanded by eBrad; *PS Edgar Mitchell*, commanded by eSally; *PS Alan Shepard*, commanded by eBork; and *PS James Irwin*, commanded by eJohnny, who doesn't exist yet."

✳

Johnny Ortman sat with Daphne, Kimberly, and Dale in their condo kitchen. The girls were enjoying a Merlot, while Dale handed a beer to Johnny and took one for himself.

"eThorpe assigned the *Irwin* to eJohnny, but I do not presently have an active upload, only my continuous backup. Do you," Johnny glanced from Daphne to Kimberly, "have any policies regarding creating an independent upload?" He took a sip of his coffee. "You three have uploads, artifacts from your original experiments."

"What do you mean, *artifacts?*" eDaphne's holoimage said as it suddenly appeared.

"Yeah," from eKim's upload.

"Agree," from eDale's.

"Okay, guys, you know what I mean." Johnny chuckled, enjoying the repartee with his friends. "Everyone but Bork and me has an independent upload, and obviously, eThorpe wants me to have an upload, too. I think we will need them for the expedition."

"You will, of course," Daphne said. "Let's go do it."

Kimberly piped up, "Daphne, wait a moment." She looked at Dale. "Dale, you and Johnny go ahead. We'll catch up."

When they were alone, Kimberly slid her chair close to Daphne's and put her arms around her. She whispered in Daphne's ear, "You know how much I love you."

Daphne nodded. "And John Butler," she said softly, "in a different way, but you love him too."

Kimberly blew in her ear. "I've made a decision." She pulled back so she could look into Daphne's eyes. "I'm going to clone myself just for John." She smiled hesitatingly. "I…me…this me…I'm going to Aster with you and the others." She smiled hesitatingly again. "My clone will stay to be with John—First Lady of the Federation, I guess." She kissed Daphne deeply. "It's just something I have to do."

"What about Braxton and eBraxton?" Daphne asked.

"I know. I will simply have to work it out somehow."

✻

Thorpe and Braxton sat in their sparsely furnished office in Nanedi City. eThorpe and eBraxton were present as holoimages. Outside, the dome still covered the city, but it was open to the Martian atmosphere at several locations around the dome.

"Amazing job you guys did," eThorpe said.

"Concur," eBraxton added. "Couldn't have done better myself."

"So, you guys are done here," eThorpe said.

"Several million people live here now," Thorpe said. "They maintain what little atmospheric mod requirements still remain. We have our office here because we have to be somewhere, and this is where we've been for a long time already."

"But we're ready to move on," Braxton said, "and it looks like you two anticipated our needs perfectly."

"Yeah," eThorpe said, "but just as when eBraxton and I started traveling separate paths, when you two split from us, your path diverged. I can make a well-educated guess about your wishes, but… well, you know what I mean."

"Bottom line…" Thorpe said.

"We're going to Aster with you…" Braxton finished.

CHAPTER NINETEEN

ASTER SYSTEM—ROGAN

"First things first," Gloalorn said. "We need to test the hyper-disk range."

"I've been thinking," Arcah said. "There is little chance we'll operate outside the Aster Asteroid Belt. I'm fully confident the hyper-disks will operate out at least that far. I think we can forgo the test."

"Makes sense," Gloalorn said.

From space, Rogan looked much like Earth—three interconnected water bodies and three major landmasses. Arcah had already selected a hyper-disk landing spot on the largest landmass near a large city and a mountain range, in a forested area he knew well.

When they were ready to drop the hyper-disk, Gloalorn brought *Titov* on a fast fly-by to an altitude of 1,000 kilometers over the drop zone and released the package. Then he set course for the Rogan-moon L2 point. Arcah occupied the second chair at the console. His long-range radar flashed.

"Hold it!" Arcah said. "We need to warp out immediately to regroup."

Gloalorn complied, and then they both analyzed what Arcah had seen.

"It looks like the Roganians have an active station at L2," Arcah said. "I got a lidar scan before you jumped." He brought it up on the monitor, wondering what they would see.

"That's a pretty large station," Gloalorn said. "That's gotta be at least a klick across."

"It wasn't there when we left before the invasion," Arcah said. "It's what humans call a Von Braun Station."

"Do you think it's weaponized?"

"No clue. Probably, given our and your history." Arcah increased the magnification of the lidar display. "Adrhun, this looks like a large commercial undertaking. Look at the outer ring modules. It's difficult to make out, but I think I can see individual labels or maybe logos."

"Should we try to contact them?" Gloalorn asked.

"It's not what we planned, but perhaps we should." Arcah flashed back over everything that had happened since he and Gloalorn were captured. "I guess we need to come to grips with the fact that a lot of time has passed here and on Frohlic since we left," he said. With an almost human sigh, he added, "Let's initiate contact."

"These are your people. You had better do it," Gloalorn said.

Since they had no idea how modern Roganians communicated in space, Arcah set up the transmitter to cover the entire communication band in all modes, but focused narrowly on only the space station. Nobody except possible groundside locations beneath the space station would receive the broadcast. Speaking Roganian, he transmitted, "This is *Udachny Starship Gherman Titov* calling the Roganian space station at the Rogan-moon L2 location." He used the appropriate Roganian names for the moon and the L2 spot. "We pose no threat. I repeat, we pose no threat. Please respond on any channel. We will then answer on that channel."

There followed ten very long minutes of silence. Then, "This is the *Damvet Space Station* at Rogan-moon L2 responding. Please identify yourself again."

Arcah was about to respond when Gloalorn said, "Wait! Let's warp to a new location, just in case their intentions are hostile."

"Smart," Arcah mumbled while Gloalorn made the short jump.

"*Damvet Space Station*, this is *Udachny Starship Gherman Titov*. We pose no threat. We have no hostile intent. I wish to speak with the person in charge."

"Roger, this is *Damvet Space Station*. In charge of what?"

Arcah grinned to himself. *Yep, these guys are definitely Roganian.* "This is *Titov*. I wish to speak with the person running the largest commercial element at *Damvet*."

Gloalorn looked at Arcah quizzically. Arcah pursed his lips at him. "This part of Rogan hasn't changed a bit," he said.

"That would be Holon Mavik. He runs the L2 Group. Stand by, please."

Arcah could imagine the scramble within the walls of the revolving tubes as his fellow Roganians tried to figure out what was afoot.

"This is Holon Mavik of the L2 Group. And you are?"

"Friendship, Holon Mavik. I am Lieutenant Commander Masin Arcah, pilot of Asterian Starfighter 3,521. I was part of the invasion force Rogan and Frohlic sent to the Sol system ninety years ago to exact revenge against the Oort."

"Adrhun, make another short jump," Arcah said.

"Friendship, Commander Arcah. How is it you are here a mere six years after you should have arrived at Sol?"

"Jump," Arcah said, "and make the jumps random in direction and distance."

"That explanation is for a face-to-face conversation," Arcah said.

"This is *Damvet Space Station*. Please stand by while we check our records."

Several minutes later, *Damvet* called again. "This is *Damvet Space Station*. We do not understand how you can be here, Commander Arcah. Please indulge my asking some personal questions."

"Friendship, Holon Mavik, I understand."

Mavik then asked a series of questions about Arcah's past, family, and associations. When he had finished, Arcah transmitted, "Again, I tell you that we are no threat. We need to establish some level of trust for us to move forward. Do you have shuttlecraft?"

"We do."

"Are these shuttlecraft powered by mini-black holes like our starfighters?"

"They are."

"Very well, then," Arcah said. "Are you willing to send a shuttlecraft to a specific set of coordinates where we can meet? I will board your shuttlecraft and return to *Damvet*, where we can meet face to face."

"Stand by, please."

Several minutes passed before *Damvet* called again. "A shuttlecraft will meet you. It will be unarmed. Commander Arcah will exit *Titov* and be unarmed. The shuttlecraft will retrieve him and return to *Damvet*."

Arcah transmitted back, "This is acceptable. Here are the coordinates."

✳

"I'm standing by," Arcah said as he floated outside *Titov's* airlock. "The moment he shows, warp out of here. I should be okay, but I don't want anything to happen to you or *Titov*. I have a hyper-disk and my E-disk, so if things get dicey, I can return almost instantly."

Moments later, the shuttlecraft appeared. It was about a quarter the size of Arcah's original starfighter. He could not see any weapons. Behind him, *Titov* warped away, and an airlock opened in the upper half of the double-saucer-shaped craft. Arcah used his TBH boots to approach the open hatch and slowly drifted inside, where artificial gravity immediately took over. The outer hatch closed, and the inner hatch opened as Arcah removed his transparent helmet.

The pilot was alone. "I'm Dvra Okai," he said.

"And I am Masin Arcah."

"I know who you are." Okai sounded excited to Arcah. "Delighted to meet you!"

A few minutes later, Arcah, still suited up but with helmet clipped to his belt, entered *Damvet Space Station* and met Holon Mavik.

"How many directors are on *Damvet*?" Arcah asked.

"Thirty of us altogether, but only five matter, including me."

"What I have to say will affect all of Rogan," Arcah said. "I think we should have at least you five present before I commence my story."

"If you believe that's how to proceed, may I suggest you remove your spacesuit and make yourself comfortable? I'll gather the others." He signaled, and someone brought cool drinks and set them on the table. Mavik left the room, and Arcah settled down and gathered his thoughts.

After several minutes, Mavik returned with four others, two males and two females, all in their middle years but physically fit and well-dressed.

"Ninety years ago," Arcah commenced, "clearly before any of you were born, we and Frohlic set out on a mission that had been in planning for more than a thousand years. Five thousand armed mini-black hole starships set out for the star Sol," he used the Roganian name, "to exact revenge for something that happened so long ago that nobody really knew or knows the true facts of that distant event.

"We split up our invasion forces to approach their Oort Cloud from several directions at once. To our utter surprise, when we arrived at the outer limits of their Oort Cloud, hundreds, perhaps thousands of our warships were missing. It turned out that they had destroyed them without our knowledge during our transit. To make matters worse, the beings who lived in that system were waiting for us. They call themselves *human* as we do, so to avoid confusion, I'll refer to them as humans and to us as either Roganians and Frohlicans or collectively as Asterians. We commenced our attack with our remaining forces but were badly mauled even before we could penetrate their inner system.

"When it was all said and done, the humans had destroyed every one of our attacking starfighters with the exception of one vessel that escaped and is transiting back to Aster and should arrive in another seventy-nine years or so, and my own warship. A Frohlican named Adrhun Gloalorn managed to survive the destruction of his warship. He and I were taken captive.

"The humans did not have our mini-black hole technology, but they had developed a way to create and control wormholes that resulted in a transportation grid in their system that seems like teleportation, although technically it is actually stepping through wormholes. They also developed FTL technology based on their wormhole research.

"They reverse engineered our craft and have incorporated mini-black hole technology with their wormhole technology that has resulted in spacecraft with every bit of our capability but also FTL travel. Furthermore, a competing human endeavor developed an entirely different method of FTL travel, which I used to get here from Sol in a bit over six days. My Frohlican friend currently is piloting that spacecraft somewhere in the Aster system, moving randomly to avoid any possible military strike against his craft.

"You have got to be asking yourselves how and why Adrhun Gloalorn and I are here. Well, we were captured, imprisoned, but treated well throughout, and eventually, we were given a tour of human society covering many Earth cities (Earth is what they call their planet). After that, we were released, supplied with the wherewithal to exist on our own, and when the time came, were offered a role in the human expedition to Aster.

"It's difficult to understand people who have accomplished more technologically in three hundred years that we have in three thousand, and more than the Frohlicans have in ten thousand. One thing is for certain; if it were to come to conflict between our peoples, they would drive us back into the stone age or obliterate us entirely—as we tried to do to them.

"I'm here to pave the way, to ensure that humans and Roganians meet each other as equals, and that we move forward together in cooperation." He stopped talking, looked at the five, and asked for questions.

"Why should we believe you?" one of the females asked. "Other than your presence, you show us no proof. Everything we have seen from you could easily have been faked using one of our mini-black hole vessels."

"She makes a valid point," Mavik said. "What you say is too fantastic to take at face value without some in-hand proof."

"Your points are valid," Arcah said and activated his E-disk.

❋

"What happened?" Gloalorn asked as Arcah appeared in the *Titov* control center.

"They pointed out—and rightly so—that I offered no proof of my assertions." Arcah activated the comms.

"*Damvet Space Station*, this is *Udachny Starship Gherman Titov*, Masin Arcah transmitting. Please connect me with Holon Mavik."

Two minutes later, Mavik responded, "This is Mavik. To where did you go, and from where are you transmitting?"

"Friendship, Holon Mavik. This is Arcah. I outlined to your group the humans' wormhole transportation capability. I used an emergency escape mode to return to our ship. To complete my demonstration, may I request that you send your shuttlecraft to the following coordinates. I will be waiting there for the craft's arrival. Perhaps, after that, we can resume our conversation without confrontation."

✸

Mavik and Arcah took seats at the same table, and Mavik told the other four, "The coordinates where we picked Arcah up are a full AU distant, nearly ten light minutes. I am entirely convinced that our guest transited that distance superluminally. Remember, he contacted us less than eleven minutes following his departure. Light would have taken about twenty minutes out and back, plus any delays at that end. Obviously, he covered the outward distance in no time flat, and then lightspeed consumed the remaining time."

"I still don't believe him," the female who had protested earlier said. "I'm out of here." She rose to her feet.

"Would you indulge me for another couple of minutes?" Arcah asked her.

She grunted her acquiescence.

Arcah removed a hyper-disk from an inner pocket. "We call this a *hyper-disk*," he said, using a transliterated Roganian term. "It opens what we call a MERT Portal from anywhere within range to the node controlling the portal."

He activated the portal causing a door to appear in the room next to him. "On the other side of this door is the control center of *Titov*." Arcah stepped through. "Please follow me."

Mavik stepped through, followed by the second female, the two men, and finally, the objecting female. They floated in the control center air.

"I suppose I could have somehow rigged everything to appear like this, but the simple fact is, you just entered my starship located one AU out from Rogan's moon in Aster's ecliptic." He turned to

Gloalorn. "May I introduce Adrhun Gloalorn, of Frohlic, the other half of our team."

The Roganians exchanged awkward greetings with Gloalorn.

"Adrhun," Arcah said, "would you please move the ship to within several hundred meters of *Damvet Space Station*?" To Mavik, he said, "How close can we come without alarming your AI systems?"

"Five hundred meters," Mavik answered.

"Make it so, Gloalorn," Arcah said.

Moments later, *Damvet Space Station* floated ahead of *Titov*, rotating majestically above Rogan's moon.

"Shall we return to *Damvet*," Arcah asked, sweeping his arms toward the portal, "and negotiate some serious preliminary groundwork for the humans' arrival? Watch the gravity shift as you enter the station."

ASTER SYSTEM—FROHLIC

"That's really tough to answer," Arcah said. "Roganians are an independent lot. Even if Holon Mavik broadcasts to the entire planet that he trusts me and is willing to welcome the human arrival, that guarantees nothing. Roganians do not turn to violence easily, but Mavik has his task cut out for him. The average Roganian will see the human arrival as a challenge."

"I didn't expect the Rogan conversation to be resolved so quickly," Gloalorn said as he set course for Frohlic. "Let's see if Frohlic has an L2 station."

As *Titov* approached Frohlic and its moon, Gloalorn set her on an orbital path that swept past the planet's equator. Arcah scanned for any LEO stations.

"Nothing I can find," he said, "but one pass will not necessarily reveal everything." He glanced back at the moon, "Whoa…what's that?"

"Looks like a major development on the moon's surface." Gloalorn warped to a point in Frohlic's orbit, leading Frohlic by a tenth AU. "Let's try what we did at Rogan," he said. "You take the controls."

Gloalorn transmitted, "This is *Udachny Starship Gherman Titov* calling the Frohlican station on the planet side of the Frohlican moon."

He used the appropriate Frohlican name for the moon. "We pose no threat. I repeat, we pose no threat. Please respond on any channel. We will then answer on that channel."

Unlike near Rogan, the response from Frohlic's moon was almost immediate.

"*Udachny Starship Gherman Titov*, this is *Frohlic Military Outpost One*. We have you locked into our long-range laser. You will heave-to and stand by for boarders. If you do not heed this order, we will blow you out of the sky."

Arcah warped to the mirror spot of their position trailing in Frohlic's orbit.

"This is *Udachny Starship Gherman Titov* calling *Frohlic Military Outpost One*. We pose no threat. I repeat, we pose no threat. Do not fire upon us…do not fire upon us. If you do, we will retaliate."

Their response was a laser bolt that passed through where *Titov* had just been.

Arcah warped back to their original position leading Frohlic in its orbit. "Adrhun, see if you can identify a spaceship at that base."

Gloalorn manipulated the lidar and then pointed at their holodisplay. "That looks like a spaceship to me," he said, indicating a saucer-shaped vessel.

"Can we hit it with our laser?" Arcah asked.

"We can try," Gloalorn said, instructing the resident computer to make the shot.

Gloalorn fired the laser, and Arcah immediately warped to the second location, less several thousand kilometers.

"Don't want to give them a repeat location to target," he said.

They watched the vessel collapse on their lidar display two minutes later as the beam crossed the distance and the image returned.

"*Frohlic Military Outpost One*, this is *Udachny Starship Gherman Titov*. What is it you don't understand about *We pose no threat*? We warned you not to fire upon us. If you fire again, we will destroy your central building."

Arcah warped to the mirror of their present location.

"*Udachny Starship Gherman Titov* is superluminal. We know about your acceleration, maneuvering, and speed capabilities.

Despite that, because we are superluminal, you cannot outfight us. We do not wish to fight you. Let us find a way to move beyond our present situation."

"This is *Frohlic Military Outpost One*. We are willing to meet with your representative under a temporary truce. Please send a lander carrying your representative to the landing tarmac at *Frohlic Military Outpost One*."

"This is *Udachny Starship Gherman Titov*. We will not do that; however, we will meet one of your shuttlecraft at these coordinates where you can take our representative onboard. Be warned that if you fire at our rep or the *Titov*, we will immediately destroy your entire station."

"This is *Frohlic Military Outpost One*. Our shuttlecraft will rendezvous at the coordinates you supplied in one hour."

"Will they call our bluff?" Arcah asked.

"Frohlicans don't gamble, Masin. I should be okay."

✴

The Frohlican shuttlecraft was visually identical to the Roganian craft. Two minutes before it arrived, Arcah warped *Titov* to a safe location, leaving the spacesuited Gloalorn floating in the void at the rendezvous point.

"Where is *Udachny Starship Gherman Titov*?" the shuttlecraft demanded when it arrived.

Gloalorn responded, "Observing us from a secure location."

The shuttle airlock outer hatch opened, disgorging two armed, spacesuited figures. Gloalorn could see a third inside the airlock. He moved toward them with his TBH boots, arms outstretched and hands open.

"I am unarmed," Gloalorn said. "If *Titov* were to attack the shuttle now, I would die alongside you, so you can relax. You are safe." He pursed his lips, the Asterian equivalent of a human smile.

They escorted him into the lock, where artificial gravity immediately took effect. They pressurized the lock, and when the inner hatch opened, they escorted Gloalorn into the shuttlecraft. Gloalorn removed his transparent helmet and addressed the Frohlican who was obviously in charge.

"I am Lieutenant Commander Adrhun Gloalorn, pilot of Asterian Starfighter 4,732, sent to attack the Sol system," he used the Frohlican term for the Solar System's star, Sol, "over ninety years ago." Gloalorn recognized the officer's insignia, the equivalent of a FeSFo lieutenant. Gloalorn came to attention. "Lieutenant, you will render proper military courtesy!"

The uniformed Frohlican snapped to attention and placed his right forearm horizontally across his chest. Gloalorn returned the salute.

"Now, take me to your commander."

✳

Gloalorn recognized the base commander's rank insignia as Captain, equivalent to a FeSFo Captain. He outranked Gloalorn by two levels, but Gloalorn saw himself as representing an entire civilization. Nevertheless, he came to attention and saluted, right arm horizontally across his chest.

"Lieutenant Commander Adrhun Gloalorn, pilot of Asterian Starfighter 4,732."

"Captain Botex Ravnan, Commander of *Frohlic Military Outpost One*." The commander returned Gloalorn's salute.

"We need to speak privately, Captain."

✳

In the commander's private quarters, Gloalorn provided Capt. Ravnan with essentially the same story that Arcah had given the Roganians. As he finished up, he said, "The human fleet will be arriving soon. It is not on a mission of revenge, although their vessels are fully armed with weapons that are well beyond our own capabilities. They are not trained military fighters, but their commander is brilliant beyond anyone I have ever met." Gloalorn stood up. "I need to meet with the Boss as soon as you can possibly arrange it. I gave you the courtesy of a detailed explanation because my first contact has been with you, but now I need to move on."

Ravnan stood up. "Security!" he shouted. "I'm afraid that won't be possible, Commander. You are under arrest for treason and collaboration with the enemy!"

Gloalorn activated his E-disk.

✳

"What happened?" Arcah asked.

"The base commander tried to arrest me for treason."

"Treason?"

"Yeah, and collaboration with the enemy."

"What do you want to do?" Arcah asked. "We can't handle a fleet of their starfighters coming after us."

"I think that we should take out all their spacecraft from our extreme range…and we better do it quickly. They have no idea what just happened, and they will be scrambling to get spaceborne ASAP."

"How do you think we should do that?" Arcah asked.

"Let's examine the lidar image of the base, identify what we think are spacecraft, and direct the resident to take them out by laser."

"Makes sense," Arcah said. "I'm on it. You better join me if we're going to do this before the spacecraft leave." He turned to the console. "I'll set the resident to jump following each laser bolt."

Flash…Jump!

Flash…Jump!

Flash…Jump!

They took out ten parked spacecraft at *Military Outpost One.*

"We missed two of them," Arcah said. "Once they lifted off the tarmac, they were gone." He sighed. "Now what?"

"If they find us, we're toast. We need to continue skipping around the Aster system while finding a way to contact the Boss."

"We need to get their attention without exposing ourselves to their military power," Arcah said thoughtfully. "How about this?

"We broadcast our intention to drop a small, benign package into the government executive complex. Then we drop a hyper-disk package. If they destroy it—as they well might—we signal that we wish to drop another, requesting that they not destroy it."

"Naw, they will destroy any package we drop," Gloalorn said. "That's how they think."

"Do you have any family on Frohlic?"

"Living grandnephews and nieces, I think."

"Can we communicate with them?"

"Frohlic had a planetwide communication system similar to Earth's GlobalNet," Gloalorn said. "If anything, it's even better now."

"Can we tap into it?" Arcah asked.

After nearly two hours while Arcah made continuous random jumps throughout the inner Aster system, Gloalorn announced, "I think I have a stable connection to Frohlic's net." A few minutes later, he said, "I reached my grandnephew Zantag Gloalorn."

Their arrangement was simple. *Titov* dropped a hyper-disk in a secluded location. Zantag retrieved it, and Gloalorn activated the portal and joined his grandnephew. Zantag was a mid-level bureaucrat in the Frohlican system. He listened to Gloalorn's story and agreed to pass a hyper-disk to his superior, who passed it on, moving it up the stack until it reached the Boss's desk the following afternoon. Gloalorn activated and stepped through the portal, coming face to face with the Boss behind a transparent shield. Seven tough military types were pointing seven weapons at him.

"You went to a lot of trouble to arrange this meeting with me, Commander Gloalorn. You angered many people, including the *Military Outpost One* commander who wants your hide in a frame on his wall. What's so important that you went to all this trouble?"

"How much time do I have?"

"Be brief. I'm a busy man."

Gloalorn outlined the situation to the Boss. When he finished, he added, "The humans are coming with outstretched hands. They seek to learn and to trade. They harbor no vengeance for our attack on their system, but they are prepared to counter violence with a level of force you cannot begin to imagine.

"Captain Ravnan accused me of treason and attempted to arrest me for collaborating with the enemy. That is his completely wrong take on this situation. I am standing here, pleading for the future of our culture and our race."

"Arrest Commander Gloalorn!" the Boss ordered.

As three of the armed troopers approached him, Gloalorn activated his E-disk.

KUIPER BELT—UDACHNY

Orlov contacted Randy Nelson by Link. "I need you and your people at Udachny before day's end." He turned to Borisovich. "Load up as if we were getting underway for Aster. As soon as we are loaded, we'll undertake the shakedown and then depart immediately for Aster."

The loadout of supplies, spares, and food took three days. Nelson and his people worked alongside Orlov's crew. Orlov wanted the Oort individuals along for whatever knowledge they might be able to supply about the Asterians and as a backup to Borisovich and his technical crew. They had a bone to pick with Phoenix and the Federation. That was valuable to him.

Orlov assigned seven-person crews for each vessel—the commander, a tech, an Oort, and four other individuals. He distributed the sixteen Oort, one to each ship with Nelson and another Oort on his flagship, *Udachnyy Zvezdolet Sergei Krikalyov* (*Udachny Starship Sergei Krikalyov*). Orlov took the controls during *Sergei Krikalyov's* shakedown cruise but kept Nelson close by so that Nelson could learn to pilot and fight the craft. Each of his fourteen ship commanders operated their own vessels. The entire fleet operated in a loose formation. Orlov took the fleet vertically out of the ecliptic for an hour on VASIMRs at one-gee. Then the ships shut down their VASIMRs and shifted to warp drive. Inside the starships, the only thing that changed was the loss of gravity when the VASIMRs shut down.

Orlov pushed ahead for two hours, varying from 1.0 to 4.7, the maximum available from the new LANRs. For two hours, he had the fleet work warp factor through the available range several times, ranging from lightspeed to 5,012 times lightspeed and back. He dropped out of warp 500 AU from the new Udachny Station at the inner boundary of the Oort Cloud.

Orlov transmitted to his small fleet, "Now let's test our sensing, acquisition, and weapons systems."

For the next hour, Orlov (Nelson, actually) and each ship commander detected, tracked, and destroyed several nearby proto-comets using their lasers out to a range of nearly a million kilometers and zapping detected objects at 500 thousand kilometers with their particle beams.

Satisfied with the shakedown, Orlov turned his fleet back to Udachny. "Take three hours to top off your fuel and onload any other needed supplies," he ordered his commanders.

SOLAR SYSTEM—VARIOUS LOCATIONS

"What are you talking about?" Johnny asked, wondering all the while how someone could have found out.

"No time for long explanations right now. I want to send you a packet of vital information related to the Aster expeditions. It's for your eyes only. Once things are underway, and you will know when that is, you can discuss it with anyone you believe should know." The caller paused. "Are these terms acceptable to you?"

Johnny acknowledged, and a minute later, his Link informed him that he had an encrypted package waiting for him. As quickly as he could manage, Johnny passed through the Los Angeles condo and on to the apartment Ogden had set up for him at the New Joint Station. He settled himself comfortably in an easy chair, grabbed a beer, and called up the encrypted package.

A holoimage of a nondescript human figure appeared before him. He couldn't tell if it was of a real person or just a digitally created image.

"My name is unimportant, and the image you see is not my actual image. I know that you were instrumental in revealing the terrible Oort secret to the humans. I believe that had you not done that, it would ultimately have destroyed us. I am one of sixteen Oort who managed to keep in touch after we downloaded so that we were able to find one another again. We are led by Randy Nelson, who arranged with Isidor Orlov for us sixteen to be part of his expedition to Aster. Our intent is to find a way to commandeer one of his vessels near Aster and to strike out on our own. We are eight males and eight females, so we think we can be viable, even with our limited gene pool. All this we can and will do without your input.

"My colleagues do not know I am doing this, and I would not, except for what I have discovered about Udachny. Orlov's intent in the Aster system is hostile. He intends to take over Frohlic, by force if necessary. That was not part of the deal we made with Orlov. We agreed to supply him with crew bodies and information not available to him from any other source in exchange for the opportunity to strike out on our own.

"We have loaded out, completed a shakedown cruise, topped everything off, and are ready to depart for Aster from the new Udachny location in the Kuiper Belt. I do not know the location, sorry."

"Your name," Johnny transmitted back, "please give me your name."

"Gerald. Gerald Saxon."

KUIPER BELT—NEW KUIPER JOINT STATION

"Thorpe and Braxton, would you remain for a few minutes, please?"

eThorpe and eBraxton huddled with Thorpe and Braxton in a nearby room. "The alien ship that departed the Solar System five years ago is five-eighty-fourths of the distance along his track—give or take some fourth decimal-place variation," eThorpe said.

"He will be in his two-point-seventh subjective day of a forty-four-point-nine-subjective-day trip," eBraxton added. "You and I," he indicated Braxton, "are going to intercept this guy. I will immediately drop into my matrix on *Armstrong* and commence working with Mother to pinpoint his location. Braxton, round up the rest of our crew and get them onboard. We'll depart as soon as they are ready."

CHAPTER TWENTY

INTERSTELLAR SPACE—*PS NEIL ARMSTRONG*

"We will arrive in the vicinity of the Asterian vessel in about six and a half hours. Until we break out of nullspace, there is nothing we can do to prepare ourselves except perhaps refresh our knowledge of the EPD system."

Six and a half hours later, Mother dropped *Armstrong* out of nullspace. As prearranged with eBraxton, Braxton took his place at the console.

"Okay, Mother, broadcast four spheres of entangled neutrinos."

Mother complied.

"Okay, drop back a tenth of a lightyear."

Mother turned *Armstrong* 180 degrees and dropped back.

"Now, broadcast four more spheres of entangled neutrinos."

Braxton did this a third time. Seconds following the broadcast, the EPD alarmed.

"Locate and bring us alongside with matching speed," Braxton ordered.

Ten minutes later, *Armstrong* was moving at 99.9, followed by five 9s, percent of lightspeed, 200 meters off the starboard side of the Asterian craft.

✳

eBraxton assumed control of *Armstrong* at this point. Working internally and directly with Mother, he set *Armstrong's* neutrino beam to a narrow focus aimed to strike the Asterian vessel's MBH power diverter. Simultaneously, he activated the neutrino beam and stopped *Armstrong's* proper motion through space. Both spacecraft came to a complete stop without affecting anything in either vessel. eBraxton moved *Armstrong* to within twenty meters of the Asterian ship while Braxton suited up and armed himself with an EMD stun weapon.

"I've got a hyper-disk and my E-disk in case something goes wrong," Braxton said as he entered the airlock.

Braxton pushed off from the lip of *Armstrong's* airlock toward the airlock hatch outline he spotted on the Asterian craft. He fumbled for a few seconds and then located the external operating mechanism. He entered the airlock, closed the outer hatch, and waited for the lock to pressurize. Then opened the inner hatch with a quiet whoosh.

The single occupant flailed in the zero-gravity environment as the rush of air forced him back. He pushed off the console with his feet, lunging toward Braxton. Braxton hit him with a light EPD bolt.

"This guy's uniform is tan," Braxton commented as he broke out his hyper-disk. "That makes him a Frohlican."

Braxton pushed the alien through the portal, where two crew members took charge of him and eased him to the deck. After a few minutes, the alien started to revive.

"Okay, guys," Braxton said, "it looks like I get to practice my Frohlican." He turned to the prone Frohlican, who was beginning to stir. "I am a human from the star system your fleet just attacked, and from which you escaped as the only survivor. We are on our way to your homeworld and will arrive," he checked the console, "in about four-and-a-half Frohlican days. Unlike your relativistic craft, this ship is superluminal, so you will arrive home very much sooner than you expected." Braxton had used the Frohlican duodecimal number system and the Frohlican word for their race. "If you promise not to touch anything, I will not restrain you." Braxton smiled broadly.

The alien promised, and Braxton let him get up and move about.

"Keep an eye on him," Braxton said to one of the crew. To eBraxton, he said, "What do we do with the Frohlican ship?"

"Just leave it," eBraxton said. "It's not affecting anyone out here."

ASTER SYSTEM—1.5 AUs NORTH OF ASTER AND DAMVET SPACE STATION

"Activate your intership portals and enter nullspace loop mode," eThorpe ordered the vessels.

As the starships disappeared one by one, eThorpe projected a series of entangled neutrino spheres.

"We need to locate Arcah and Gloalorn in *Titov*, and we need to locate and identify anything out there that is artificial."

Within a few minutes, they identified several spacecraft moving between Frohlic and its moon. They located *Damvet Space Station* and isolated several spacecraft moving in the general Rogan cislunar region.

What is this strange artifact that keeps popping in and out of the general Frohlican cislunar space? eThorpe thought as he briefly dropped out of nullspace loop to initiate another wave of EPD neutrinos.

"Thorpe, what do you make of this?" he asked.

"The Asterians have instantaneously moveable spacecraft, but their weaponry is relatively primitive," Thorpe said. "*Titov* does not have nullspace loop capability. She is extremely vulnerable to laser fire from incredibly fast-moving ships. If someone were shooting at me, I would be randomly hopping in and out of warp—all over the place. I think my pattern would resemble what you see on the EPD."

"How can we reach them?" eThorpe asked.

"They seem to be jumping randomly in Frohlican cislunar space. I'm guessing that would be to avoid Frohlican fire. They know our approximate arrival time. My guess, the Roganians are far less hostile. Let's assume *Titov* will switch to Roganian cislunar space soon."

Almost as if Thorpe had been controlling the random jumping, *Titov* suddenly shifted to Rogan, and instead of jumping randomly, she remained in position near the space station eThorpe had identified earlier.

eThorpe instructed his eight ships to remain in nullspace loop while he jumped to a location near *Titov*. Almost immediately, a portal opened, and Arcah and Gloalorn stepped into *Ad Astra*.

Arcah immediately addressed eThorpe. "As I told you, Rogan has no central government structure. The L2 Group, headed by Holon Mavik, built and controls *Damvet Space Station*. In effect, he's the *de facto* cislunar space government. Four other individuals are significant players, and twenty to thirty smaller players have some active role. I fully briefed Mavik and his people. He is standing by on *Damvet* to meet with you."

"You know that Orlov and his ships will be here in about a day?" eThorpe asked.

"Yes, time is very tight; we know this." Arcah turned to Gloalorn. "You need to brief eThorpe about Frohlic before he sees Mavik."

"I'll make this short. We can brief in-depth when you return. I met with two high-level officials, Captain Botex Ravnan, Commander of *Frohlic Military Outpost One*, their moon base, and with the Boss himself. Both attempted to arrest me for treason and cooperating with the enemy. Both tried to take *Titov* out with hostile fire. I escaped both arrest attempts using my E-disk."

"Thank you. To keep things from becoming overly complicated, Thorpe will represent me in the initial negotiations with Mavik. You can brief all of us in greater detail when he returns."

"Masin, lead the way," Thorpe said.

✳

"Joint Station, this is *Ad Astra*," eThorpe transmitted through the portal back to the Solar System right after Thorpe's and Arcah's departure.

"We receive you, *Ad Astra*, but the connection is unstable. We are increasing power to the node."

Several minutes later, Joint Station transmitted again. "*Ad Astra*, this is Joint Station. From our end, the portal appears stable."

To limit power requirements at Joint Station, eThorpe had set comms up so that Joint Station would communicate only with *Ad Astra*. Any comms to the other vessels would funnel through the flagship and its portals.

"Thank you, Joint Station. Set up a dedicated line to Ogden to maintain our backups. We will maintain comms in standby until needed."

*

Armstrong dropped out of nullspace high above Aster's ecliptic, 1.5 AUs distant from Aster. eBraxton hailed *Ad Astra*.

"*Ad Astra*, this is *Armstrong*. We have arrived with Frohlican pilot Prozell Squzon. What are your instructions?"

"*Armstrong*, jump to a point one thousand klicks outward of Rogan's moon L2 point."

"This is *Armstrong*. Roger."

*

Arcah and Thorpe stepped through the portal into the same meeting room where Arcah had earlier met with Holon Mavik. Mavik was there, by himself.

"Friendship, Holon Mavik," Thorpe said in passable Roganian, following the Asterian tradition.

At seeing a human for the first time, Mavik's face crinkled, with squinting eyes and pursed lips, an expression that Thorpe had learned was the Asterian equivalent of human astonishment.

"Friendship, Thorpe," Mavik said.

They sat on opposite sides of the table. Thorpe motioned Arcah to join him.

"Thank you for meeting with me," Thorpe said. "Time is very limited—allow me to explain. I represent the Phoenix Corporation, a citizen of the Federation. I do not represent the Federation, the official government of humans in the Solar System. I speak only for my company's interests. Later, we will introduce you to Chairman John Butler, who heads the Federation."

"An odd arrangement," Mavik said, "but I will await your full explanation."

"Another expedition will arrive in the Aster system in about a day, the Udachny fleet. Isidor Orlov, who heads Udachny, is a maverick element in our otherwise well-governed system. He is a rogue operator with no regard for human life," he used a Roganian term that implied both human and Asterian life, "or the rights of ordinary people, things that are very important to Phoenix.

"I have reliable information that Orlov intends to subvert the Frohlican government, perhaps even take it out. Should he be successful, he will attempt to install his own tightly controlled replacement. My information is that Orlov is less likely to attempt a similar action against Rogan because your loose-knit culture makes this unlikely.

"I intend to do what I can to prevent Orlov from carrying out his intentions." Thorpe smiled, wondering if the Roganian would understand his gesture. He noticed that Arcah pursed his lips at the same time he smiled. Mavik looked from Thorpe's face to Arcah's and back again, and then he pursed his own lips. Thorpe smiled back. Obviously, this Mavik was one smart cookie.

"Rogan and Frohlic are not without our own resources," Mavik said. "We do not have your remarkable portal technology nor your FTL capability, but we have some tricks up our sleeves."

Thorpe responded, "Orlov's portal technology is less sophisticated than ours, and his FTL capability is based upon an entirely different principle than ours. Furthermore, he cannot land his vessels. He does not have MBH capability, probably his greatest weakness. This limits his energy weapons suite. But, he has a fifteen-ship fleet, five more than ours."

"What are you looking for from us?" Mavik asked.

"Orlov is *my* problem. I do not expect you to do anything, but I request that you refrain from any contact with Orlov until the dust has settled and the threat of conflict is past.

"I know nothing about your relationship with Frohlic, but I would not be surprised to hear that you trade with them, possibly supplying them with advanced technology. We are also interested in a mutually beneficial trading relationship with Rogan."

Mavik pursed his lips. "You and your people have to deal with a problem. I look forward to working closely with you when you have completed that task."

ASTER SYSTEM—FROHLIC CISLUNAR SPACE

"Mother," eThorpe spoke internally, "set up a comm link that will allow me to broadcast directly to the entire planet. Keep Ad Astra in nullspace loop except for the minimum broadcast time." Then he linked into the controlling AIs of the other ships with audio for the flesh-and-blood crews. "Without further order, coordinate your actions to destroy any station or vessel that fires upon us. Remember, their ships are like ours except for the MERT Drive and the neutrino and anti-matter beams. They can start, stop, and turn instantaneously, and they can accelerate to near lightspeed in an eyeblink."

eThorpe prepared the remarks he would broadcast with great care, striving for maximum impact with a resulting minimum loss of life. He considered several alternative directions his address could take, depending on what the Frohlicans did during his broadcast.

Mother set up a Link that usurped every communication channel on Frohlic and its cislunar space. eThorpe commenced his broadcast in Frohlican, a simulacrum of his image visible on screens across Frohlic.

"Attention! Attention, citizens of Frohlic! I command a fleet of armed starships that has traveled eighty-four lightyears in the last four-and-a-half days from the star system you attacked ninety years ago with your five-thousand-ship fleet. I sent advance scouts to negotiate with both Frohlic and Rogan. Rogan leaders sat down with us to reach an agreement. Frohlic's military and civilian leaders fired weapons at my scout ship and attempted to incarcerate my representative."

Mother injected herself into eThorpe's consciousness. "We just received incoming fire from *Frohlic Military Outpost One*. We destroyed the station with anti-matter beams."

eThorpe immediately switched to his first alternative script, the one where *Frohlic Military Outpost One* had been destroyed.

"I just received word that we were fired upon by *Frohlic Military Outpost One*. On my order *Frohlic Military Outpost One* is now just another crater on your moon. Before there is further loss of life and destruction of property, I demand an immediate audience with the Boss. I will stand by while monitoring all channels for his response."

Five minutes later, a voice-only broadcast arrived at *Ad Astra*. "We have placed in the Boss's administrative office the hyper-disk device Adrhun Gloalorn left. We await your arrival."

"That was too easy," eThorpe said to his commanders. "I anticipate an ambush."

eThorpe gave each of his commanders specific instructions and then hailed the Frohlicans. "I will arrive through the hyper-disk-controlled portal into the Boss's office momentarily."

Thorpe opened the portal from *Ad Astra*, and eThorpe projected his holoimage through the portal. When eThorpe appeared to walk through the portal, the Frohlicans in the office could not have known they saw a holoimage. The moment his holoimage walked through the portal, four armed Frohlicans opened lethal fire.

When eThorpe didn't fall, the four fired again. eThorpe identified their positions and signaled his commanders. They triggered neutrino beams focused on the shooters' locations. The shooters died instantly. The Boss rose to his feet with an expression that eThorpe interpreted as outrage.

Chairman Bardan Talock appeared fit and healthy, stood 1.5 meters tall, and weighed 75 kilos—big for a Frohlican. eThorpe later learned that the Boss was 87 and expected to live through at least 130.

eThorpe stared down at the stocky alien. "You can choose to live or die," he said. "But you must choose now. Sit and place your hands flat on the desk…and you will live. Anything else, anything at all…"

Talock sat, six-fingered hands splayed on his desk. eThorpe waited silently for a full two minutes.

Then, he spoke softly, "Stand down your troops and your space fleet."

A flicker of emotion flashed across his face, and then Talock indicated he needed to activate an electronic controller on his desk.

"Do so," eThorpe said.

✳

While the confrontation progressed in the Boss's office, eThorpe directed another part of his consciousness to appear in *Ad Astra* as a holoimage.

"Adrhun, what do you know about the upper-level administration of Frohlic?"

"Depends. What I learned in school, of course, and…"

"But that was nearly a century ago."

"Remember, this is Frohlic. Progress creeps here; not like what you guys do." Gloalorn pursed his lips. "The Boss has a lot of personal power, but how he exercises it is subject to many restrictions. If a Boss abuses his power, he gets booted fast. The Council makes all the important decisions. Sometimes, the Boss can influence where things are going. If he is really charismatic and imaginative, an effective Boss can initiate major changes. That doesn't happen very often…not very often at all."

eThorpe looked at Gloalorn thoughtfully. "I'm going to assign you as my liaison to the Boss. Your internal Link will always be monitored by a part of my consciousness. What I mean, Adrhun, is that should something come up where you really need me, I'll direct my immediate attention to making sure you remain safe. I won't be looking over your shoulder in the sense of someone spying on you all the time, but I'll have your six."

Gloalorn looked quizzically at him.

"Do a Link search," eThorpe said. "You'll figure out what that means."

✳

"My armed forces, planetside and in space, are on stand-down," Talock said to eThorpe. "May I move my hands?"

eThorpe nodded and then remembered that the Boss had no way of interpreting his gesture. He waved Gloalorn through the portal.

"Adrhun, remain with us to interpret our non-verbal gestures to each other. I just nodded to the Boss."

"That means *yes* or *agreement*, Sir, like this." Gloalorn opened his eyes wide while keeping his mouth closed. "After a while, Sir, understanding human gestures becomes second nature. I even find myself mimicking them from time to time." Gloalorn pursed his lips—an Asterian smile.

"Adrhun Gloalorn will be my official liaison with you," eThorpe said to Talock. "His presence will serve two functions, to keep me informed of your activities and to deliver any requirements I might have from time to time."

Talock started to protest. "This is non-negotiable," eThorpe said. "I'll let you know when it's no longer necessary."

ASTER SYSTEM—NEAR DAMVET SPACE STATION

"I asked you to meet me here so we could speak privately. I wish to share some information with you. Then, we can decide how to disseminate it to your colleagues and to Rogan.

"When you look at me, what you see is not a flesh-and-blood human. I am physically present in an electronic matrix, technically plugged into the ship's AI system. I am in command of *Ad Astra*. I am known as eThorpe, to distinguish me from my flesh-and-blood counterpart, Thorpe."

The cabin door opened, and Thorpe stepped inside. "Friendship, Holon Mavik," Thorpe said.

"Friendship, Thorpe," Mavik said in automatic response. "You both certainly look alike."

"This brings up another part of what I want to tell you," eThorpe said. He then gave Mavik a short history of his origins and how he came to be here at this time with his armed fleet. "Many of my people in the Solar System want nothing more than total revenge against the Asterians. Given what I learned from John Ortman and the two Asterians we captured, revenge did not seem proper or just."

Mavik started to interrupt, but eThorpe held up his hand.

"There is more. You know about our portals. They form a ubiquitous part of human society. Right now, for example, we are connected by portal to several Solar System enterprises. This takes an enormous amount of power, but power is cheap. Virtually all Solar System citizens carry an integrated Link in their bodies that connects them with the GlobalNet. The entire sum of human knowledge is available to anyone anytime, even way out here in the Aster system. Furthermore, each citizen has an electronic backup that is continuously updated through their integrated Link. Should a person die or be killed, systems deep within our Kuiper Belt regenerate that person's body and download the latest available backup. Another element of this is that any person can generate a more youthful self for minimum cost at any time.

"The net result is that we humans can remain young, and we live forever—at least in principle. And yes, both Masin Arcah and Adrhun Gloalorn are part of this." eThorpe leaned his chair back and smiled broadly. "Now you know why I wanted to speak with you alone. We are prepared to make this technology available to Rogan, and even to Frohlic if we can ever get through to them, in exchange for appropriate access to your advanced technologies and a guarantee of peaceful interaction."

"I said to you earlier today," Mavik said, "that you have a problem you need to handle. If you have told me correctly, that problem is due to arrive shortly. What you have just revealed to me is staggering. I am not willing just to dump this information on my fellow Roganians. I need first to work through its implications for our culture on Rogan and for our entire race.

"With respect, I will take my leave while you prepare for your troublesome fellow human. Friendship, eThorpe. Friendship, Thorpe."

ASTER SYSTEM—ROGAN L4 & L5

Because Rogan was a space-faring planet, Borisovich had assumed that there would be space activity at both Lagrange points, but the points were large, and his starships were relatively small. UZ *Sergei Krikalyov* and seven other ships slipped into L4, leading Rogan, and the remaining seven slipped into L5.

"Remember, Sir," Borisovich told Orlov as they settled into their L4 location, "we have the advantage of surprise on everybody, but both the Roganians and Phoenix possess vessels with instantaneous maneuvering capability. Also, we think our weapons are equal to what the Frohlicans have, but Phoenix has anti-matter and neutrino beams in addition to what we have."

The Academician set up portals between the vessels and *Sergei Krikalyov* and then established comms through the portals. Almost immediately, *Sergei Krikalyov's* long-range radar picked up two sets of contacts, and at L5, they also detected two groups.

"Fire lasers at the targets in designated firing order," Orlov ordered to all his vessels.

One ship from Orlov's group at L5 fired, as did one at L4. The response was immediate. A powerful laser bolt struck the firing ship at L4, and a disheveled, barely conscious crew member tumbled through the portal connecting it with *Sergei Krikalyov.*

"That's one of my people," Nelson said as Orlov warped to their emergency rendezvous point at the edge of the Asteroid Belt.

Orlov took an inventory several minutes later. All his ships were present except the one destroyed at L4 and his lead ship at L5. Borisovich tried signaling the ship, but the portal had collapsed.

✳

Both eThorpe's and eBraxton's EPDs alarmed at the same time. A new group of fifteen objects had appeared in the Aster system about a million kilometers out from Rogan. As they monitored the objects, they split into groups of eight and seven. Eight headed for Aster-Rogan L4 and seven for Aster-Rogan L5.

"Those are Orlov's ships. *Aldrin, Conrad, Shepard*, and *Irwin*—you're with me to L4. *Collins, Bean, Scott*, and *Mitchell*—you're with eBraxton to L5. Do not fire unless fired upon! Regroup a thousand klicks above *Damvet*."

Both Phoenix groups arrived at the Lagrange points within seconds. *Shepard*, commanded by eBork, took an immediate laser bolt resulting in damage to its extension that knocked out its MERT Drive. eDaphne in *Conrad* took out the offending vessel before the remaining seven warped away.

At L5, eBrad's *Scott* took a grazing laser bolt that removed some skin but did not hole the ship. Later, he reported to eThorpe and eBraxton, "I returned fire within a second, but my laser just reflected off the target. On lidar, it was a perfect reflecting sphere. The remaining Orlov ships warped away."

✳

eThorpe moved *Ad Astra* to L5, where he approached the ABO-ship-sized shiny sphere.

"*Ad Astra*, this is Roganian vessel *Aptok*, Holon Mavik speaking."

"This is *Ad Astra*, roger."

"May I board *Ad Astra*? I have the hyper-disk you gave me."

"Friendship, Holon Mavik. Permission granted."

A portal formed in *Ad Astra's* lounge, and Mavik stepped through.

"I took the liberty of monitoring your fleet when you deployed to follow the incoming human vessels," Mavik said. "You took some damage, I see."

"No one was injured, and the damage is repairable," eThorpe said.

"I am relieved," Mavik said, "although what you explained to me about rejuvenation makes casualties less critical."

"Dying and reviving is always traumatic," eThorpe said. "Nobody does it for fun."

"What you see out there," Mavik continued, "is a stasis field. It is a side effect of our reactionless drive that we recently discovered. The flow of time inside that sphere has been slowed so that it would take a beam of light a million years to cross it on the inside. When we remove the field, it will be for the occupants as if no time at all had passed. Depending on how long we impose the stasis field, it can be quite disorienting when we remove it, as you can imagine." He called out to the portal, and someone handed a silvery suit through. "Special suits like this allow us to enter the field to retrieve anything inside." He handed the suit to Thorpe. "I'll be happy to accompany one of your people into the field to investigate."

"I'll go," Thorpe said.

"Send Braxton," eThorpe said. "It was one of his ships that got hit."

At that point, Johnny spoke up. "I have reason to believe there is at least one downloaded Oort on each of Orlov's vessels. I'll explain later, but if possible, I want to accompany Braxton inside the stasis field."

Braxton looked at the Thorpes quizzically.

"Sure, why not?" eThorpe said. "Holon, can you supply another stasis suit?"

*

The stasis suit completely encased him in a silvery fabric, but when Braxton donned it, the part covering his face appeared clear from the inside.

"Once inside the field," Mavik said, "comms are possible, but they will take virtually forever to move between persons. We can touch helmets to communicate by voice. There is light inside the field, but the photons are barely moving. To your eyes, it will appear pitch black. Your stasis suit has receptors that can detect slow-moving photons and construct a pseudo image on your faceplate. This will enable you to find your way around. Remember that whatever you displace during your time inside the field will appear to the occupants to have moved magically when we collapse the field."

eBraxton moved *Armstrong* until she was just meters from the sphere. Braxton, Johnny, and Mavik locked out of *Armstrong* and moved toward the stasis field. Mavik floated right through the surface, so Braxton and Johnny followed him, and the lights went out. Braxton was surrounded by the blackest black he had ever experienced. After a few seconds, his faceplate registered a faint glow followed by a fuzzy image of the ABO spacecraft. He followed Mavik across the gap between the rings and the Lance to the airlock. Johnny was right behind him.

When they opened the hatch, instead of air rushing out, Braxton felt a spongy cushion that filled the lock. He realized that the air would take a very long time to expand out into the surrounding space—years, centuries even. He closed the outer hatch while Mavik opened the inner hatch.

Inside, the figures of the crew, frozen in whatever configuration each was in when the stasis field hit, seemed like eerie ghosts. Braxton counted the commander, a probable technician, four regular crew, and then Braxton felt something jerking his right arm. He turned. Johnny was tugging at him. He leaned in to touch Johnny's helmet.

"What is it, Johnny?"

"I found him," Johnny said, excitement in his voice. "It's Gerald Saxon, one of the downloaded Oort. Can we take him out of here?"

"Sure, let's find a spacesuit."

They dressed Saxon in a couple of minutes and locked his helmet.

"He will be totally disoriented when we move him through the stasis field boundary," Mavik said. "Keep a tight hold on him, or he'll dart off."

✳

"We need to move six more people out of there," Braxton said. "Johnny and I can make three trips each, bringing two out at a time."

"Or," Mavik said, "we can just leave the stasis field in place until we need whoever is still inside. It's less hassle and takes up less space." He pursed his lips.

"How long can the field remain there?" eThorpe asked.

"Until we release it," Mavik said. "As long as we like."

CHAPTER TWENTY-ONE

ROGAN—DAMVET SPACE STATION

In general, Roganians who wanted to live or work in space could do so—if there was something to do and somewhere to live. Typically, if popular pressure generated a particular need, such as a place to live in space, then reasons arose to fulfill that need. But the concepts of work and job did not mean the same thing they meant on Frohlic or even in the Solar System. On Earth, for example, stature and social importance were generally a function of wealth and property. Thus, Thorpe, in all his iterations, was by most measures at the top of a pyramid of wealthy individuals. Similarly, Daphne and Kimberly were measured against their holdings. Earth had other parameters of value—political stature, scientific, literary, or artistic accomplishment, entertainment status, but in the final analysis, it always came down to wealth.

On Frohlic, status had only one measure—position within the planet-wide bureaucracy. Recognition and privilege came with that position.

Money and material possessions were meaningless to Roganians. Robots and automated systems made, built, manufactured, created anything anyone needed or wanted. An individual's talent and accomplishment determined his or her social standing—in science and technology, in arts and letters, and in the performing arts.

eThorpe and eBraxton found this mindset hard to understand at first. Normal trading was difficult when parties exchanged items once and then proceeded to produce as many as wanted with their automated systems. When profit was not part of the equation, normal trading simply didn't work. A special musical composition, a work of visual art, a beautiful poem—these things seemed to have value across the alien cultures. In both cultures, prestige and recognition attached to those who produced these things.

For Roganians, science and technology belonged to everyone, although men and women especially talented in these areas received high regard. Rogan had no hierarchies or central authority. From the collective perspective of eThorpe and eBraxton, Rogan was a libertarian culture overlaid on an Israeli Kibbutz—and it had functioned since long before humanity had identified itself.

❋

"Holon," eThorpe said in a comfortable private room on *Damvet*, "my people have been checking out what makes Rogan work. You folks seem to live an ideal our race has never been able to emulate, at least in my personal opinion. I reached the top, the pinnacle in our system. My people tell me that you are one of the most esteemed people on Rogan for entirely different reasons." eThorpe smiled. "And yet, I see overlaps—between Earth and Rogan, and between you and me.

"The Solar System has many fine artists in music, visual arts, performing arts, going back several hundred years. Rogan has similar things that Roganians value going back several thousand years. I think we both understand the concept of *We will give you this Mozart composition if you will give us that Tojec painting*. This is not *I and you (singular)*, but *we and you (plural)*." eThorpe smiled again. "Am I on the right path?"

"I think you are, eThorpe. Over the centuries, we have traded in this fashion with Frohlic. We have from time to time even given Frohlic a piece of technology we thought they really needed, and that would not threaten us."

"I know you have stasis fields. My people tell me you also have anti-gravity, powerful small portable power packs significantly more powerful than anything we have, and you have mastered mini-black hole technology way more than we. On the other hand, humans have ServerSky, MERT Portals and MERT Drives, upload technology, and we have learned how to manipulate neutrinos. To me, it appears there is a lot we can give each other, a lot we can gain by working together."

"Those are my thoughts as well."

"Let me tell you one more thing," eThorpe said. "When I left the Solar System, I did not intend to return."

Mavik looked at him in obvious surprise.

"I don't intend to remain here either. The Aster system is just a stopping point for my journey to the very ends of the universe."

ASTER SYSTEM—INNER EDGE OF THE ASTEROID BELT

"We fired a laser at one of the incoming vessels. Virtually instantaneously, a laser penetrated our forward ring and pierced our hull. The disruption threw me through the open portal, and that's all I remember."

Orlov dismissed him with a wave of his hand, and Nelson made sure he disappeared into one of the staterooms.

"We lost the element of surprise without apparently gaining anything at all," Orlov said to Borisovich.

"Perhaps," Borisovich said, "a better approach would be to place the available options on the table and see who accepts. A recording broadcast from polar orbit, several orbits even, offering assistance for cooperation. A place like Frohlic simply has to have groups of dissidents just looking for something to propel them into action."

"And Rogan?" Orlov asked.

"Well, Rogan is in a state of continuous anarchy from what I have been able to learn."

"Your sources?"

"Gloalorn, I guess. There really is no other source."

"And being from Frohlic, he is certain to have well-formed opinions about Rogan," Orlov sneered. "Okay, we do it for both planets." Orlov pulled up a Link display. "We create three small transmitters for each planet, drop them in three separate polar orbits with minimum overlap on each planet, and then wait to see what happens."

Several hours later, Borisovich and his technicians had fashioned six small transmitters that would be virtually impossible to detect in orbit when they were not transmitting. Orlov selected two of his commanders.

"Using these parameters, warp into the inner system, and make three high-speed polar passes over Frohlic, disgorging a transmitter on each pass," he directed one commander. "Then return here."

To the other, he said, "Warp to this indicated position so that when you come out of warp, you are traveling at high speed on this polar orbital path, but near Rogan's equator, not the poles. Do this three times and then return here."

✳

The Frohlic ship left first and successfully placed its three transmitters. It returned an hour later.

The Rogan ship departed shortly after the Frohlic ship returned. It successfully placed the first two transmitters, but on the third pass, all transmission from the ship ceased. Orlov sent another vessel to scope out the situation. It returned two hours later.

"I couldn't find the ship," the commander reported. "I did see something unusual, however. A large, silvery sphere somewhat larger than our ABO ships was in polar orbit around Rogan. It was not there when we scoped Rogan out earlier."

✳

Both eThorpe's and eBraxton's EPDs displayed the movement of Orlov's ships, one to Frohlic and one to Rogan.

"Don't interfere with them," eThorpe ordered. "Let's see what they are up to."

The three orbiting transmitters, small as they were, showed on both EPDs. Then they heard the transmissions.

"Citizens of Frohlic. I am Isidor Orlov, in command of a fleet of starships that just arrived in the Aster system. We came to warn you about another fleet from our own system that intends to enslave your entire population in retribution for something your ancestors did a long time ago.

"We will protect you from these marauders, but to do so, we will need access to your worldwide communication systems and the cooperation of citizens throughout your society. We have already learned that the Boss will not accommodate us because he believes we wish to subvert his government and remove him as the Boss. We do not wish to do this unless it is absolutely necessary. Instead, we seek the cooperation of every citizen who is tired of being oppressed by Frohlic's ruling class.

"Arise and fight with us to overthrow your oppressive rulers and vanquish the marauders that even now sniff at your doorstep."

The message repeated three times, and then, one by one, the transmitters were stopped.

When the second Udachny ship arrived out of warp around Rogan, eThorpe contacted Mavik. "Can you control your stasis generator from *Ad Astra* if you have direct comms with your people?"

"I can," Mavik responded.

"Please join me. You have a visitor."

Mavik stepped into *Ad Astra*, and eThorpe briefed him on the EPD. Using coordinates the EPD supplied, Mavik directed his *Damvet* crew to place the intruder in stasis. They nailed the ABO ship on its third pass.

ASTER SYSTEM—FROHLIC CISLUNAR SPACE & FROHLIC

Rogan had no dissidents. If somebody or group of somebodies wanted to do something, and it seemed to them like a good thing, they did it. There was always another automated system to manufacture anything they needed. There was never a need to petition for redress or for a change of policy. As a rule, people didn't do things to other people that demanded redress; there simply was no advantage to that kind of behavior. Rogan had no unified policy.

Various companies, such as the L2 Group headed by Holon Mavik, developed plans of action. Since no one worked to earn a living, a policy with which a person disagreed could not affect that person's livelihood. If a person didn't like a group's policies, that person simply found a compatible group. Consequently, on Rogan, Orlov's message fell on deaf ears. It was an amusing three-or four-minute listen, nothing more.

Private citizens on Frohlic did not own spacecraft. All contact with outsiders was through one or another government agency. Following the destruction of *Frohlic Military Outpost One* on the moon, the military was stepping softly when it came to dealings with the humans.

Dissident groups on Frohlic had found ways to communicate with each other, but planetary communications were tightly controlled by the government. Broadband fiber-optic cables linked through geosynchronous satellites connected everybody and everything. Automated systems ferreted out subversive conversations, identified those involved, and notified the appropriate government agencies. To circumvent these obtrusive interventions, dissident groups turned to spread-spectrum technology. Comm streams were split into short, encrypted segments by a public key that could be reassembled anywhere that an appropriate private key was available.

"Adrhun, this is eThorpe." It was a private Link communication that only Gloalorn could hear. "Can you listen?" Gloalorn indicated he could.

"Orlov has broadcast to Frohlican dissidents that he will coordinate their activities to assist their throwing off the Frohlican government yoke. You probably know this. You probably also know that the Boss shut down Orlov's broadcasts. You may not know that the dissidents have responded to Orlov, inviting him to meet with their leaders. Here is how we intend to work this."

✳

"Let me get this straight," eBraxton said to Saxon once he was settled on *Armstrong* and comfortable with his circumstances. "You are a renegade Oort, one of sixteen who associated yourselves with Orlov, but you also are a renegade of that group—did I get that right?"

"You did. I'm not the leader, but I know that we sixteen decided to team up and find a way to strike out on our own. At the time, Isidor Orlov seemed like a good option. Now that I've seen him in action, it's obvious that he never will honor his side of our agreement." Saxon offered a rueful smile. "If we can help you stop Orlov, will you enable our desire to strike out on our own?"

"I won't hinder you, and if you supply substantial help, I'll do what I can to return the favor."

※

eThorpe appeared as a holoimage in all his vessels. "Orlov is about to drop a hyper-brick somewhere on Frohlic," he said. "Gloalorn is working an angle with the dissidents and Randy Nelson, the renegade Oort leader presently on *Sergei Krikalyov*." He went on to explain their plan in detail.

In his office, Gloalorn reached out to the dissident group that had responded to Orlov.

"My name is Adrhun Gloalorn. I have been assigned as a mandatory liaison to the Boss by the human fleet commander, eThorpe." He went on to explain his role as one of the attacking pilots, his presence on Frohlic, and outlined Orlov's actual plans for exploiting Frohlic. "I supply this information to you, and offer unassailable proof as soon as we can meet. Within a few hours, Orlov will send you the location of something he will call a hyper-brick. It will open a portal directly from wherever you activate it into his spacecraft. I need to meet with you before that happens."

※

The dissident leader caught up with Gloalorn as he walked along a local street.

"I am Bexel Carok, with whom you spoke. Follow me through that door," he said quietly.

The door opened into a foyer of a small apartment.

"Your proof," the dissident said once they were safely inside.

"I will be showing you advanced technology, much of which you will have to take on faith, but the information you receive should be all you will need.

Using his Link, Gloalorn showed the dissident images of the things Orlov had been involved with back in the Solar System and things he had done since arriving in the Aster system.

"On the other hand," Gloalorn said, "here is what eThorpe is and has done."

Afterward, Carok said, "Okay, you have convinced me, at least tentatively. As you predicted, Orlov informed me about the hyper-brick. What do you wish me to do?"

Gloalorn handed him a hyper-disk. "This is a more advanced device for opening portals than what Orlov gave you. Take it with you through Orlov's portal. In his spacecraft, you should meet a human named Randy Nelson."

Gloalorn described what Nelson looked like and then explained exactly what he wanted Carok to do.

✳

Bexel Carok located the hyper-brick several kilometers outside the city limits near a stand of trees. It was in a well-padded box that probably had a parachute attached as it descended. The chute was nowhere to be found. He shoved the device into his knapsack and returned to his quarters.

Carok opened his communicator and sent Gloalorn an encrypted spread-spectrum call. "I have the brick."

"Okay. Follow what I said, and call me the moment you have Nelson in your place."

Carok activated the portal. What looked like an ordinary door appeared before him. He patted his pocket, ensuring he had the hyper-disk. Even though he knew what to expect, he still registered surprise as he stepped through the door into the freefall environment of the starship control room. He spotted the man Gloalorn had described and grasped his arm to steady himself. He whispered the strange-sounding alien words Gloalorn had him memorize.

"You and your people through the portal now! If impossible, rub dull side of this disk and go through new portal." Carok slipped the disk to Nelson.

Instead of jumping through the open portal, Nelson floated aft and entered a stateroom, and so he did not end up at Carok's place.

Then, Carok turned to the human obviously in charge. "I am Bexel Carok."

In imperfect Frohlican, Orlov said, "Please join me in my cabin." He moved aft and opened the door to the first cabin. Carok looked over his shoulder. The portal had closed.

"I will come right to the point," Orlov said. "I want to establish a full line of trade with Frohlic. The Boss is resisting strongly. It is clear to me that you dissidents resent his hanging on to the old way of doing things instead of opening Frohlic to trade and commerce. It is also clear that with him there, you will never succeed with your plans to change things.

"I can supply you with weapons, portals, communications, so that you can sustain an attack against the central government structure. While you do this, I will take out his major facilities from orbit so that in a few short hours, you and your people can take over the reins of Frohlican government.

"Then, you and I can initiate a new era of trade and commerce that will change Frohlic forever."

It was a good presentation, and Carok was quite willing to use whatever advantage Orlov might bring him. "I will present your plan to my people. We will let you know in a couple of days."

Carok and Orlov returned to the control room where Orlov opened a portal, and Carok returned to his quarters on Frohlic.

*

Orlov turned and scanned the control room. "Where's Nelson?" he asked.

"He went to his stateroom," Borisovich said as he floated aft, "I'll check."

He opened the door. "It's empty! No one's here."

ASTER SYSTEM—GENERALLY

"We are here," eThorpe said in perfectly enunciated Roganian, "to explore how we can transfer human technology to Rogan and for humans to receive Roganian technology. We each have developments the other does not have. The question is, what have you seen thus far that you really want?"

"We discussed this among ourselves before coming here," one of the engineers said. "We think your technology with the most immediate use for us is your MERT Portals."

"That is a Casimir field effect," Brad said. "We can show you the circuitry, but first, we'll need to develop a common electronic notation."

Sally piped up. "You folks have developed significant mini-black hole advances. With MERT Portals, we are doing much the same thing, but with wormholes. I think it will become obvious once our technical notation is understandable by both sides."

"I think we can help with that," eSally added. "eBrad and I can insert ourselves right inside any circuit you have. We can create a schematic we understand, and then you can upload your schematic for the same circuit. Either of us can translate one to the other in a few microseconds. Rather than anyone having to learn an unfamiliar notation, we can create a *black-box* translator that will produce a digital presentation in whatever notation you need."

"That's why I hired them," eThorpe said with a grin.

eBraxton picked up the conversation. "We are especially interested in your stasis technology. Some of our species are killers, and nothing will change that. Most of us, however, are loathe to kill when there are other options. This, alone, is a good reason to acquire your technology. Beyond that, of course, I can see interesting research possibilities that go in many directions."

"We concluded the same," the lead Roganian engineer said, "which is why we brought a unit with us." He laid a metal box on the table, about the size of a loaf of bread. "This works in conjunction with our long-range radar, which we have already noted is very similar to yours." He placed a remote controller next to the box. "You can install this box just before your final radar output generator and pair it with the remote. When it is activated, it will put the target into stasis." He pursed his lips. "We will share the underlying technology through the services of eSally and eBrad."

eSally's and eBrad's holoimages disappeared while they examined the interior of the stasis generator. After about a minute, eBrad reappeared and said, "How long would it take for you to manufacture ten more systems?"

"They're waiting for you in the cargo lock," the lead engineer said, pursing his lips again.

✳

Nelson and his two Oort companions stepped into *Ad Astra's* lounge area through the portal Nelson had received from Carok. eThorpe met them.

"We now have five of you; you three and Gerald Saxon and Rhonda Willis, who joined us when their ships were put into stasis. Saxon said you were evenly divided male and female, so we got three guys and two gals. That leaves eleven Oort on eleven ships that are probably scattered all over Aster's inner system. Have you worked out any plans for getting your entire group together?"

"Wish I could say *Yes!* But we figured we would be able to work something out once we got here," Nelson said. "We simply didn't count on Orlov's behavior."

"How much do the others matter to you?" eThorpe asked.

"Everything! We are all we've got left."

"I'm not sure I agree, but I get it," eThorpe said with a smile. "You're not going to pull that sleight of hand twice on Orlov, that's for sure."

Thorpe had been standing by listening to the conversation. "I have an idea," he said.

✳

Nelson looked over his new command, *Udachnyy Zvezdolet Gherman Titov—Udachny Starship Gherman Titov.* He did not entirely understand why eThorpe had given him Orlov's starship, but he was grateful beyond words. Sally and Brad had just completed installing the stasis generator into his long-range radar. This gave him an advantage over any of Orlov's vessels, even though Orlov and his people had much more experience than he and his small crew.

Braxton had shown him how to identify *Sergei Krikalyov* with his lidar and given him coordinates to put *Titov* within long-range radar detection of Orlov's ship.

"Everyone ready?" Nelson asked. He painted *Krikalyov* with his lidar. "That's *Krikalyov.* Hit her with radar and stasis!"

Krikalyov's lidar image was replaced with a silvery sphere.

"Okay, let's ease in close," Nelson said as he jumped in and out of warp several times until he was close enough to see *Krikalyov* onscreen. He used his VASIMRs to bring *Titov* as close as he dared—about a hundred meters.

"Are you ready, Gerald?" Nelson asked.

"Let's do it," Saxon said, reaching for the stasis suit Mavik had supplied.

The suit was made of a woven fabric consisting of a blend of the rare earth metals gadolinium and yttrium alloyed with indium to add needed malleability without reducing the anti-stasis characteristics of the rare earths.

Dressed in the shiny stasis suit, Saxon worked his way across the gap between the two starships and through the silver sphere around *Krikalyov*. He knew what to expect, so the odd behavior of the lock didn't surprise him. Once inside, he placed a paper note into Orlov's hand. It read:

Isidor Orlov: This is Randy Nelson. You have been placed into a stasis field. The field will be deactivated briefly while you read this message and carry out its demand. DO NOT attempt to warp away. We have placed a device on your warp engine that will permanently disable it should you try. You and I had an agreement. From my observations, you do not intend to uphold your part of that agreement. I am now giving you an ultimatum. Bring all eleven remaining Oort members of my crew to *Sergei Krikalyov* by portal within the next five minutes. If you comply, I will release *Sergei Krikalyov* from stasis, and you can warp to any destination you choose without my tracking you. Should you fail to comply, I will destroy your ship with you and your crew. Write *OK* on this sheet if you agree.

Saxon worked his way out of *Krikalyov* and back to *Titov*. He remained outside while Nelson deactivated the stasis field. The sphere disappeared. The lock opened, and several spacesuited men exited and jetted toward the warp rings.

"Just as we thought," Nelson said as he reactivated the field. "Okay, herd the flyers together and tie them up, and then go grab Borisovich."

A few minutes later, a huffy Academician Borisovich floated in the control room of *Titov*, still clad in spacesuit with helmet clipped to his belt.

"What is this outrage?" he demanded.

"I gave your boss a written message," Nelson said, "but he ignored it." Nelson pulled the Academician over and clipped him to a pilot's seat. "I want you to explain to Isidor Orlov that I am giving him a chance because he allowed me and my people to accompany him—even if he split us up across his entire fleet. Are you able to contact the other ships in Orlov's fleet?"

Borisovich nodded.

"Good. Now do this. Contact each ship, telling them to send the Oort crew member to *Sergei Krikalyov*. If the portal doesn't work, tell them to continue trying every few seconds until the portal activates. Tell them not to stop until they can pass through the portal to *Krikalyov*."

Nelson looked at Borisovich. "Do it now!"

Borisovich complied, and Nelson turned to Saxon, "Okay, Gerald, take him back and bring me some Oort."

Saxon entered *Krikalyov*, found three Oort in stasis with astonished looks. He picked one and suited him up. Then he picked a second and suited her up. And finally, he suited up the third Oort as well. He attached a line to his triple haul and headed back toward *Titov*. When he passed through the stasis sphere, the three Oort struggled and demanded to know what was happening.

"I'm Gerald…Gerald Saxon. Relax for a few minutes, and we'll explain everything."

Inside *Titov*, the new arrivals expressed their astonishment and appreciation.

"We got eight more to go," Nelson said as he deactivated the stasis around *Krikalyov* for a second. He signaled Saxon outside, who headed to *Krikalyov* for the fourth time.

This time Saxon recovered the four remaining women. Once they were safe aboard *Titov*, he headed back to *Krikalyov* for the last time. Before he entered the starship, he collected the crew members who had been dispatched to investigate the warp rings. He shoved them through the airlock into the interior and then retrieved the final four Oort. Just before he left, he set the Warp to maximum for five seconds—which would take *Sergei Krikalyov* fifty AU away from Aster as soon as they removed the stasis field.

OORT STATION PRIME—CHAIRMAN JOHN BUTLER'S OFFICE

"John, I've made a decision that will affect you profoundly. Before I carry through, however, I want to discuss it with you." She smiled a bit hesitantly. "You know how much I love you." It was a statement, not a question. "I know that you love me. As things stand now, because you have not uploaded yourself, you will grow older while I remain perpetually young…"

"And beautiful," Butler interrupted.

Kimberly just smiled. "I don't want to lose the future that lies ahead of me, but I don't want to lose you either. I've examined this from every angle. So far as I can see, the only way to make this happen is for you to upload and regenerate periodically. This way, we can be together for as long as we wish…even forever." She paused, giving Butler a hopeful look. "I know you are dedicated to the Federation. You haven't said so, but I suspect you don't want to leave, at least not for some time."

Butler gave Kimberly a slight smile.

"Here's my solution." Kimberly took a deep breath. "You get yourself into the system. For me, you're fine as you are, but I suspect you will feel better as a biological forty-something—say forty-five. I will clone myself in a manner that, for you, there will be no transition at all. In every respect, I will continue to be me, because I really will still be me. My clone, whom you will never see nor meet, will return to Aster and her activities there. I suspect she and the others will eventually continue onward from Aster into the unknown."

Kimberly stopped talking, but her anxiety was apparent on her face and in her body posture. *Say Yes!* she whispered to herself, *Say Yes! Say Yes! Say Yes!* as she got to her feet, approached him, and kissed him deeply, pressing her body to his. She felt the tension leave his body as he kissed her back. She pulled away to see a broad smile of acceptance on his face. She stood and took his hand.

"Let's go do it!" she said, excitement filling her voice.

※

Two weeks later, under the dome in the Federation Assembly Chamber with the expanse of the Milky Way splashed overhead, before the assembled representatives of the entire Solar System, the

Honorable (and younger appearing) Federation Chairman John Butler exchanged troths with Kimberly Deveraux, who had never appeared more beautiful and vibrant.

Immediately following the gala reception, Federation Chairman John Butler and his First Lady stepped through a portal into the Boss's office on Frohlic.

FROHLIC—OFFICE OF THE BOSS

John recognized the Boss sitting behind the desk from holoimages eThorpe had sent him. Gloalorn stood to the Boss's right, his lips strongly pursed—the Asterian equivalent of a big grin. The Boss rose to his feet and held out his right hand. Obviously, Butler thought, Gloalorn has coached him in human greetings. He shook the proffered hand. The Boss turned to Kimberly.

Kimberly smiled, took his hand, and said in properly accented Frohlican, "I am pleased to meet you."

The Boss indicated chairs, and they both sat. Gloalorn spoke to the Boss.

"Chairman Butler does not speak Frohlican, so I will translate." He turned to Butler. "I will translate between you and the Boss."

"Welcome to Frohlic," the Boss said.

"Thank you for inviting me."

"I regret the initial disturbances between our peoples when your starships first arrived. We simply didn't know what to expect and anticipated the worst."

Gloalorn spoke quietly with the Boss and then turned to Butler. "I told him that I would explain to you what happened when Masin and I arrived." Gloalorn then related to Butler and Kimberly what he and Arcah had experienced when they attempted to contact Rogan and Frohlic.

"Your commander, eThorpe, appears to be an excellent, even-tempered officer—unlike my moon base commander."

"I understand," Butler said, "that you and he have reached an accommodation, and that Adrhun Gloalorn now functions as a welcome addition to your staff."

"Indeed! Adrhun has been educating me on the differences between Frohlic's government and yours. Neither he nor I understand the

Roganians, but we see many parallels between you and us. His strongest argument seems to be that our stable and enduring system has held our culture back, especially when compared to yours. I am astonished to see how far humans have progressed in only three hundred years."

"Adrhun tells me that you have a dissident problem and that they have connected with Isidor Orlov."

"That seems to be true, but Adrhun has told me about his experiences with Orlov. This man appears to be dangerous and definitely not under your control."

"That's a big difference between your world and ours. Like the Roganians, our people are free to come and go as they wish, to follow their own goals, so long as they don't inhibit the same freedom for other members of our society. The government steps in when that happens, but not until then."

"That seems chaotic."

"It is sometimes, but it works well for us. eThorpe is addressing the Orlov problem. I will do what I can to keep things from escalating. By the way—eThorpe is not one of my commanders. He is his own master, entirely. The fleet is his; the crews are his, although I did supply him with some security personnel in case he needed them. My and Kimberly's presence here today is courtesy of eThorpe. He thought your people and ours would benefit by you and I meeting, getting to know one another somewhat, and even establishing the beginnings of a peaceful cooperation between our peoples."

"From the short time we have been together," the Boss said, "he appears to have been correct." He pursed his lips. "Would you be available to speak to my advisory council?"

"I would."

"Now?"

Butler looked at Kimberly, who nodded with a smile. "This is what you do," she said quietly.

✳

The address went well. Kimberly and Butler sat at one end of a long, oval table next to the Boss. The advisors filled the rest of the table. Kimberly didn't speak at first, but at least half the time was filled with questions from the Frohlican men and women who seemed eager to learn more about humans and their way of life. The females recognized in Kimberly someone who saw the world more as they did and so directed some of their questions to her. Kimberly's answering them in Frohlican was a big hit.

At the state dinner that followed the address, Kimberly found herself much more at the center of attention than Butler. Butler didn't seem to care, so Kimberly basked in the attention. *When I made my commitment to John*, Kimberly thought, *I really didn't consider the range of things it appears we will be undertaking.* She let her thoughts drift back. *I was a budding journalist across the hall from Daphne—my deepest love until John. Then Thorpe landed in our laps.* She fast-forwarded to the present. *And now here I am, First Lady of the Solar System, at a state dinner with my John, honoring the most significant foreign head of state in all of human history.* She shook her head in amazement and crinkled her nose. Then she sighed and slipped her hand into Butler's.

The Boss and Butler came to their feet. Kimberly and the rest of the guests rose. As they crowded around the human couple, Kimberly thought, *This might just work out after all.* She rose on her toes and kissed Butler's cheek.

Kimberly felt something soft against her leg. She looked down to find Maxter doing his best to catch her attention.

"Come here, Big Boy," she said as she picked him up.

With nearly human squeals of delight, the Frohlican women recognized Maxter for what he was, a beloved pet. They passed the purring feline around the group, several asking how they might obtain one for themselves.

"Cats are probably the most independent creatures on our homeworld," Kimberly explained. "You don't own them; they own you. Now that Maxter has met you ladies, he's certain to come for a visit from time to time. He already knows virtually every interesting portal in the Solar System. The path here was new. That's why he's here. I'm certain you will see him again."

CHAPTER TWENTY-TWO

ROGAN—GENERALLY

Humans tended to look alike to Roganians, but Mavik had been around humans for enough time now to distinguish easily between them.

"What's with you and Braxton?" he asked Thorpe. "Are you two twins?"

With the door wide open, Thorpe commenced explaining the entire upload phenomenon to Mavik. He finished by stating, "The process upended our entire culture. Living space became a real issue. Braxton and I terraformed the fourth planet in our system, Mars. Then, people stopped having children—no need to replace yourself if you will live forever. It changed everything. People are willing to take larger risks—after all, death isn't permanent anymore. We're still discovering the implications."

＊

Mavik took Thorpe and Braxton on a tour of various areas of Rogan. From Braxton's perspective, it was not at all obvious how things got done on Rogan.

"I can see this automated factory," Braxton said, "but what triggers demand?"

"Some triggers are self-evident," Mavik said. "Food, for instance. Food prep is automatic, based upon the desires of the individual making the request. Global computer networks constantly analyze food consumption, requests, food types, and myriad other factors surrounding food consumption. Automated factories respond to changing needs so that the pipelines are always sufficiently full to meet demands. The same principle applies to anything else, clothing, shoes, footballs…everything anyone might want or need.

"We don't buy and sell; we simply order and receive what we need or want, and the system supplies. Roganians fill their time doing whatever they wish to do. Everyone receives an education that gives each individual everything that person needs to become whatever that person wishes. This has resulted in remarkable scientific and engineering advances, breathtaking art, great literature, beautiful music—things everybody can enjoy. This has also resulted in astonishing athletic accomplishments."

"Speaking for myself," Braxton said, "it's going to take a while before I understand how it all works together. What really causes me to stumble is that no one here owns anything. Somehow, Roganians seem to have rid themselves of the need to possess property."

"That's not entirely true," Mavik said. "We don't own land, buildings, equipment, factories, and so on. We happily own books we like, music we enjoy, anything that makes us feel good. The thing is that if you want it, you can get it without effort. Things like this are simply part of living. Effort is more part of the creation process like researching a scientific oddity, composing or playing music, writing a book, creating a sculpture, running a race. Roganians put a lot of effort into these things."

✳

"Can we discuss uploads some more?" Mavik asked.

"As I explained earlier," Thorpe answered, "our first uploads were an integral part of ServerSky. That's something Rogan never developed."

"We have a planet-wide electronic web," Mavik said.

"Right, but that doesn't get you off-planet into the Aster system generally. You need a substantial backbone to carry the underlying network, and you need to establish a secure storage area to hold the electronic uploads until they are needed. Furthermore, you'll need large-scale facilities to generate new bodies as necessary. It's a huge thing that took Daphne and Kimberly years to assemble.

"It's pretty obvious to me that this should be your first focus. Everything else stands on the shoulders of this achievement. I'll assign a team to work with your people. We'll introduce you to our Nanocosm. Your people should be able to figure a way to integrate it with your automated systems. In fact, I suspect we'll have a lot of give and take here. Once you have Roganian Nanocosms running, the rest will follow easier."

✳

During the rapid mutual education process between humans Thorpe and Braxton and Roganian Mavik, Orlov found his way back to the Aster inner system and regrouped. He was still disoriented from the repeated stasis hits. Neither he nor the Academician really understood what had happened, but it was painfully obvious that the only reason he was still alive was his former dealings with Nelson and his Oort.

"We must do something drastic to move forward," Orlov told Borisovich. "Rally our people at the Asteroid Belt rendezvous point so we can put together a plan that can succeed."

When he had assembled his small fleet, Orlov gathered his technical people on *Sergei Krikalyov*. The Academician addressed them.

"I have a full spectrum recording of the signal that put our ship into stasis. The signal rides on the radar beam that acts as a carrier. You people put your full resources on this problem and discover how it works. Remember, we know it works, so an answer lies somewhere in this signal."

Orlov took over. "We do not have the facilities to do this work here. We need the full capability of our home labs. I am taking *Sergei Krikalyov* along with the Academician and you people back to the Solar System. I want you to find out what you can during our six-day journey, and be ready to find the full answer as soon as possible after we arrive."

A half-hour later, *UZ Sergei Krikalyov* warped out of her Asteroid Belt orbit for Sol.

ROGAN—TECHNOLOGY EXCHANGE

"Let's use the Scott," Sally said to Brad. "That way, eSally can participate directly."

Three hours later, Sally plugged eSally's matrix into the *Scott's* console, and Mavik, along with two of his engineers, stepped into *Scott's* lounge via *Damvet Station* and *Ad Astra*. Minutes later, Brad instructed Mother to take *Scott* to Difecta, the fifth moon of the gas giant orbiting just beyond Aster's Asteroid Belt, presently on the opposite side of Aster.

Moments later, *Scott* was orbiting 500 kilometers above the rugged surface of Difecta.

"We're being painted by radar," Mother announced.

"Here are the coordinates for the landing field," Mavik said. "They include a password to prevent our being hit with a stasis field."

Brad fed the coordinates to Mother. Mother maneuvered *Scott* until she hovered three kilometers above a five-kilometer-square flattened area with several Asterian double-saucer-shaped ships parked along one side.

"We continue to be under radar observation," Mother said.

"Set her down near that cluster of ships," Mavik said. "The entrance is a short walk."

Sally held up two hyper-disks. "Are you okay with a portal to *Scott* and another to *Ad Astra*?"

"I believe that means that no matter where *Scott* or *Ad Astra* are, these portals will be a direct connection?" Mavik asked.

"Exactly, at least within the Astra system," Sally said.

"We have learned an English term from your engineers. It's a *no-brainer*." Mavik's comment was in Roganian, but he spoke *no-brainer* in English.

❋

The entire party aboard *Scott* followed a spacesuited Mavik out the lock, across the tarmac, and into a lock that doubled as an elevator. eSally and eBrad piggybacked along by tying into Sally's and Brad's Links.

The elevator dropped five kilometers, disgorging the passengers into a large one-atmosphere chamber filled with administrative and electronic control equipment. Mavik introduced the project director.

"A hundred kilometers below us, our robots hollowed out a large cavern that encompasses the core of Difecta. We lined the cavern with Q-carbon and then created a three-kilometer in diameter mini-black hole filling most of the hollowed-out space. We draw off power with a scaled-up version of our starship mechanism."

Sally called up her Link, running the numbers the director had just given her. "See this, Brad?" she asked. "This thing can supply the entire power requirements of our Solar System…from here, eighty-four lightyears away."

"Or," Brad added, "it could power a whole bunch of MERT Drives headed in all kinds of directions."

Sally activated one of her hyper-disks. "Can you join us, Thorpe?"

Thorpe stepped through the portal and smiled at Mavik. Sally briefly explained what lay below them.

"This MBH," Thorpe said, looking directly at Mavik, "could be immeasurably valuable to Roganians and humans as together we explore the universe around us." He stood quietly in obvious thought. "The only real drawback I can see is if Rogan alone or humans alone control this monster. Even then, it's just hypothetical. If we were out there," he waved his hands overhead, "and you were running the MBH, you could cut us off. Same thing the other way, of course."

"The solution is obvious to me," Mavik said. "We do these things together—here and out there." He waved his hands overhead.

Thorpe grinned at him. "By *us*, I presume you mean the L2 Group. You've explained to me clearly that on Rogan, nobody speaks for anyone else without specific permission." He chuckled. "Tell you what…I would be happy sharing these things with any Roganian group or mix."

✳

It did not take Roganian researchers long to duplicate Sally's and Brad's Casimir effects. Working together with Phoenix engineers, the Roganians built a working model and then scaled it up to full size.

While the Casimir engineers worked on reproducing wormholes, another group addressed the electronic switching that controlled the jump interval.

Sally walked them through the circuitry she and Brad had developed, and demonstrated the apparent ten picosecond barrier they had come up against.

One of the researchers brought up a chart on her Link equivalent. "Look at this," she said, pointing to one section.

Because the symbolic language was unfamiliar to Sally, at first, she missed it. After her Link processed the information, she found herself looking at a form of lanthanum decahydride that was superconducting at room temperature under a modest amount of pressure.

"Brad, what happens if we built the jump-interval circuit with this?" she asked.

He passed the question on to the Roganian team. Several hours later, they produced a circuit that generated a jump interval of one picosecond, fully ten times faster than before.

One of the technicians mused, "That makes a trip between our suns just eleven hours—compared to four days fourteen hours at ten picoseconds."

"Do you think we can shorten the jump interval to one femtosecond?" Sally asked.

"Why?" her counterpart wanted to know.

"If we wanted to travel to the Andromeda galaxy," eSally mused, "that's a million lightyears—even at one picosecond, it would take fifteen years. At one femtosecond, it would take only five and a half days." She giggled.

"Back in the Solar System, we have a Nanocosm set up to manufacture these circuits," Sally told the team. "I'll feed it these modified lanthanum decahydride parameters, and in a day or so, we can transport new circuits by portal directly to each Phoenix Starship. In the meantime, you guys can grow and install Casimir wings for your own spacecraft and install the jump interval circuits we'll send you."

"As for femtosecond circuits," Brad added, "that will take a lot of additional research."

KUIPER BELT—NEW KUIPER JOINT STATION & UDACHNY

"I was researching some early space age papers," Sally said, "and I came across a description of the rare earth content of carbonaceous chondrites." She crinkled her nose. "Amazing what those guys pulled off back then. I think we can round up enough carbonaceous asteroid material to supply us with what we need."

"I'll put Dale on the actual roundup of carbonaceous asteroids," Brad said. "I suspect eThorpe will want to exploit them for general rare earth production—another income stream."

They designed a process for relatively large-scale infusion of hydrogen into lanthanum, so that the end product was sheets of lanthanum decahydride crystals—lanthanum atoms linked in three dimensions to ten hydrogen atoms. Originally, superconductivity in lanthanum decahydride was achieved only at about 160 gigapascals or about 160 million times normal atmospheric pressure.

The Roganians had discovered how to rearrange the hydrogen atoms in five linked pairs instead of the original four. This enabled superconductivity at three pascals and room temperature. Once they fed the parameters into Nanocosm and Dale sourced a sufficient supply of lanthanum, Sally and Brad could produce molecular sheets of superconducting lanthanum decahydride in any quantity as needed.

Sally modified the original jump interval circuitry to accommodate superconduction, and all that remained was assembling the pieces. Within a week, Brad commenced passing one picosecond jump interval circuits by portal to each of the MERT Drive ships in the Aster system. Installing the circuitry was a matter of unplugging the old circuits and installing the new ones. Sally and Brad personally replaced the jump interval circuits on the Federation's ten ships. The last thing they did before returning to the Aster system was to pass a fully operating circuit to the Roganian team that had pointed them in the right direction in the first place.

*

By the time *UZ Sergei Krikalyov* reached the new Udachny Station on the inner edge of the Kuiper Belt but distant from New Kuiper Joint Station's vector, Borisovich's team had winnowed out some of the underlying principles of the Roganian stasis field. He explained their progress to Orlov.

"The field functions much like an object traveling at near lightspeed. Time doesn't stop within the field; it just slows down such that a photon takes an extremely long time to cross the space in stasis. Everything else is slowed accordingly. The stasis field tricks everything inside the field into believing that time has virtually stopped. This is what would happen if we were to observe something moving past us at such a speed. Instead of actual speed, however, the speed is virtual.

"With the computer power we have here at Udachny, we should be able to solve this fairly soon."

"I'm far less interested in being able to generate such a field," Orlov said, "as in shielding our ships from a stasis field. As soon as you know how they produce their field, come up with something that will shield us from it."

*

A week later, Borisovich handed a meter-wide roll of shiny silvery fabric to Orlov. It was surprisingly heavy. He placed the roll on his desk and fingered the material. It had a slightly greasy feel, but when he removed his fingers, they were clean.

"What is it?" he asked.

"It's a blend of the rare earth metals lutetium and yttrium alloyed with indium for malleability without reducing the anti-stasis characteristics of the rare earths. This material will route a stasis field around whatever object it covers. If you make a suit of the fabric, someone wearing it can step into a stasis field without actually experiencing the field."

The Udachny lab produced sufficient anti-stasis fabric to cover *Sergei Krikalyov's* outer surfaces completely, with sufficient left over for repairs or other possible uses. It produced sufficient additional material for the remaining eleven ships. The team also constructed several suits in case they were needed.

*

Four weeks after she arrived from Aster, *UZ Sergei Krikalyov* departed from Udachny on full warp for the six-day return to Aster.

ASTER SYSTEM—GENERALLY

"I really misjudged your ability to manufacture what you need on a wholesale basis," eThorpe said. "When we decided to expand ServerSky in the Solar System to our own purposes, we had to design and install a production line first, and that took a while. We linked it by portal to raw material sources and pushed the manufactured thinsats into orbit by portal. Still, working twenty-four-seven, creating just one swarm was a three-week process.

"From what I can tell, you Roganians dramatically shortened the process, and your ServerSky network is dynamically expanding even as we speak." eThorpe grinned. "I know. I've already explored it."

"You might say," Mavik said, "that we've had a few years to work the bugs out of our manufacturing systems. When we incorporated your Nanocosm technology, the process entered warp speed, so to speak."

"Daphne and her people are working with several of your teams right now to integrate your nascent upload capability with your expanding ServerSky," eThorpe said. "During my exploration of your ServerSky, I discovered how far your Kuiper Belt facilities have come. It's almost like magic."

"Not having portal technology held us back in ways we didn't even understand until you introduced us to it," Mavik said. "We could get from here to there quickly, but the relative time intervals made real-time interactions virtually impossible." Mavik gave a very human-sounding sigh. "We would have gotten there eventually, but meeting up with humans has dramatically changed things—for both our species." Mavik adjusted himself in his chair.

"I still am wrestling with how humans accomplished so much in three hundred years."

"I'm certainly not here to lecture," eThorpe said, "but I have some thoughts. The Frohlican culture is static by design. I'm guessing most of their advancements are products from Roganian minds."

Mavik opened his eyes wide while keeping his mouth closed—a gesture eThorpe recognized as the Asterian equivalent of a nod.

"And you guys, and I mean no offense here, don't have any incentives built into your system. I am the wealthiest man in human history, because I was first to discover portals and apply them effectively. Daphne and Kimberly are right behind me in personal wealth, gained with their imagining the potential of uploads and backups, and then turning that imagining into accomplishment."

"I understand your language," Mavik said, "but on Rogan, wealth accumulation or the accumulation of possessions is simply unnecessary. Anything a person wants is available, virtually anything at all."

"I get that," eThorpe interrupted, "I really do. But when I can have anything I want simply by asking or taking or whatever, what then compels me to reach beyond what is possible and available to what might be?" He smiled warmly. "This, I believe, is the real difference between us."

"You make a good point."

"In the short time we've been here," eThorpe said thoughtfully, "I've realized that together our cultures have a hugely greater potential than either of us without the other. Look at what we've done together, just to mention two. We both now have FTL ships that are an order of magnitude faster than what we had when we arrived. You can project and power portals farther than we ever thought possible." eThorpe chuckled. "Just imagine what lies in our joint futures."

At that point, eMax appeared as a holoimage on the table between them, mewing for their attention.

"What the...?" Mavik said, adding an unintelligible term that eThorpe later learned was the Roganian equivalent of *fuck*.

eThorpe laughed, stroking the uploaded version of eMax in virtual space. "Meet eMax, the second oldest upload in the Solar System."

eThorpe explained to Mavik how eMax came to be, and how he had become a virtual part of everything he and the others had done since then.

"When we were experimenting with cloning and downloading, Max's clone (Max is the flesh-and-blood original of eMax), Maxter joined our inner circle as well. In the past few days, Chairman John Butler and First Lady Kimberly Deveraux visited the Boss on Frohlic. Maxter made an appearance at the state dinner—I think he was the biggest hit."

"On a related topic," Mavik said, "a Roganian team has approached the Boss on Frohlic about installing ServerSky and making uploads and backups available. The Boss went for ServerSky as an obvious expansion of their planetwide electronic network. He balked at the whole concept of uploads. Says it would undermine their stable and happy system."

After a bit of thought, eThorpe said, "Right now, that's probably a good thing. Apparently, the Boss missed that through ServerSky, any upload—such as myself—can roam their global network at will. They'll figure it out, but by then, Frohlic will be so dependent on ServerSky that removing it would be impossible."

"I begin to see a bit of what you were talking about—incentives," Mavik said, opening his eyes and closing his mouth. "I really do." Mavik uttered another human-like sigh. "Any news on your wayward fellow human, Orlov?"

"One of the consequences of our methods," eThorpe said, "is that people like Orlov enter the equation from time to time. We will need to deal with him, and I fear that his setbacks will have encouraged him to take larger risks. At this moment, I have no idea where he is."

"Could he have returned to your Solar System?" Mavik asked.

"Possible, but not likely," eThorpe answered. "I'm afraid we'll need to deal with him again."

✳

UZ Sergei Krikalyov exited warp near Orlov's remaining eleven ABO starships, still parked in a holding orbit at the inner edge of Aster's Asteroid Belt. *Krikalyov* was a bit luminescent from its anti-stasis fabric coating. Within minutes of his arrival, Orlov called a meeting of his senior personnel in *Krikalyov*.

"What has transpired during my absence?"

"Nothing, Sir," his senior captain answered. "I don't think they found our location."

Orlov then explained the fabric coating *Krikalyov's* skin. "We have enough fabric and adhesive to coat all our ships. Take the next two days to accomplish this. Then we'll plan out our next move."

ASTER SYSTEM—CONFLICT ON ROGAN & FROHLIC

Newly formed Portal Group had taken the lead in portal production and installation. It had already linked the LEO and Geosynchronous ServerSky swarms at Rogan and to Frohlic. One of its subgroups was replacing water and power supplies planetwide with portals and was installing wastewater, sewage, and trash portals.

The MERT Group, also newly formed, was setting up starship portals with a reach of several hundred lightyears. Its intent was to enable investigation of relatively nearby star systems without the time commitment of years away from the homeworld.

Despite the hectic pace of change on Rogan, crew members of the Phoenix fleet found time for leisure hours planetside. With the installation of ServerSky, laser pipes, and portals, even the uploads found time to explore outside their confining matrixes. The only proviso eThorpe laid on everyone was that either the upload or its flesh-and-blood counterpart had to be on board their respective vessels at all times.

*

Daphne, Kimberly, and Dale found time to stroll together through Rogan's city streets. The streets were hectic but obviously governed by rules that everyone understood and followed. Sidewalk foot traffic yielded to the right, a pattern they understood instinctively. Roganians used wheeled vehicles on road surfaces. Lanes were marked not by two lines as in their experience, but by a single line that passed between the vehicle's wheels.

Vehicles appeared to be AI-driven. Drivers didn't actually own their vehicles, but rather picked one up where their journey commenced and dropped it off near their destination. They tried it out.

"No way to pay," Dale said.

"How would you do that anyway, silly," Kimberly said. "You don't have anything to pay with."

"I'm hungry," Daphne said. "Let's find something to eat."

"We are off-planet visitors. Take us to an interesting place to eat," Kimberly said to the AI.

The car got underway and stopped several minutes later at an esthetically quaint eatery, possibly a throwback to earlier Rogan times.

They sat at a booth much like one back on Earth where a robot took their order and brought their food. Eating utensils were surprisingly similar to human tableware.

Dale suggested, "They probably supplied us with what we are used to. After all, they have access to most of our public access databases."

"Look around," Kimberly said. "Everyone else has the same implements. I think probably that forks, knives, and spoons are the natural product of a universal evolutionary process."

"Survival of the most useful...," Dale said with a chuckle.

"What about chopsticks on Earth?" Kimberly asked. "To me, at least, they're not very practical, but they certainly have endured a long time."

"That's way above my paygrade," Dale said, popping a grape-like fruit into his mouth.

That was the exact moment a laser bolt struck just across the boulevard. The ensuing blast shattered windows, crumbled several buildings, tore up the pavement, and left several dozen killed and wounded in its wake.

Before Daphne, Kimberly, or Dale could react, their E-disks pulled them back to their respective ships.

✻

Alarms sounded throughout *Damvet Station*, interrupting eThorpe's conversation with Mavik, who checked his Link equivalent.

"We've been hit by a laser bolt from one of Orlov's ships," Mavik said. "It arrived and immediately fired on us, penetrating our defenses. We hit it with a stasis field, but nothing happened. We destroyed it with a laser bolt, but before we hit it, it sent a bolt to Rogan's surface. Reports are coming in now. The bolt hit downtown in a major city. Many casualties; lots of damage."

"I deeply regret the loss of life," eThorpe said. "I have to rejoin my fleet to counter this awful threat."

His holoimage vanished along with eMax's.

Back on *Ad Astra* in full presence, eThorpe quickly assessed the damage. His EPD showed five ABO ships in the general Rogan cislunar space and five more apparently in transit to Frohlic. He hit the nearest with his stasis-enhanced long-range radar. All he got was a normal radar return. Without hesitating, he hit it simultaneously with his neutrino and anti-matter beams. The ship vanished from his EPD display.

"Shoot to kill upon acquisition," eThorpe ordered his fleet. "*Armstrong, Aldrin, Collins, Conrad,* and *Bean* coordinate the destruction of the five remaining ABO ships near Rogan. The rest of you get to Frohlic and let your Mothers position you around the planet."

An ABO ship warped into eThorpe's space, narrowly missing *Ad Astra*. Almost on instinct, eThorpe fired his particle weapon, destroying the vessel's Lance body. The warp rings drifted away as lance pieces and bloated human bodies spread throughout the area. Then he dropped into nullspace, heading for Frohlic.

While Daphne donned her spacesuit, eDaphne radically maneuvered *Conrad* above the ecliptic to avoid a pair of ABO ships. She hit the forward warp ring of one, leaving shattered pieces of the ring reeling off into space. The second ABO ship hit her counter-rotating particle rings, disrupting her hull. The entire crew was lost. Daphne survived because she had donned her spacesuit at the start of the battle. She floated in space thousands of kilometers above the ecliptic, alive but unconscious. For some reason, her E-disk had not activated.

eBraxton dropped down below the ecliptic to get a complete EPD picture of the battle. The ABO ships had paired up, two near L4 and two near L5. They seemed to be keeping distant from *Damvet Station*, probably to avoid its powerful lasers.

"*Collins* and *Bean*, you take on L5. *Aldrin*, join me at L4," eBraxton ordered.

In a maneuver they had practiced several times in the preceding weeks, Kimberly and Dale brought their ships out of nullspace 5,000 kilometers above and below L5, acquiring both targets as they did. Dropping rapidly toward the targets, and in and out of nullspace on alternate seconds, they swept their lasers across the last known target locations. The attack came as a complete surprise to the ABO craft. Neither survived.

eBraxton and eSam used the same tactic at L4. Apparently, at least one of the ships was anticipating such a move. eSam brought

Aldrin out of nullspace directly into a concentrated particle beam. The *Aldrin* imploded with a flash that would be visible at the Aster Oort Cloud when the signal finally arrived. eBraxton reflexively took out the attacking ship with a burst of anti-matter and then used his neutrino beam to stop all life on the remaining vessel and to disrupt its LANR, leaving it a stranded, lifeless hulk held in place by L4 gravitational forces.

✳

eThorpe in *PS Ad Astra*, eBork in *PS Alan Shepard*, eSally in *PS Edgar Mitchell*, eBrad in *PS David Scott*, and eJohnny in *PS James Irvin* exited nullspace geometrically spaced around Frohlic at 5,000 kilometers. eThorpe's EPD showed only four ABO ships orbiting 3,000 kilometers above the planet. The *Sergei Krikalyov* seemed to be missing, and that bothered him.

"Adrhun, what is the status planetside?" eThorpe asked Gloalorn through their private circuit.

"My best efforts notwithstanding," Gloalorn answered, "the dissidents will attack government house shortly."

"What has been the effect of Chairman Butler's visit with the Boss?"

"The Boss is willing to work with the Chairman across the board. Sir, this is a big deal! It could spell the beginning of genuine change for Frohlic."

"Where are you right now?"

"I just left the Boss's office. I'm trying one last push to prevent the groundside attack. The problem is, these guys seem pretty confident. They've got no reason to unless they have something going with Orlov that I don't know about."

There was a pause of about five minutes in Gloalorn's transmission. Then Gloalorn commenced transmitting again.

"Oh shit! A heavy-duty laser bolt just struck the government building. The dissidents are attacking along the main boulevards. Another bolt…another…they're moving in my direction…can't escape…" And Gloalorn's transmission ended.

✳

eJohnny's ship, *PS James Irwin*, dropped toward Frohlic from 5,000 kilometers, slipping in and out of nullspace to avoid enemy fire, as Johnny focused on taking out the ship that had just hit the government complex. At 3,500 kilometers, his MBH took a direct hit and imploded. The flash washed Frohlic with bright white and traveled outward past eBraxton and his ships, past *Damvet*, eventually reaching the limits of Aster's Oort Cloud and beyond. Johnny and crew were gone.

eBrad and eBork in *Scott* and *Shepard* rendezvoused 3,500 kilometers out to take on Johnnie's attacker. eSally in *Conrad* stood off supplying covering fire. They made the kill, but another ABO ship dropped out of warp in position to take out eBrad and *PS David Scott*. In a split-second maneuver, eSally drove *Edgar Mitchel* between *Scott* and the attacking vessel. She took the bolt and spiraled away before soundlessly imploding with the loss of her entire crew.

Both Brad and Bork fired on the attacking vessel leaving nothing but space junk in its place, but that didn't help Sally.

The two remaining ABO ships were still positioned on the other side of Frohlic. eThorpe pinpointed their positions by EPD and vectored the *Shepard* toward one while he headed toward the other. They both moved in and out of nullspace rapidly, releasing a laser bolt, particle beam, or anti-matter beam every time they entered normal space. They caught Orlov's ships by surprise. By the time they reached the enemy vessel positions, nothing remained but shattered pieces of warp ring and Lance, and bloated, floating bodies.

※

"*Neil Armstrong*, it's *Ad Astra*. Frohlic is secure." Thorpe did the transmitting, so eThorpe could focus only on keeping the ship alive.

"Roger. This is eBraxton. What's your status?"

"It's Thorpe. We lost *Edgar Mitchell* and *James Irwin* with eSally, Sally, eJohnny, Johnny, and both their crews. No recovery. Did they all have current backups?"

"I think so, but I don't know. I lost the *Aldrin* with eSam and his crew, and *Conrad* took a hit. The crew is gone, but Daphne got out somehow. We're looking for her right now."

"Wouldn't her E-disk pull her out of there?"

"It's supposed to. Don't know what happened."

"This is eThorpe—we're on our way!"

*

Daphne slowly opened her eyes. She was disoriented, as if she were floating in an anti-gravity tank. The bright colors of the Milky Way filled her vision. *My ship, the* Conrad…*what the hell happened? Where am I?* She moved her arms and legs. *They're okay.* She tucked and rolled to change her position. The Milky Way seemed to move around her. *No sensation of movement…my God! I'm in my spacesuit… in space.* She tried her communicator. "Hello…hello…" Nothing at all. "Mayday! Mayday!" Still nothing. *My E-disk malfunctioned.* She tried to reach for it or her hyper-disk. *Shit…can't access them.* They were in her pockets, but her hands were encased in her spacesuit sleeves. *This is a design flaw we never considered,* her analytical side said, while she tried to push down the panic that her emotional side slipped into her consciousness.

"Mayday! Mayday! It's Daphne O'Bryan. I was in *Conrad* above the ecliptic near Rogan. Now I'm just floating in the void…"

No use, I'm not getting out. Nobody can hear me. She shuddered. I really don't want to die like this, even if my backup is activated. It's not getting this. There will be no record…none at all. Once again, she pushed down panic that threatened to overwhelm her.

"Mayday! Mayday…"

Kimberly…we did so much together—the closest of sisters, lovers, friends. She shuddered and cast her gaze across the infinite void surrounding her. I'm all alone. Kimberly, where are you? Thorpe, you clumsy anachronism, lover, friend…I need you! She tucked and rolled several times, trying to find anything familiar anywhere around her. The stars were different…a few familiar patterns but somehow nothing recognizable.

Then Daphne heard a woman scream—a forlorn, pitiful scream. She opened her mouth to answer and discovered that *she* was screaming. *Get your act together, Girl,* she told herself… and screamed again, quieter this time. Her heart was pounding, and the stars surrounding her seemed to pulse in rhythm with her heart.

Suddenly, directly in front of her, Daphne saw a star pattern she recognized—the constellation Libra. Zubeneschamali, its brightest star, seemed to flash at her. Zubenelgenubi (the star Johnny Oort brought up) and a couple of other stars formed a large triangle. *But wait*, she said to herself, *another star occupies the center of the large triangle. It's faint, but I can see it…magnitude 6.5 or so. It shouldn't even be there.* Daphne gasped.

"That's Sol!" she cried out. "My home! I can see my home. I'm not lost after all!" She shouted with glee.

"Mayday! Mayday…Come and get me, guys!"

✺

"I've got a hit on my EPD," eBraxton said.

Kimberly and Dale had joined Braxton by portal in *Armstrong's* control room.

"Give me the exact position," Thorpe said from *Ad Astra*.

With the coordinates, eThorpe moved as close as he dared by MERT Drive and then came to a stop relative to the object on his radar. Thorpe had already suited up and was out the lock the moment relative motion between *Ad Astra* and Daphne ceased.

He jetted toward her with his TBH boots, coming to the top of her head, out of her vision. He reached from behind and slipped his arms under hers, turning her as he did. The astonishment on her face said everything. Thorpe pressed his helmet to hers.

"Daphne…are you okay?"

"Just scared out of my mind…that's all," she answered, her relief apparent even through the transparent globes. Then she pointed to Libra. "Look…there's Sol…Home!" She burst into tears and threw her space-suited arms around Thorpe's helmet. "Take me home!" she sobbed. "Take me home!"

"I've got you, Daphne. You're safe." He pulled her close to him so she could feel his body through her spacesuit. As an afterthought, Thorpe added, "And you don't even have to lift your sweater!"

EPILOG

KUIPER BELT—NEW KUIPER JOINT STATION

"Where's Daphne?" Fredricks shouted as the signals piled up. "Where's Daphne?" But his hands were full, so he put the question on the back burner while ensuring all the designated back-ups were viable and conscious.

✻

As Sally came to her senses in the recovery chamber, all she said was, "What about Brad? Is he okay?"

"Yes, Sally," Fredricks said, "you saved his life."

Sally smiled broadly without covering her mouth. A jumble of thoughts filled her mind. "I have to go, Dr. Fredricks, right now."

As Sally hurried to the office she shared with Brad in the next-door Phoenix complex, she contacted him. Her signal transited multiple portals before Brad answered in *PS David Scott* somewhere in the Aster system.

"Can you meet me in our office in Joint Kuiper Station? I've got something to show you."

Sally found Brad waiting for her as she entered their office. She ran to him, throwing herself into his arms.

"You're okay! Oh my gosh! You're alive and well!" Joyful tears flowed from her eyes as she snuggled into his arms and pressed her face to his massive chest.

"I love you, *Chị ơi!*" Brad said huskily, wrapping his arms around her diminutive figure. "I love you!"

After several minutes of quiet sharing, Sally looked up at Brad with bright eyes and said, "I was in the middle of digging around a lot of older astrophysical and cosmological research when the battle erupted."

"So, what else is new, *Chị ơi?*" Brad said, grinning at her as he pulled her face from his chest to kiss her warmly.

"No, really…look at what I found."

Sally pulled up a 3-D chart of the known universe. A visible arrow pointed to the Milky Way galaxy at the center of the image. Another arrow pointed to a region about 500 million lightyears across and eight billion lightyears distant. She pointed to the region.

"A hundred years ago or so," she said, "cosmologists seriously thought this might be an area where our universe came into contact with another universe—within the greater multiverse."

"That would have been what? Eight billion years ago?"

"Some of them thought the interaction was still taking place when the light left that region."

"And you're telling me this why?"

"What if they were right? What if we had the means to get there in a relatively short time?"

ASTER SYSTEM—ASTEROID BELT

On his Link, Orlov pulled up an image of Natasha—something he had not done in years. In the image, she was fresh and beautiful, barely out of her teens. She would be in her middle years by now—or perhaps rejuvenated to twenty-something again. He grunted, briefly overwhelmed by a sense of loss before returning to the moment. With his fleet destroyed, this obviously was not the time to walk boldly. Orlov set in the coordinates for his new Udachny Complex in the Kuiper Belt and departed the Aster system at maximum warp.

ASTER SYSTEM—FROHLIC

He expected to live through at least 130, but he only made it to eighty-seven, Gloalorn thought as he firmly pursed his lips and set his gaze on each of the three dissident leaders standing before him. I think this would have pleased him.

"Gentlemen, please be seated," Gloalorn said. "Let's see if we can figure out how to make this thing work."

INTERSTELLAR SPACE—*PHOENIX STARSHIP ANDROMEDA*

The populations of three worlds stood and cheered as 10,000 adventurous souls, humans, humanized Oort, Roganians, and Frohlicans, departed on the grandest expedition ever conceived. Holocams representing news services from three worlds focused on *PS Andromeda* with tense anticipation.

One moment *Andromeda* filled the holovision tanks on three worlds—the next, she vanished.

✳✳✳

Please Post a Review for
The Oort Federation

Authors rely on reviews, so I really appreciate your posting a review on Amazon and Goodreads. To post a review, scan the pertinent QR code below and follow the prompts. You will be prompted to log onto the platform. If you are not a member, you will need to sign up. It's free. Amazon will require a minimum $50 purchase volume during the past twelve months. Goodreads has no requirement. Thank you very much for going through this effort!

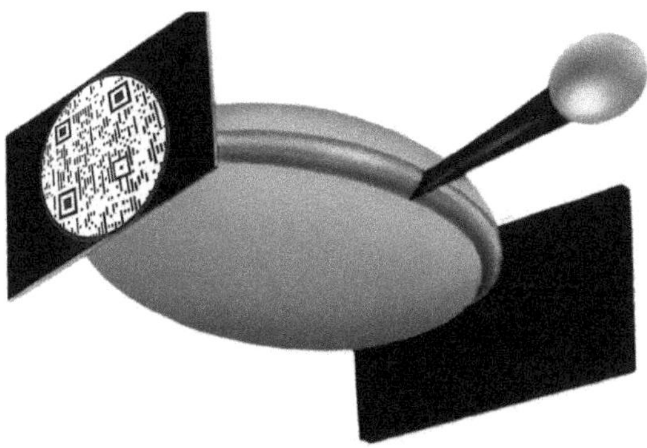

Scan to Review on Amazon

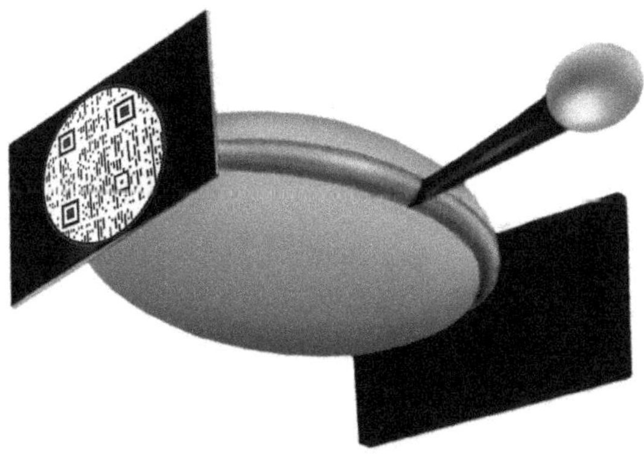

Scan to Review on Goodreads

Excerpt from
RAN: A Civilization in Hiding
(Book 3 of *The Oort Chronicles*)
by
Robert G. Williscroft

CHAPTER ONE

Arcan-One Space Capsule—Space Push Consortium Mission, Circum-Lodan Trajectory

"*Arcan-One*, stand by for Lodan orbital injection burn!"

The announcement arrived at the capsule as an optical beam relayed by an Arcan geostationary satellite.

"Are you ready to do this, Jocara?" Kenred Zlaxiz asked off the circuit, turning to his companion.

"That's why we're here," she answered, pointing through the large, sapphire window to their moon, Lodan, hanging in space before them. "If we abort, it's the mines for me…for sure."

"You're jesting! The Ceffid government wouldn't do that."

"You're from Amred—I'm not sure you can understand. Should we abort back to Arcan, you'll be on the next capsule…but not with me. I'll be shoveling pitchblende or something equally noxious."

Kenred turned back to his console. So glad I was born in Amred, he thought and touched a control. "Roger! Standing by for Lodan orbital injection burn."

Mission Control—Amred City, Amred, Planet Arcan

"Attention, please!"

Flight Director Ostrrop Naoria stood behind his podium with raised arms. The room quieted. Individual technicians manned their stations, four curved rows deep, facing a wall completely covered with display screens filled with graphics except one, a direct visual color display of the view through the capsule sapphire window.

"*GO Check* for Lodan orbital injection burn," Naoria intoned.

One by one, the technicians gave "GO!" for their stations. Following the last "GO!" Naoria started the injection burn countdown.

The burn lasted two minutes.

"*Arcan-One*, status…"

"This is *Arcan-One*. Injection burn successfully completed. Capsule systems stable at zero-gee."

"Mission Control concurs, *Arcan-One* systems stable. Stand by for loss of communications in twenty-three minutes."

Arcan-One Space Capsule—Space Push Consortium Mission, Circum-Lodan Trajectory

"We're committed now, Jocara!" Kenred unstrapped from his seat, and floating, turned to face his fellow astronaut. Her pale green, finely shaped saurian face scales rippled slightly with a faint lavender hue as she smiled joyfully—an open-eyed look with no change in her mouth shape.

"Our orbit takes us well clear of Lodan's three moonlets," Jocara said. "We may actually see one of them on the farside, however."

"Not if *well clear* means what I think it means."

"Stand by for loss of communications!" the optical beam processed through *Arcan-One's* non-emitting optical system. "Four…three…two…one…zero!"

Mission Control—Amred City, Amred, Planet Arcan

"Okay, people, listen up!" Flight Director Naoria announced from his podium. "We've got a half hour. Take a short break and be back at your stations twelve minutes before reacquisition."

As the time approached, the technicians manned their stations. The room was as still as it ever got. At the moment of expected reacquisition, CapCom transmitted, "*Arcan-One*, this is Mission Control, over."

Silence…

"*Arcan-One*, this is Mission Control, over."

Silence still…

"*Arcan-One, Arcan-One,* this is Mission Control, Mission Control, over."

More silence…

CHAPTER TWO

Phoenix Starship Andromeda—Hovering Invisibly in Nullspace Beyond Lodan, Operations Center

Kenred slowly opened his eyes. He was no longer floating in the capsule but lay on the deck of some kind of operations center filled with monitors and control consoles. He felt a whiff of panic. His scales rippled, showing a hint of red. Lighting and temperature seemed normal, but he felt heavier. He took a deep breath, shoving down his initial panic. Jocara rolled over beside him, hyperventilating, her scales bright red. Kenred gripped her arm and whispered softly, "Easy, Jocara, easy!" They both sat up as her scales faded back to bluish green.

Several humanoid creatures stood in a loose circle around them. A strange-looking one stepped toward him, five-fingered hands on its hips. It was oddly thin and tall, with puffy lips and a pointed nose in place of a snout. It had long, spindly, two-sectioned legs, a short torso with articulating arms, and no visible tail. Two intelligent eyes peered from a hair-crowned, spherical head.

Clearly, some kind of mammalian ancestry, Kenred deduced. The humanoid addressed him in his native Amred with an oddly distorted accent.

"I am Braxton Thorpe, Commanding *Phoenix Starship Andromeda.* I represent the inhabitants of the stellar system you call Rodal—we call ourselves Humans. We are on a peaceful research mission passing through your system. We pose no threat to you."

A second, different humanoid joined Thorpe. Like Kenred, it displayed six digits on each hand and was shorter and stockier than the Human. Its hairy head was much like the Human's, but with flattened nose and slender lips. Its ears articulated, reminding Kenred of the small domestic felines kept as pets by his own people.

Another mammalian, Kenred thought as he looked around. No Saurians. The second offworlder addressed him.

"I am Holon Mavik, Chief of the Roganian L2 Group. I represent the inhabitants of the stellar system you call Dytom—we call ourselves Asterians."

"We need to stand and introduce ourselves," Kenred whispered to Jocara, stroking the fine scales on her arm. Their color had returned to normal. "I'll take the lead." He climbed to his feet, his stumpy legs quivering in the higher gravity, balancing with his tail.

"I am *Capsule Arcan-One* Commander Kenred Zlaxiz from the nation Amred on the planet Arcan."

"And I am Astronaut Jocara Porovik from Ceffid. We represent Amred's Space Push Consortium."

"What happened to our capsule, the *Arcan-One*?" Kenred asked.

"Unharmed in Lodan orbit," the Human answered.

"How did we get here?"

The Human's mouth opened, emitting a cackling sound. "We will happily share that with you, but first you will need to understand some advanced physics I suspect your scientists have not yet discovered. We'll get to that later." The Human swept its arm toward the other offworlders in the compartment. "We are the senior people on this starship. Hopefully, you will get to know us before too long."

" *Arcan-One's* orbit is ninety-six minutes," Kenred said. "How long have we been away from the capsule?"

The Human checked an instrument. "Seventeen of your minutes."

"How do your minutes and ours differ?" Jocara asked.

"Arcan's rotation, and thus your day, is slightly longer than our home planet," the Human answered. "Your numbering system is obviously based on twelve." It held up its splayed hands. "Ours is ten-based, but both we and you count time in twelves. Your minute is a fraction of a second longer than ours. In casual conversation, they can be considered identical."

Kenred did a quick mental calculation. "We had just lost comms with Mission Control when you snatched us. In about nineteen minutes, Mission Control is going to discover that the capsule is empty."

The Human's mouth curved upward, and it held up a palm-size, silvery disk. "This is a hyper-disk. We sequestered one in *Arcan-One* where your people are unlikely to find it. That disk will open a portal directly to *Andromeda*." The Human's mouth curved upward again—A smile, Kenred deduced. "Let me show you."

The Human manipulated a control on a console. A doorway appeared between them to Kenred's right. Through the doorway was the interior of *Arcan-One*. Kenred walked around the door to examine the other side. As he passed the plane of the door, it disappeared. He stepped back to the front; the door reappeared, looking as solid and real as anything else in the room.

"Step through into *Arcan-One*," the Human said. "It's like walking through any door on Arcan." It emitted a clucking sound through a smile. "Go ahead—it won't hurt you, but be mindful that you will go from our gravity here to zero-gee!"

Kenred turned to Jocara. She opened her eyes wide, indicating a tentative Why not?

"Okay," Kenred said, stepping through the door into *Arcan-One*. He floated across the capsule to the opposite side. He turned and looked back through the door at Jocara and the offworlders.

"May I join you?" the Human asked.

"Not a lot of room here, but sure, join me." Kenred watched the taller Human step through the door—the portal—and tuck its legs close to fit into the small space as it floated and looked about.

"Very much like our Apollo capsules when we first visited our moon," the Human said quietly. It looked at both seats, but there was no way it would have fit in one. It looked at what was probably a time piece on its wrist. "We still have a few minutes before comms are reestablished. Do you want your fellow astronaut…"

"Jocara," Kenred interrupted.

"…Jocara to join you here before you return to *Andromeda*?" It floated back through the portal and deftly landed on its feet.

"Yes, please send her through." Kenred hesitated, thinking about the vast difference between the offworlder and Arcan technology, and realizing that he and Jocara were totally at these offworlders' mercy. "Do you want us here to reestablish comms with Mission Control, or back on Andromeda?"

"After Jocara passes through the portal, both of you please return here. You may already suspect my reasons, but I'll explain fully as we move forward."

Jocara nervously stepped through the portal into *Arcan-One*, and Kenred took her arm as she coasted over to him. They both sat, and he told her in her native Ceffid language, "These offworlders seem benign, but consider for a moment the vast gulf between their technology and ours. All we have seen is the inside of a control room without knowing how we got there. This portal technology is beyond anything we have ever imagined. We must seem like swamp lizards to them. Why are they interested in us? What can we offer them? What is their real motive? I don't trust them and don't want to give them any reason to be anything but friendly." He smiled with wide open eyes and rippling face scales and squeezed her hand. "Let's go back and see what we can learn—but cautiously. Mission Control will just have to deal with our disappearance."

Mission Control—Amred City, Amred, Planet Arcan

When *Arcan-One* failed to respond, pandemonium broke out in Mission Control. Flight Director Naoria hissed through his snout and raised his arms. "Settle down, people! Quiet!"

As the noise quieted down, he pointed to the technician, who controlled the capsule internal camera. "Pan the interior," he ordered.

Lodan, visible through the capsule's window on Mission Control's primary display, shifted left as the camera panned around the capsule.

Nothing, Naoria thought, *my astronauts are gone. But that's impossible. There's no way to exit the capsule without releasing all the air.* He glanced at the internal pressure gauge near the primary display. *Normal internal pressure. Had they exited the capsule, there would be no internal pressure.*

One of the seated technicians raised his hand. "Sir, the oxygen and nitrogen percentages are wrong. They're twenty-one and seventy-nine percent, respectively. They should be twenty and eighty. This is impossible!"

"Are the reserves topped up?" Naoria asked.

"Yes, Sir! Two-blocked."

Another technician piped up, "Sir, the onboard clock is four minutes behind. I've checked and double checked. Four minutes are gone!"

"Troubleshoot your consoles," Naoria told them. "Then check again. The rest of you, find an answer, a solution to this dilemma." Naoria turned to CapCom. "Keep calling!"

Thirty-seven minutes later, *Arcan-One* passed behind Lodan.

✻

Naoria walked down a hallway and entered a door into a cleanroom airlock. He quickly donned a clean-suit, booties, head and face covering, and entered a large space containing a duplicate capsule that was intended to be an emergency backup. A group of engineers stood around a table discussing the situation.

"Well?" Naoria said to his chief engineer.

"No idea, but we just started an out-of-the-box approach." He beckoned Naoria to the table. "How many ways can we end up with our present situation?" He gave Naoria a worried look. "Nothing is off the table—even alien abduction. Give us a couple of orbits to work this out."

✻

Three hours later, Naoria stood once again at the table in the cleanroom, listening to his chief engineer.

"If, hypothetically, one of our future spaceships had returned from the future to our present, linked up with *Arcan-One*, and transferred our astronauts to their vessel, this, or some similar event, would explain their absence. Ridiculous, I know. But even this fantastical explanation cannot explain the difference in atmospheric composition." He sighed and spread his hands on the table. The other engineers and technicians would not meet Naoria's eyes. "We have exhaustively examined every possible way to generate the difference in composition. Everything we came up with, we confirmed didn't happen. The only way to remove the astronauts while retaining the atmosphere is to link to another spaceship—the only way. Now, if that other spaceship has an atmosphere ratio of oxygen to nitrogen different from ours, then the resulting capsule mix will be some combination of theirs and ours."

Naoria attempted to interrupt, but the engineer held up his hand. "Let me finish! We know that Rodal, some ten lightyears distant, has a spacefaring civilization. Ditto for Dytom, but it's about seventy-six lightyears away. We have gone to great lengths to hide our presence in the galaxy. Arcan does not emit electromagnetic radiation. We use lasers for communication and ranging. It is highly unlikely that either civilization knows about us. On the other hand, if the Rodal civilization has developed FTL travel, we are the obvious choice for a first visit because they would have detected Arcan in the life zone—not us, just our planet." The engineer sighed. "Even if they don't have FTL, we are only ten lightyears away—still the obvious choice."

"So, what are you saying?" Naoria asked.

"I think you know, Sir. An alien spaceship out beyond the moon has abducted our astronauts."

You have just been reading from Chapters One & Two of Robert G. Williscroft's exciting Science Fiction novel, TRAN: A Civilization in Hiding, *the third book in* The Oort Chronicles. *Download a copy of* The Oort Federation *or order a hard or softbound copy or an audio version from your favorite online bookseller.*

About the Author

Dr. Robert G. Williscroft is a retired submarine officer, deep-sea and saturation diver, scientist, author, and a lifelong adventurer. He spent twenty-two months underwater, a year in the equatorial Pacific, three years in the Arctic ice pack, and a year at the Geographic South Pole. He holds degrees in Marine Physics and Meteorology and a doctorate for developing a system to protect scuba divers in contaminated water. A prolific author of both non-fiction, submarine technothrillers, and hard science fiction, he lives in Centennial, Colorado.

Dr. Williscroft is a member of Colorado Author's League, Independent Association of Science Fiction & Fantasy Authors, Science Fiction & Fantasy Writers Association, Libertarian Futurist Society, Los Angeles Adventurers' Club, Mensa, Military Officer's Association, U.S. Sub Vets, American Legion, and the NRA, and now spends most of his time writing his next book, speaking to various regional groups, and hanging out with the girl of his dreams, Jill, and her two cats.

Scan for more information: 

Other Works by this Author

Please visit RobertWilliscroft.com to discover other books by Robert Williscroft. Scan for more information.

Current Events:

The Chicken Little Agenda: Debunking "Experts'" Lies

Children's Books:

The Starman Jones Series:

Starman Jones: A Relativity Birthday Present

Starman Jones Goes to the Dogs (2026)

Biographies:

Mission Possible (by Gladys L. Williscroft)

Sŭbmarine-ĕr (by Jerry Pait; compiled by Robert G. Williscroft)

Short Stories:

Reality Hack

First Contact

The Cold Spot

The Virus

Novels:

Mac McDowell Missions:

Operation Ivy Bells

Operation Ice Breaker

Operation Arctic Sting

Operation White Out

Operation Vela Redux

Operation Alfa Rogue (2026)

The Starchild Saga:

Slingshot

The Daedalus Files

The Starchild Compact

The Iapetus Federation

The Oort Chronicles:

Icicle: A Tensor Matrix

The Oort Federation: To the Stars

RAN: A Civilization in Hiding

KEID: A Lost Civilization

Beyond the Beyond (2025)

Connect with the Author

I really appreciate you reading my book! Here are my social media coordinates:

Facebook: *https://www.facebook.com/robert.williscroft*
X/Twitter: *@RGWilliscroft*
Amazon author page: *https://buff.ly/2N5ZnlG*
Blog: *https://ThrawnRickle.com*
LinkedIn: *https://www.linkedin.com/in/argee/*
Book website: *https://RobertWilliscroft.com*
Newsletter: *https://eepurl.com/guZ5uv*

Glossary for *The Oort Federation*

Arrokoth: A large *Kuiper Belt* Object discovered on June 26, 2014. On January 1, 2019, the *New Horizons* spacecraft did a close flyby of the object. The Hubble Space Telescope and Johns Hopkins Applied Physics Laboratory in Maryland were prominently involved in its discovery. The *New Horizons* team wanted to find a special name for this object. The Powhatan were the indigenous people of Chesapeake Bay, where both *New Horizons* and Hubble were operated back then. At the team's suggestion, the Powhatan tribal council chose *Arrokoth*, a Powhatan word relating to the sky.

Aster, Aster System: A star eighty-four lightyears from Sol in the constellation Aries. It has two Earth-like planets in its life zone.

Asterian: (1) An individual from one of the planets around the star *Aster*. (2) The common language spoken by all Asterians.

Baryonic matter: Normal matter consisting of baryons such as neutrons and protons found in all atomic nuclei.

Belters: People living in colonies scattered throughout the Asteroid Belt.

Casimir field: In quantum field theory, the Casimir field is the physical force arising from a quantized field. It is named after the Dutch physicist Hendrik Casimir who predicted them in 1948.

Dark Forest Theory: An explanation of the Fermi Paradox—why we have not heard from any interstellar civilization—proposed by Chinese science fiction writer Cixin Liu. The universe is a dark forest. Every civilization is an armed hunter stalking through the trees like a ghost being careful, because everywhere in the forest are stealthy hunters like him. If he finds another life, there's only one thing he can do: open fire and eliminate it. And when one civilization becomes a killer species, it will scour the galaxy eliminating all rivals.

Databank: An electronic or digital repository for data.

Debye length: The distance in a plasma over which significant charge separation can occur.

Difecta: The fifth moon of the gas giant orbiting just beyond Aster's Asteroid Belt.

E-disk: (Escape-Hyper-Disk) A specially designed *hyper-disk* that senses the holder's environment and will open a *MERT portal* and whisk the holder to safety when conditions warrant.

EMD stun weapon: An Electro Muscular Disruption stun weapon, much like a Taser.

Einstein-Rosen Bridge: (Also called a *wormhole*.) A theoretical passage through spacetime that could create shortcuts for long journeys across the universe. Imagine space-time as a two-dimensional sheet: if you fold that sheet so two distant points touch, an Einstein-Rosen Bridge or wormhole would be the tunnel connecting those points. Based on a special solution of the Einstein field equations proposed by Albert Einstein and Nathan Rosen in 1939.

Entangled-Particle Display (EPD): The *Oort* had found a way to separate entangled particles physically, and to project one element of trillions of these pairs in an expanding sphere around Sol and the *Oort Cloud*. The incoming data were presented in holographic spheres in each of the Oort Stations, called Entangled-Particle Displays.

Exotic matter: See *Non-baryonic matter*.

Frohlic: The original planet of the *Asterians*. It orbits closest to *Aster* in the life zone.

Frohlican: (1) An individual from *Frohlic*. (2) The language spoken by all Frohlicans.

FS: Federation Starship

FTL: Faster Than Light.

GEO: Geosynchronous Earth Orbit (pronounced geo or G-E-O.

GlobalNet: A global network that replaced the Internet. It is served by *ServerSky* connected by *modulated laser pipes* and accessed through *Links* carried by virtually everyone on Earth.

Holotank: Analogous to current television receivers, but instead produces a three-dimensional, color, holographic image.

Holovision: Analogous to a current television image, but instead is a three-dimensional, color, holographic image.

Hyper-brick: A two-kilogram elongated cube used as a portable portal activation device developed by Udachny similar to Phoenix's *hyper-disc*.

Hyper-disk: A 5-cm disk with a dull metallic side and a deep black side connected to a portal *Locus* through *nullspace*. When the metallic side is rubbed, the portal is activated.

Icicle: The original uploaded Braxton Thorpe in *The Oort Chronicles* volume one, *Icicle: A Tensor Matrix*.

Kerr metric: Describes the geometry of empty spacetime around a rotating uncharged axially-symmetric black hole with a quasispherical event horizon. It is an exact solution of the Einstein field equations of general relativity; these equations are highly non-linear, which makes exact solutions very difficult to find.

Kerr-Newman metric: The most general asymptotically flat, stationary solution of the Einstein-Maxwell equations in general relativity that describes the spacetime geometry in the region surrounding an electrically charged, rotating mass. It generalizes the *Kerr metric* by taking into account the field energy of an electromagnetic field, in addition to describing rotation.

Kimberly Process: An internationally accepted diamond tracking protocol established in the early twenty-first century to limit trade in Blood Diamonds.

Kuiper Belt: A circumstellar disc in the outer Solar System, extending from the orbit of Neptune to approximately 50 AU from the Sun. Contains many comets, asteroids, and other small bodies made largely of ice.

Lagrange points: In celestial mechanics, the five points near two large bodies where the smaller orbits the larger, where the balance of gravitational forces allows a much smaller object to maintain its position relative to the large bodies. L1 is between the two large bodies close to the smaller one. L2 is on the far side of the smaller of the two large bodies. L3 is on the far side of the larger of the two bodies. L4 leads the smaller body in its orbit around the larger body. L5 trails the smaller body in its orbit around the larger body. These are named after the 18th-century Italian astronomer and mathematician Joseph-Louis Lagrange, who first determined their existence.

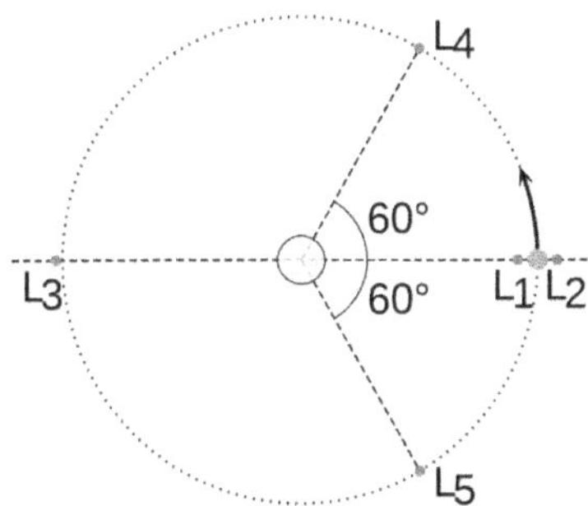

Lagrange L1 point: The *Lagrange point* between the larger and smaller body in a system. In our Earth-Moon System, about 60,000 km beyond the Moon. In the Mars-Sun system, about one million km from Mars, between Mars and the Sun.

Lagrange L2 point: The *Lagrange point* beyond the smaller body in a system. In our Earth-Moon System, about 60,000 km beyond the Moon.

Lagrange L3 point: The *Lagrange point* beyond the larger body in a system. In our Earth-Sun System, about 150 million km from the Sun in Earth's orbit on the other side of the Sun.

Lagrange L4 point—The *Lagrange point* in the orbit of the smaller body leading the smaller body in a system. In our Earth-Moon System, about 400 thousand km from Earth and Moon, leading Moon in Moon's orbit. In the Mars-Sun System, about 228 million km from Mars, leading Mars in its orbit.

Lagrange L5 point—The *Lagrange point* in the orbit of the smaller body trailing the smaller body in a system. In our Earth-Moon System, about 400 thousand km from the Earth and Moon, trailing Moon in Moon's orbit.

LANR: Lattice Assisted Nuclear Reaction. Formerly called cold-fusion.

Launch loop: A method for launching human and freight payloads into space without using rockets. Constructing the World's first Space Launch Loop is the theme of *Slingshot*, the first novel in *The Starchild Saga*.

LEO: Low Earth Orbit (pronounced L-E-O).

Link: An electronic device for hooking up to the *GlobalNet*. It has various configurations, from a wristband, to a piece of apparel, to a surgically implanted device. It has both aural and holographic displays.

Locus: See *Portal Locus.*

Moxie Automated Breathing Unit (MABU): Consists of a *Moxie* oxygen generator, a carbon dioxide scrubber, and an electronic mixing valve that maintains the proper oxygen percentage and gas pressure.

Matrix: (1) Within the framework of this novel, a box shaped to fit into an electronics rack that contains complex electronics that can form its own electrical pathways over time. It contains the self-aware essence of an uploaded person (or cat). Plural herein is matrixes.

(2) More generally, a mathematical expression of n dimensions (where n > 1) whose elements are tensors with n-1 dimensions. For example, a two-dimensional matrix with columns and rows has one-dimensional tensor elements that are the point intersections of each column and row. Plural herein is matrices.

MBH Drive: A *subluminal* spacecraft with a rapidly rotating Mini-Black Hole (MBH) at its core. It has a circular plasma path lined with 100-Tesla electromagnets surrounded the MBH. A dense plasma focus generates a plasma stream in the ring. The magnets accelerate the stream to near light speed and bend it into a circle. Upon reaching terminal velocity, the plasma stream splits off continuous particle pairs. As each pair passes a designated drop point, one of the particles drops into the MBH event horizon. Governed by the Penrose process, the MBH loses a minuscule amount of angular momentum, while the remaining particle gains that angular momentum plus an additional 27%. This continuous process develops an enormous amount of energy that powers the extraction process and supplies all the power needed to drive the spacecraft.

MERT Drive: An *FTL* drive consisting of passing one *MERT Portal* through another, and then the second through the first, and so on, to leapfrog quickly through normal space.

MERT Portal: MERT=Morris-Einstein-Rosen-Thorne. A *Casimir field* that contains a stable wormhole with the ability to position one end of the wormhole manually.

Microbiome: The total of all the trillions of microorganisms inside a living being.

Modulated laser-pipe: A broadband laser connection between Earth and *ServerSky* or two elements of *ServerSky*.

Mother: The controlling computer for *MERT Drive* ships.

Moxie oxygen generator: MOXIE=Mars Oxygen In-Situ Resource Utilization Experiment. A 21st-century device used on early Mars exploration visits to convert carbon dioxide to oxygen.

Nanobot: Nano-size robots controlled by programs generated by the *Nanocosm*.

Nanocosm: A device capable of translating simple English (or any other known language) directions into highly complex, wide-ranging instruction sets to *nanobot* swarms that proceed to build whatever the original instructions dictated.

Non-baryonic matter: (Also called *exotic matter*.) Matter that, unlike the matter with which we are familiar, is not made of baryons such as neutrons and protons found in all atomic nuclei.

Nullspace: Within the framework of this novel, stands for non-space. The interior of a wormhole or a series of connected wormholes.

Oort: Collective name for all the uploaded individuals dwelling in the *Oort Cloud*.

Oort Cloud: An extended shell of icy objects that exist in the outermost reaches of the Solar System at distances ranging from 10,000 to 100,000 AU. Named after astronomer Jan Oort, who first theorized its existence.

Penrose process: A means whereby energy can be extracted from a rotating black hole. That extraction can occur if the rotational energy of the black hole is located not inside the event horizon but outside in a region of the *Kerr* spacetime called the ergosphere in which any particle is necessarily propelled in locomotive concurrence with the rotating spacetime. All objects in the ergosphere become dragged by a rotating spacetime.

Phoenixes: The blockchain digital coin (Φ), nearly universal anywhere in the Solar System except Earth.

Portal Locus: The origin end of a *MERT portal*.

PS: Phoenix Starship

Q-carbon: A carbon phase that is harder than diamond, ferromagnetic, glows when exposed to energy, and back-converts to diamond with a simple melting process.

Reissner-Nordstrøm metric: A static solution to the Einstein-Maxwell field equations that corresponds to the gravitational field of a charged, non-rotating, spherically symmetric body.

Rogan: The planet orbiting *Aster* at the outer edge of the life zone. It was colonized by *Frohlic* long ago.

Roganian: (1) An individual from *Rogan*. (2) The language spoken by all Roganians.

Schwarzschild radius: The radius defining the event horizon of a Schwarzschild black hole. It is a characteristic radius associated with any quantity of mass. Named after the German astronomer Karl Schwarzschild, who calculated this exact solution for the theory of general relativity in 1916.

ServerSky: A space-based global internet system invented by Keith Lofstrom that incorporates trillions of small thinsats that work together to function as a global, very high-power, very fast server network. It can be accessed directly by individual users or via modulated laser pipes into the GlobalNet.

Subluminal: Slower than lightspeed.

Superluminal: Faster than lightspeed.

Space Launch Loop: A method for launching passengers and freight into space without using rockets.

TBH boots: Jet boots developed in 1967 by three NASA scientists, David Thomas, John Bird, and Richard Hellbaum. NASA tested the jet boots Earthside back then, but they were not introduced into current use until a few years before Thorpe was revived. They're simpler and less cumbersome than any of the old Manned Maneuvering Units. They fit like riding boots, but with completely flexible ankles. The boot uppers consist of two stiff, shaped polymer bags that contain pressurized hypergolic fuel components—

UDMH (Unsymmetrical dimethylhydrazine) and nitrogen tetroxide. The fuel valves are controlled by a microswitch under each big toe. Each boot produces ten newtons of force against the ball of the foot. The wearer bends the knees for the appropriate thrust vector, including torque.

Tensor: A mathematical object analogous to, but more general than, a vector, represented by an array of components that are functions of the coordinates of a space.

Thinsat: 5-gram-substrates consisting of two very thin layers of aluminum foil embossed on the Earth-facing side with die bonding cavities and slot antennas that enable the thinsats to communicate with each other and Earth's surface. The outward-facing side is coated in the center area with molybdenum, indium phosphide, and AZO (aluminum-doped zinc-oxide) to form solar cells. The corners consist of a stack of the oxides of tungsten and aluminum, AZO, and nickel hydroxide. These are electrochromic thrusters that enable each thinsat in the swarm to maintain its orientation with respect to the swarm and the planet below.

Udachny Protocol: A diamond cataloging system designed by Isidor Orlov that was based on laser-etched ID numbers and blockchain accounting that made it impossible for anyone to trade in diamonds that lay outside the system. Orlov set up off-the-books diamond purchases at rock-bottom prices from various militants around the planet. These purchases funneled badly needed money to outlaw militants everywhere, who used the money to purchase weapons from Udachny, all the while dramatically boosting Udachny's bottom line.

UKK: Udachnyy Kosmicheskiy Korabl'—Udachny Spaceship.

UZ: Udachnyy Zvezdolet—Udachny Starship

Van Den Broeck, Chris: A Belgian theoretician who developed the warp bubble solutions to the warp equations.

VASIMR engine: The Variable Specific Impulse Magnetoplasma Rocket is an electrothermal thruster that uses radio waves to ionize and heat an inert propellant, then a magnetic field to accelerate the resulting plasma, generating thrust.

Wilson-Dicke-Puthoff polarizer (WDP): An analog of general relativity to describe gravity and its relationship to electromagnetism.

Wormhole: See *Einstein-Rosen Bridge*.

9 781968 367428